Praise for *Qu...*

'A sassy, light and sweet rivals-t... ...
best kind of heroine' Elizabeth Drummond, author of *The House Sitter*

'A funny, honest and deeply relatable novel about the highs and lows of navigating your twenties. It feels at once like a crash out prompted diary entry and deeply reassuring hug from your best friend. Brimming with heart and humour, Burke's debut is a warm exploration of love, friendship and the delightful messiness of being in your twenties' Rufaro Faith Mazarura, author of *Let the Games Begin*

'An utterly relatable rom-com with all of my favourite tropes. Jasmine Burke is one to watch' Carlie Walker, bestselling author of *The Takedown*

'A sparkling, buoyant debut that so deftly captures the highs, lows, and everythings-in-between of that period in your twenties where you know you've got the rest of your life ahead of you, but you also can't help but feeling like you're already falling behind. The romance between the leads absolutely sizzles, but the true star is relatable badass Maddison with her big dreams and even bigger heart. What a moving, authentic, joyful ode to one's twenties' Pyae Moe Thet War, author of *I Did Something Bad*

'A smart and hilarious romcom, Jasmine has deftly mixed iconic 2010s nostalgia with sizzling chemistry and finished with a modern twist. *Quarter-Love Crisis* is an instant classic' Annabelle Slator, author of *The Launch Date*

QUARTER-LOVE CRISIS

JASMINE BURKE

Dear reader,

Thank you so much for reading!
Hope you have the _BEST_ time
with it!

B x

ЯENE
GADE

RENEGADE BOOKS

First published in Great Britain in 2025 by Renegade Books,
an imprint of John Murray Press

A CIP catalogue record for this book
is available from the British Library.

Paperback ISBN 978-1-408-74969-2

Typeset in Caslon by M Rules
Printed and bound in Great Britain by Clays Ltd, Elcograf S.p.A

Papers used by John Murray Press are from well-managed forests
and other responsible sources.

Renegade Books
An imprint of
John Murray Press
Carmelite House
50 Victoria Embankment
London EC4Y 0DZ

The authorised representative
in the EEA is
Hachette Ireland
8 Castlecourt Centre
Dublin 15, D15 XTP3, Ireland
(email: info@hbgi.ie)

www.dialoguebooks.co.uk

John Murray Press, part of Hodder & Stoughton Limited, an Hachette UK company.

To anyone who's "not where they should be" in their life –
you are enough.

And to my parents Dionne and Hugh.
Thank you for being my biggest cheerleaders.
Remember to skip Chapters 24, 28 and 29,
they're not important.

Prologue

Ten things I would go back six months and scream ferociously at myself:

1. There is no point keeping your outdated clothes from sixth form 'just in case'. They are too small for you and you are in your late twenties.

2. It's not a bad thing that you don't know how to drive ... But you can spare yourself that late-for-the-bus run and order a taxi sometimes.

3. You can paint as clear a picture of 'adult you' as you like, but life will show up, tear it to pieces and throw those pieces out of the window.

4. You are not a big drinker. Don't try to be a big drinker, even if you are trying to prove a point.

5. If a man walks like a villain and talks like a villain, he's absolutely a villain. DO NOT keep texting him.

6. There is no such thing as too many notebooks no matter what anyone may try to say. Buy another, actually! You know you deserve it.

7. You are far too good at sticking things out. If something's not right for you, leave it, I beg.

8. Bottling up is not fun. You have friends for a reason and they are the best friends in the entire world.

9. Maybe, just maybe, you can know someone for most of your life and yet still not quite perceive them right.

10. You may have thought the day you blew your life up would stem from one big push. It has not. It has stemmed from six months of gentle nudges to the edge. And now the day has come. You know what to do ... It's time to jump.

Nudge 1

The Bus Pass

'Wake up!' I slam on the door, yelling. 'Or I swear I will crease every single pair of your trainers.'

I promised myself that today would be different. I made a schedule, a tick-list and set a new wake-up time. And, yes, I snoozed two alarms before I got out of bed, but it still should have worked.

5 a.m. – Wake up; gym wear; go downstairs.

5.05 a.m. – Transfer last night's clothes from washer to dryer; put on a forty-five-min cycle.

5.15 a.m. – Thirty minutes of yoga in the living room.

5.45 a.m. – Brisk morning shower (playlist pre-made).

6 a.m. – Remove clothes from dryer; pick an outfit.

6.15 a.m. – Body lotion; get changed; light natural make-up; try new hairstyle.

7 a.m. - Make green tea; pack lunch into black leather shoulder bag.

7.30 a.m. - Walk to the bus stop in new wool trench; log steps on new app.

8.30 a.m. - Arrive at work; use extra half an hour gained of workday for meeting prep.

But nothing is ever that simple and I should have known that from the moment I found my brother's clothes in the dryer. The same clothes that have been sat there for over a week despite my multiple reminders. At that point I would have folded them myself, but Mum said we needed to 'teach Anton a lesson'. What lesson? He's learnt nothing and is only getting worse, and now the perfect outfit I'd planned is still sat, soggy, damp and likely smelly, in the washing machine. After digging around in my wardrobe, all I could come up with was a pair of thick tights, and a top and skirt that I haven't worn since sixth form. I'm in a *Peter Pan* collar, for God's sake! When I do not have the neck to pull those off!

There was a version of me from thirty minutes ago that believed I could get my perfect morning back on track. I ditched the yoga, skipped the tea and resolved to grab lunch on the go, and for a moment all seemed somewhat OK. Then I hit the bottom of the road, stuck my hand in my pocket and realised Anton still had my bus pass. A quick round of expletives and a speedy U-turn later, and here I am back at home at 7.50 a.m., having an almost one-sided screaming match with my little brother.

I slam three sharp, hard slaps on his bedroom door before immediately following with rapid-fire knocking. If I had any real courage, I'd barge through it, but I've already learnt the hard way that he doesn't wear a stitch of clothing to bed.

'Seriously, Anton. I mean it,' I hiss through the closed door. 'I'll ruin every single pair you own.'

'Go away, Maddison!' His voice is a husky growl.

Anton has never been a morning person and it's only got worse with age.

'Where's my bus pass?' I ask, banging once more for effect. 'I asked you to leave it on the table when you got in last night.'

I could ask him to take *money* from me and he'd still do it wrong just to spite me.

He grumbles something unintelligible and I hear the shuffling of his duvet, and scraping, before his door inches open. I can just about make out his face, set into pure resentment as he peers through the gap and recoils at the hallway light. He is a gremlin if I ever saw one. One who cannot go back to university quick enough, if you ask me.

'Aren't you too old to be getting the bus to work?' he asks, reluctantly passing the card through the crack in his door.

'Buy your own bus pass next time.' I snatch it off him.

'Move out.'

'Grow up!'

There's no use. The door is already closed and the shuffling behind it suggests he's already back in bed.

I'm already so behind I could cry, and at this rate I may actually be late to the office again. So, I speed out of the door for the second time this morning, the gripless soles of my loafers be damned. There's no time to be practical – it's make or break. Get this bus or be late for the most important meeting of the year.

The heavens open above me, a non-forecasted torrential rain

pouring demonically from the sky. I rummage through my bag as I continue to skid down the street, a mum on the school run eyeing me for my choice of language as I curse the clouds. I have an umbrella, of course – I always pack prepared – but what I do not have today is a hood – the only thing that could possibly keep my hair from frizzing. High-powered businesswomen walk down the road in wool trenches, not parkas they've hung onto since they were sixteen.

High-powered businesswomen, however, probably have their own drivers, or at least their own very fancy cars. I have a worn-out bus pass and a head of hair that's frizzing the longer I remain in denial. I do a quick mental calculation.

Bus – Eleven minutes away from bus stop.

Bus stop – Seven minutes away from my house.

House – Three minutes away from where I had got to.

Raincoat – On our banister. A one-minute grab at most.

Time behind schedule: Zero if I move fast enough to be back at bus stop in eight minutes.

'Back again?' Mum asks as I run through the door. 'What did you forget this time?'

But I have no time to give her more than a grunt in response as I lunge for the banister. I have no doubt I'll hear all about my supposed attitude later, but my mother's wrath is a price I'll simply have to pay.

I plough through the rain once more, shimmying to keep my handbag from sliding down my arm, fingers grappling as I try to frantically close the zipper on the coat before realizing it's on the completely wrong side. I look down. I grabbed Anton's coat. It's larger, bulkier, not tailored at all. But at least I will be on time, with my hair mostly intact. That is, of course, if the bus app stops acting up. Why the jump from six minutes to three when I'm five minutes away? I pick up the pace, my rain-soaked loafers hooked on my feet with nothing but the sheer force of my toes. It's a race against time, gravity and the forces that clearly want me dead, but I power on. I must. My future hangs in the balance. I cannot have suffered all this for nothing.

By the time I reach the end of the road I can make out the bus, a once-distant blob becoming clearer and closer. I run. My lungs hate me, but there's too much at stake. It's close – far too close, but I reach the stop just in time, my sigh of relief synced with the stilling engine and the whoosh of the doors opening.

I press my card against the yellow reader.

A double beep and a red light flashes up.

I try again. The same happens.

'You're out,' the driver snaps at me through his little glass window.

'Excuse me?' I'm panting, still catching my breath.

'Out of money. It needs topping up.'

Of course it does. Anton is the devil incarnate. Why would he think to reimburse me after using the card I pre-load with the exact amount I need to get the bus to and from the office each month?

'I don't think I have my bank card.' I'm still disorientated as I riffle through my bag.

'Just use your phone, darling.' He tuts. 'Everyone uses the phone these days.'

And I know that. I've not lived under a rock. But after running through the rain and making this bus by the skin of my teeth, he'll have to forgive me for not recalling the best practices when it comes to bus etiquette. He doesn't acknowledge the apologetic smile I give him as I tap my phone on the reader, so I can only assume his morning is going just about as well as mine. But today can only get better. It *has* to get better. I have too much riding on it.

I got on the bus at 8.13. This bus ride is forty-two minutes with traffic. It is super close, but I should just about make it with a couple of minutes to spare. I take refuge in the first empty seat I find, and take a moment to breathe and re-centre myself. I skipped yoga (as I do every morning), but that doesn't mean I can't meditate on the bus. I take a deep breath, but my phone buzzes in my pocket before I can start.

Morning, sunshine. I've missed you.

Kimi's message is followed by a whopping twenty-minute-long voice note.

'Hey, bighead, I'll try to keep this brief, but, honestly, I make no promises. The group chat went off last night and I know you won't read back anything over forty messages, which ... honestly, Mads, we really need to talk about. Anyway, I thought I'd check in and let you know you're needed round Devi's tonight – she finally closed on her flat and she wants to celebrate with one last wine night at her parents' place. She's supplying the wine, we're ordering pizza and Raina's gonna pick up some flowers and a card. Don't even try to come at me with your whole "it's a weeknight" thing – we won't keep it too late and I can pick you up on my way. I haven't been to yours in ages, actually, so it would be nice to pop in and say hi to your mum. Speaking of Auntie, is she going to ...'

I zone out as I stare out of the window, making a mental note to listen properly before I see her later. Kimi, bless her, while one of my favourite people in the world, sure knows how to drag a simple point into five separate ones with additional backstory and side quests.

I text back. Is wine night straight after work? Her status jumps online the second it's sent.

> **KIMI:** Yeah, ASAP – why, you got plans?!
>
> **ME:** The gym. I can meet you guys after?
>
> **KIMI:** You weren't gonna make it to the gym.
>
> **KIMI:** Be honest with yourself.

She's right and I know it, annoying as it is. The second I ran for the bus it was pretty much decided that my grand return to the gym could wait. That doesn't, however, mean that Kimi has to be so loud about it. Especially so early in the morning.

> **ME:** You are an enemy of progress.
>
> **KIMI:** You can progress tomorrow when it's not wine night x

I heart the message. She knows I'll be there as much as I know I'll be there. One of my best friends just bought her first home; I wouldn't miss that for the world. But back to now. Deep breath. I pull out my journal and set my intentions for the day.

1. Apologise to Mum for not saying bye – throw in some kisses for good measure.

2. Don't shy away from the facts with Pippa. I have worked hard. I have proof. I deserve a promotion.

3. Drink two litres of water (at least 1.5 while at work).

4. ~~Go to the gym after work (you have the membership! Use it!)~~. Wine night with the girls.

5. Plan revenge on Anton. Make it good. Make it super evil.

Nudge 2

The Reintroduction

Everyone told me that finding a job straight after graduating would be hard. They kept advising me to 'pace myself' and 'not to worry too much' and I nodded along and agreed to their faces. I saw all the stats and I heard about the state of the job market again and again. I also, however, secretly believed that I would be the exception.

That delusion made the shame and sadness I felt when I became part of the statistic absolutely unbearable. I cried and applied to everything I was even remotely suited for, only to be met with toneless, standard rejection emails.

Unfortunately, we have decided not to move forward with your application . . .

We have chosen a candidate whose qualifications more closely align with . . .

We have received a significant number of applications from qualified candidates and we regret to inform you that . . .

It went on for months. I was never experienced enough or, in most cases, even good enough for a reply. I watched my friends slide into their degree-determined grad roles and tried not to resent them as they vented about their hard workdays, but it got dark after a while. So devastatingly hopeless that I even considered going back and doing a masters.

I needed a break. An escape. I threw my energy into literally anything else I could get my hands on, which just so happened to be my dad's fiftieth birthday party. At the end of the night, as everyone danced and ate from the incredible buffet I'd organised from four different caterers, it was actually Anton who suggested that organising parties might just be my calling. So, I refocused my search to anything to do with events.

Eventually, along came a beacon of hope, offering rudimentary pay in a shiny personal assistant role to the head of events and project management of Abbingtorn Accessories. I applied in a rush on the closing date and got invited to an interview the very next day.

Abbingtorn has earned their place as one of the best luggage providers around, dominating the UK and beyond with their chic but practical items and accessories. Not only has their aggressively flashy marketing got every content creator around flaunting their bags, but their launch parties and collaborations dominate the news sphere for weeks at a time.

Before I started at Abbingtorn I imagined that each morning would take place like a flawlessly choreographed dance, in which I floated through the revolving doors, whipped my coat off and glided up to my desk. Each team would greet me with smiling faces, and cute sassy one-liners, complimenting my shoes and my effortless style. I'd go for afterwork drinks with Design, lunchtime coffees with Production, and gossip with the IT girlies over shaken espressos. But then I joined, and it took about two weeks to realise that workplaces are just school-level arenas with fewer repercussions. My dream came crashing to a rough halt and here I am, four years later, still caught in the wreckage.

'Sorry I'm late – had a nightmare with buses!' I pant as I weave my way through the sea of office chairs.

'It's 8.58,' Gus says, looking up at me in confusion.

'Exactly. Pippa's here already?' I ask. Her lilac handbag sits in pride of place on her desk, taunting me with its earlier-than-usual arrival.

'She got here before me and she's wearing a *blazer* today.' Gus grimaces.

'A blazer?' I ask, my heart sinking.

I know my outfit's not cute, but at least it's still smarter than Pippa's normal attire. She wholeheartedly ignores the 'smart' in 'smart casual'. The blazer must mean something – a mind game or a statement to snatch that pay rise right out of my already shallow hand.

'How early did she get here?' I ask, sniffing for more clues.

'Jackson said she signed in a little before eight. It's got to be because of this big meeting, right?'

The words make my heart plummet even further down in its new pit. My appraisal's been booked in for the better part of a year, rescheduled more times than I've been able to count, and each time it's been called just that – an appraisal. There's no reason she'd be referring to it as the 'big meeting' unless there's more to it now. Unless it's been continuously moved to bide time for a bigger purpose ... a dismissal.

'What big meeting?' I try to level my breathing.

I need clarification before I fully freak out, but Pippa saunters through the door before Gus has a chance to answer.

Pippa Shaw was the first person I met at Abbingtorn. She collected me from Reception with a freshly whitened smile and gushed over how excited she was to have another girl around. She was chirpy and bubbly, and gave me a whole twenty-four hours in the role before asking if 'that was my real hair'. Her constantly upbeat nature and intrusive questions took some getting used to, given that most of it is rooted in how easily everything has come to her, but, once I realised that she'd lobbied for me to get the job, my resistance to her lessened. Mostly.

'You're not usually this late in – everything OK?' she asks, taking a sip of her mint tea.

She wouldn't know – she's never here when I get in. She's never usually here within the first twenty minutes of the workday. Of course she'd pick today to outshine me, to dress smarter and portray the image of a perfect manager. An image she has never once kept up.

'Bus troubles,' I say, my heart beginning to thump in my chest.

She coos. 'Bless! In this rain as well? No wonder you look so . . . tired.'

Of course, I look tired. Anyone would look tired if they'd been up since the crack of dawn fighting for their life.

'Wild night?' Gus asks from across the desk. 'I can barely function the morning after the night before!'

'Nah, just dinner with my family and some reading in bed,' I reply.

'Ugh. I wish I was more like you. Someone suggests one drink and that's it, I'm out until two.' Pippa sighs wistfully. 'By the way, Maddison, your hair suits you like that! All frizzy and puffed out.'

I flinch and try my hardest not to link Pippa with every mean girl I've encountered rolled into one. Then I grab an elastic band out of my desk drawer and drag my hair into a sad little bun that hangs limply on my scalp with no structure. It's the best I can do without a hairbrush or edge control, and it's not like anyone in the office will even notice. Pippa plops down onto her seat, running a hand through her own hair and giving herself a quick once-over in the reflection of her blank desktop screen.

The two of us have pretty similar stories, in the sense that we graduated with no clear career path or professional events experience. The main difference, however, is that she then turned to her uncle, whose golf buddy happens to own significant shares in Abbingtorn. One informal 'interview' at a family party later and she jumped into a project manager role that she was entirely unqualified for. A year later, the head of department quit, two weeks before one of Abbingtorn's biggest events. Left with very little time and no other real options, Pippa was thrust into her current role as head of events and project management.

'Look at the time – we should probably start heading upstairs.' She fishes a purple notebook from her bag.

'Upstairs?' I flick through my calendar. 'Weren't we booked in for Meeting Room H?'

'Shit, I was meant to email you.' Pippa sighs, unapologetic as can be. 'I have to move your appraisal – we have a team meeting upstairs.'

'Oh? The three of us?' I ask.

'Yep. And Olly and Max.'

She lifts her bag from the desk, avoiding my glare as she smooths down her skirt and makes her way to the exit.

'A meeting, right now, with Oliver and Maxwell?' I say slowly.

She nods, confused as to why it's not clicking. Like she didn't just drop an atomic bomb on my lap.

Maxwell Abbington and Oliver Tornton built Abbingtorn Accessories from the ground up (depending on how far down you'd consider the 'ground' to be when you already have the money, capital and a network of popular influencer friends that will flaunt your products for free). What started as a drunk conversation between two friends quickly transformed into a finely oiled machine, with a hundred and fifty-plus direct employees and factories worldwide. After an exclusive deal with a very famous actress and a gold-medal-winning athlete, they have rapidly scaled up their operations, headquartering themselves in a repurposed warehouse building in Clapham and bringing all of their events and marketing in-house.

'Why do they want to meet with all of us?' I ask, swallowing the panic rising in me.

'I'm not sure, didn't ask,' she says, waiting at the door.

'You didn't ask?' I try to hide my horror.

'We'll find out upstairs, hun. I want to be a couple of minutes early.'

With her flightiness, her story is almost believable. Except for the fact that I have access to her calendar and do the majority, if not all, of her scheduling. I do a quick scan and this meeting isn't in her diary. Nor is the appraisal that she has supposedly rescheduled. But there's no time to dwell. There's no time to do anything but slap on a smile and head for the elevator.

It is then, for the first time today, that I catch my entire outfit in the mirrored door. It is worse than I feared. Far more juvenile and bordering on offensive to the eyes. As I tug at the eight-year-old velvet skater skirt, I pray it might bring some maturity or at least some decency, but it still hangs obscenely, the hem ending two or so inches from my crotch (if I'm being generous). I subtly twist to the left, trying to catch my side view in the reflection without raising eyebrows from Pippa or Gus, but, as I move, the silly, stiff collar rubs at my neck, scratching a tiny mark by my collarbone.

I need to focus. Turn my anxious thoughts to the exact way Anton will pay for his crimes against my wardrobe, and away from whatever Oliver and Maxwell could possibly want with us. Also, more importantly, why Pippa went to such lengths to keep the meeting a secret from me in the process.

'There's my favourite team!' Maxwell gives a cheer as we walk through the door. 'How's it going down in Events and Project Management?'

'Great as always!' Pippa flashes her most winning smile.

'Great to hear!' he says, clasping his hands together. 'Take a seat, take a seat.'

I shuffle around the table and into a seat as quickly as I can, hiding the belt of a skirt under the boardroom table before anyone else has a chance to clock it, but they barely acknowledge Gus and I as we sit. My stomach churns, pushing against the cheap blouse as the buttons start to close in. I can't help it – in my four years of working here, we've never all met with them at once. Something has got to be up and the sooner we find out, the sooner I can stop feeling so queasy.

Maxwell glances over to Oliver, who takes a painfully slow sip of his coffee, revelling in the quiet as the rest of us wait on his every move.

'Do you all know who Evie Eesuola is?' Oliver asks eventually.

'Everyone knows Evie!' My exclamation is meant to come off as cool, but it's more of an involuntary, awkward laugh. I can't help it, I'm pumped full of adrenaline from the nerves, and the relief that the first topic of discussion isn't firing us all. Maybe that's why I'm met with staunch silence. I look from Pippa to Gus, who seem completely thrown by the question, and even more by my spontaneous and bubbly answer. 'The lifestyle blogger turned business mogul?' I continue, starting to doubt myself. 'Ridiculous numbers on socials . . . ? Recently got her own TV show?'

I thought that everyone had heard of Evie Eesuola. It's impossible not to have at least seen her name. She is a Black woman in a field dominated by white blondes; she sticks out like a sore thumb, but she makes that thumb the best finger. But the way Gus and Pippa are staring back at me, it's clear they're encountering a blind spot. A very specific and somewhat telling blind spot, if I say so myself.

'Oh, yes, of course, that Evie! I totes love her.' Pippa blags her way through without an ounce of authenticity.

'Good' says Oliver. 'Well, I don't know if you've seen, but she's created a travel-tailored loungewear line as part of her business—'

'Evielution!' I say excitedly. 'She launched it a couple of years ago. It's stocked by most high-end retailers.'

Oliver nods. 'Yes. And now she's launching a luggage line to go with it. A luggage line that she has signed on to release with us.'

'No way!' I gasp.

'It's our biggest brand collaboration to date.' Maxwell beams. 'Working with Evie could open a new set of doors for us.'

Pippa claps her hands. 'That's an awesome get, guys! Where do we come in?'

'With the Summer Splash, the annual July extravaganza she holds at her place. I'm sure you've seen them in the tabloids – big production, flashy décor, real expensive. This year she wants to use it to launch the new range and we've convinced her to give our events team a chance before outsourcing,' Oliver says. 'If she's impressed with what we do with her launch, it could lead to future collaborations and events with her and, in time, her large network of rich friends.'

'We would be honoured to plan it.' Pippa's cheeks have reached their limit with just how far they can stretch into a smile.

'Good to hear it.' Oliver nods approvingly. 'We've arranged a meeting next Friday to survey her grounds and figure out exactly what she wants from us, and we want you all there so we can show her that we are a friendly and united front. In the meantime, Evie has popped in to say a quick hello. She likes to meet large suppliers in person.'

'She's here?' Pippa straightens herself in her seat.

'On her way up as we speak. I trust you'll all give her a proper Abbingtorn welcome.'

Only a man like Oliver would think it non-sociopathic to spring this on us last minute. Pippa's putting on a front and Gus is trying to bottle his worry, but it's clear they're both more than ready to blow. They may not know exactly who she is, but they know that she's important and needs to be impressed, and that's enough to rattle them both to their core. I'd revel in the irony and the fact they now know how I felt having this meeting sprung on me, but, unfortunately, I'm right there with them. Evie Eesuola, trend-setter and absolute fashion icon, is about to walk through those glass doors and I am in a crumpled skater skirt with my hair in a bedraggled bun.

There's a light tap on the door and Maxwell shoots out of his chair.

'Evie, welcome!' he says, as the rest of us look on in awe.

I know Evie Eesuola is gorgeous – I've followed her online for years – but in person she is ethereal. She exudes glamour and elegance with each miniscule movement, every eyelash in place and every wisp of an edge laid. Her glittered French tips catch the light as she extends her hand to shake Maxwell's, creating a small kaleidoscope of colours on the white office wall.

'So nice to meet in person! This must be the team you told me so much about.' The words tinkle as she speaks and scans our faces intently.

She pauses when she gets to me, a fleeting but genuine smile flicking across her face as I twitch nervously and adjust the stupid collar digging into my neck. I know she must be disgusted by the outfit. I try to make it clear I hate it too with a subtle, self-deprecating grimace, but there's only so much you can do while being completely starstruck.

'These three are our events and project management team, who will take your Summer Splash to new heights. This is our head of department, Pippa, her assistant, Maddison, and our junior project manager, Gus.'

'Nice to meet you, Pippa, Gus, Maddison!' She nods at us in turn. 'I'm Evie.'

'We know!' Pippa lies through her lying teeth.

'I never like to assume.' She smiles softly. 'Thanks for taking some time to meet me today. I know some companies can be quite weird about last minute pop-ins, but we just wanted to put some faces to names before the whole formal meeting next week.'

'It's never a bother here at Abbingtorn,' Oliver says, strolling over to shake her hand. 'I'm Oliver by the way – Managing Director. It's lovely to meet you both ahead of next week.'

Oliver's eyes flick past Evie to acknowledge the stone-faced, casually dressed man standing next to her. I hadn't even noticed him in my Evie-induced trance and now, as I digest the sight of him properly, I feel my blood run ice-cold. He stands there, tall in a crisp white T-shirt, a pair of soft black trousers and a silver chain. It's simple, effortless, and yet anything but plain, accentuating his defined chest and muscular arms without trying. His face has changed ever so slightly, more chiselled and dignified with age, but the way he makes my stomach turn on itself remains the same all these years later.

'Nice to meet you, Oliver! I'm Evie, as you know, and this is my talent manager—'

'Aiden Edwards,' I murmur under my breath, the name tasting like pure venom on my tongue.

But I'm not quiet enough. The words ring out across the room and bounce off the walls as clear as day. His deep-brown eyes reach my face and flick up and down as he takes me in slowly. He doesn't move – he doesn't have to – the raised hairs on my arms and my racing heart are enough. I feel like I've seen a ghost, which is fair because as far as I was concerned, he was well and truly dead to me.

Nudge 3

The Wine Night

The FGA

Stands for: The Feral Girls' Alliance.

An inseparable group of friends consisting of Raina, Devi, Kimi and Maddison, founded after a teacher at school called them feral.

'You only got red?' Kimi asks, face scrunched in disgust.

'I asked if you had any preferences!' Devi cradles one of the bottles defensively, stroking its neck as if it needs soothing from Kimi's insults.

'I didn't think that you would go *this* wrong,' Kimi scoffs, shaking her head slowly in dismay.

'I like a red,' Raina weighs in as she hands out the glasses.

Kimi grunts. 'Nobody *likes* a red. They just pretend to because it sounds more mature. Red wine tastes like Ribena that's been left out in the sun. And not in a good way.'

'There's a good way?' I ask as she pouts harder.

'So, no wine for you then?' Devi asks, pouring them out and dodging Kimi's glass.

Raina and I smirk as Kimi continues to purse her lips.

'No, I'll still drink it. I just want you to know that I am *appalled*,' Kimi says.

Ever since listening to Kimi's voice note this morning, the idea of tonight has weighed on me heavily. Not because I didn't want to see my darling friends, but because being an adult is more exhausting than I would like. Between the messy morning and the draining commute, and the general fatigue that comes from sending and receiving emails, the last thing I wanted to do was slap on a smile and play happy for my friend's near-impossible milestone. However, after seeing Aiden again, the idea of wine in my loungewear with my best friends has never sounded sweeter. Even if it is with the corner shop's cheapest red wine.

'You all right, Mads?' Raina asks as she hands me a glass.

I swear, I could sigh from a million miles away and Raina would be able to hear it. She is the only person in this world that I will allow to unironically call themselves an empath. It was clear even in the formation of our friendship when she took pity on me in sixth form and beckoned me into their fold. With ten years and six degrees behind us, you wouldn't even guess that I was a later addition to their close-knit group of three.

'Yeah, sorry. Work is kicking my butt right now.' I snuggle further into the sofa.

'So your appraisal didn't go well?' Raina asks.

'It didn't go at all, actually. Got rescheduled. Again.'

I do my best to wave the topic away, but it's not enough. She moves to sit opposite me and stares me dead in the eyes, face scrunched with determination.

'I know your Pippa face, Mads. This isn't your Pippa face.'

Kimi and Devi stop their squabble to join her pursuit, each one hanging on the promise of my forced brain dump.

'It's honestly nothing.'

Because it has to be nothing. It has to disappear, in the same way that I hoped and prayed that *he* would disappear from my life before. I can't go back to who I am when he is around. Not now. Not again.

'We don't have to talk about it, we can just drink,' Devi says.

Kimi shakes her head. 'Nope. We are talking about it. It's something to you, Mads.'

And they're right. As much as I would like to move on unaffected, I cannot ignore the gnawing pain in my gut. Today dragged up raw emotions I didn't believe I was still capable of feeling.

'Aiden Edwards showed up at my work today,' I say into the rim of my wine glass.

I might as well have dropped a physical bomb with the way the room shakes with the sheer force of their collective gasp at my news. Kimi clutches her chest, Raina's mouth drops open and Devi's eyes widen, as they all stare with tender concern.

'He was in your actual place of work?' Kimi asks.

'In the flesh.'

Devi stands up. 'I'll open the second bottle.'

'And I can Deliveroo a third if needed – I know a place.' Raina reaches for her phone. 'Is he working on one of the events?'

I huff. 'Worse. He is Evie Eesuola's talent manager.'

Talent manager to an icon at my age, while I'm stuck booking Pippa's bikini waxes and chasing her expense receipts. My stomach fills with a thick, sticky jealousy.

'*The* Evie Eesuola? How the hell did Aiden Edwards score that?' Devi pours out a fresh glass.

'Knowing him, it probably just fell into his lap.' I sigh.

'What did you do? What did he say? Please tell me you spilled coffee on him or something?' Kimi downs her glass and joins Devi's second pour.

'Unfortunately not. I chose to be an adult about it and asked him how he'd been,' I reply bitterly.

'Very mature,' Raina says.

'Did he match that energy?' Kimi asks, eyebrow raised.

Of course, he didn't. But Kimi knows that. They all already know that.

'Everyone was confused, so Evie asked if we knew each other.' I sigh again, feeling the anxiety and frustration build in me. 'He responded, in front of my entire team, and my bosses, by saying, "I think she was maybe in my class for something at school."'

My throat burns, the words somehow harder to swallow now than they were when he said them to my face. We spent years at war with each other, we set each other's blood on fire, and now he just looks right through me. It's borderline offensive to be reduced to just another background character in his life, especially after the way our last altercation ended.

'That utter prick,' Devi whispers. 'What is it we used to call him again?'

'The Primary School Prick!' Raina chuckles. 'It lost the ring to it after what happened at uni, though.'

'Yep. That was far too sinister for any nickname . . .' Kimi sighs. 'Girls.'

My warning brings them to an abrupt halt, each one freezing in panic and unsure of what to say next. I watch as their eyes cautiously dart between each other, before silently agreeing on a way forward.

'Sorry, moving on. I hope you slapped him,' Kimi says.

I shrug. 'I shut my mouth and avoided eye contact for the rest of the meeting.'

'Actually, can we backtrack to this meeting for a second ... Evie Eesuola?' Devi asks, helping herself to another glass.

'Oh, yeah – turns out we're planning this year's Summer Splash.'

This new collective gasp could power a wind turbine, blowing the last one out of the water.

'Why, and I cannot stress this enough, *why* aren't you more excited?' Raina asks.

Kimi claps her hands. 'I swear this is literally part of your whole five-year plan?'

Honestly, in the midst of all the drama, I hadn't even thought about my five-year plan. The list that has refreshed itself cyclically since I was fifteen; the list that's got me where I need to be and will now take me to thirty. Kimi's right – Evie's Summer Splash would be the portfolio gold dust I'd need to cross 'organising an event I can be proud of' off my list. But the mere presence of Aiden Edwards has wiped all sense and logic from my brain. I have seen him for one day – a couple of hours at best – and I'm already starting to revert to someone I don't want to be.

'Maybe you can mostly avoid him. Didn't you say your boss usually takes the lead on big events anyway?' Devi asks gently after seeing my expression.

She's right. Pippa has this fun little quirk where she will ask me to plan out an event, liaise with suppliers, then take my work and pass it to the client 'for me'. Does she tell them it's me who did it? I'll never know. But I would put money on that being a no. While frustrating, it might just be the silver bullet I need to save myself from completely losing my mind this time.

'Yeah, maybe you're right.' My chest already feels lighter.

Maybe, in this less-than-ideal world, Aiden and I can co-exist purely through our bosses. I can go back to burying all the times he made me feel inferior and he can go back to pretending he doesn't remember the history between us.

Nudge 4

The Group Project

This is never going to work. I am going to kill him. And everyone here will have to watch.

Even now, as we survey Evie's illustrious grounds, I can't maintain a normal composure. I've been here for three hours, strolling directly next to him, and he has done absolutely *nothing*. Not a 'hello', not a 'remember when . . .', no small flinches at my presence. I could be anyone or no one, and I don't know which is worse. It's infuriating and embarrassing, and incredibly rude.

'Are you all right?' he asks gruffly.

'What?' I ask, snapping out of my rage-filled haze.

'Your hand. It's going pale from how tightly you're holding that pen.'

'Just taking notes,' I lie curtly.

'Yeah . . . and lots of them.'

His eyes scan pointedly over my paper full of annotations. It awakens a deeply savage instinct inside me that demands I gouge his eyes out right here on this grass.

The first time I ever really interacted with Aiden, he looked at me not too dissimilarly to now. It was a tale as old as time – I was a quiet, young people-pleaser and he was a disruptive class clown, eager to be everyone's best friend. The teacher, dying to destroy some formative years, thought, *How could I make both of these small children miserable?* and ripped us from our friends and sat us next to each other, in the hope that my quiet nature might tame him.

'They're not dissimilar to the type of notes I took when we were at Winterdown.' I study him closely, but his face remains neutral. It's psychotic. 'You remember Winterdown? The school that we went to? Together.'

'I know the place,' he replies coolly.

Of course, I never tamed him. I don't know why she thought it would be possible, for the devil cannot be turned with such ease. Even back then, he took one look at my page of notes, asked why I bothered writing so much and that was the beginning of the end. Although, the innocent eight-year-old me couldn't have possibly imagined just how awful that end would be.

'But not me?' I keep pushing. 'You don't remember anything except me being "in your class for something"?'

I think it's a perfectly sane, normal thing to ask. So, I have no idea why he's staring at me like I have grown an extra head.

'What are you doing?' he asks, lowering his voice significantly.

I know he's smart enough to pick up on context. I've experienced the unfortunate strength of his mind games first-hand. But I will not waste any further time explaining myself to someone who does not have the basic empathy to engage. It's undignified and stupid, and, most importantly, another instance where he comes out the winner.

'Just forget it,' I hiss.

'You're angry with me.' The corner of his lip twists into a smile that could launch a thousand deathly missiles.

I lie again. 'No.'

He responds with a chuckle that activates my fight-or-fight-harder instincts. 'You seem it.'

I take a deep breath, close my eyes and remind myself that I am not a person that would fare well in jail. I have spent years building everything on my way to success, and I will not allow him and his stupid laugh to knock it down for me. But it's so loud and so pressing, and bounces around my brain with so much vigour, that I can't drown it out despite my best efforts.

'Will you be quiet?' I snap back louder than I intended. 'You ruin *everything*.'

He shrugs. 'I'm just standing here.'

'Standing here and judging me when you should be paying attention,' I reply.

'I can't multitask?'

'This is important!'

'Well, if it's so important then maybe you should stop talking to *me*.'

'Can you please go and stand next to literally anyone else?'

'There she is – there's Moany Maddy!'

I hear the triumph in his voice and time stops, trapping us both in it. Blood pounds in my ears as I turn to face him, my icy stare a contrast to his proud warmth.

'What did you say?' I hate how thin and weak my voice sounds.

'Moany Maddy.' He cocks one eyebrow. 'I thought you might have grown out of her by now.'

He does remember me.

I lose all concept of space, time and all that surrounds me as my eyes narrow in on his face. There's a challenge in his eyes, a dare almost. *That's* the guy that's haunted my thoughts for over a decade.

'Maddison!' Oliver's call breaks the moment and I turn to see everyone else, Evie included, looking my way expectantly.

'Evie asked if you had any thoughts,' Pippa says, the words squeezing through her incredibly false smile.

'My personal thoughts?' I ask.

'Yes, your personal thoughts.' Evie chuckles. 'You've taken so many notes – what do they say?'

'Oh, Maddison's just like that – she always takes loads of notes!' Pippa rushes to say, attempting to sweep me back under the rug. 'She gives such detailed write-ups; it's so helpful when Gus and I are getting stuck in.'

'I love that! And I'd like to know what she's thinking,' Evie says, perfectly mimicking her sickly-sweet tone. 'I am really keen to hear what plans you've got brewing, Maddison.'

She looks at me with an open, earnest smile.

Don't get me wrong, I have plenty of ideas, but, in the four years that I have worked at Abbingtorn, nobody has ever asked me for any of them. I'm not used to voicing my ideas and I don't really know where to start. There's a line of communication, which is always filtered through Pippa, and we do not ever break that mould.

But Evie is staring at me now, glossy lips pursed into the softest and most supportive of smiles. I try to speak, but the words get stuck somewhere in my throat. So, I do the only thing my anxiety-riddled body will allow and hold out the notebook. She crosses the space between us and I hold my breath as I let her scan the pages in my hand. Delight and confusion dance across her features, nose scrunching at sentences, fingers tracing over my wobbly letters and shoddy diagrams. She *actually* wants to know. She *actually* cares. And even from here, I can tell it's making Pippa furious.

'There's a question mark by water features. You don't like the idea either?'

I hear Pippa's sharp inhale at Evie's query, daggers shooting into the side of my head.

Two years ago, Pippa decided she needed an 'event signature' – something people would see and know they were at a Pippa Shaw soirée. Why she decided on water features, I could not tell you. I also couldn't tell you why she consistently picks the tackiest ones around. I just can't bear to see Evie brought down to her level. They're not her brand – they're not even remotely close – and she shouldn't endure them at the expense of Pippa's weak attempt at having a personality.

'We all love water features, of course. They're a Pippa Shaw staple,' I say as diplomatically as possible.

'But?' Evie asks.

She can already tell what I'm thinking and she's pressing me to go on, despite Pippa's death stare.

'I just don't know if they should be the main feature for this event.' I hesitate, but Evie nods for me to continue. 'It's called a "Summer Splash", which to me implies more water *park* than it does water *feature*. You know?'

'I do,' she says, musing this over. 'So, you think we should go down a water-ride route?'

'Your brand screams luxury, and luxury is not found in family water parks.' I wrinkle my nose, thinking of the garish colours, the smells, and the screams of children. 'I think you could still have some fun with it, though – water parks and pool parties with a twist, you know? More adult, more upmarket, more . . . you.'

Her face grows more animated the longer I speak, at least until she surveys the crowd and narrows in on the less-than-impressed man to my right.

'Aiden, you're frowning.'

Of course, he's frowning. I could tell him he's just won the lottery and he would frown at me. Aiden hates my guts, and, by the looks of it, he's done pretending otherwise.

'It's all good.' He shrugs, feigning apathy.

'Well, it's clearly not.' Evie continues to watch him closely. 'Speak your truth.'

'I just feel like it's a bit obvious.'

'Obvious?' I say.

I'll tell him what's obvious. The way he dresses like a nineties R&B singer because he hasn't got any style of his own, *that's* obvious.

'Resort ... Summer ... It just seems a little basic, you know? An obvious link,' he says.

Pippa barely masks her snort of derision and I scoff at his words.

'We would *obviously* make sure it wasn't basic,' I say.

'And how would you do that exactly?' he asks.

Well, I don't know, Aiden. I just came up with it and no one was supposed to read my half-thought-out notes until they were fully formed and typed up.

I think for a moment, trying to recall the key points from the brief Aiden emailed around.

'The point of the event is to launch a luggage line, so we could make this place a holiday resort – multiple holiday resorts.' I wave a hand around the grounds, sectioning it off as the vision springs to life in my brain. 'If we have multiple water rides – one in each quadrant, there could be a theme with each representing a different country you've been to. So, we—'

'It has potential, but I don't think it's big enough,' Aiden cuts in.

'And how, exactly, would you make it bigger?' I say.

I don't quite understand what's not big enough about multiple holiday resorts, and, frankly, I'm not convinced that he does either.

'I don't know ... I just feel like it needs more,' he says.

'Like more rides?' I grill him further.

He shakes his head. 'Like more substance. Anyone can throw a party – Evie always does things with meaning.'

He makes an annoyingly good point. Evie has always been someone that posts with a purpose, be it a good cause or someone she can lift up.

'We could reach out to tourism boards for the gift bags – include fact cards and links to causes people can donate to,' I say.

'Yeah, and serve authentic cuisine from each region, from smaller family-run businesses who would really benefit from the money and exposure,' he adds.

'And of course, if we're going immersive, we've got to go all the way. What about if we have the waiting staff in cabin-crew uniforms or traditional cultural dress?'

'That works, then theme the invites around travel kits,' Aiden continues. 'I'm thinking boarding passes, custom passports ...'

'We could ask Production if they can make some event-exclusive passport cases just for guests as pre-event promotion.' I throw out the idea.

Aiden nods. 'Actually, if it isn't too late to add passport cases to the range, they could be released on the website a week after the party. We wait a couple of days to announce it, so fans have time to ask where they can get one and then boom – surprise drop with instant sell-out potential.'

'We make it clear that it's limited edition – that way we not only get hype, but massive resale value,' I say.

We both stop to catch our breaths, the rush of the back-and-forth knocking us speechless. The moment is fleeting, but it's just long enough to notice the five now-startled faces staring at us.

Evie gasps. 'That was electric.'

I still can't speak. I'm forced to stare back at her silently, and by the sounds of the poorly concealed panting to my left it seems that I'm not alone.

'Oliver, Maxwell. You heard that, right? I want all of it, just like they suggested. How possible would you say that is?'

'Well, we'd have to look into suppliers and run some numbers, but if you've got the budget I can't see why not,' Oliver replies.

'We can get a deck together by, let's say, this time next week?' Maxwell looks to Pippa for confirmation.

'Perfect. Friday works for me,' Evie says, flicking through her phone calendar. 'How does eleven a.m. sound? We can swing by the office.'

'Oh, absolutely!' Pippa forces herself back into the spotlight. 'We'll get on it right away!'

The deal's in the bag; everyone is visibly more relaxed at the knowledge. We've got Evie's Summer Splash and I managed to play a part in it.

'Brill! So we're done.' Evie's eyes are still glued to her phone. 'And I want those two leading on this.'

The sentence sends a visceral ripple through the group, ripping apart any trace of status quo as all eyes follow her pointing finger to where Aiden and I stand. I can barely process the words myself; a rush of adrenaline vibrates through my body. If this is everything I've wanted for years, why does it feel so terrifying?

Pippa splutters, plastering a strained grin on her face. 'Well, as a team, we tend to work in a certain order … Maddison will, of course, be heavily involved, but she works in an assistant capacity. I really don't want to overwhelm her at this stage in her career. Especially with something as important as this.'

The words drip off her tongue like honey, but I see them for the lumps of coal they really are. She was not concerned about how 'overwhelmed' I was when she made me take over hosting duties at our last Christmas event so she could shed some mulled-wine-fuelled tears, or when she was passing all of her incomplete tasks to me before going off for unscheduled annual leave, or while sending me off on three buses and two trains to location-scout because she just had 'too much on' to do the half-hour drive in her car. It doesn't fool me one bit and it doesn't look like it fools Evie either.

'I believe in empowering people, especially young women in the workplace. I would never have got to where I am otherwise. I am sure you agree that if Maddison is big enough to come up with the idea, she's big enough to execute it, right?' she asks bluntly.

'Oh, yes, we believe in empowerment and have a strong focus on diversity at Abbingtorn too,' Pippa recites robotically.

Evie's done with Pippa. Bored, even. Her eyes swoop over her head and land on me.

'Maddison, do you feel capable of leading this, if you are supported?' she asks, her face softening.

I've always known what I could do if I were just given the chance, but it feels validating to know that someone else can see it too. There's something about the way Evie carries herself and the support in her eyes that lights a fire in me that I have not felt for a long time.

'One hundred per cent,' I reply, holding her gaze and trying to block out the sets of eyes burning into my skull. 'I won't let you down.'

'Perfect.' The smile she gives me is like a warm bear hug. 'And, Maxwell, you trust in your team, right?'

He's flustered under her gaze, his face matching the salmon of his shirt as he mumbles a response. 'Well, I suppose ... provided you are happy with the deck she produces, and it doesn't interfere with her other tasks, Maddison can lead with Pippa's supervision.'

'Then I don't see a problem!' Evie claps her hands together and keeps grinning as they all nod in tandem, dazzled by the power in her stare.

'I reckon I can part with Aiden two days a week so he can work with Maddison on the logistics.'

And that's when the second part of her sentence truly hits me.

I want those two *leading on this.'*

Two of us.

Me and Aiden.

'Wait, when you said "both" ... you want me doing events?' he asks, sounding about as horrified as I feel.

I'm not being dramatic when I say that I'd rather chew gravel than work side by side with him.

'I need more of that fire.' She sweeps a perfectly manicured finger between the two of us.

I feel my blood run cold. I have been waiting for four years for any modicum of recognition – a new title or a pay rise that wasn't a fraction of the inflation rate. And now, I have been handed the ultimate chance to show just what I'm capable of and prove that I'm worthy of more. It's the exact rocket up the ladder that I need to make up for stagnant time, and Aiden has shown up to rip it all away.

He tries to argue. 'I'm sure Abbingtorn won't need my input for the deck.'

'Yes, we're good to handle it on our end!' I nod in agreement.

I will not have him walk his way into something I've spent years preparing for and outshine me. Not this time. Not ever again.

'I think this will be good for you, Aiden. I like what just happened and the ideas came from you both equally.' Her tone is final. 'I want that deck by Friday. Got it?'

And just like that, Aiden Edwards has cemented himself back in my life for another round.

Nudge 5

The Mood Board

'Aiden's here,' Pippa says as she hangs up her phone. 'Will you collect him from Reception yourself, or shall I?'

'No worries, I'll go,' I reply, ignoring her tone as I push back my chair.

I can see Gus staring intently at his screen, jaw clenched in an intense effort to stay neutral. Pippa's been so passive aggressive since the tour of Evie's grounds and I can tell it's grating on him just as much as it is me. First there were the backhanded compliments, then the exclusion from daily coffee runs and, finally, the thinly veiled snipes about who is in charge. Plus, she looks like she's sucking on a lemon every time someone so much as mentions the Summer Splash. It's deeply uncomfortable for absolutely everyone involved, especially me – which is clearly the point.

But, unluckily for her, a good planner always has Plan B at the ready and I skipped a few letters to initiate Plan H the second Pippa started acting funny. Meeting Room H to be exact.

'Just so you know, I've booked out one of the third-floor meeting rooms for the rest of the day,' I say politely.

'You're not planning down here?' she asks, gripping her coffee a little too tightly.

A voice interrupts before I have the chance to reply.

'Where shall I sit?'

Pippa's spine straightens at the intrusion, her fingers flying to her hair to oh-so-not-subtly let out her ponytail.

'I was just on my way to come and get you,' I say pointedly.

He opens his mouth to respond when Pippa interjects.

'Aiden! Such a pleasure!'

'Thank you ...'

'What do you think of the office?' she asks, twirling her hair. 'We should give you a tour before you two get started. Come, I'll take you.'

I don't know what's more off-putting – the fact that Pippa is flirting or the fact that she's flirting with *Aiden*. Aiden is, I guess, objectively attractive, though his fresh trim and rich, spicy bergamot aftershave are doing a lot of the heavy lifting. Plus, no haircut or flexed biceps can do anything to make up for his horrible mess of a personality.

There's a part of me that wants to send him off with Pippa and have a few extra moments to myself while he suffers. But she works fast, and never without an agenda. Who *knows* what she'd say about me if I left her alone with him. The last thing I need is Aiden Edwards having more ammo against me than he already does.

'I don't think we have time for that, Pippa. We really need to get started upstairs.' I grab my bag and head towards the door.

Aiden follows me gladly before Pippa has time to object, but I can feel her eyes burrowing a hole into the back of my skull as we leave.

We stand in the lift in complete silence and I do my best to keep my eyes focused intently on the plain metal door ahead of me. One time I do accidentally glance over and I catch his mouth opening as if to speak, but he snaps it shut just as quickly when he notices me staring. It's an agonisingly slow ride despite being only two floors, and I release my long-held breath the second we make it to the meeting room. Aiden enters cautiously, circling the office slowly like he's in some sort of a trance.

'Are all your meeting rooms this small?' he asks, squeezing around the table.

'Only the ones that allow for recurring bookings.' I wince, thinking back to Shirley from Office Administration glowering at my six-month-long list of meeting-room dates.

'You know, no one books these rooms this far in advance but you,' she said with a lipstick-coated scowl.

I know she resents me for it. The room allocation made that clear as day. Meeting Room H is the drabbest in the building, reserved almost exclusively for disciplinaries and dismissal meetings. It boasts about six feet in both length and width, and reeks of damp, desperation and despair, which is not made any cheerier by Aiden's sullen face. However, I refuse to let that derail me and spread an A3 sheet of planning paper across the table.

'We have twenty-five weeks until the Summer Splash and you're in the office two days a week. The way I see it, we do weeks one to five fully in here while we curate the deck and finalise details. For weeks six to fourteen, we move down to my department one day a week, as the team will be assisting more. Weeks fifteen to twenty-four we meet in here once a fortnight, just to go over where we're at and record progress. Week twenty-five will obviously be entirely on site. I've reserved this room for two weeks post-event in case of any loose ends that need tying.'

'Right …' he says, staring at the newly annotated sheet soullessly.

'What?' I ask, trying to keep my voice calm.

'I figured we'd just see how things go,' he replies.

Of course he did. That's literally all he does. He's spent nearly three decades 'just seeing how things go' and he assumes that the rest of us can afford the same privilege.

'That's why I have a real job and you work for an influencer.' I recoil the second the words leave my mouth, my whole body going stiff with shame. I didn't even mean it – I genuinely respect influencer hustles, especially ones of the calibre of Evie Eesuola. I've been following her for years. I have photos of her on my vision board. 'I'm sorry, I didn't mean—'

'It's whatever.' His tone is clipped. 'So, should we get going or what?'

He plonks himself down in a chair, his knees pressing against my thigh as he shifts himself under the table. This room really is tiny, especially with the two of us in it. I'm a few inches away from being able to feel his breath. I turn slightly and realise with a jolt of horror that I can see every pore on the side of his face closest to mine. Perhaps Plan H isn't the golden ticket I needed it to be after all.

I clear my throat. 'I brought examples of some pitch decks we've done in the past, so you can get an idea of what a deck entails.'

'I know what a pitch deck is,' he says dryly. 'Super surprising for a lowly influencer worker, right?'

He's offended – I knew it. I don't know why he wouldn't be – if he said something like that to me, the FGA would have never heard the end of it. I am messing this up before we've even got started.

'I'm sorry,' I repeat my apology a little louder.

'I spend half my time going through brands' pitch decks for Evie. And I have a degree in business management.'

'You do?' I ask.

'First class honours. So, we can skip the "Pitch Decks for Idiots" segment.'

Fair enough. I just need to keep it calm and cool – work-focused and stripped of the personal. He can't be mad forever – eventually we'll get wrapped up in this enough to forget my bitchy comment.

'OK, so did Evie choose the four countries she wants?' I ask.

'She's leaving it up to us. The only one that must be there is Indonesia, because "Bali changed her life".'

'Cool. OK, first task is clear, then.' I grab a fresh sheet of A3 and put it in the centre of the table. 'Let's start by brainstorming popular destinations on social media – they're the ones her attendees will want to see the most. Then we can . . .'

Aiden leans over and I watch in horror as he grabs my orange highlighter, dividing the paper into quarters.

'What are you doing?'

'Evie's Nigerian, so naturally that can be number one. Then we've got Indonesia for two; her most-liked picture is from Mexico – that's three – and for the fourth one we can throw in something for us.' He pauses. 'You're St Lucian, right?'

'Yeah,' I say, eyes fixed on his scribbles.

'Me too, so that makes number four.'

He draws a line under his ugly scrawled writing, pushing it closer towards me so I can take in the atrocity in all its horrific glory. There it all is in bright orange, a colour not meant for writing, fresh from a highlighter pen clearly not made for notes.

'How'd you know I'm St Lucian?' I ask, trying to distract myself from the abomination under my nose.

'My mum. She used to beg me, day in and day out, to make friends with "the nice St Lucian girl" from my class.'

'You never did,' I say.

He scoffs. 'Yeah, 'cos I was like ten years old. Who lets their parents choose their friends at that age?'

I concede. 'Fair enough. For the colour scheme, I was thinking—'

'I've got the hex codes for each bag colour from her new range. I also think we should make a mood board.'

'A mood board?'

'Yeah.' He doodles on the corner of the already disorganised sheet. 'This perfume brand came to her with one once and she absolutely loved it.'

He digs out his phone from his pocket, scrolling quickly before revealing a shaky photo of the mood board. Evie was right – on top of being an aesthetic dream, it's personal and looks like it required a lot more effort.

'Mood board it is.' I reach into my bag.

'What are you doing?' he asks, face scrunched in disgust.

'Writing all of this down.'

I've got some notebooks in front of me and a pen in my hand – it could not be clearer what I am doing.

'You have two notebooks.' He looks horrified.

'Yes? The pink one for lists and the spiral-bound for jotting down meeting minutes.'

Two notebooks aren't that outlandish. If anything, he's the weird one for making it such a big deal. I straighten my spine and stare at him, solid in my convictions, but then I watch his eyes dart from my face to the third notebook poking out of my bag.

'Fine. There's two more.' I ignore my burning cheeks. 'My daily journal and my intention-setter. But they're irrelevant right now.'

'Your intention-setter?' he asks.

'Yeah, for my goals, aims, objectives. Professional, physical, five-year plan ...'

'Five-year plan?' He has a judging look on his face.

'I like documenting where I want to be in five years, every five years. It helps me stay motivated,' I say, exasperated.

I don't know why I'm justifying my notebooks to him; I know he doesn't care. But I am not, and will not, be ashamed of having my life together, or at least trying to.

He mutters under his breath. 'You haven't changed one bit.'

'And you have?'

'I didn't need to.'

I think back to my first day of secondary school and my determination to be a new, cooler version of me. That was, of course, until I got to my chemistry class and found none other than Aiden Edwards in the assigned seat next to mine.

'Are you serious?' his friends groaned, wasting no time.

'Not this again!' I heard another one wail as they guffawed behind us.

I couldn't bear to look at him, or any of them for that matter. I took my notebook out of my schoolbag, put my head down, and resolved to focus all my attention on the task at hand. The new plan was to blend in – the less I was noticed, the better. But Aiden made that impossible for the rest of my time there.

'Problem?' he asks, snapping me back into the present.

He knows he's got me. He knows I'm upset, and the way his lip is curling only makes the whole ordeal worse. I could not think of anyone I would detest sharing this tiny room with more. Not Pippa, not Gus, not the devil himself.

I huff, trying to hide my distress. 'Let's just get back to work.'

I know he can sense it; his infuriating little smile says it all. 'Of course.'

I can't bear to look at it any longer or give him his twisted satisfaction; every second I stay here with him is another second I die inside.

'What now?'

'What now?'

'Your tone.'

His eyebrows raise in shock.

All those years next to him and I never actually bit; I knew all his little comments and gestures were just bait. But I'm older and wiser now, and he's at *my* place of work, and I cannot go on like this for the next six months.

'You got anything else to roll your eyes at or can we actually get started?' I ask, doubling down on my snark.

His head cocks to the side, tongue rolling in his mouth as he carefully formulates his next response, but then decides against it.

'Sorry.' He shrugs, smile changed but unwavering.

There's a new light to it – it's brighter – he's finding this fun. It flickers over his face, softening each feature on its way. But it quickly ceases once he realises that he's let down his guard. I feel a fizz of excitement at this new upper hand.

'Am I good to continue?' I ask smugly.

If only I'd bitten back like this in school.

He nods quickly, avoiding eye contact as he brings the scribbled paper back into the centre.

I pull out my daily journal and flip to a blank page, making sure he sees.

Countdown:

Days until the Summer Splash - 175

Days until no more Aiden - 189

Nudge 6

The Agreement

'I hate him,' I cry out as I throw my back against the mattress. 'Tell me I don't have to go in tomorrow.'

'If I tell you that, will you get off my stuff?' Anton asks, roughly tugging his hoodie out from underneath me.

Evie got pulled away on a shoot with Fenty, so she pushed our meeting back by a week. I nearly cried with relief when I heard; it's hard meeting deadlines when you're tied to a lead balloon.

I worked with Aiden on a fair number of occasions over our fourteen years at school together. I have not, however, worked with Aiden in a situation where my job and future are on the line. Turns out that comes with a whole lot more frustration and a week's worth of headaches and stress screams to anyone who will listen. That includes Anton, who is enduring the latest one as he packs to go back to uni.

'And everyone *loves* him. Gus and Pippa can't stop sucking up to him when he's there and gushing over how amazing he is every time that he leaves.' I can hear the whine in my voice.

'That tracks. I was only at Winterdown at the same time as you for a year, and I *still* heard about him my whole time there. That man was a legend. But I don't get why you still care. That was, like, fifty years ago for you now anyway.'

He ducks, effortlessly dodging the T-shirt I throw in retaliation. It flies past his shoulder and dips to the floor to land perfectly in a crumpled heap in his suitcase.

'Thank you,' he says, smirking as I scowl back at him. 'Seriously, though. You're obsessive, but you're not "hold a decade-long grudge" obsessive. There's no way this is still over beef you had at school.'

Flickers of memories slice through me, packed full of biting comments, fragmented eye rolls and frustrated sighs. Alone, each one would have been fine – forgettable, even, but they went on for years, spanned decades and haunted me for so long after. Perhaps things would have been different, perhaps I would have forgotten it all if not for the trauma of our last interaction. But that last time . . . I can't. I feel my stomach curl into a tight, fixed knot.

'It's not about school,' I say.

'When have you seen him since? There's no way you two run in the same circles. He's too cool for that.' Anton tuts.

'Are you calling me uncool?'

'Was there a world where you ever believed you *were* cool?' he says, deadpan.

I get him this time, triumphantly watching him flinch as a pair of jeans hit him square in the face. I'd like to chalk it up to my fantastic aim, but I know he let me have it.

'D'you know he was responsible for my first taste of failure?' I shift my focus to a far less traumatic interaction. 'End of Year Three. Mrs May took me to the side and said "it was such a shame that I couldn't change his behaviour" while sitting next to him.'

She may as well have slapped on handcuffs and sent me to prison. 'I cried all evening. Mum and Dad didn't know what to do.'

'You know that's pathetic, right?' Anton asks.

I sigh, sinking further into his duvet. 'I don't think I can do this.'

'We both know that's not true,' he scoffs. 'You've never met a challenge that you can't make the best of. It's really annoying.'

I turn to look at him, sat unassumingly on his floor as he folds his clothes without a care in the world.

'That was almost nice.'

He grunts as he zips up his case. 'Don't get used to it.'

But the words stick with me past the hug goodbye the next day and carry me all the way to my next session with Aiden. I *have* always managed to make the best of a challenging situation and Aiden is just that – another challenge. When I enter the Abbingtorn building I am, above all else, a professional working individual. And I should be able to stay that way even around the likes of Aiden Edwards.

I let his little comments roll off me, his blank face fade into the wall and every little grating moment dissipate around me. That is, however, until Raina's message hits the group chat.

HE DID IT!

The words are bold and bright underneath a picture of a dazzling diamond ring. It's immediately followed by a slew of non-stop *OMG*s and *FINALLY*s from Devi and Kimi. I join in, of course, sending a garbled string of capitalised letters and liking their messages about planning the hen, but I can feel my face grow cold and the air draw sharply from my lungs. She's engaged. Getting married. Married. At my age.

'You look rough as hell,' Aiden says. 'You need to start taking your lunch break.'

'I'm fine,' I mutter, eyes still glued to my screen and that ring.

'Cool, well, I'm gonna head off then.'

Not only did Raina's news throw me for a loop, but it helped me finally succeed in forgetting Aiden's existence. So much so that I didn't notice him pack up his bag, ready to abandon me and our half-finished pitch deck.

I glance down at my watch. 'It's only four-thirty.'

'And we never took a lunch break. I'm owed an hour. You should feel lucky I'm only taking thirty minutes.'

I stare at him in disbelief. 'But we're not even close to being done.'

'That's a problem for tomorrow morning, when I'm back on the clock.' He swings his backpack onto his shoulder.

I've always known he was unserious, but I didn't think that even he would be so stupid as to leave something *that* last minute at the expense of 'owed time'. He wants to continue tomorrow morning. The same morning in which we are presenting to Evie at eleven o'clock. My brain fizzes and splutters, breaking down as a result of his sheer idiocy.

I take a pause, take a breath and swallow my rage as Anton's words echo in my head. I can be professional, understanding, face this challenge head on. Even at the limits he's pushing me to.

'Have you got plans tonight?' I ask, giving him the benefit of the doubt.

'Nope,' he replies, plain and simple, as he heads for the door.

'Then why would you need to—'

'I told you – we worked through lunch. Our paid time was done thirty minutes ago. You should be leaving too.'

'There's still so much to do.'

'Whatever, see you tomorrow.'

I know that he's smarter than this. We've made progress for sure, but not Evie-ready progress. The script and mood-board accents are still things of fiction, and neither of us has even started proofreading the binder. Leaving it all for the two hours we have tomorrow morning is a sure-fire way to guarantee that this whole thing crashes and burns. The fact he even suggested it makes me question how he got all the way to being a talent manager in the first place.

'You've never stayed late a day in your life, have you?' I tut.

'I've probably done it more times than you've chilled out,' he retorts.

'I know how to chill,' I reply, rolling my eyes.

I'm just also aware that there's a time and a place, and work is not one of them. Especially the day before a presentation like this. A presentation I'd happily stay all night to finish if it meant it went well.

'I beg to differ.' He chuckles. It's extremely grating. I feel my blood simmer, flames crawling up my body.

I don't know who I offended to get this level of karma, but somehow my friends are killing their careers, buying property and now getting married, while my chance at making it past assistant level hinges on a guy who hates my guts. And if that weren't enough, if the odds weren't already unfair, he also thinks he deserves to leave early the day before I face the most pivotal moment of my career so far. I lunge for the door at lightning speed, barricading it with my body before he can reach it.

'We're not done yet,' I say, my jaw clenched.

'Are you serious?' he asks, one eyebrow raised.

We are face to face, one step away from our chests touching as he stares, flummoxed, at the new five-foot-six obstacle in his way. But I'm not moving. I stay still, rooted to the spot, my fist squeezed around my ballpoint pen.

'We're not leaving until we at least finish the presentation content,' I say as calmly as I can.

He makes a play for it – arm brushing ever so slightly against my waist as he reaches for the one thing that could make his escape. But I'm faster, more agile and way closer to it. I grip the door handle tightly before he has the chance. His hand clasps over mine, palm warm to the touch but eyes cold and angry.

'We'll finish it in the morning,'

His voice is low and gruff, his breath close enough to tickle my face as he speaks. He hasn't moved his hand. It stays pressed on top of mine over the metal handle, resolute. He means business. It's time to show I do too. I puff out my chest and feign intimidation, the buttons of my dress brushing his T-shirt in the process.

'This isn't school, Aiden – you can't just do things half-arsed and still expect to come out on top.' I point my pen angrily at his chest. 'They don't think I can do this as it is, and I am not giving Pippa Shaw the chance to take this away from me.'

I stand my ground, rigid with indignation and the sheer resolution to see this through. Looking at him now, it's clear that his grip on the handle has brought him lower. If I turned, my nose would graze against his. But he still doesn't move, so neither do I. No matter how close we seem to be.

'What would you prefer? That I be more like you and plan every breath and second of my life?' he asks.

His lips are dangerously close to mine as he sneers each word, a callousness to his tone that wasn't present in the empty threats from before. I'm making him angry, but I couldn't care less. I spent years pretending I didn't see his eye rolls every time we were paired together, pretending that snide comments from his friends didn't cut me to my core, and I will no longer pretend that I don't matter. I'm taking up space today and I am showing him that I am not someone he can just brush aside.

I block out his lips and his face, and the feel of his breath, and remind myself of the task at hand. I could get closer to promotion like Kimi, or own property like Devi if I make this project a success. The first step in doing that? Ensuring that the man leaning over me goes nowhere. And by nowhere, I mean I want him to stay in the room ... not leaning over me, obviously.

'Tell you what, I'll plan your evening for you,' I say. 'You stay here with me, finishing this mood board until further notice.'

'You're insufferable.'

'That makes two of us.'

His eyes say 'move'. Mine say 'make me' as I press my back further into the door. He has one of two options: give in now or give in later. Either way he gets out of here past five o'clock.

His shoulders sink slowly and he gives a low exhale as he skulks back to his seat. I can feel the silent rage that overcomes him from the moment he reopens his laptop. It should be worrying, or sad, or guilt-inducing, I guess, but all it does is fill me with intrigue. In all my years with him I've seen every possible shade of indifference, but I've never actually seen him angry. I've never seen him display anything towards me that requires passion, but here it is, burning bright as he clicks his mouse.

'About time,' I say, eager to push it further.

His mind is racing – I can tell by the creases in his forehead and the clench of his jaw. I dare not imagine what's brewing, begging to get out and eviscerate me in the way I know he wants to. He keeps it to himself, though, the only sounds in the room our shaky, recovering breaths and synchronous typing. The fog of the conflict shrouds the room in a damp, sticky heat that fills my lungs with discomfort and makes my whole body tense.

After ten minutes of agonising silence, it is he who finally breaks it. 'You don't like me.'

It's plain, unfeeling.

'Neither do you,' I retort. 'Like me, I mean.'

I've known it for years and yet the words still sting as they come to the surface. But he doesn't react, eyes fixed on the peeling motivational poster behind my head.

'I think today's proven that this doesn't work, despite our best efforts,' he continues.

He's right. I vowed that I'd be professional, and I've tried, but the truth is that we just can't work with each other. Two weeks into the project and the knives are already drawn ... Six months down the line and one of us will be on life support.

'So, what do we do?' I ask bitterly.

I want him out of my life more than almost anything, but my stomach drops at the thought of where this might be headed. At the end of the day, he's the one with the strong tie to Evie ... The way he's sitting here makes it clear that he has more control than I could've summoned for a moment. Of course he let me win the battle. He already knew that he had the war in hand.

He cocks his head. 'I'll do this presentation, stay late for today, but after tomorrow I'm telling Evie I'm off the project.'

'You're giving it up?' I ask in disbelief.

He shrugs it off like it's as simple as who has the last slice of pizza.

'We can't do this together and I don't even work in events.'

I'm speechless. I simply can't relate. There is nothing on this earth that would make me drop something like this. If he's willing to throw it away over two weeks together, I severely underestimated just how much he hates me.

'But Evie said she wanted us both to do this,' I say.

He waves me off. 'Evie's word isn't law. She listens to reason and I'll give her a good one.'

My mind runs wild with the string of 'reasons' he'll throw Evie's way, all of which I have no doubt will reflect poorly on me. I know how he sees me and soon Evie will feel the same, marring any chance I had of winning her over.

He looks up at me, squinting at my scrunched features, and sees my apprehension instantly. 'It'll be calm. We'll present and then I'll chat to Evie straight after. Tell her you've got it covered and I'd be better spent somewhere else.'

My jaw remains tense. 'You mean it?'

It's childish. I'm back in primary school, forcing a pinky promise with a boy who wouldn't even take my hand.

He nods firmly. 'One more day and we're done.'

The words, deep in delivery, echo across the walls as the low vibrato shakes all the way to my core. It's too spine-chillingly good to be true, but, if I want to be free, then I have no choice but to believe him.

'Thank you,' I mumble.

'No problem.'

Then he goes back to typing without another word.

For a moment, everything settles. All seems right with the world. My six months of torture turns to two weeks, all over tomorrow.

Nudge 7

The Disagreement

<u>Presentation Day Schedule</u>

8 a.m. - Arrive at work. Proceed to wait seventy-eight minutes for Aiden, who promised he'd 'make it for 8.30' and severely oversold.

9.20 a.m. - Wait for Aiden to reluctantly unpack, harass him to be ready for:

9.30 a.m. - Run through presentation from start to finish.

10.15 a.m. - Quick-fire feedback about said run-through.

10.30 a.m. - Reattach items to the mood board and make note for next time to buy better glue.

10.45 a.m. - Set up in the boardroom; ensure coffees and herbal teas are ready for consumption.

11.15 a.m. - Wow Evie with perfect pitch, smile and wait patiently while she takes it all in.

Evie is flawless as ever, a pop of pastel against the otherwise mo-
notonously slate-grey boardroom. She has us all under her hold
without even trying as she flicks through our handout with rigor-
ous focus. Her eyes jump from word to word, giving nothing away,
every small movement a tease. Pippa, Oliver and Maxwell look
about ready to burst, and, as I stand at the front, right next to our
mood board, I do my best to ensure I don't look as bad as they do.

There's a shift in the room, a quick catch of breath from all, as
she flicks back to the beginning of the printout and closes it for
good. She smooths down the paper with a soft but intentional
stroke, before staring back at our expectant faces.

'I love it!' she says, a wide grin on her face. 'It's a fabulous concept with tons of potential. I want it bigger, though.'

'Bigger?' Aiden and I echo in tandem.

'Huge. This is a transformative time in my life, so this Summer
Splash must be one for the ages. I want no expense spared – if it's
right, then we get it. And you two certainly get the vision enough
to help me grow it.' She beams, looking between us with pride.

'Thank you.' I try and fail to hide my joy.

Evie Eesuola thinks I 'get her'. I can die happy now.

'Don't thank me; this is where I start riding you hard. I'll need
you all to bring your A-game, twenty-four-seven. And obviously
you'll be adequately compensated.'

'Compensated?' Maxwell asks, eyes widening.

He's practically frothing at the mouth at the mention of financial gain. It's very on brand for him, but it doesn't make it any
less sad.

'Your team pulls this off and you can have my Christmas launch
too. I'm thinking ski holders, cute bumbags . . . you get the gist,'
she says.

Maxwell gushes, reaching out his hand. 'We'd be honoured.'

Evie pretends she does not see. 'I'm sure you would. And, obviously, Aiden and Maddison would be rewarded for leading. Do you do bonuses here?'

She turns to Oliver, who seems to fold under the weight of her direct gaze.

'Well, yes, at Christmas, and sometimes with KPIs ...' He's scrambling for an answer that will grant him her favour.

The answer doesn't pass. She cuts him off with a brief nod before turning her attention back to me and Aiden.

'I've put a lot into this collaboration and I need the party of all parties to reflect that. You make it happen and there's a thank-you bonus in there for you. A big one.'

'A bonus for each of us?' I say.

'If you follow through, yes. Good work warrants good rewards'

For her, it's a drop in the bucket; she barely notices the way it shifts our whole demeanours. But shift our demeanours it does. Aiden's spine is straightening out and my eyes are widening as I attempt to keep it together.

'Wow, thanks, Evie,' Aiden replies, taken aback.

'Yeah, thanks so much,' I say, watching him closely.

There's a joyfulness in his smile – a genuine excitement and appreciation for what Evie's just offered. It is touching really, or at least it would be if he was going to be on the project to receive it. But he said he's leaving today, so he must be putting on an act for someone. I just don't know if it's for Evie or if it's for me.

'I'd say we're done here. Everyone agree?' Evie asks, casually reaching for her phone.

'Totally,' Maxwell says, clearly trying to think of something cool to say.

'Perfect. Maddison, I'll finalise my notes and send them with Aiden next week. From here, it's go, go, go.'

And then she flounces out of the room. Maxwell and Pippa finally snap out of their trances in time to trail after her with words of affirmation and 'helpful' suggestions, and Oliver asks if we have everything under control before leaving my soon-to-be-ex-partner and I to pack up our presentation.

'You know she never gives out bonuses like that,' he says, still giddy from the news.

He turns to look at me – to celebrate, or at least exchange a smile, but I can't shift past the act he's putting on.

'What's wrong?' he asks, smile still inexplicably wild. 'A bonus not on your list for today?'

He waits for me to smile, laugh, roll my eyes, simply do something, but my face is frozen into something far more serious. I don't have time to waste on his little jokes. Last night was the first full night of sleep I've had since the day he walked through that door, and it was entirely down to the fact that, after today, I would only have to see him in fleeting moments from *afar*.

'You said you'd give it up. Tell her you were done with this.'

He scoffs. 'That was before I knew there'd be a bonus. You can't expect me to walk away from that.'

'I can. You promised.'

And whiny as it may sound, I stand by every word. He can't go back now. I was promised an Aiden-free life and that is what I deserve.

'You can't be serious.'

He looks entirely unfazed, the corner of his mouth curling, lifting higher as my chest tightens. My head is spinning just thinking about working with him again, let alone being by his side for the next six months.

'Are you laughing?' I ask.

'Yeah, I'm laughing at the fact you think I'd give up my first chance at some real money for you.' He shakes his head in disbelief. 'When Evie gives out bonuses, she is very generous. One guy in the team paid off his car with his bonus last year. Another girl used hers for a deposit on a house. If you can't firm working with me for a little longer, then *you* can back out.'

A snort of derision leaves me before I can help it, catching Aiden's complete attention, but I stay tall. If he thinks this project could even get off the ground without me, then he is sorely mistaken.

'Problem?' he asks.

'I just think it's ridiculous that you believe that's even an option.'

'Exactly! Because you wouldn't give up the money either. No one in their right mind would.'

He gestures for agreement. He thinks we're on the same page, but he could not be more wrong.

'No. Well, yes. But I was focused more on the fact you believe that you'd be able do this without me,' I say.

'You think I couldn't?'

'I know you couldn't. If I had let you go last night, we wouldn't have even *had* a pitch to give this morning.'

He scoffs louder this time, not even daring to hide it between his snide little comments and brisk eye rolls. 'You haven't changed at all. Thought you were better than me then and still believe you're better now.'

'I don't think I'm better than you.' I've never thought I was better than him. If anything, he was notorious for acting like *he* was better than me.

'Then you do a good job pretending,' he retorts.

'And how have I done that?' I don't expect him to answer, because we both know there's absolutely no proof. He can throw around baseless accusations all he wants, but when it comes to the meat of it, he has absolutely nothing to his name. We were *both* in that school together – we both witnessed the way that he acted and there's no way he can turn that around. He does not get to flip the narrative now and come out with the sympathy vote.

He picks up one of the printouts of our deck that are strewn across the table. 'You throw around all your plans and your charts and your highlighters and look down on anyone who doesn't have their own. You did it when we were younger and you've done it again these last two weeks – like it's your way or total turmoil, but it's not. I matched you mark for mark, award for award, and I managed to do that without a single diary.'

I sneer. 'Because things come easy to you.' I snatch the paper from him and crumple it into a ball.

He grabs the ball back. 'Because I work hard. It got me where I am now and it will get me through the Summer Splash.'

His words are low, coarse and sinking to the floor with undeniable gravitas. They're eerily quiet, audible only because our argument has brought us face to face. Perhaps it was the back-and-forth, or the clear-up, or the fact that our bodies were drawn together through the sheer force of our pent-up anger. But whatever it may be, our eyes meet, with a tension so sticky it clogs my lungs faster than I can breathe. This is it. Years of silence coming to the surface, right here in the Abbingtorn boardroom.

'My way breeds results,' I say definitively.

'Your way breeds disappointment. Your whole life is so obsessively rigid.'

'Obsessively rigid?' I echo his words.

'Yes, obsessively rigid.' He shuffles closer, the front of his trainers rubbing against my loafers. 'And it actively only makes your life worse.'

'You know nothing about my life.' I stand strong.

In all the time we've known each other, he's never made any effort to know. So, who the hell is he to come out now, after all these years, and act like he understands one thing about me?

'I know what works for me. Goals work for me,' I say. 'Having something to aim for keeps me pushing on forward.'

'Does it though?' he asks, his voice semitones from a growl. 'That list you wrote yourself – your five-year plan – what's on it?'

I don't know what's more shocking – the question itself or the fact he remembered the five-year plan in the first place. It was a quick aside in a conversation he barely engaged in. He's up to something – a larger point, a closing argument – and I have no choice but to fall victim to it. If I shy away from telling him then I look like I don't believe in it. I do believe in it. I own my five-year plan and my methods.

'Car, house, senior position at work, husband or boyfriend with marriage potential at least . . .'

'And that's before thirty, right? So, by your standards, you've only got a few years to do all that or you've failed.' He looks at me challengingly.

'Well, I—'

'And how much have you completed? Like fully completed and ticked off your list?'

'None,' I reply, feeling my cheeks grow hot.

'Exactly, because it's stupid to try to plan out your whole life,' he says. 'You're gonna stress about it and feel like a failure for what? Nobody asked you to do that but you.'

I want to say something back – eviscerate him – but every word I've ever known has escaped my brain. I've been slapped in the face by the one thing I've been actively trying to avoid for far too long. All the churning in my stomach, all the bubbling in my blood ... Everything I've been trying to ignore is brought to the surface by his stupid utterance of the exact thought that I have tried so hard to keep at bay.

When I started my twenties, I was so excited for this fruitful and exploratory chapter of my life. I was finishing university and venturing into the real world with the promise of a future I could shape for myself. Everything was new and exciting, and completely unmoulded. All the routes were untouched and however I wanted them.

But then I blinked, and now I'm on the brink of turning thirty, and the buzz of 'potential' is a thing of the past. I have friends getting married, buying houses and getting promoted, and I am in the same position I've been in for the last four years. That work promotion's still an empty promise, I'm in the same bedroom I've been in since I was fourteen, and the closest thing I've had to a committed relationship is the guy who delivers my food shop every other Sunday. Everybody else has worked their way to the finish line and, no matter how positive I try to be about it, I can't help but feel like I've been left behind.

'Are you all right?' Aiden asks, his brow furrowing.

He's paused his vitriol to take a long, hard look at my face, his own growing awash with concern. I've never seen him so worried. I've never seen him look worried at all, for that matter, and it is only contributing to my fast-beating heart. He's looking at me with such pity and it's making me want to claw his eyes out. I don't want pity, or worry, or anything from anyone – let alone Aiden Edwards, the bane of my existence.

But I can't tell him to stop, because my words have disappeared and been replaced with sharp breaths. They're spilling from my mouth and taking hold of my lungs, wrapping around my chest and squeezing as tight as they can.

'Look it's OK. I was just making a point ...' He tails off, face dropping further as he studies my own.

I try to nod, or shrug, or do anything at all to make it clear that this isn't about him. I don't want him thinking that he of all people can affect me like this, because he can't.

Apparently, my body has other ideas, because it can't seem to do anything but shake uncontrollably. I feel my head growing lighter and my vision narrowing. Everything is a blur. All I can feel is the weight of my ribs as they cave into my body.

'Hey,' he says, lifting his hand to my chin. 'Look me in the eyes. Do you think you can speak?'

I manage one feeble head shake, choking on the tears that have started to run down my face. If I could grapple together even one measly word, I could let him know I can get through this without his stupid help. But my chest keeps tightening and my breaths overwhelm me, punching my nervous system as I continue to shake.

'OK, that's fine.' He lightly grabs my arm. 'We'll just do this with head shakes and nods, OK? Has this happened before?'

I nod, gasping for breath. Yes, it's happened before, but not for years at this point. I haven't had a panic attack since final-year exams, and I've only had one this bad once in my first year of university. It is just my luck that one would pop up on a day like today, in front of him.

'And do you have a preferred way of getting through these?' he asks.

I shake my head, shrinking further into my huddled frame. I haven't done this in years. I can't remember how to act. I thought I'd left these attacks sealed in a box next to my Crocs and my overplucked eyebrows.

'OK, cool, we're going to try something, but I need you to listen. First, let's breathe together. Copy me – in and out.'

He looks into my eyes as he delivers the instructions, steadying me softly as he guides me with his actions. I fix my pupils on his and mirror his movements, our chests rising and falling to the same silent rhythm.

Oh-so-slowly, the air starts to calm in my chest, frantic rushes declining into much calmer sweeps.

'Good,' he says, cradling both of my arms. 'Now tell me which letter I'm drawing.'

I focus all my energy on the feel of his thumb as it traces a pattern through my chiffon sleeve. He keeps his dark brown eyes firmly on my face as his finger swirls the letter over and over again.

'*A*.' I muster a response, the word a pathetic tremble.

He smiles faintly, nodding with pride. 'And now?' His thumb switches direction.

'*I*,' I whisper, feeling my spine unfurl.

'What about this one?' he asks, his brow softening.

'*D*.'

'Good.' His thumb lifts off my hand momentarily. 'Keep breathing.'

'Is that an *E*? *A I D E* …' I pause. 'Are you spelling your name?'

'Maybe,' he replies, a knowing glint in his eye.

I shake my head. 'That is so self-centred.'

'Perhaps. But it got you grounded again.' He gives my arm a soft, supportive squeeze.

And he's right – I'm back to breathing without thought, the shakes have stilled and my body's expelling its last fragile tears. Aiden Edwards has just talked me down from the edge. Aiden Edwards. The man with no soul.

I mumble a thank you, shrugging my arms from his hold and quickly gathering the mood board under my arm. 'We should go. I'm pretty sure this room's booked after us.'

I cannot stay in here with a man who's now seen me cry.

'I'm sure they won't mind if we stay longer. Are you sure you're OK?' he asks, timidly studying my face.

'I feel fine. I'm fine. You should go and find Evie,' I say.

'No, wait. I can come with you?'

But it's too late. I'm already by the door, and I run. I grab my bag and head for the annex, not even daring to wait for the lift and risk more time with Aiden.

I barrel down the stairs, across the lobby and out of those double doors before anyone has time to ask who, what or where. My face is dry from the salt, my lungs close to ruin, but I march on through the winter rain anyway. I race down the street, through the common, trudging through the mud without even thinking about soiled loafers. It's not until I reach the neutral sanctity of the second-closest Pret that I allow myself a moment to calm down and refocus. I catch a glimpse of myself in the reflection of the pastry-cabinet glass. I'm an emotional wreck at 12.45 p.m. on a Friday. The ground may as well open up and swallow me whole. I can't possibly go back to work and face Pippa or, God forbid, Aiden. Not while I'm still struggling not to shake.

I dive into my bag, reaching for the only thing that could possibly help at a time like this.

GIRLS. TODAY I HAVE REACHED A NEW LOW.
ANYONE FREE?

Nudge 8

The Comment

'A panic attack?' Raina asks.

'A panic attack,' I say over the café chatter around me. 'My first one in years, right there, on the floor of the boardroom.'

She nods sympathetically. 'Are you OK?'

'Yeah, I'm fine, it was fine.' I shrug it off quickly. 'What's important is that Aiden Edwards has now seen me cry. And not just cry – ugly cry. While shaking uncontrollably. I'm never going to be able to live that down.'

'I doubt he'll bring it up. And, honestly? If he does, he's a dick,' Raina says.

'A bigger dick than we already know he is!' Kimi adds.

Raina frowns. 'Let's not be too harsh – he did just help her through a panic attack.'

'Was he supposed to stand there and let her rot? That was the bare minimum. And let's not forget that he kind of caused it,' Kimi tuts.

Raina and Kimi, diamonds that they are, jumped to action the second I sounded sirens in the group chat. They nodded patiently over a crackly FaceTime as I spurted out the shaky series of events, masking their shock and worry to the best of their abilities. I am eternally grateful for the urgent response, but that has not stopped the ever-quickening beat of my heart.

'He didn't cause it. It wasn't about what he said, I just . . .' I trail off. I can't do this. 'This is mortifying,' I groan.

Another person brushes past me on the way to pick up their drink, but I hardly register the feeling. My mind's still in the boardroom, between Aiden's arms as he coaxes me through the worst moment I've had in years.

'He won't mention it. No decent person would mention it,' Raina says.

Kimi shrugs. 'But he's not a decent—'

'Drop it for two minutes, Kimi! We don't need petty, we need reason. And reason stands, he won't talk.' Raina's voice is firm. 'It's all going to be OK, Mads – I promise. Now wipe your face off, get a falafel wrap and go back inside.'

And I know that she's right. Aiden is many things, but I don't believe he'd be one to lord that kind of thing over me. I keep her words with me all weekend, soothing my thoughts every time they get a little too frantic. I take them as far as they'll go, all the way to work on Monday morning. He wouldn't talk about it, he's not that guy.

But then my desk phone rings the second I sit down, his name flashing across the screen, and I can feel my heart drop to the pit of my stomach.

'Good morning, Aiden.'

There's a small shake in my voice as I deliver the greeting, but not enough to pick up on if you didn't care to. *And he doesn't care*, I remind myself. He's probably already forgotten Friday happened.

'Checked your emails yet?' he asks.

'I just got in.'

'Nice, so I get to hear your live reaction.'

There's a slight teasing to his words that makes my stomach flip over and my breath catch under the weight of them. I crook the phone between my ear and neck as I frantically log in, my pulse pounding so hard it could solo on drums.

Friday got pretty heated and my episode gave him the perfect means of revenge. What if he emailed Evie and told her that it was too much for me – that I can't handle overseeing something so big? And the sicko has chosen to stay on the line so he can hear me cry about it in real time. I should have expected nothing less. Raina was wrong and she owes me apology brownies.

'Oh, my God,' I gasp, as my screen jolts to life.

'Welcome to Evie-land.' Aiden is clearly amused.

When Evie said she was going to start riding us hard, she was severely underplaying it. My inbox sits at 147 from the weekend alone, more pinging in each second that I stay on the phone. The subjects range massively from *What about?* and *Idea!* to slews of random calendar invites. She must have phoned in favours with every connection she has, because suddenly I'm booked in for site visits, canapé tastings and flower-arranging classes.

'Is she always like this?' I ask, speed-scanning my screen.

'Pretty much. Evie's very much "strike first, think later".' He chuckles. 'Don't worry. You'll soon learn to filter through the garbage to get to the gold.'

'And how much of this would you say is gold?' I ask, frantically rummaging around in my drawer for my rough notebook.

'So far? I'd say about fourteen per cent. But I've only read as far as Saturday, two p.m., so I've still got like eighty emails to go.'

I don't know how he deals with this all the time – the sheer volume is making me feel sick to my stomach. I don't even think these can go straight into the notebook. It's a print, highlight and filter kind of job.

'Your head must be gone. Get the notebooks out,' he says. There's no malice to be found in his words, even a hint of a smile creeping through in his voice. He's choosing the high road and, in turn, a second chance at our partnership – panic attack and heated arguments a thing of the past.

'Not at all.' I'm lying through my teeth.

If he can be a new person this Monday, then so can I.

'It's a lot, yeah, but obviously just part of the job. I'm pretty good at going with the flow,' I say as breezily as I can.

'No one relaxed actually uses the phrase "go with the flow".'

'Sorry, can't hear you, too lost in the flow. Please try again later.'

It's a dorky joke and I regret it the second I finish, but his laugh is instant. He tries to hide his chuckle as it leaves his mouth, muffling it with a sleeve or something, but I can still hear it clear as day over the line, permeating through the speaker and soothing my stampeding stomach.

'It's not all bad. Did you get to Sunday, 3.12 p.m., yet?' he asks.

I quickly scroll through and click on the email in question. It's another calendar invite, this Friday at 9.30 p.m., with *WILL PAY OVERTIME* written alongside the subject.

I read out loud. 'Cocktail tasting.'

'At the La La Lounge, yeah. Evie's friend's the owner, designs her bespoke cocktails each year. It's proper fancy,' he says.

'Like black-tie fancy?' I ask.

He laughs again. If it wasn't clear before that I don't get out much, it certainly is now.

'Every time I've gone, men wear shirts and jeans, but all the women have been in high heels and tiny dresses.'

I huff. 'Lovely.'

'I'm not complaining,' he replies.

And once again I am reminded of just who I am dealing with: the boy who was such an inexplicable hit with every girl we went to school with. They would swoon over him and whisper about him in the hallways. He was a natural-born flirt. Except when, of course, he sat next to me.

'You still there?' he asks, filling the silence I've left.

I lie quickly. 'Yeah, sorry. Just reading through. Shall we make notes and exchange them on Wednesday?'

'Sure, but we might have to do it over email. Evie wants to steal you our first day this week.'

'Steal me? Alone?' My voice is higher than I'd like.

'Yeah. Can you make it? I'll send you timings once she gets back to me.'

'Why?' I ask.

'So you know when to show up . . .'

'Aiden . . .' I plead with him, too stressed to waste time rolling my eyes.

'Look, I don't know – she just told me to get you here Wednesday. I didn't care enough to ask any more.'

It makes complete sense for him – why would he bother asking a question? God forbid I'd want any info or to prepare.

'Shall I tell her you're a yes?' he asks, already obviously bored.

'Of course, I'm a yes.'

Who would say no to Evie Eesuola?

'Calm, I'll let her know. See ya, Maddy.'

'No one calls me that.'

'Good. Makes me special.'

And with that he hangs up, leaving me with nothing to work with other than the fact that Evie 'wants to see me' alone on Wednesday. Why Evie, blazing star and business baddie, would want to spend time alone with *me* is baffling, especially when she made such a point of insisting Aiden ran this event with me. I know it can't *possibly* be bad – I've been killing this project so far and one workday ago she literally offered me a bonus. But that was over forty-eight hours ago, which is more than enough time for something to have gone wrong, or, more importantly, *someone* to have made them go wrong for me.

'Who was that?' one of the main suspects asks, concern as fake as her morning smile.

Pippa strolls into the office, breezy as ever. I check my watch: 10.24.

'Just Aiden. We have some details to lay out for Evie,' I reply. 'She wants to see me on Wednesday.'

'Oh, really? Do tell!' She plops down in her seat.

After Pippa realised that her cold shoulder was proving futile, she pivoted to subtler and far more disingenuous tactics. It has been nothing but wide smiles and gentle prods into my work, all in the name of 'genuine interest'. The sickly sweetness emanating from her could tar the walls of our office, and I can see it makes Gus's skin crawl almost as much as mine. I have a sweepstake going with the FGA on how long she'll keep it up for, and I was convinced Evie's bonus would be the thing to break her. But, surprisingly, here she still is, faux excitement in tow as she tries to hide the fact this whole thing is killing her inside.

'She's just sent us some meetings and tester appointments – different suppliers, contacts, all that jazz.'

The vaguer I can be the better, because the last thing I need is her weaselling her way into places she's not needed. Regardless, she scurries to peer over my shoulder at my open calendar.

'Cocktail tasting? Do you even know your mojito from your margarita?' she asks, masquerading her insult as a joke. 'I'd be happy to come for a second opinion!'

'Aiden and I have got it covered, plus Evie only booked for two. By the sounds of it, this place is pretty fancy,' I say.

She peers closely at my screen. 'The La La Lounge. My friends and I almost went the other week.'

Pippa twirls her hair a specific way every time she lies, wrapping it around two of her fingers, twice to the right and then unfurling. It's a tell I've picked up over the years and you'd be surprised at how often it comes up.

'Oh, cool. I'm excited,' I lie in return, only to be met by a near-silent chuckle from Gus.

He swallows it almost immediately, eyes darting bashfully between me and his blank computer screen. He knows that I heard it, but he's praying I won't bring it up. Unfortunately for him, I have a little fire under my belt this morning.

'You all right, Gus?' I ask, the question startling him ever so slightly.

'It's nothing, don't worry.' He is typing suspiciously fast and likely fake notes on his screen.

We've never had an issue because we keep our relationship as base level as we possibly can. It's all ambiguous descriptions of our weekend and what we're having for dinner – it never stretches further and it does not need to. He does not care to know about me or my life or my extra-curriculars, and I afford him the same privilege. He turns a blind eye to my afternoon coffee run, and I don't comment on him buying Funko POP!s on eBay during work hours. Which is why his little giggle is so confusing and deeply out of pocket.

'You scoffed,' I say, refusing to drop it.

'It was hardly a scoff.' He is still avoiding my gaze.

'Should I not be excited for the La La Lounge?' I press on.

'It's not that. It's just ...'

He's desperately hoping I'll back off, eyes frantic as he searches for the best way out. But there is none. I stare back, being as strong as I can, making it as clear as day that this will not be dropped until he answers me.

'I just can't imagine you there,' he mumbles after what feels like a lifetime.

'Meaning what?' I ask, continuing to stare him down.

That I'm not hot enough?

Don't wear short enough skirts?

Don't own enough designer?

'You know ... You're just a little ...' He looks to Pippa for backup.

'Go on.' I dare him to answer, bringing focus back to me.

'Predictable.' He winces, clearly deeply uncomfortable.

A small giggle quickly escapes Pippa's mouth. She catches it between her perfectly puckered lips, trapping it there with a dignified smirk, but I already heard it. I know that she's loving this. I grit my teeth to distract from the sudden wash of shame.

'It's not a bad thing! It's just ... The people there are usually a little wild,' Gus continues.

He's desperately trying to claw himself out of this hole, but it's too late.

'I can be wild,' I say.

But it's to no avail; neither Gus nor Pippa can contain themselves this time.

'The world needs people like you to balance out people like us.' Pippa is blatantly trying to hold in a laugh.

'People like me?' I repeat, as they try to straighten their faces.

'The sensible ones, that keep the rest of us in check.' She flicks her hair. 'Not everyone can be a go-getter. Some people need to sit on the sidelines and make sure the rest of us don't go too wild. And you are *fab* at it.'

'I'm not . . .' I don't even know what to say.

Pippa coos. 'Don't take it personally, babe. We all have our things and yours is being exactly what you'd expect.'

She has a really great talent for taking a seemingly harmless statement and delivering it in the most bludgeoning way possible. I'd respect the craft of it if I respected her in any way at all.

I turn back to my computer, typing furious and nonsensical words into a blank email before succumbing to my anger and dropping it entirely. I can't focus. I'm too sick and tired of people making assumptions when they only see a rundown fragment of who I actually am.

So, I do what I do best. I reach into my bag, practically snatching my list book from its place and smoothing down the crease before getting to work.

To-Do List

Find an outfit for the La La Lounge.

Google ways to be unpredictable to colleagues.

Find out if IT can block eBay on work computers,
    specifically Gus's PC.

Nudge 9

The Offer

'Name?' A voice grunts over the intercom.

I squeak back, 'Maddison Clarke.'

There's a quick buzz and a click as the latch unlocks and the door releases.

'Floor five,' the man says.

Evie told Aiden she thought I deserved a lie-in, so scheduled our appointment for 11.30 a.m. What she did not realise, however, is that Pippa does not share that sentiment, and I was immediately told to use the extra time to finalise Pippa's expense report and send it to her for approval before I went.

By 'finalise' she meant 'start', as well as empty her desk drawer to find half of her receipts myself. She knew for a fact that it was a full day's-worth of work easily, especially if she were the one doing it. But nothing was going to stand in the way of me and Evie. One early morning and a rushed train and Tube ride later, here I am, only three minutes late, at the foot of a shabby-chic brownstone building just off Bond Street.

The lobby is just as gorgeous as the outside, complete with light stone walls and pale-pink sofas leading straight to the lift that takes pride of place in the centre of the room. I press the button without even looking for an alternative. After the way I power-walked from the station, the last thing I need is to battle five flights of what I can assume are probably inexplicably gorgeous stairs.

'Maddison!' Evie exclaims as the door slides open to reveal the most beautiful loft I have ever seen.

She runs over to me, engulfing me in a hug, hints of oak and vanilla and cocoa butter dancing their way up my nose. She smells as amazing as she looks; I knew that she would, but it's different to experience it in person. The tighter she squeezes, the more I try to process the fact that Evie Eesuola is hugging me right now.

'Let me take your coat. Did you get here OK?' she asks, taking a moment to look my sweaty face over.

'Yes. Sorry I'm late! I got caught up with some work!' I try my best to not sound out of breath.

'Oh, don't be silly.' She gives a breezy flick of her wrist as she beckons me to follow her across the room. 'You're right on time. Come in – Anika is so excited to meet you!'

The place is decked out in a variety of plush furnishing and an-tiques, a bright and colourful theme running through the space. It feels full of life, packed with ornaments, mirrors and knick-knacks, each one placed far too intentionally to be considered clutter. Large bay windows adorn the furthest wall, proudly displaying a crisp view of the London skyline. The light that shines through them casts speckles of golden sunshine across the white-and-yellow-patterned wall opposite. She leads me across the open-plan floor, turning the corner to reveal racks upon racks of clothes, all hung on beautifully antique metal railings. Standing by them is a woman, her braids wrapped on top of her head in a bun. She meticulously flicks through the pieces with such firm concentration that she doesn't even notice us appear.

'This is my stylist. The *only* one I trust with my look. Anika, this is the wonderful new event planner I was telling you about!' Evie says cheerily.

Anika breaks from her focus, dark skin glistening in the window light as she turns to face us with a gentle smile.

'Maddison? Lovely to meet you!' She walks over to welcome me with a hug.

She hovers as she withdraws, resting her hands on my shoulders as she slowly but kindly looks over my frame.

'You are stunning. Good bone structure, *beautiful* complexion. This is going to be a piece of cake.' She turns back to one of the racks and starts vigorously fishing through the items. 'Do you have any preferences?'

She patiently awaits my response, but I can't answer because I have absolutely no clue what's going on. I look to Evie, the deer in headlights that I am, as she smiles back at me softly.

'Anika's dressing you for Friday. You didn't think I'd let you go to the La La Lounge unprepared, did you?' she asks with a tinkling laugh.

'I, erm ...' I'm stunned, somewhere between flattered and offended. 'You really don't have to. I know I didn't look my best the first time you came to the office, but I swear I don't wear skater skirts everywhere!'

She stares back at me quizzically.

I try to explain myself fully. 'My brother didn't take his clothes out of the dryer and then there was no time to get to the office. I practically ran to the bus stop in the rain and then—'

'Maddison,' she says, gently stopping me in my tracks. 'This isn't because I don't think you can dress.'

'It's not?'

'No!' She takes in my panicked expression. 'Do you know why I started my channel?'

I know she's gone from strength to strength in the fashion industry and covered pretty much every area she can. I know she is synonymous with luxury and beauty. I know that her YouTube channel grew so huge that the major streamers had a multi-million bidding war to turn Evielution into a studio-style show. I don't, however, know why it all started. What made Evie *Evie*.

'I started because there was a huge disparity between the life I wanted and the life I was told I should settle for.' Her voice is firm. 'I knew that working twice as hard for half as much was bull. If I was going to work twice as hard, I wanted twice as much.'

I blink. Her intensity is startling and maintaining eye contact with her is like staring straight at the sun, but I can't look away. She is pulling me in, making me hang on to her every word.

'My parents begged me to get a real job, but I wanted to use my obsession with clothes and hair and make-up to give every other Black girl the chance to be as frivolous and stylish as they wanted to be.' She takes my hand. 'I'm doing this because I can. And because you deserve this.'

I don't even know what to say. It's too kind and too much, and has prompted a knot in the back of my throat.

'If your boss asks, we worked *super* hard today,' she says, winking before she scoots to the side so Anika can measure me.

'How'd you feel about glitter? I know it can sometimes be tacky, but not the way I do it,' Anika says, boasting.

She turns back to her racks, tape measure balanced between

her lips as she pulls out the most beautiful dress I've ever seen. The design itself is simple – mini, with a sweetheart neckline and off-the-shoulder sleeves that drape lightly on the shoulders. It's a deep grey – smoky and mysterious, and adorned top to bottom in fine glitter detail. Each fragment catches the light, radiating perfect tendrils on the patterned walls. It's understated yet showy, elegant but simple, and I can't stop staring at it.

'Oh, I love it,' Evie says. 'You *must* try it on.'

The pair excitedly hurry me behind the bamboo room-divider, shoving the hanger in my hand and paying no heed to my polite objections. I unzip it slowly, careful not to snag it as I'm sure it's worth more than I make in a month. I can hear them chatting animatedly – already brainstorming accessories and cheering for me from the other side – but I'm not prepared for this. I'm in mismatched socks and the completely wrong bra for *anything* that remotely shows cleavage. I try easing the straps off my shoulders and shoving them into the cups. It's bulky and unrefined, and so wrong for the dress.

'You OK?' Anika asks carefully. 'We'll be tailoring, so I can let it in or out.'

'Uh ... I haven't got it on yet, just figuring out what's best ...' I'm trying to find the most appropriate way to phrase things in front of my sort-of boss and her accomplished stylist. 'The neckline is a bit lower than I—'

'Go braless, hun,' Evie shouts out, somehow reading my mind. 'It's best for the fitting anyway.'

I pull my trousers to the floor, cautiously stepping into the dress and shimmying it up my legs. It tugs slightly at the hips, which is to be expected. Kimi always lovingly reminds me that what I lack in boobs I make up for in butt.

'I need a little help with the zip,' I say, scurrying out from the divider once I have it covering most of my modesty.

I swivel back and forth, trying to reach round the back for myself while I wait for one of them to rush over to assist, but neither does. Instead, they both stand and stare.

'Anika. You have outdone yourself,' Evie whispers, hand on her chest in sheer awe.

'We need photos – she's going in my portfolio.' Anika nods.

They beckon me over to the mirror, turning me to face it as Anika ducks behind me to get the last of the zip.

'*Woah.*'

It sounds conceited, I know. But it's not. Because I don't feel like I'm looking at me. I've worn dresses and cute outfits, and done my *best*, but none of that compares to the way I look in this dress. Everything from the colour to the shaping makes me glow in a way I didn't know I was capable of.

'Sorry, but your *bum*!' Evie grabs my hand and twirls me around. 'This is the one. What do you think?'

'I love it,' I say softly, eyes still glued to the mirror.

The material hugs my curves, the boning in the top snatching in my waist and curving out to accentuate my hips. Even my boobs – a modest B-cup (approaching C on my period) – have the kind of cleavage I've only dreamed of, and that's *without* a bra. I'm lost in its sparkles, its shaping and structure, and the indescribable way it's making me feel. I don't want to take it off ever, let alone before I leave.

They both stay standing behind me, taking it in as I turn to catch myself from every angle.

'We'll keep the accessories simple. I'm thinking black bangles, small earrings,' Anika says, jumping back to work. 'Maybe dangly, maybe large stud – I'll pull some options.'

She faffs around me, rummaging through drawers and holding pieces of jewellery up to my neck, wrist and ears. She shoves various clutches into my hand, slips my feet into different shoes, has me twist and turn and bend until she's happy with what she sees. But I can barely engage. I'm floating on the high that overcame me the moment I stepped in front of the mirror. I can focus on nothing but the dress until I'm reluctantly back in my own clothes and sitting down with Evie in a nearby restaurant, having said my goodbyes to Anika.

'I'm so excited for you.' Evie is babbling away between bites of her scallop. 'I wish I could experience the Lounge for the first time again. Are you much of a clubber?'

'Occasionally,' I say, trying not to sound too boring.

'Understandable. I only like going with the right people.'

She finishes her bite, chewing vigorously and swallowing it down, before dropping her cutlery and staring intently at me.

After we left Anika's, dress and accessories in hand, Evie insisted that she had to take me for lunch and wouldn't accept no for an answer. She swore it was 'nothing' and that the lunch wouldn't take too long. Now here we are, a good two hours later, still munching away. Do I feel bad? Of course, but I've been having a ball just listening and soaking up all her expertise. At least, I have been until now. Now Evie's staring closely in a way that's making my heart rate rise rapidly.

'I like you, Maddison. You're so bright, so hard-working. You have the drive that I *wish* I'd had at your age.'

'Didn't you have, like, your first million followers at my age?' I ask.

She chuckles softly, a proud nod at my clear research.

'Yes, but if I'd had your drive, I'd have turned that into a profitable business far sooner than I did.' She pauses to take a quick sip of her champagne, before tilting her head and continuing, 'How long have you been at Abbingtorn?'

I sigh. 'Four years.'

'Do you like it?' Her eyes narrow conspiratorially. 'Be honest.'

'Of course.'

'Be *honest*.'

Her gaze is soft – I want to trust her. I feel like I *can* trust her, but there's a niggling at the back of my mind that keeps me quiet. I'm a professional and this is a work lunch with a client. A client I absolutely shouldn't slate the company she's working with to.

'I think you're underutilised there, from what I've observed,' she says, willingly filling in the blanks that I left with my silence. 'Would you agree?'

Her fingers trace the rim of her drink as she patiently awaits my response.

'I definitely have more that I'd like to achieve in my role. That's why I'm grateful for you letting me lead on the Summer Splash,' I reply. 'Hopefully after this, I can take on more responsibility.'

'That was so diplomatic, I love it,' she says, giggling. 'That's the kind of professionalism I look for on my team.'

I can't stop myself from smiling at the end of her sentence. Empty comment or not, on some level, Evie thinks that I'd be good enough for her team. But she doesn't smile back, just keeps looking straight at me, a serious expression on her face.

'I want you, Maddison. As a part of my team.'

She states it without an ounce of emotion, like she didn't just drop a chunk of gold into my lap. I grit my teeth in an effort to stop myself from choking on my prawn in shock.

'I plan to take all my events in-house and I need a head of department,' she continues.

I probably look constipated, but it's the only way to stop my jaw from dropping open. A job like that would be everything I've wished for and more, headed up by someone who I've admired for years.

'You want me to head your events department?' I say to clarify.

The words sound absurd. Absolutely unheard of. Who goes from assistant to head of events? Head of Events for Evielution, no less, one of *Forbes*' Most Innovative Companies of the last financial year.

'It's a big step up from assistant, I know. And I can't just *give* you the role – my board of investors would kill me.' She rolls her eyes at the red tape. 'But I like what you're doing with the Summer Splash and I see a lot of potential in you. I've been singing your praises to the board and they'll all be at the event, so if you pull it off in the way I know you can, you could bag that bonus *and* a new job. That's if you're interested at all?'

She continues to swirl her finger round the glass, anxiously watching my reaction. It's ridiculous to think this is something I'd even waste time considering. There's only one answer.

'Oh, I'm interested. Definitely.' My spluttered reply is met with a smile.

'Perfect!' She lifts her glass, prompting me to cheers. 'Here's to next steps.'

We clink our drinks, the sound rippling through me and hugging my heart.

Nudge 10

The La La Lounge

When everyone said that the La La Lounge was fancy, they should have been more specific. There's regular fancy and then there's the kind of place that shames your bank balance the second you walk through the door. The La La Lounge is the latter, with a smattering of general insecurity thrown in for good measure.

The staff nabbed my tone-lowering parka the moment I stepped through the door. I tried to hang on to it, but they just gave me a pointed look and told me they'd take it to the cloakroom. What they didn't know, however, is just how naked I feel without it draped around me, so I've been cowering in the corner ever since.

Even adorned in the dress of my dreams, I can't help but feel like I stick out. I don't have the regular clientele's faces, or their surgeons, and the heels Anika gave me are several inches taller than what I'm used to walking in. I'm praying that the two warm-up shots I took at home kick in any moment now.

'There you are,' Aiden bellows across the room as he strides towards me.

He's stood tall with a fresh trim, dressed in a simple black suit with dark-grey detailing and a white shirt. The pattern is subtle but catches the light in a way that lets you know he's not basic. There's not a crease in sight or an ill-fitted seam, sleeve hugging his forearm as he moves to adjust his cufflink. He looks like someone who belongs on the front of a magazine and I have to bite the inside of my cheek to stop my jaw from dropping to the floor. I am almost embarrassed, although, judging by his own roaming eyes, I'm not the only one having a problem with staring. He looks me over from top to toe with the kind of intensity that makes me want to shrivel up inside this tiny, shiny sheath of a dress. It lasts a second too long. Long enough for me to catch the shift in his breath, and for him to see me do it.

'You look like a disco ball,' he manages to say, regaining composure.

'And you look like a petrol-soaked penguin,' I retort.

He chuckles heartily at the comment, shaking his head. Issues aside, game respects game.

'Evie bought this for me, actually. A couple of years ago,' he says, throwing in a cheeky little spin for good measure. 'I used to show up to events in chinos and shirts, and, once the invites got more regular, she decided that wasn't good enough.'

'She got me this dress too,' I tell him.

'She's a pretty generous boss. Not bad for just an influencer job, eh?'

His eyes glint as he says it, delighting in the way I squirm at his reference to that first day together.

'I didn't mean it,' I say.

'I know, Maddy. It's just fun to bring up – it gets you all flustered,' he teases. 'Right, let's go. I hope you're thirsty.'

He ventures further into the heated room, beckoning me to follow, and we twist and turn, the music swelling the closer we get to the core. We weave our way through society's flashiest patrons, from reality stars to cover models to social media veterans. Each face is both aloof and yet so strangely familiar, and each stare looks straight past us, focused on swilling drinks and taking selfies. It's enough to make anyone feel smaller than dust, and yet Aiden seems entirely impervious to it all. He ploughs through the dance floor at lightning speed with no regard for his surroundings, only turning back every so often to check that I am still following. Just when I become accustomed to the crowd, he breaks us from routine, taking a quick and sharp left turn. We arrive at a steel door, hidden in the darkness in the corner of the bar.

'We're not staying here?' I shout above the music.

'There's no way we can discuss drinks in this noise.'

He disappears through the door, prompting me to follow suit as we leave the crowd of prim partygoers behind. The sound mutes instantly, the hustle and bustle of the club a distant memory as we ascend the stairs. All I can hear is the sharp, tinny click of my heels against the steel steps, bouncing off the walls and echoing around us. We spiral up one flight, two flights and finally a third, winding up at a door much like the one we just entered. Aiden knocks lightly, smoothing his jacket, before grinning at the man who swings the door open and welcomes us in with wide, stretching arms.

'Aiden!'

'Lucien! Nice to see you again!' Aiden brings the man in for a hug. 'This is Maddy, the one Evie emailed about. We're excited to see what you've got in store for us!'

Lucien is the walking definition of a silver fox, with an

effortlessly suave demeanour. Even in his tailored jeans and plain T-shirt, he emits nothing but class.

'Hi! Yes, I'm *Maddison*,' I say, extending my hand and giving Aiden a reproachful glare.

'Nice to meet you, Maddison. I'm Lucien, friend of Evie's. I hear you're planning her Summer Splash this year?' He continues as I nod, 'Brilliant. Never liked the old guy anyway. Shall we get started? Lucie's already inside.' He disappears through the door, beckoning us to follow.

'Their names are Lucie and Luci*en*?' I ask Aiden before we head inside, his smile confirming it to be true.

'It's great, right? I'm convinced they planned it,' he whispers. 'Her and Evie go way back ... Something about a trip to France and a shoddy dive bar.'

The room is large but abnormally sparse, its main feature being a long, drawn-out table. It stands proud in the centre, laden with crystal glasses of every shape and size imaginable. A young woman stands behind it, her hair flowing down to her waist as it escapes her increasingly unravelled chignon. Lucie's smile matches Lucien's in warmth, but boasts a deeper, richer excitement as she hurries us over to the seats in front of her.

'What you got for us then? Evie said she sent concepts,' Aiden asks, elbows sinking into the silk tablecloth.

'That she did, and of course they were as Evie as ever.' The three of them chuckle lightly.

Something's shifted in Aiden – from the smile to the tone, he exudes something one might go as far as to call charm. He's a natural among them – a full-fledged part of this world, cementing me as the only true outsider here. I can feel my chest plunging as I stand and observe, desperate to hide my hands in sleeves this dress is so dearly missing. I'm smiling – of course I am – it's all I can do. But at this point my anxiety is surely palpable. It should not be this hard to make nice with people I've never met before. I'm not some shy kid at school; I am a full-blown adult in a job who has earned the right to be here. If Pippa was in my place, she'd already be exchanging numbers and swapping diaries to plan holidays abroad.

But Pippa's not 'boring'.

Pippa's not 'predictable'.

'Maddison?' Aiden whispers, his eyes set on mine.

They burrow deeper, searching my face for some sign of worry. It's just a look, but it's enough to tell me that I'm safe. Enough to instantly quell the shake at the pit of my stomach. I nod back, my smile gaining some semblance of sincerity as I slide back the chair and start to get settled.

'So, cocktails,' I say, my breath steadying.

Aiden cheers. 'Yeah, Maddy here is raring to go! Let's get stuck in, shall we? Can't wait to see what you've done.'

Our eager entertainers jump straight into action, pulling bottle after bottle out from under the counter. They work in tandem, reaching and diving for spirits, and generously pouring into the shakers with glittering smiles on their face. I can't help but watch the way that they move, the way they dance with such unbridled joy in their craft. The ice clangs against the metal as Lucie's shaking comes to an end. She flicks the lid off, bringing a glass into play. A vivid electric-blue concoction emerges from the tin, flowing into the cup effortlessly before meeting its spiralled-lemon-peel garnish. It's mesmerising.

'We call this the "Evie Peasy Lemon Squeezy",' Lucien says as the drinks are placed in front of us. 'It's an iced tea, mixed with gin, tequila and citrus vodka, with a dash of blue curaçao, triple sec and a lemon garnish to finish. You'll find the mildness of the tea balances the harsher citrus flavours. Would taste beautiful on a hot summer's day.'

Lucien retrieves a rose-gold bucket from below, placing it gently between me and my cocky co-worker.

'This one's a little strong, and the first of many, so please don't shy away from the spit bucket,' Lucie says.

Aiden wastes no time rolling his eyes and laughing at its presence, before sliding it directly in front of me and throwing a wink at Lucie, who fondly shakes her head back at him.

'Now, when have I ever needed one of those?' he asks brashly, bravado on the maximum setting. 'Maddy, on the other hand, may need a couple.'

'A couple of spit buckets?' I roll my eyes too, shaking my head at another one of Aiden's bad jokes. But as I stare at him, he's calm and exceptionally genuine. He's not kidding.

'Seriously?' I whisper.

He stares back at me, unfazed. 'I assume you're still in "work mode" so you can make all your notes.'

My cheeks flush with heat. Gus was right – I am a sensible, predictable person. Of course I'm in work mode – this is for work . . . Am I wrong to take my job seriously? Why does everyone else just know how to chill – when to be serious and when to let loose? Did I skip a class? Did I decide to care too much? Or am I just incredibly and inherently uncool? God, I hate him and the way that he is completely right. I can't let him be right. I can't let any of them be right. Not today and not ever again.

I stare him dead in the eye, lifting my glass in a mock salute before downing its contents. It stings as it attacks the back of my throat, the citrus coming at full throttle, but I swallow the cough down with the liquid.

'Damn, Maddy,' Aiden says, shock not going unnoticed by me. 'Remember, this is only drink number one.'

'You're right. We have way more to get through and you're slowing us down,' I retort, eyebrow raised in challenge.

Lucie and Lucien cheer in encouragement, one whisking away my empty glass and the other prepping ingredients for drink two. A blender whirls to life in the background, but I can't focus on anything but Aiden as he lifts his glass to his lips and takes me up on my challenge.

'You can't outdrink me,' he says, slamming the empty glass on the table.

It's a dare. Strong and threatening, but inexplicably alluring.

Reason dictates I should leave it – ignore him just like I did every time he tried to bring me down to his level at school. But this feels different – stronger and burning hot.

We lock eyes.

'Challenge accepted.'

Nudge 11

The Seven Notebooks

A definitive rating of the La La Lounge Lucie(n) cocktails
from a totally unbiased and definitely not drunk source

1. The Evie Peasy Lemon Squeezy: 7/10
   Nice palate cleanser. A little stingy, but good.

2. The P'eve'na Colada: 8/10
   Classic and beautifully blended. The name warrants the
   electric chair, though.

3. The Torp'eve'do: -5/10
   I thought Lucie and Lucien were nice until they let me
   drink this.

4. The minty one (didn't hear the name, too scared to
   ask): 6.5/10
   Tastes like liquid toothpaste, but it kind of grows on
   you after a while.

5. ??? It was fruity?: 9/10
   Aiden drank this one soooo quickly. I don't think
   that's fair.

6. This one: 5.5/10
   It's giving girl next door. Shockingly average. Is that
   gin? It could be vodka, idk.

'There she is, Moany Maddy and the notepad.' Aiden is staring down at my sheet with thinly veiled disgust.

The words jump around the page, leaping between lines and dancing in their own little circles. It's wildly confusing and disorientating, and the longer I stare, the less I can trace their movements without feeling motion sick. I glance away, reverting my gaze back to Aiden and his judgy face.

'We have to relay this to Evie. How were *you* planning to recall which one should win?'

'It's a cocktail,' he says. 'I will send her an email saying, *number three tastes good. Go with that one.*'

'Number three tasted like fragrant toilet water,' I slur as I lean in closely to whisper the last bit.

I was going for smooth and suave – the act of someone who does this all day. And honestly, it would have worked had the room not been so *spinny*. The floor comes zooming up to meet me and Aiden smirks as his hand anchors me into place, keeping me on my seat and off the floor. He does the best that he can, but my head lurches forward, a giggle escaping me as our foreheads collide. I hear the knock more than I can feel it – I'm too distracted by how funny he looks from this angle. I keep my head right in place, pressed up against his, as he tries and fails to swallow his bemused grin.

'I'm cutting you off,' he says, his breath tickling my lips as he continues to take the majority of my weight.

I protest, leaning back in my seat, confident in my balance and his firm hold on my knee. 'I am fine.'

'You need water.' A glass appears at my fingertips.

'You guys are amazing, you know that? Like wizards!' I coo at a smirking Lucie and Lucien. 'Except instead of magic, it's drinks that you make.'

'I'm gonna take her outside, get her some air,' Aiden says, nodding towards them. 'But this was great, thank you! I'll be in touch with our notes.'

I feel his arm swing around me and scoop me off my chair, and we make our way back down that quiet stairwell. Except this time, the stairs are smaller and more slippery, with less room for feet and overall movement. Whoever designed this place should have been more consistent. No person wants to walk down a moving staircase.

'How are you doing this?' I ask.

'What?'

'The moving stairs!' I say. 'You keep walking on them like normal stairs!'

He glances at me, perplexed, before his brain starts to connect my words with the flushed cheeks and glassy eyes. His mouth crooks into a smile, a small chuckle escaping his lips as he grips me tighter and shakes his head.

'God, when you commit, you really commit, don't you?'

He guides me down the final set before we plunge back into the roaring crowd from before. They're louder this time, the bass striking my heart as it beats to the rhythm of the gyrating bodies. It is magnetic – impossible to watch, but far more impossible to look away from.

'We should dance,' I say.

'You dance?' Aiden asks, shocked.

'When there's music to dance to!' I grab his hand before he has a chance to laugh at me again, dragging him into the middle of the floor. He's reluctant at first, but soon he's left with no choice; the drinks have unlocked a new strength I didn't know I had. We're swallowed by the infinite bodies and swept away by the tide of their movements, ebbing and flowing just as they do. What I once thought would feel suffocating is no more than a tight, sweaty hug, embracing me as I lose myself to the music.

The song switches to something I actually know, the beat pouring directly into my soul. I sing every word loudly, hips swaying to the rhythm as Aiden stares at me in disbelief.

'You *don't* dance?' I ask, mirroring his tone from before.

He picks up on it, chuckling back at me. 'I'm not a robot – of course I do.'

'Well, come on, then!' I reach for his hand once more.

He stares at it timidly at first, glancing up to double-check I'm definitely holding it for him. So, I stretch it out further, shaking it for dramatic effect. He laughs, the sound rumbling through his chest and loosening him up on its way out of his mouth. His fingers close around mine, his body effortlessly tuned into the music as he spins me around and pulls me in towards him. His arm wraps round my front, holding me in place tightly as my back stays pressed against his chest. We move as one, Aiden, me and the music working in sync like the three of us were born to be together. When I roll, he rolls. When I grind, he grinds back and he smells really good as he does it. I turn my neck and crank my head up to sneak a better whiff of his cologne, losing my balance ever so slightly as I do. But he doesn't let me fall. He keeps me locked into place, his face dipping down to meet mine, laced with intrigue.

For a moment, it's really just Aiden and me, the music a dull and unimportant thud in the background. His face is so close I can see every detail, from the hair of each brow to the small but intentional part in his lips. They dip further towards me, magnetic in their pull, acting purely on instinct. I feel a jolt in my stomach, like a flash in a pan. First exciting, but quickly overcome by something far more violent.

'I don't feel good.'

He freezes. 'What?'

'The drinks,' I manage to say, before throwing my hand to my mouth and clasping it shut.

I can practically hear the acid roar in my stomach, working faster than I ever thought possible. I turn to face him properly so he can read the panic on my face loud and clear. He's panicking right back, eyes wide and breath caught as he quickly devises next steps in his head.

'Can you make it to the toilet?' he asks, surveying the room.

'How close?' I ask.

'Across the crowd.'

I shake my head. 'Absolutely not.'

'OK, fine – this way.'

He clutches my arm, sweeping me through the crowd and across the room faster than my legs could manage alone. I fear each dancing person, a tall obstacle along the way, but I have no reason to as Aiden steers us through the maze effortlessly. In no time at all, we reach his target destination – a nondescript door at the back of the club. The cool air slaps me across the face, the night stilling once again and allowing me time for a much-needed deep breath.

'Sit down.' Aiden lightly tugs at my arm as he takes his own seat on the step where I stand.

I follow, softly lowering myself onto the step as gracefully as someone with tunnel vision can. His arm reaches out to guide me, scooping me into place on the stoop. It's colder out here by far, but I have hardly any time to feel it before he drapes his suit jacket over my bare, goosebump-ridden shoulders.

'Elbows on knees, eyes on floor. Breathe as deeply as you can.'

I follow each command in order and he watches closely as I do, hands at the ready in case of any missteps.

'I'm fine,' I say, looking down at the ground.

'I know you are.' He gives my back a light and pointless rub.

'But that's not true.'

'That you're fine?'

'That you believe that I am.'

'Just keep breathing, Maddy. I'm not cleaning up vomit.'

We sit in silence for what feels like an eternity, me taking my breaths as he waits patiently next to me. Each inhale fills my lungs with a cold, chilling air that pierces harder than the thudding that sat there before. But, somehow, it's working – somehow, it's sobering me faster than the glass of water upstairs ever could. The steadiness starts returning, the ground stops its swaying, and, though still hazy, the world begins to take shape.

'This isn't the same,' I say, drunk courage taking the reins.

'What?'

'This – you helping me – this isn't like the other day,' I say. 'You're not, like, a hero, or something. This isn't a panic attack. I just drank all those cocktails too quickly.'

'I know. I never said that it was,' he says softly.

'Good, because it's not. I'm not like this. I'm just drunk.'

It was meant to sound forceful and super direct – but judging by the quick chuckle that escapes his lips, I would argue that it had the opposite effect.

I whinge, throwing my head in my hands. 'Don't laugh at me!'

He's not allowed to laugh at me while I'm incapacitated like this – it's rude.

'Would you believe that I'm laughing with you?' he asks.

'I'm not laughing.'

'OK, you're right. I was laughing at you.'

There's a warmth to his goading that makes everything feel just that little bit safer. I will be OK, even if my head still feels like it's rocking. Aiden and his jacket will not let me down.

I groan. 'You're the worst.'

'And not a hero,' he says. 'You sure do have a way with words.'

'Please, you're no better,' I say, scoffing. 'What did you say the other day? That I was ruining my life with my own planning methods?'

I glance up long enough to watch his smile fade, retreating back into his mouth and leaving a frown in its place. His brow knots, eyes glazing over as he harkens back to that day, that never-ending moment in the boardroom that I've dared not speak of.

'You know I didn't mean to do that. To cause that,' he says softly, his sentences fragmented as his eyes shift to the floor. 'I would never want to actually hurt you. I wanted to push you, I guess, but I didn't think it would trigger . . .'

'A panic attack?' I finish for him.

The phrase visibly washes him in discomfort, an unspoken sadness circling above his head and weighing over him. I look over the last week in a new light and it suddenly dawns on me – he hasn't brought it up because *he's* the one who's ashamed.

He looks haunted by the idea that he caused that level of pain and

I cannot have him continue to believe he's responsible. He may have said what he said, but it was deeper than that. Even if I've refused to admit it until now.

'It wasn't about you,' I say, attempting to put him out of his misery.

He lifts his head and looks towards me again. 'But I said all those things and then suddenly you were ...'

I can almost see the scene play out in the depth of his eyes, darkness swirling in his pupils as he relives the nightmare.

'You've said a lot worse and I probably have too. Plus, nothing you said was particularly false. I knew it already, and I felt it inside. It was all just briefly too much,' I explain.

His hand's still on my back, the once half-hearted rub transformed into a gentle yet comforting hold. I nestle into it closer, taking in the stillness of the night as it battles the booze still swirling round my brain.

'What was?' he asks. 'What was too much?'

'Just ... everything.'

It would be hard to string these words together if I were sober, so starting this conversation now was his worst idea yet. But I can see in the way that he looks, that he breathes, that here and now was the only way that he could have. He needed the lowered inhibitions to ask these questions just as much as I need them to be able to answer. So, I answer.

'There were a lot of factors – the argument, the presentation, the *you* of it all ...'

'The me of it all?' He frowns, searching for the connection.

I didn't want to talk about this ever, especially not with him. I counted myself so lucky that nothing was said afterwards. But now, here on this stoop, I'm left with no real option.

I gesture towards him. 'You're Aiden Edwards.'

He looks back at me, confused. 'That is my name . . .'

'And you walked through the doors of my workplace and called me boring,' I say. 'After everything.'

'I've never called you boring.'

'But you've wanted to. And, honestly, it's fine, because everyone else agrees with you.'

His shirt ruffles as he shifts from his pose on the stoop, turning back towards me so he can properly take in my face. His expression is stern now, fixed in place, his eyes a pool of confusion and something that, if I'm not mistaken, looks a lot like anger.

'Who's everyone? Who called you boring?' he asks.

'Gus and Pippa. They said "predictable", but it's the same thing. They basically said it's my best quality.' I sigh, lying back on the stoop in distress.

Aiden reaches out to try to catch my head before it knocks against the concrete, but it's no use – we've already made contact. He scoops his hand under my head anyway and I give a deep, long groan, my focus shifting from our conversation to the star flurrying above me. It whizzes and loops with such impressive speed that it takes me longer than it should to realise that it's a plane.

'The worst part is that being sensible has got me jack shit,' I continue, using his palm as a pillow. 'I'm still nowhere near my goals for thirty *and* everyone thinks I'm a bore who wouldn't know fun if it whacked her round the head. If I'm gonna be this far from my original plan I should at *least* have a trail of wild stories to justify my derail, but I don't! All I've got is this sensible label and seven colour-coded, itemised notebooks.'

'*Seven* notebooks?' he asks.

'Yeah, I lied the other day,' I say. 'There are seven, not four.'

I don't know where the confession came from – I blame the last cocktail – but, drunk or not, I can't do this all looking up at him. I tug at the lapel of his jacket, pulling it out from under my back to cover my face as I hide from the impending judgement.

'One's more of a file than a notebook, but they serve the same purpose and they're all updated on a regular basis,' I mumble.

Even *I'm* sick of me, so I can't even fathom why Aiden of all people still remains by my side. But remain he does, still and silent, as I regain composure and eventually shrug off my suit-jacketed cone of shame.

'That's too many notebooks. Even for you, Maddy,' he says, getting up from his step and scooping me from the bed I have made of the stoop.

My calves tremble in the new standing position, giving me no choice but to grip Aiden tighter as I wobble unevenly in my heels.

'They all serve a purpose!' I try to steady my legs.

He holds firm, patiently waiting while I bring myself back to a less shaky stand.

'I'm sure they do. Now take this and put your address in,' he says.

His phone feels warm and slippery in the palm of my hand, taxi app shining brightly on the pre-loaded screen.

'The best thing they ever did was let people add stops.' He watches as I clumsily type in my postcode.

'I can get my own car.'

And I mean it, as well. The last thing I need is another favour owed to Aiden Edwards.

'Don't think you can,' he responds, lightly bemused.

He practically lifts me into the taxi, doing up my seatbelt and resigning me to the middle seat so he can keep a closer hold of me. It would be demeaning if I were able to do any of it myself, but with the way the car is basically just a blur at this point, I suppose I could use the help. We drive mostly in silence, me too focused on not throwing up and him too focused on checking on me. But, after a while, I feel him shift slightly, chest rising and falling with purpose as he takes a deep breath to prepare for something big.

'Maddison?' he asks nervously.

'Yes, Aiden?' I manage to reply.

'While we're here, can I ask you one thing?'

'I guess.'

'Why do you hate me so much?'

I let out a deep, accidental laugh, cringing as it echoes around the taxi.

'That's what we do, Aiden. We've been playing this game since we were, like, ten years old.' I search for his face in the dark. 'Though the last round was pretty cruel of you, I have to say.'

I wait for the inevitable pained pang in my gut that comes every time I revisit our last encounter. But it gets drowned out by my sudden yawn as a wave of tiredness washes over me.

'Since we were eight years old, actually,' he says. 'I think about that last round a lot. And how you seem to *really* hate me now.'

The car swerves violently around a corner and it takes all my strength to keep my body rigid, leaving me with no strength to sit upright again. I let myself go limp, but it's fine because Aiden is there, his arm like a solid, toned pillow.

'Because you're the worst!' My exclamation is muffled by his shirt.

I let my head sink lower as another yawn takes over my body. My stomach grinds to a halt, eyelids growing uncontrollably heavy. I let them fall, first for a moment and then for a while longer as a light tingling sensation spreads around my body. Aiden's saying something, I can feel the bass of his voice vibrate through me, but I can't register any of the words. Only the feel of his chest, rising and falling underneath my head, as I drift off to sleep.

Nudge 12

The Lie

'*That's too many notebooks.*'

I bared my soul to the guy on that step and all he could say was, 'That's too many notebooks.'

What a strange way to turn an evening of what almost felt like bonding into foolish drunk ramblings to an impassive ear. The words have played on my mind since I woke up (the first time, and every time since) in all of their plain, dry, offensive and subtext-less glory.

'*That's too many notebooks.*'

He may as well have called me ugly and boring there and then.

My phone vibrates harshly against the glass of my bedside table, the sound grating violently against my deeply tender eardrum. I groan at the sound, rolling over and blocking my ear with my hands, but it's no use. It keeps going, message after message.

It's 11 a.m. . . . Are you dead?

The latest in a string of texts from Kimi. I turn the brightness down completely before even starting to reply.

Me: Worse. Hungover.

Kimi: Oooo, so the Lounge was good?

Me: It's so blurry. But I think I danced on Aiden . . .

Kimi: ON?! FaceTime debrief. Now.

Me: No one is seeing my face today. Not even you.

'Maddison?' Mum calls from the bottom of the stairs.

It's her chores call. Her 'help me peel three tons of carrots for dinner' call. Any other day I'd take it on the chin as part of my living-rent-free tax, but today it makes me want to be sick.

'Maddison?!' she yells louder, sounding slightly more irate.

I'm hit by the blinding light of the corridor the second I step out from the comforting darkness that was my cave of a room. Each step down the stairs is my own personal Everest, complete with the icy chill of my dad's stinginess.

'Can we please turn on the heating?' I call into the distance and my voice comes out gruff and croaky, ringing between my ears.

'It's practically spring!' my dad says from the comfort of the front-room sofa.

I moan. 'It's February.'

'Exactly!'

I don't know why I even bothered trying. The central heating is his third and favourite child, and no one touches it without his explicit permission. I'm met with a look of horror as I finally land at the foot of the staircase.

'You look awful. Are you ill?' Mum presses the back of her hand against my forehead.

'No, just tired. And I drank quite a lot last night,' I say.

'I thought you were working?' she asks, grabbing my wrist to check my pulse.

'Yes, I was, and I'm fine.' I snatch my wrist back. 'Just need coffee. Or water. Or ... bread, I don't know.'

My parents were in full support of me living at home for as long as I saw fit. 'Why rent when you could stay here and save to get on the property ladder?' they would say. I agreed wholeheartedly. It's a massive privilege to have. I did not, however, still see myself living here at almost thirty years of age. But, to be fair, I also didn't see the mortgage rates and rent prices climbing to where they are right now. My parents do their best to make me feel better about the whole thing, insisting I have 'full freedom as an adult' and attempting to treat me as such. But, at the end of the day, I will always be their child in this house and they can't help but remind me of the fact.

'Why did you drink so much?' Mum follows me into the kitchen.

'It was a cocktail tasting; I had no choice.' I let out a small whimper as the fridge light smacks me across the face. She thinks I'm being dramatic; I could already tell by her tone, but her new eye-roll-and-sigh combo pretty much solidifies it.

She tuts. 'Sit down.' She pulls out a kitchen stool and takes my place in front of the refrigerator. She grabs a few eggs, some peppers, red onions, milk, bacon and cheese, and gets to work at the counter immediately. Within a matter of minutes an omelette mix is ready to go, butter sizzling in the pan in anticipation.

'I was going to ask you to come shopping with me,' she says as she tips the eggy mix into the pan. 'But it looks like you need your rest, so I'll have to either force your dad or go alone.'

'I could go,' I wince, folding under her gentle manipulation.

'No, you couldn't. You're eating this and going back to bed. And put a jumper on – you'll catch a cold.'

She presents me with a wooden tray. On it lies the omelette, a glass of water, a pack of painkillers and three plain cream crackers, all organised neatly in their own little sections. The smell of egg wafts around the kitchen and under my nose, irritating the very little contents left in my stomach. I don't dare say anything – not after she's gone and cooked it for me. She'd kill me before the hangover gets its chance and I can assure you it'd be a far more gruesome death.

'Sorry,' I say.

'For what?'

I don't know why I'm apologising either, I just couldn't shake the feeling that I should probably be in trouble. Being like this on a Saturday – or any day, for that matter – is so deeply unlike me. And to be like this in front of my parents of all people is practically unheard of, even in my younger days.

'Getting drunk?' I say.

'Honey, you're an adult,' she says plainly. 'And frankly, it's quite nice to see you actually out hitting the town.'

'I go out.'

She chortles. It's loud, fast and sharp. Far kinder than the ones from the office, but somehow hurts just the same. She catches my sunken eyes.

'Aw, baby, I don't mean anything by it. It's just nice to see you relax, that's all.' Her voice is gentle, but it's still not enough.

'Mum … Do you think I'm boring?'

It's been on my mind since Monday and it won't leave no matter how much I try to shake it. Who better to ask? She's known me literally all my life and she certainly won't shy away from being honest.

She stops her tidying, turning back to face me with a look of shock and disgust on her face.

'Of course I don't think you're boring. Why would I think you're *boring*?' she says, offended at the mere idea.

'It's fine. I was just wondering,' I mutter, sweeping it back under the rug.

I can't get into it with her. Not while she's prepared to go full mama bear. She shuffles over and wraps me in her arms, my head resting against her stomach as she gently rubs the back of my head soothingly.

'Did someone call you boring?' she asks.

I snuggle into her closer as she squeezes me tighter, with the silent promise that she won't let go.

I think back to Gus and to Pippa, to Aiden and my seven notebooks, to all the looks and the laughs and the eye rolls between them. I run through conversations like scripts in the back of my head. *Predictable, responsible, too many notebooks*, but never boring. *I* came up with boring and stuck with it – kept pushing the agenda until there was no other word I could describe myself with.

Do I think I'm boring?

I sink further into her embrace, shut my eyes and try to shake off the last of my headache. It's no use. It stays with me, pounding violently against my skull all the way through to Monday morning. I try to keep it easy, plugging my headphones in the second I get to my desk and slowly making my way through Evie's latest batch of weekend emails over a cup of tea. But Pippa won't stand for it. Her voice cuts through my lo-fi playlist, bright and bitchy, twenty minutes into the workday.

'Is there a reason your calendar's blocked out today from ten a.m. till five p.m.?'

Of course there is, and she'd know that if she'd bothered reading the email I sent her last week when I blocked the day out.

'Evie emailed – she needs me offsite today. I've swapped my Wednesday Summer Splash focus day for today to make up for it.'

'Oh. Anywhere exciting?'

'I don't know. She's kept it very hush hush.'

And I hope, for my head's sake, that wherever I'm going is just as hushed.

'Oh, yeah, how was Friday? What did you think of the Lounge?' Gus asks.

'It was fine; nothing to report,' I reply.

I have no energy, or desire, to run through the antics of Friday's misfortune with Pippa or Gus. They don't actually care and, honestly, the less it's mentioned, the quicker I can forget about how I once again acted a fool in front of Aiden Edwards. I reach for my earphones, pointedly sticking them in my ears yet again in the hopes that they'll finally take the hint, but the man himself walks through the door before the Bluetooth even has time to reconnect.

Pippa's face lights up the second Aiden appears, her hand flying to smooth her hair back quicker than I can inhale. Even Gus smiles wider and looks brighter under Aiden's ever-disinterested gaze. Their behaviour is vapid and shallow, and far beneath them. Or maybe it isn't – frankly, they're pretty low already.

'Aiden! How's it going mate?' Gus asks, his voice deepening. 'Heard you went to the La La Lounge Friday – bet it was sick.'

I have never heard Gus use the word 'sick' once in my four years here, or refer to anyone as 'mate'. One glance at Aiden and I can tell he's just as baffled at the faux familiarity as I am.

'Yeah, it was good, thanks. Ended up being a pretty late one.' He is so clearly uninterested in the conversation.

'Oh, I bet it was!' Pippa jeers before launching into a chorus of knowing giggles. 'What time did Maddison head off?'

I can't deal with this today. I'm sick of her giggles and hair flicks, and snide little comments about how predictable I am. I can't bear to listen and I certainly can't bear to watch as they delight in how Aiden had to ferry me home. I take a deep breath, squeeze my mouse and start desperately clicking through old emails in an attempt to appear like I couldn't care less. If I try hard enough, I can tune all three of them out while they revel in my lame too-many-notebooks-filled life.

'Actually, she ended up outlasting me.' I look up just in time to watch Pippa's face fall at Aiden's lie. 'I couldn't keep track of her, from the dance floor to the tabletops . . . This girl is a *menace* once you get a few drinks in her. But you guys should know that already, right? With a party animal like her in your team, she must invite you out twenty-four-seven.'

I would pay disgustingly large amounts of money to have Gus and Pippa's current expressions immortalised. The utter shock, confusion, and, dare I say, *jealousy*, has formed the kind of look worthy of preservation in the Louvre. And I need it preserved, because at this moment in time I can't enjoy it the way I so dearly want to. I'm too busy frozen in my own state of shock and confusion.

What game is Aiden playing now?

'We should head out,' Aiden says blankly, turning to me. 'Evie's waiting outside – we don't want to be late.'

I nod back tepidly, gathering my things and following him towards the lift. He doesn't look back, so I don't either. I leave Gus and Pippa behind. They're probably still frozen, probably still dumbfounded. I get it; I know that I certainly am.

Nudge 13

The Bet

I've never seen anybody move through life with the sheer ferocity of Evie Eesuola. It is captivating just as much as it is terrifying, and each second I spend with her fills me with adrenaline. From the moment I got in her car (chauffeured, of course), I was handed a bottle of sparkling water, then given piping-hot tea over the following two hours. She spoke at the speed of light, covering more ground than Aiden or I could possibly even try to digest. I've been trying to be cool about it, especially after Friday night, but after a while I realised it's an impossible task. I have a job to do, and therefore no choice but to whip out a notebook and pen.

Plan of Action

When: Today (twenty minutes from now, exactly)

Where: Tennerton House, Colchester, Essex

What: Brooke Tennerton's launch party for her new wellness gummy 'Salyva'

<u>The Tea:</u>

Brooke Tennerton, big-time influencer and long-term frenemy to Evie Eesuola, is launching a new wellness multivitamin chew called 'Salyva'. To launch, she is throwing a 'Start of Spring Soirée' with two hundred of her closest friends and business partners. Suspiciously familiar? Of course. Even down to its 'boho glamping' theme, almost identical to Evie's 'Camp with Style' Summer Splash theme from last year.

<u>Goals, Aims, Objectives:</u>

We are, ultimately, here to support, because Evie doesn't compete - she uplifts (even 'bitches who steal her whole concept'). That doesn't, however, mean that Aiden and I can't scope it out on her behalf. Take pictures, take notes, look at what works and be sure to document what doesn't. Take stock of how she throws it, how it's running, what she puts in the gift bag. Look out for key players ... Are they invited to the Summer Splash? What can we do to ensure Evie still has the hottest ticket of the year?

'You all right?' Aiden whispers we make our way through the second of three sweeping flower archways to the grounds. Brooke's grounds. The grounds for her house. She has three sweeping flower archways down the path to the grounds for her house.

'It's incredible, right?' he says, catching me staring. 'When you've been in the game as long as Brooke and Evie, the world is truly your oyster.'

I still can't respond. I haven't been able to speak to him since we left my office two hours ago. Evie and her ranting made it easier to focus and pretend it was about the work. But now she's gone – already off doing her round of hellos, and we're back just the two of us for the first time since Friday. I can't do it; I can't talk to him. I don't know how to act around him after what he did earlier.

We continue down the path in silence, music growing louder the closer we get to the action. At last, we reach a towering hedge, sculpted into a vaguely phallic-looking mushroom. It looms over us, casting shade in our path and blocking us from the party on the other side. In the middle of the hedge sits a pale-pink wooden door with a small, shiny golden doorknob and an *Enter for Wellness!* wooden sign hanging on it. Aiden reaches for it.

'You ready?' he asks.

I nod silently. It's enough – he twists the doorknob and we begin to creep through.

I can't help but gasp as we enter, taking in the extensive grounds that stretch on for miles, adorned with balloons, fairy-light-strung trees, and row upon row of deluxe tents, each boasting ten feet at least. We walk past a few of them, all clearly labelled for different functions, from drinks, to shisha, to hair braiding, to massages and more. Crowds of people frolic among the flowers and ornate statues, posing for pictures in beautiful boho gowns despite the seven-degree weather and popping multivitamins in their mouths for videos before promptly spitting them back out. I look down at my flared mini dress and platform cowboy boots, and silently thank Evie and Anika for preparing an outfit for me to change into in the car. I felt so unlike me when I first put it on, but, being among the rest of Brooke's guests, I can see how needed it was. Who cares if the wind is using my few inches of exposed thigh to chill me to the bone? At least I fit in here, which I certainly wouldn't have done in my button-down tunic dress, tights and loafers.

'She's certainly gone all out,' Aiden says. 'I'd expect nothing less.'

I nod back, still busy surveying the events around us. 'How similar is it to last year's Summer Splash?'

But before he can answer, Evie comes bounding out from a tent towards us. She's still dressed the same – flowy boho dream of a dress, long wavy hair and Chanel slingbacks – but she seems to have acquired some new accessories. Her eyes, partially hidden behind sunglasses, cautiously glance to each side as she scurries our way, using one hand for drinks and the other to clutch the neck of the scarf wrapped around her head so as to remain inconspicuous. I try to stifle my laugh. She is Evie Eesuola at a high-profile influencer event. She couldn't be more conspicuous if she tried. But I appreciate her commitment to the cause and her willingness to skulk around as if she's gone undercover.

'There you are!' she says, three circular Martini glasses balancing awkwardly under her grip. 'Here, try this.'

We quickly take them from her, avoiding probable disaster as she looks on at us expectantly. I stare down at the liquid. It's pink and glittery, the cool winter sunlight painting iridescent swirls that float around the glass. It's harmless … probably. It doesn't exactly look tasty, but it certainly looks Instagrammable, which I suppose is the point.

Aiden sips quickly, pushed by the force of Evie's impatient foot-tapping. He holds it in his mouth before gulping, tilting his head and taking another swig.

'This is your "Pink Dream" cocktail.'

'YES, IT IS! From last year's Summer Splash!' She flails her arms and lets the headscarf drop to the grass. 'I *knew* I wasn't imagining it.'

'You're not. This is exactly it.' He downs the rest as Evie beams triumphantly.

I give it a sip and have to stop myself from recoiling as an all-consuming rush of sugar hits my tongue.

'Is that candyfloss?' I ask.

Evie nods. 'Yep. And tequila and prosecco and sherbet and raspberry. The trick is to drink it fast without really thinking.'

'It's absolutely awful,' Aiden grimaces.

'Uh-huh. But *so* photogenic!' Evie says. 'This one won't be getting a photo, though. Did she really think putting it in a different glass would make it a different drink? That little . . .'

'Evie!' a voice exclaims, as Evie's face shifts from mad to glad in an instant.

'Brooke! *Beautiful* party!' she says, throwing her arms around Brooke in an embrace. 'Though seems kind of familiar.'

'Yes, glamping's all the rage right now!' Brooke ignores Evie's thinly veiled snide remark entirely.

I've seen Brooke Tennerton online of course; she's quite hard to miss with her endless campaigns with every skincare, make-up and toothpaste brand known to man. But much like Evie, seeing her in person is a considerably different experience. Her skin is just as smooth and smile is just as bright, but she seems smaller – more muted . . . More human.

'Ah, let me introduce you to my team! You already know Aiden, but this is Maddison,' Evie says, as Brooke follows her gaze over to me. 'Look out for this one – she's gonna be the next big thing in events.'

She finishes her sentence with a proud smile towards me and

a wink that sends a flush of warmth through my body. It sounds true when she says it. Maybe I *could* be the next big thing in events. All that's left in my way is the Summer Splash and my unwanted co-organiser.

'Nice to meet you, Maddison!' Brooke comes in for a hug. 'And, Aiden, always a pleasure.'

'The pleasure is always mine, Brooke – you know that.' The pair exchange a look that's a little too sultry for a professional event.

I try to stop my face from going sour, but I feel my cheek muscles twitch and know it's pretty much inevitable. What is it with these women and Aiden? First Pippa, now Brooke … Are we interacting with the same man?

'This is a beautiful event!' I say, eager to break the tension. 'And I'm excited to learn more about "Salyva". What an interesting name.'

'Thanks, sweetie!' Brooke happily turns to me. 'I just think that "saliva" is such a pretty word with an unfair reputation. I'm working to change that.'

'There's none in the gummy, right?' Aiden asks.

'Of course not!' Brooke gushes before biting her lip in worry. 'At least, I don't think so … I don't know … You'd have to ask the lab, I guess. Evie, can I borrow you for photos?'

'Of course, babe!' Evie replies. 'You two explore and have fun; I'll catch up with you in a bit.'

They're less than a metre away before Aiden springs into action, grabbing my glass and dumping it on a nearby barrel-turned-table.

'You heard Evie, let's go. There's got to be something to drink that's better than this sugary nightmare.'

I'll give Brooke's team their dues – if there's one thing they know how to do, it's cohesion. The place is a Pinterest board come to life. I snap far too many pictures, balancing my notebook on every uneven surface I find as I attempt to pen my reactions onto the page. Aiden says nothing – he wouldn't dare, but I know what he's thinking. He made that all pretty clear on Friday night. Which is what made this morning's reaction so confusing … I still don't get who he was trying to fool – Pippa and Gus, or me.

We eventually find the bar – the biggest of the tents, stretching long and wide across one of the edges of the grounds. There are three other bespoke cocktails according to the picture menu, each of which looks as terrifying as the last, boasting an equally un-natural, glittery colour as the Pink Dream rip-off we started with. I can't stomach another. Not on a Monday, when I still haven't recovered from Friday night. Luckily, Aiden seems to be on the same vibe and returns from the bar with two bottles of Coke Zero.

'So, what's your issue today?' he asks as we continue to stroll along the grass. 'You've barely spoken two words to me since we got here.'

I swivel my neck the second his gaze turns towards to mine, repelling his stare like a magnet. My eyes land on a new tent with an open front, showcasing tons of glowing women and men sat beaming as aproned professionals jab needles into their veins. Trust Brooke's party to have an IV-drip station, all in the name of wellness, I suppose. The mere idea sends a chill down my spine but I'd rather look there than at Aiden.

He stops us in our tracks, grabbing my hand and checking for a pulse.

'Are you OK?' he asks sternly.

His hand feels warm against my wrist, fingers twisting around it, sparking the blood underneath. I feel it fizzle at the new, foreign feel of his fingertips as they brush over the delicate skin. It's too much. I shrug my wrist out of his grip, but it doesn't stop him from staring and waiting for my answer.

'Why did you do that?' I ask.

'Check your pulse? You haven't spoken much, and after Friday I just—'

'This morning, when you lied to Gus and Pippa. Why'd you do that?'

His face shifts instantly from concern to a more tightly wound confusion. 'Oh, that? That was nothing – just seemed like you needed it.' He shrugs. 'And they needed humbling. Don't know how you deal with that every day.' He smiles back at me. I'm not smiling. In fact, my scowl renders him visibly shocked. 'Look, I just thought I was helping you out. If it's that deep, I won't talk to them again.'

'It's not that. It's just . . .'

I look up at his big brown eyes, deep and apologetic and rooted in concern. It makes me dizzy. I can barely hear myself over the music and chatter and the decorations and him . . . It's all too much.

I drop my gaze immediately, looking around for something, anything, that could help me out, and spot a wooden arrow labelled *Private Meditation Tents* pointing far south of the garden. Perfect. I start to walk, pacing across the green and trying to ignore the footsteps directly behind me. He is *relentless*. What's his problem, and why must it involve me and making me talk about what's going on in my head?

'You can't leave it there,' he says, meeting me at my side.

I don't let it stop me. That tent will be mine.

'I just don't see why you'd go through all that trouble to lie when I know that you agree with them,' I say as I walk.

'Who said that? Agree with them about what?'

'You, literally all the time. You think I'm this boring, predictable girl who owns too many notebooks.'

We reach the meditation corner – a series of eight single-sized tents, tucked away from the rest of the party in the lower eighth of Brooke's garden. The music's quieter here, the air slightly cooler and the light so much dimmer thanks to the shade of the trees. I press my eyes shut and breathe for a sweet, tranquil moment, before opening them to address the man in front of me. His forehead crinkles in confusion for a moment before something clicks in his brain, piecing my words and his from Friday night together.

'Seven notebooks *is* too many notebooks, Maddy,' he says, a slight tease in his tone.

'I got it the first time,' I sigh.

His lips twist as he studies the dip of my brow and the defeat in my eyes. Eventually he sighs too, shoving his hand in his pocket before casting his eyes back over my face.

'You remember that trip we took at the end of Year Six? With that old crusty river in the middle of nowhere?'

'It was a brook. And it was less than ten minutes from our campsite,' I say.

'Which explains its crustiness – my point stands. Anyway, remember when we found it? Everyone was so excited because it was mad hot and we were desperate for anything to cool us down.'

His face contorts into a smile at the mere recollection of his silly, rambunctious days as a youth. It's endearing, sweet, even, or at least it would be if the day in question hadn't been the epitome of stupid.

'I remember. Everyone started kicking their shoes off and diving headfirst into that filthy pond water.'

'And Mrs May was screaming, and I stained my white vest and got a bollocking from my mum, but it was totally worth it,' he says. 'Do you remember what you did, while we were all jumping?'

Of course I do, but I'm surprised that he still does all these years later. Especially since he was out in the middle having fun with his friends, far, far away from me.

I shrug. 'I dipped a hand in to test the depth and when the teachers gave the go-ahead, I waded in up to my knees.'

It sounds really lame when I repeat it back, but at the time it made the most logical sense. Who jumps willingly into a pool of murky green water? People with no home training, that's who. There was a wave of illness after that too, nasty rashes and stomach bugs sweeping through everyone who went on that trip.

'Yeah, you did, because that's the kind of person you are,' he says, a somewhat fond smile on his face. 'Some people wade in until they know what's out there for them, and some people dive in, headfirst, not knowing what's at the bottom. You're a wader. You always have been and there's nothing wrong with that. You still get there eventually. That's the important part.'

'But you think I'd get there sooner if I dived in headfirst?' I ask.

'This isn't a lake, Maddy – it's life. It's not a competition.'

And of course I know that, but deep down I think we can all admit that life feels like it is. Everywhere I look, someone I know buys a house or gets married or makes a thirty-under-thirty list and leaves me in the dust. Even Aiden – a boy with every start that I had – is a talent manager to an icon, and probably goes to events like this all the time. How am I meant to compete with the quick divers and jumpers who already have their houses and six-figure salaries while I'm still dipping a toe in the shallow end?

'I can be a diver,' I say in protest.

He chuckles again. 'No, you can't, and that's fine. You don't need to be.'

He's resolute in his tone – far too set in his beliefs for a person who barely knows me. We've been in each other's lives for nearly two decades but these last three weeks are the most we've ever spoken. How dare he take twenty-one days of contact and use that to determine who the hell I am? I don't know if it's the residual hangover from Friday, or Gus and Pippa this morning, or the over-stimulation of this event, but I can't be around him and his weird pseudo-psychology anymore. My shoulder brushes against his as I make a beeline for one of the empty meditation tents.

I sigh, long and deep, the second I'm inside, back resting lightly against the flimsy canvas wall. For a piece of cloth, it has semi-decent soundproofing. I shut my eyes tight and let the party fade into the background.

'That was supposed to make you feel better.' Aiden's voice cuts through the quiet.

I guess the soundproofing doesn't work that well if somebody stands right outside.

'Well, it didn't!'

'I'm coming in.'

'No, you're not!'

A quick zip and a shuffle, and there he is. Who buys a privacy tent you can unzip from the inside *and* the outside? What, exactly, is so 'private' about that?

The second he enters, it's clear that these supposedly private meditation tents are specifically designed to fit one person and one person only. And, likely, a person of Brooke's five-foot-nothing stature – something Aiden does not resemble. His head bends forward against the curve of the tent ceiling, pushing his nose closer to mine. This is a *squeeze*. A tight one. His trainer tips brush my boots as he moves around in an attempt to find some comfort.

'You need to stop doing this.' I can only describe his tone as akin to a fed-up headteacher. 'It was never that deep. You are who you are, and I am who I am, and you don't need to try to be anything else.'

It's meant to be sweet, I think, or helpful, or something of that sort, but it does nothing but fill me with a hot, burning rage. He doesn't know me. He never has and he never will, and he certainly doesn't get to think that he does because he witnessed one panic attack and a drunken confession.

'OK, yeah, I like to plan things and I always have ... I'm a wader by nature and everyone knows it,' I say. 'But, of course, I know how to dive. I've been known to, actually. On many occasions. Witnessed by people I *actually* spend time with.'

A snort rushes from the back of his throat, his lips clasped tightly in an effort to trap it inside. I squint up at him coldly in return as he attempts to look me in the eye, the muscles in his cheeks working overtime to stop a stupid grin forming.

'OK, I get it – you can be spontaneous.'

I huff. 'But you don't get it. I can tell that you don't believe me.'

'That shouldn't matter.'

But it does. *Badly.* There's a burning fire in my chest that will not be soothed until he understands. I square up to him, tilting my chin harder and leaning into the minimal space that existed between us in the first place. I need him to see me, to feel the rage in me as I convince him and everyone else that I'm not the predictable girl they think I am.

'I don't need to plan every second of my life.' I enunciate each word as well as I can. 'If I gave up my notebooks and calendars tomorrow, and started to live like you, I'd be absolutely fine. You think I'm up myself because I like to plan, but you're no better than me because you don't.'

He sighs. 'I don't think I'm better than you, Mads.'

My eyes narrow. 'My friends call me Mads. My name is Maddison.'

His eyes widen, spine straightening at my firmer, more biting tone. It awakens something in him; his soft, apologetic stare alight with a new energy.

'OK, Maddy,' he says, a devious hue seeping in through his irises.

I roll my eyes. It's still not 'Maddison', but one battle at a time.

'Your little laissez-faire attitude comes with its own inflated ego and I'm sick of you parading it round like it makes you superior.'

He crosses his arms. 'No one says "laissez-faire".'

'Well, maybe they should. It's fun,' I say through gritted teeth.

A quick chuckle escapes from his mouth, head shaking at my tightly packed animosity.

'If you tried to live like me, you'd barely make it through a week.'

I snarl. 'I could do it without trying.'

His eyes seem to grow more alive. He shuffles closer, pressing against me until our chests touch and his stare drills right into my soul.

'Prove it.'

His words are a notch above a whisper, dangling forbidden fruit. I feel my breath hitch.

'How?' I ask.

He pauses for a moment, rolling his lip against his bottom teeth before revealing a sly, wicked smile. It sets off every warning signal inside my body, but I can't look away.

'I'm guessing Evie told you about the events job?' he asks, his voice slower, focused and rife with an agenda. I nod.

'Did she tell you about the board?'

'She mentioned them.'

He shakes his head. 'So, she didn't tell you. It's cool – she didn't tell me either. I just get copied in on her emails.'

'Tell me what?' I ask softly.

I keep it as cool as I can, but it's to no avail. He knows he's got me hooked.

The delight dances across his features as he takes his sweet time to respond. 'The board thinks you lack the experience – which, to be fair, you do. You can do the work for sure, but you've never been a manager.'

'I know, that's why they're using the Summer Splash to determine—'

'Even with the success of the Summer Splash, they want you with a partner. A co-head of department if you will. Someone who is good with numbers, budget, and has experience of business management.'

As much as it stings, I do get the board's worry. It's the same kind of worry Maxwell and Oliver should have had before they appointed Pippa. I'm not opposed to a partner – in fact, it would be quite nice to not have everything fall solely on my head. That is, however, depending entirely on who the partner is. And the devious look in Aiden's eyes tells me the answer's not good.

'Evie didn't think to put me forward for it – she knows I don't do events and I've been grumbling about this one since she assigned it to me.'

My chest eases immediately, a relieved breath escaping my lungs.

'That is, however, until I asked her to consider me. Which she did instantly, and quite enthusiastically, actually.'

And just like that the tightness returns and my breath falls short, brain muddying with the nightmare dropped upon me. A million thoughts run through my head, but one screams above the rest.

'You don't even *like* throwing events!'

'I like promotions.' He shrugs, crushing my dream between his shoulders.

Of course, he's made this happen – he has never let me be happy. But even at his cruellest, I did not believe that he was capable of something this low. And he doesn't even care about the role! He's doing it for what reason? To torment me? To one-up me? To finally win?

'And I've actually really been enjoying the event-planning recently,' he continues.

The tent starts to close in around me as I aim to steady my breath. What was, mere days ago, a trip across a perfect stream to success, has become a murky river of unending torture with Aiden at the helm.

'There is no way you'd volunteer yourself to work with me full time,' I say.

Tolerating each other for six months is one thing, but by doing this he's resigning himself to what could be a lifetime with me.

'Oh, I'm sure you can't think of anything worse. Which is why I say we make this interesting.'

He bends his neck down even further, the depths of his brown eyes trapping me in his gaze. I ignore every feeling and focus directly on the man above me. I will not break under him. Not at a time like this. No matter how badly he is pushing me.

He continues. 'If we make the Summer Splash as epic as it could be – really blow everyone away – get the kind of media attention and sales that not even Evie has experienced – then we might be able to convince the board that one of us is capable of doing this alone.'

'You want the full job?' I ask.

'I want one of us to *earn* the full job,' he says. 'You have to admit, it'd be better than whatever *this* is.'

'What are you proposing exactly?'

He pauses for a moment. 'There are what? Six months until the Summer Splash? In that time, show me you can be a diver, not a wader. If you can, I'll tell Evie and the board that the event was all you. If you can't, then you go to them and you tell them that *I* ran it all.'

He says it so plainly, like it's simple logic, but they're the words of a man who has never seen sense. A man who is only further proving my point that he clearly does not know me at all.

'You think I'd stake a promotion on you?' I ask.

'With your ego, yes, I do. Especially since it's a promotion we don't even have right now,' he replies. 'If you're as laid-back as you claim you can be, then surely it's an easy win.'

His voice is seductive and cocky – assured that this will work, that he's moments away from reeling me in. But unlike him I think rationally, and I would never throw away the biggest chance of my life on a man like him.

'You can't do this. You can't just manipulate me into giving away a promotion.'

'I wasn't trying to manipulate you,' he says, steady and strong. 'I just figured that after our talk Friday night, you'd maybe be up for something different.'

I recoil immediately. The mention of Friday is enough to snap me out of his hold and remind me just who I'm dealing with. I may have risen to his bait before, but I will not rise to something this insultingly low-hanging.

'Something different like parting with my dream job?' I say with a sneer.

'Something different like taking some risks. And let's not forget, two weeks ago in that boardroom you were pushing me to give up my job first.'

That was entirely different – he would have been giving it up without having to do all the work. And yes, it wasn't my most level-headed moment, but, in my defence, he'd already promised he would. Whether the bonus existed when he promised it is frankly none of my business.

The mere thought of that argument sends chills up my spine. The same chills I felt just before that panic overtook my body. I can't keep going through that. I can't keep working with him. Especially not for what could be the rest of my working life.

'Just think about it. If you can make it that long just winging life, with little to no planning and more spontaneity, then I will step aside and sing your solo leadership praises to Evie without complaint. It's a no-brainer,' he says.

The air is thick between us, slick with the terms of the agreement as they marinate between our two bodies. That job could be mine for the taking if I simply bet on myself. Bet against the man who does nothing but pray for my failure.

'You would really bet your promotion on this?' I ask.

'Like I said, it's not like it's a job I had before.' He shrugs. 'Plus, for me to lose it, you'd actually have to follow through.'

'And you don't think I will,' I say bitterly. 'What makes you think I'll fail?'

'Your aggressive Type-A personality.' He smirks as my face scrunches into a scowl. 'So, is this you saying that you're in?'

He's doing something to me. Messing with my brain, making me all hot and bothered in this tight, overcrowded tent. I can't think straight – everything jumps around, screams then shakes, and I can't organise it, as hard as I try.

'I need clearer terms,' I say.

He rolls his eyes instantly, but, on this occasion, I'm standing by my request. I'm not putting my future on the line over a sentence and some vibes, and if he were smart, he wouldn't either.

He curls his tongue in his mouth as he looks to the top of the tent, contemplating a stronger set of rules. His jaw tenses every second that he stays in deep thought, bringing with it the kind of definition that could cut like a knife.

'Six months of saying yes to everything – every spontaneous night out, every random invite. No thinking, no debating – just a cold, hard yes. Do that for six months and the job is yours.'

'I can't say no to *anything*? Seems a tad problematic,' I say.

'Within reason,' he adds, rolling his eyes again. 'There's obviously an implied element of consent. I'm asking you to live a little, not sell your soul.'

'For six months?'

'We end at the Summer Splash, just before the job is allocated.'

My eyes flit to the floor – focus in on the grass beneath us, desperate to look at anything but Aiden's face. I need logic, I need reason, I need all the things that seem impossible whenever I am too close to him.

Think, Maddison.

I could say no to this – stick with Aiden through the Splash and then resign myself to a life of working by his side. Go from one miserable job to another, all in the name of 'safety' and 'security'.

Or I could take a risk.

I could say yes and prove him wrong and walk away with the prize. The sole leader of the new Evielution events department. That's the kind of thing that would kill with my parents and my annual LinkedIn post. And, most importantly, it's the one thing that I could definitely tick off my five-year plan before thirty.

I have always been pretty smart with my choices. I've always planned my path and made the necessary steps, and it all seemed worth it until I got to Abbingtorn. I *know* you have to work your way up the ladder and I *know* that good things take time. However, after four years in the same entry-level position, I have really got to start questioning whether the careful path really is the smartest option.

'OK, six months.' I watch his face light up. 'But you want that job? You've got to prove something for it too.'

'Go on,' he says, motioning to give me the floor.

'You've got six months to plan everything you do. I want calendar entries, tick-lists, even a five-year plan. I'll be inspecting your notes at the end of the period.'

He scoffs. 'You're setting me homework?'

'I'm teaching you basic adult skills. Trust me, you'll realise you're better off.'

'I doubt it. But, yeah, sure, I'll give it a go. Now give me your phone.' He holds out his hand.

'My personal one?' I ask, taken aback.

'Yeah. With so much on the line I'll need proof, and I'd rather not have it by email.'

I roll my eyes at his stupid smirk, but hand over my phone nonetheless. My spine tenses ever so slightly as he takes it in his hand, calmly tapping his number into my contacts.

'Why so scared? You think I'm gonna read all your hate messages?' He's clutching my life in his palm like it's nothing.

'Hate messages?' I say, poker face in tow.

'I imagine I'm a hot topic in your group chats.' He shrugs.

'Bold of you to assume that you're that important.'

He looks fondly at me as I snatch my phone back from his outreached hand. If I didn't know any better, I would say he enjoys the animosity that he brings out of me.

'I want pics and vids every time you do something reckless. For something to count it needs to be caught in 4K,' he says.

'Every single thing?'

'Let's be real, there won't be that many,' he says tauntingly.

He stretches out his toned arm, the weight of the deal resting dangerously in his palm.

'You've got yourself a deal.' My hand swings towards his.

'I look forward to my promotion.' He smirks, settling with a firm shake.

And just like that, the deal is done – my route out of Abbingtorn hanging in the balance over something I'm not sure I know how to do.

Nudge 14

The Group Effort

There are certain things you come to expect when your friend moves into their first solo place: wine nights, a designated hangout spot, a sofa to crash on after a night out. What you actually get? Full weekends sat on the floor, attempting to assemble poorly labelled flat-pack furniture. Unfortunately, if one of us calls, we all run, no questions asked. So here I crouch, dubiously balancing a bed frame above my head.

Kimi shrieks, dramatically dropping the manual. 'Are you an idiot?'

'You *told* me to screw these pieces together!' Devi waves the screwdriver. 'I knew they looked too big to fit.'

Kimi shakes her head. 'Not you, babe. I'm talking to our new resident daredevil. You just handed over the perfect job to an evil genius!'

If I'd known she'd react like this, I might have chosen a different time to bring up the deal. But I'd hoped that our current DIY focus would be so strong that they'd let my news roll off their backs.

'I didn't give it, I wagered it in exchange for an even *better*, solo job. Let's circle back to that part. I like that part.' I slowly release the frame on Devi's cue. 'Ready?'

We all hold our breath as my hands leave the metal, placing all faith in the strength of our efforts. It stays where I left it, supported by the new hinge, as Devi grins with pride at our handiwork.

'Yeah, a better solo job if you can stop being yourself for six months,' she adds a second later, shrugging out from underneath the frame.

'Not stop being me! Just stop being so organised all the time! It shouldn't be *that* hard, right?' I ask.

The room goes silent, their telling eyes and pursed lips saying more than their words ever could. It's insulting how little faith they have in me. Or, at least, it would be if I weren't feeling just as worried. But I will not have them give up on me, at least not this quickly. *Someone's* got to rally for me, especially while I'm struggling to rally for myself.

'I can do it.' I snatch the manual from Raina and begin to arrange the next set of screws. 'You believe me, right, Raina?'

She's my best bet for an ally; her heart can't take the tension. But I can tell by her face that even she's struggling.

'Raina?'

'Of course I do, you know I always believe in you,' she says. 'But couldn't you have bet a tenner or a doughnut, or something?'

'A head of department role is a whole different ballgame,' Devi sighs.

'That's what makes it fun!' I say with a squeal, distributing the new parts between everyone.

Kimi tuts. 'No, hun, that's what makes it idiotic. And since when did we start doing deals with the devil?'

If there's one thing Kimi is, it is consistent. And I do have to rate it, honestly; someone needs to keep Aiden in check and I'm sick of carrying that burden by myself. But I can tell my fire doesn't burn as hot as hers – at least, not any more. Not after the last couple of Fridays we've had and the way he's carried me through them, against my will.

'He's not been too bad recently. Kind of helpful sometimes,' I say, tracing over the events of the last few weeks.

'*That's* how he got you.' Devi nods solemnly as she reaches for the Allen key. 'Charmed you into losing that sweet, sweet promotion. I blame the arms. You didn't stand a chance.'

'It wasn't the arms!' I say defensively. 'And he didn't charm me – I wanted to.'

'That makes it worse. You weren't manipulated, you were just being stupid,' Kimi huffs.

'She's not stupid, she's just stubborn. Especially with him,' Raina says as she holds the diagram up to our work.

It's my turn to scowl at Raina now, in response to her pointless aside, but she takes little to no note of my anger, shrugging lightly in response.

'What? It's true. You two have always been like this. You spent all of A-level English competing for who could give the coldest shoulder. Then you see him once at uni and—'

A sharp nudge from Kimi stops her words in their tracks.

'It was never a competition,' I huff, ignoring the last part.

I won at practically everything Aiden ever threw my way. When he didn't want to talk to me, I made sure my silence was louder. When he joked with everyone else but me, I made sure my eye rolls laughed for me. Every time he went out of his way to make me feel like he was the one stuck next to me, I endeavoured to make sure that he was humbled – that he knew he was no grand prize either. This will be no different if I have anything to do with it.

'Come on, guys. You know I'm not stupid; I have a plan.' I reach across the carpet for my phone. 'I've written down a list of activities that seem super reckless for me and separated them into a series of stages. Stage One starts now and sets the tone, and Stage Five – the final stage – takes place just before Summer Splash.'

The three of them stare back at me, faces a mix of horror and confusion. Then they exchange glances, clearly weighing up the best person to take this. Eventually, Raina steps up with a well-meaning sigh.

'Mads, baby . . .' She reaches for my hand. 'You just made a plan to not make a plan. And it was deeply and unnecessarily thorough. Even for you.'

'I can't just think on the spot! I'm not wired to do that and frankly don't think it makes sense,' I say.

'We know, babe. That's why we're so furious.' Devi has given up on the bed frame and is leaning back against the wall. 'This whole bet is ridiculous and we need to figure a way out of it before it's too late. Did you sign anything?'

'SILENCE.' Kimi's bellow is unprovoked and the command stops us all in our tracks, rattling the half-done bed. The doubt's been wiped clean from her face, not a trace to be found. All that remains is the tough, fixed resolve of a winner.

'If we are going to win this, then we need to stop acting like we've already lost,' she says.

'We?' I ask.

'Yes, we. You think you can do this alone? You've had five days and you've practically handed him the prize.' She tuts. 'This is group property now; we're getting you that job. Devi, start researching. Raina, take notes.'

Militant as she is, Kimi's orders send a ripple of relief through my soul. Alone, I won't lie, the bet was looking a little shaky. But together I reckon we can do this.

'Give me your phone, Maddison. I'm deleting your apps,' Kimi says confidently, holding out her hand.

'My apps?' I ask.

I don't know what's worse – how ominous her statement is, or the fact she believes that something so vague will work with someone like me. Who just hands over their phone to a friend to 'delete apps'? I trust Kimi with my life, but my phone is a whole other thing.

'We're deleting anything you rely on to plan. Calendar, habit tracker, journal, period tracker . . .' She goes on, but she's lost me already. I can't hear anything that she says over the loud alarm bells ringing in my mind.

'The period tracker seems a little extreme,' I say.

'It's six months! Like me, you will learn to quite literally go with the flow.'

'But the algorithm,' Raina whispers. 'All of that data . . . It will take months to get it accurate again!'

'Don't encourage her!' Kimi says warningly, flicking through my app screens after I reluctantly hand my phone over. 'I'll let you keep your notes app, but I expect it to be used chaotically.'

She hands my phone back, watching as I scroll through the home pages. I try to quell my imminent breakdown. The order's all wrong. The remaining apps have shifted in place. I try to oh-so subtly reorganise them in my head, my thumb mapping them out as it hovers over my screen.

'You want to organise them,' Devi says.

'I do not!' I'm lying.

'Mads! Do you want to win this money or not?' Kimi lightly slaps my hand.

When Kimi gets serious, there's nothing you can do to derail her and she is indeed serious about this new bet. I breathe a sigh of relief. With Kimi and the girls on my side, there's absolutely no way I can lose. Aiden Edwards will rue the day he staked his future on my failure, and he will do so from his remaining position as talent manager.

Nudge 15

The Paper Note

'**Y**ou're late.' Aiden is waiting for me by the door.

'You try taking two trains, a Tube and a poorly timed bus during rush hour, first thing in the morning. *Especially* after you've deleted all your transport timing apps to stop being such a planner!' I say, panting.

There is no way that this is just the way 'normal non-planners' live. It is far more stress-inducing this far on the edge. People may call me 'uptight' and 'predictable' and 'too organised', but I'm now convinced that they're masochistic.

'I don't get why you didn't just drive here. Evie would have expensed your mileage,' he says, grabbing a trolley as we start to stroll.

'Because public transport is cheaper than parking.'

Also, because driving requires a licence – a fairly vital piece of kit that I'm yet to obtain.

'She would have paid your parking too,' he says. 'I'll certainly be expensing mine. And I'll be dropping you home.'

'What? No.'

He shrugs plainly. 'That taxi home from the Lounge showed you don't live that far from me, and after the hour I'll have to drive, another ten minutes out of my way is nothing. Speaking of, why *did* I have to drive fifty minutes out of London and pay extortionate parking to come to a napkin store?'

He grimaces as he glances around the aisle, eyes tracing over the rainbow of napkins on the shelves, in every shade and hue imaginable.

'It's not a napkin store, it's a general-supply warehouse. This is just the napkin aisle. And it's the best one in the country, with the highest quality and incredibly glowing reviews. We want nothing but the best for the Summer Splash.'

I pick a set of soft yellow ones off the shelf, bringing them to my phone so I can compare them with the accent colour swatches I saved down. It's close, but not close enough, and I'm not quite sure if yellow's the vibe. I make a note to strike yellow from the napkin-and-linen-colour shortlist.

'Anyway, are you not impressed?' I ask, bringing the conversation back a notch. 'I expect my lack of apps to be recorded as evidence for my new job.'

He shrugs as he pushes the trolley. 'Small potatoes.'

Small potatoes? Small potatoes! Tell that to my ballet pumps – soaking wet from my walk through Crystal Palace after I missed the bus. With the weather app gone, I had to trust my eyes, and the sky was misleadingly clear this morning. When this is over, I will never take it for granted again. And I will be writing countless notes reminding me to put my umbrella back in my handbag.

'What, were you expecting me to quit my job, jump on a plane and start backpacking round the world?' I ask.

'A guy can dream,' he says jokingly, barely swaying as I give him a playful shove. 'I just feel like losing a couple of apps is not that deep.'

Not that deep to him, perhaps, but I've been walking around feeling like I've lost a whole part of me. I don't believe for one second that he is able to go about every single day without checking anything in advance. 'So, what would be deep?'

'There's no specific thing – you're just supposed to be winging life. I can see your head spinning.'

He can't – he's not even looking at me, just glancing at napkins as we continue to stroll down the aisle. But why wouldn't it be spinning? 'Winging life' is not a quantifiable thing to comprehend. There's nothing to measure or track, and, honestly, at this stage, I don't know if I'd even be allowed to track it if I could. How am I supposed to know what actions are small or large potatoes if I'm not supposed to even be looking into things that hard?

'My head's not spinning,' I say, lying.

He actually turns to me this time, eyes casting over my face as he raises an incredibly sceptical eyebrow.

'OK, not spinning per se – more of a light little baby turn,' I say.

'A baby turn?'

'A pirouette, if you will.'

'That's a spin, not a turn.'

'Says who?'

'My sister did ballet for fifteen years. I had to supervise a lot of classes.'

Mental image of Aiden helping teens in tutus aside, we are both losing sight of the problem at hand. How on earth am I supposed to be wild and spontaneous if I don't know what wild and spontaneous constitutes? I live in south London; I can't exactly start jumping off cliffs and paragliding above treacherous oceans. I have work and the city and the number three bus to work with; there's only so exciting my life can get.

'Don't overthink it.' He reaches for some teal napkins and motions for me to hold my phone screen up to them.

'But how will I . . .' I don't even know what to ask.

'If it doesn't feel like you, then it's probably right,' he says in jest.

Thinly veiled attack aside, it's not the worst logic to go by . . . Although not the easiest thing to put into practice. If it doesn't feel like me, how am I even supposed to think of it in the first place? The napkins still aren't right. He puts them back and we turn into the crockery aisle.

He gives me a once-over. 'We should probably lay out some further ground rules, though – stop you showing up like *this* every day. You need to check the weather and know when your bus is coming.'

I purse my lips, trying to hide my excitement at the thought of redownloading my apps.

'A normal degree of planning is fine,' he continues, grabbing a seashell bowl from one of the shelves. 'Pose with this.'

He holds the bowl out to me as I stare back, flummoxed by the sudden interruption.

'What do you mean?' I ask.

'Pose with this. I need a picture for Evie,' he says, straight-faced, as I still stare back in confusion.

I take it from him in silence, holding it up to the side with the kind of pride reserved for championship trophies. His lip curls at my bravado, smile conveniently hidden by his phone as he snaps a photo.

'Beautiful. Now, as I was saying, you can schedule things in as far as a week ahead, but you have to say yes to plans on the day if you don't already have something in.'

'Within reason,' I say to remind him.

'Of course, within reason. Let's test it. You doing anything Saturday?'

'I don't think so. Why?' I ask dubiously.

He stops the trolley in its tracks so he can reach into his bag and pull out a fresh leather notebook. He catches the surprise in my eyes as he opens it up, smiling at my evident bewilderment.

'I'm keeping true to my end of the bargain too,' he says, gesturing proudly at it. 'Even brought my own pen – in a pencil case, no less.'

He wiggles it lightly in his hand before resting it against the handlebars, scrawling something down and handing the ripped page over to me. It's an address, written messily but clearly enough for me to know that it's nowhere I would recognise.

'Grab some friends – you have those right? I can get you on the list for Saturday evening.'

'A list for . . .?'

'Don't worry about that. Just be there at nine-thirty.'

A sentence that would be harrowing enough without the knowing glint in his eye. Notebook packed away again, he moves on. We're nearing drink receptacles now, stretching all the way from plastic to fine china. He powers on quickly, forcing me to walk in double time just to match his pace.

'This isn't like, a sex club or drug thing?' I ask.

'It's actually both. It's a sex club *and* drug thing,' he replies mockingly.

I squeal. 'It's a valid question! I don't know what you're into.'

'I told you not to overthink.'

And it was bold of him to assume I was capable of that in the first place. He slows down ever so slightly, glancing behind to clock my deeply furrowed brow and pouting lips. It's enough to trigger a long, deep and pained sigh.

'It's not a sex club. There are no drugs involved,' he says dryly. 'You will not be kidnapped or taken advantage of.'

'Thank you.' I nod back at him.

I rub the piece of paper between my thumb and my finger, carefully tracing over each letter of the address with my eyes. East London. That's all I can really deduce without rushing to type it into Google Maps.

'One more thing …' I look up at him, pausing only to leave room for another of his exasperated sighs. 'Dress code?'

He huffs impatiently. 'Clothes. You've dressed yourself before, right?'

'What kind of clothes?' I grit my teeth.

'I've already done too much. You've got to be able to do something yourself, Maddy.'

And he's right, I suppose – for a moment I forgot that he too has stakes in this game that we're playing. If the roles were reversed, I probably would have let him flounder for the six months and easily claimed that job for myself. But for some reason – perhaps pity or utter boredom – he's decided to throw me a somewhat terrifying bone. So, I whip out my phone, take a picture of the paper and send one vaguely threatening text to the FGA.

Saturday. 9.30. If I'm going, so are you.

Nudge 16

The Sex Club That Isn't a Sex Club

Aiden sabotaged me. I can already tell, as I stand in this alley-way of urine and crushed dreams. And in front of my girls, no less, as some sort of sick, twisted joke.

'I think we're here.' Raina stops us in our tracks as we crowd around the desolate-looking door.

It's tall and ominous, perhaps once dark green in colour, but now a chipped mess of peeling paint and scribbled graffiti. There's no one in sight and nothing to hear, just silence and a unified air of regret.

'And you're sure that—'

'I already asked. He promised it is not a drug thing or a sex club,' I say.

'Do we trust him?' Kimi asks. 'Because this really looks like a sex club.'

'Jury's out right now. And how do you know what a sex club ...? You know what, never mind.'

'We really need to rethink this whole herd-mentality thing,' Devi mutters.

Our gazes stay fixed ahead, taking in the dubious door. Where have I taken them? Or better yet, where has Aiden made me take them?

Raina speaks first. 'There's a ringer.'

'I'm not touching that,' Kimi immediately replies.

I'm not close enough to state it with an absolute certainty, but I can just tell in my gut that the buttons are going to be sticky.

'I have hand sanitiser!' Raina says.

Devi shudders. 'Not enough.'

'You're up, Mads,' Kimi says, hand on my back as she lightly guides me to the front of our huddle.

I get it, I do – my suggested plan, my fingers on the sticky icky call bell. But that doesn't make me any more willing to do it – maybe we're all better off turning around and going home.

'We've come this far.' Raina is clearly reading my mind. 'There's nothing stopping us from at least *seeing* what's behind the door.'

'So, press the bell then,' Devi says, doubt still peppering her voice.

I can feel all three sets of eyes on me as I inch forward, the soles of my trainers gracing the dubiously speckled step by the door. My friends catch their breath in unison as my hand lurches forward, mere inches away from the button ahead.

'Girls?' I pause, looking back at them.

They're huddled tighter than before, gripping on to each other as they cower two metres from where I stand.

'We believe in you! I'm sure it's not dangerous!' Raina says.

Devi nods. 'We're just gonna wait back here till we know you're OK ...'

I can't even be mad at them. I'd be doing the exact same if I weren't the one responsible for bringing us to this godforsaken place. I turn back to the door, holding my own breath as I reach for the bell a second time, this time actually pressing. The quick buzz fills the air, short and sharp, before a muffled speaker crackles to life.

'Name?' a voice asks.

'Erm, Maddison Clarke, but I might have a booking under Aiden Edwards . . . I'm not sure.'

The silence on the other end lasts far too long, sending my stomach into a tailspin. I still can't shake the feeling this could all be one sick joke and Aiden truly has sent me into the middle of nowhere.

'Maddison Clarke, got it. With friends? How many?'

'Four! Well, three. Three . . . plus me, so . . . f-four in total.' My palms are sweaty and I can barely string a sentence together any more. We're not even in yet – how am I supposed to cope when we're inside? I still don't even know what we're facing when we get there.

'Cool. Come in.' Another short buzz sounds before the latch is released on the door in front of me. I push it open and turn back to beckon to the girls, watching as they creep closer. Their eyes are still fearful, as I'm sure mine are too. But we have come this far and I cannot back out of this now . . . I need to at least stay long enough to relay this back to Aiden.

We make our way down a dark hallway to the only other visible door at the end. There's no signage, no instruction and very little light, just our guts and the muffled shuffles of our soft-soled shoes.

'Not a sex club,' I say.

'Or a drug thing,' Raina adds, as we all motion to the handle for the final door.

We turn it together, our fingers lingering on the handle, and open the door to wonderland.

I can hear a unified gasp behind me as we creep into the room, taking in the paint-splattered walls and wooden tables. Nineties R&B blares from the speakers, echoing through our chests and immediately jolting Kimi back to life.

'OK, I see!' she says, whipping off her jacket with glee. 'Now *this* is a vibe I can get behind!'

Raina cheers happily as we settle down onto some stools and anxiously await our first drinks of the night. 'Definitely not a sex club!'

That much appears to be true, yes, but I'm still lost as to what exactly this place is. It's got all the makings of a club – DJ, stage, drinks and a healthy crowd of people. But no one seems settled. Everyone is biding their time, glancing up at the stage and getting into position.

'What's wrong, Mads?' Kimi asks as she and Devi return, haphazardly balancing eight oddly shaped glasses between them and a tray of shots.

'Happy Hour?' I ask as they begin setting them down.

'Nope. Just figured we may as well commit,' Kimi answers. 'And rightfully so – what's up with you and that face? We're here and we didn't get murdered!'

'I'm just confused.' I take a sip of my first drink. It's peppery, fizzy, with a hint of ginger and the kind of kick that sneaks up on you. It goes against everything in me not to ask what it is, but that's not what carefree people do, so I suffer in silence instead.

'You need to chill,' Devi says. 'There are drinks, there are vibes. Be in the moment! That's what you're doing this all for, right?'

And aside from the job, I suppose it is, but that doesn't shake the fact that this doesn't make sense. There's no reason Aiden would send me to a random club in the middle of nowhere, simply so I could chill and 'be in the moment'. And this place particularly feels anything *but* random. There's got to be a meaning.

'Mads, drink up!' Kimi takes in my scrunched face. 'We're gonna go dance and these need to be *gone* before we do.'

I take a breath, close my eyes and try to see into Aiden's mind . . . put myself in his far-too-informal shoes. Maybe he's here, maybe he wants to catch me out – pop out of the shadows with an 'I told you so' as I sit on my stool overthinking. Maybe he doesn't even believe I'll make it tonight . . . put my name on the guestlist just so he can check tomorrow that I didn't sign in. He's always been a fierce competitor and I should have kept that in mind from the moment he handed over the address. It wasn't a favour or help, it was part of a greater scheme. A scheme I must outsmart, even if I don't know what it is.

I lift a shot to my lips, letting the sharp smell waft up my nose before I gulp it down for all that it's worth. The girls look back at me, startled. I see both shock and pride on their faces before they look to each other with agreement, pick up their shots and quickly do the same.

Little by little, everything fits into place – from the drinks to the crowd to the people we meet as we own the dance floor. It's a room of joy and love, and shared nostalgia, wrapped in a vibrant and sparkly bow. I can feel myself move with it, breathe with it, freeing myself from my head and diving into the pool of freedom around me. If I could bottle this high I would do so in an instant, but instead I must treasure it for what it's worth now. A night with my girls in a place we don't know; a place that has managed to capture what happiness is.

A couple of hours in, sirens sound from the DJ booth and the crowd cheers, abruptly halting their moves to smile towards the stage. We turn with them to see a man enter to applause, clutching a microphone as he amps the crowd up further.

'All right, all right, you all know what time it is!' he bellows into the mic, much to the glee of the people before him. 'The drinks are down, the crowd is here – it's time for us all to ...'

'PAINT THAT MATE!' the crowd screams around us.

The chant bounces off the walls clear and strong, with a certainty that has the four of us as lost as when we first entered.

'Who's feeling brave tonight and ready to win their table a two-hundred-and-fifty-pound tab and one of our beautiful T-shirts?' he asks.

Kimi turns and shouts to us. 'Two hundred and fifty? For what? I'll do whatever it is for two hundred and fifty quid!'

The man hushes the crowd ever so slightly. 'Tonight, we're doing things a little differently. I only need *one* willing volunteer, because I've been informed that we have a special lady in the audience who has been dying to give this a try.'

Oh, no.

The gut bubbles are back and the cogs are all fitting into place. All at once I understand. I don't even need to hear him say it out loud.

'Is there a Maddy C in the crowd?' he asks, much to the screams of my friends.

Even if there was some way to hide, their pointing and screaming has rendered it utterly useless. They know as little as I do, but they've done everything but whip out a flashing neon arrow above my head.

'Get up here, Maddy!'

Through no force of my own, I'm pushed through the waves of people all the way to the stairs. Each person I pass smiles at my taut face with glee, blindly willing me on with no explanation or reassurance. They can't *wait* for me to be there and they're thrilled to be watching whatever foolishness Aiden has signed me up for.

'Here she is, folks!' the host cheers as I creep onto the stage, blinded by the lights and overwhelmed by the sea of people below me. 'Go on, Maddy, tell us a bit about yourself – where are you joining us from today?'

'South London.' My voice comes out as a squeak, bordering on a whisper. Even with the mic shoved in my face, I don't know who would have heard that. Honestly, I'm shocked anything came out at all. My mouth's gone dry, hands shaking more than I can control. I shove them into my pockets before anyone in the crowd can notice.

I don't get shy on stage – I'm a three-time junior debate champion for God's sake, but I get to prep for those; I get to know what's coming. Being shoved in front of complete strangers with no real explanation is a completely different ballgame. Plus, I'm in dungarees. Dungarees! In a nightclub!

'Well, Maddy C from south London, you ready to take on the challenge?' he asks, trying his best to soothe me with his grin.

How can I take on a challenge when I don't know what it is? Or where I am? Or what I'm doing up here?

Everyone's beaming at me in excitement and I couldn't tell you a thing about what I could possibly be doing next, but one thing is for certain. I cannot be bad vibes. My outfit has already left me with so much to prove.

'Right, who wants to go up against our dazzling contender?' the man yells out to the crowd, realising a response from me is a lost cause.

The crowd swells and cheers as arms fly in the air, pointing and waving in every direction possible. He scans the crowd for the next victim – someone far more willing than I was and clearly eager to take on whatever hell I've committed to. I watch his hand point somewhere in the crowd as a guy burrows through to the stage, a large grin on his face as he banters with our host. I can't register one word he's saying. I can barely hear. My brain is fixed on whatever ordeal lies ahead of us.

'Let's get you two dressed, shall we?' the host asks, voice cutting through my thoughts and bringing me back to the stage.

I hear a rustle behind me as a stagehand runs from the wings and hands me a plastic anorak. It's flimsy and weak, practically dissolving in my sweaty fingers, but her smile is so sweet and encouraging that I have to partake. I smile back nervously as I pull it over my head, shimmying into the overgrown sleeves.

'You both look wonderful!' our host says. 'So, the game is on! Are you ready to . . .'

'PAINT THAT MATE!' the crowd screams again.

The words are meaningless to me – foreign jumbles to my ears – but the certainty of the audience only makes whatever they are saying sound scarier. My competition is loving it – playing to the crowd and strutting around in his plastic poncho. They yelp and cheer as he makes the stage his runway, goading him into various poses and turns. I know I should do something equally fun, but my feet are stuck to the ground beneath me. Aiden Edwards will perish if I make it out of this alive. *Perish.*

'Right, I will explain this for any newbies in the audience one time and one time only,' our host says. 'Right now, our willing participants are being handed an envelope with their magic word. When the buzzer sounds, they must open their envelope and start painting that object on their canvases. First to have their word guessed correctly by all of you wins a coveted 'Paint That Mate' T-shirt, and a two-hundred-and-fifty-pound bar tab.'

The prizes elicit a 'wooo!' from the audience, all eager for the competition to start. It sounds easy enough – a high-stakes, drunken drawing game. Not my strong suit, but not the world's most distressing challenge.

'The paint can be found in the barrels at the other end of the stage and our contestants have ten minutes to get their masterpiece together.' He looks back at us to check we're OK. 'But can they paint with brushes?'

'NO!' the crowd screams in joyful unison.

'Can they paint with their fingers?'

'No!'

'What can they paint with? Everybody at once!'

'Their bodies!'

'That's right! The fastest, and most creative body part, wins!' The host sends the crowd into an ecstatic frenzy.

My smile fades into panic, cheeks losing the ability to even nervously fake some joy as it all dawns on me. Suddenly the anoraks make sense, as does the reason Aiden sent me here in the first place. He wanted me to sweat under this spotlight, shy away from the challenge and immediately default my future happiness to him. But I will not let him win. I cannot. Even if it means embarrassing myself in front of this room full of strangers.

I suppose when you think about it, that's all they are – strangers. People who don't know me, what I stand for or what I am like. I am a nobody – a blank slate in dungarees who is standing on this stage eager and up for the challenge. I can't be predictable to them; they don't know me or my next move.

I can be a girl who dives.

'Are you two ready?' he asks, grinning at both of us.

It's now or never.

'Hell, yeah!' I yell into his mic.

The crowd roars, the sound helping to steady my stomach. They're on my side. They like me. I will be OK.

'Well, then, let's get this started, shall we?' the host's voice booms. 'Ladies and gentlemen, it's time to . . .'

'PAINT THAT MATE!'

The klaxon blares almost immediately, the sound jolting through my body and pumping my blood round at two times its normal speed. My heart leaps at the challenge, the deafening screams of the crowd spurring me on as I switch into game mode with no time to lose.

I tear open the envelope, the animosity in my grip almost ripping the paper inside with it. But it survives well enough for me to make out the word *plane*, typed out in clear, unmistakable font. An aeroplane? How I'm meant to draw a plane when I can't use my hands is beyond me, but I need to figure it out asap if I want to even stand a chance.

I rush across the stage to the paint, almost skidding as I leg it to the sound of cheers. Four large barrels stand before me, coming up to the height of my ribs, filled with red, yellow, blue and black paint.

'Mix it! Mix it!'

The screams increase as my opponent gains on me, throwing his full arm into the red paint elbow-first before doing the same with the blue. He is *covered*. These anoraks may have come with 'sleeves', but they're wide open and billowy, and as fake as can be. He doesn't seem to care, scurrying back to his canvas and throwing his arm at the slate like a windmill. That's what I need to do. Throw caution to the wind and, for once, just get out of my head.

So I do.

The noise level soars as I turn my back to the first barrel, using my arms to prop me over it so I can dunk myself in. I sink into the paint slowly, the sensation dense and vaguely off-putting as I drop further in. There's no stopping me now – I am quite literally in too deep. I wiggle emphatically, ensuring that the colour will stick before repeating the same with the yellow and blue. Then I sprint for my canvas, throwing my entire back into it before smearing the canvas in the muddled blackish browny grey I've created. I need the body of the plane to take up as much space as possible – once I have the foundation, the wings should be easy. It's going to take at least three or four trips to those barrels, but I will make it work.

I should be embarrassed, ashamed, mortified, even – this goes against every fibre of my being. But the undying support from the crowd echoes around the room, blocking my thoughts and filling my head with a strong, fiery delusion. I let their cheers guide me, consume my being as I play to their smiles, ducking and weaving and grinding up on my canvas in time to the music. They want a show and I'm giving it to them, much to their glee.

'A PLANE!' They shout out the answer in unison as I smear a blue sky on my canvas with a swipe of my arm.

'We have a winner!' The host bounds over to me.

I can barely hear. My head's pounding with unabashed jubilation.

His hand grabs my own, launching it into the air as the audience hollers louder than humanly possible. Then he smiles widely, handing me a T-shirt and gift card, and gesturing for me to bow for my adoring fans. I do so somehow, my body on autopilot, powered purely by the screams of the people before me. I'm led backstage to remove the anorak and wipe off any excess paint. With shaky legs, I make my way back to my friends, who don't release me from a squished, euphoric group hug until we have returned to the dance floor.

'That was unbelievable! You are unbelievable!' Raina yells as they cling to me for the fourth consecutive minute.

'And incredibly hot. Seriously, you were on *fire* up there. Devi got it all on camera,' Kimi adds.

'Yeah, we knew you could move, but not like *that*. I don't know what came over you up there, but you should keep it,' Devi says.

She flashes the screen in my face and I watch myself come to life, owning that stage like I was born to be there. The girl in the video is confident and sexy, almost ethereal. She's the girl in the dress from the La La Lounge.

'Send me that,' I say and Devi obliges immediately, the video pinging through to my phone in its grainy glory.

Free drinks aside, there's only one thing on my mind. I slam my thumb on the forward button, leaving it caption-free. The video speaks for itself – there's no need to say more. Less than a minute later, my phone buzzes and a smile forces its way across my cheeks as I read his words once, twice, three times over. It's two messages – simple, but all that I needed to pave over a dip in my gut that I've only just realised was still there.

Not bad, Maddy.

Now that's what I call unpredictable.

Nudge 17

The Lucy Hayward of It All

I was floating on the high of Saturday night for the entirety of the next five days. No one could tell me anything, and, if they'd tried, I absolutely would not have heard it. Suddenly work felt manageable – enjoyable, even. I could block out Pippa's passive aggression without even trying. I felt radiant and utterly invincible, existing on a plane of blissful ignorance I'd only heard stories about.

It's probably why – to the surprise of absolutely everyone – I've ended up sitting in the pub after work on Thursday, pressed shoulder to shoulder in a tiny booth with an unbearably chatty Pippa. I only have myself to blame. I was girlbossing too close to the sun to properly register the emptiness of her invite.

Thursday-night drinks are an Abbingtorn tradition that I decided I needed no part in. I tried at first when I was new, because I felt like I had to, but I stopped the second it seemed socially permissible. It tends to be the same sort of crowd – the 'cool kids' of the Abbingtorn ecosystem. Pippa, Gus, the marketing boys, and a couple of girls from the design team. Occasionally Maxwell goes along too, and, of course, picks up the tab. I don't belong to that crowd, nor have I massively wanted to.

That is exactly why Pippa's eyes widened earlier when she asked, and I immediately said yes. I regretted it the second it left my mouth. But it was too late to take it back. Plus, Aiden was watching and I knew it would count against me if I said no. So, here I am, sitting at the table as they gossip about everything from work drama to their undoubtedly exaggerated sex lives.

The one saving grace? I managed to drag Aiden along with me against his will. He looks just as uncomfortable as I do – more so, perhaps. I saw his eyes practically glaze over from boredom during Pippa's last sordid tale.

'Aiden, Maddison, you've both been awfully quiet!' Pippa chirps up as the group chatter comes to a lull. 'Care to share? Maddison, you're *single* single, right?'

She's holding back a laugh as she delivers the lightly masked insult. She didn't need to ask; we've spoken about this many times. She coined the term '*single* single' just about me.

'*Single* Single' *(Adjective)*

1. Entirely single with little to no hope.

2. Not entertaining any talking stages or situationships; completely alone.

3. Maddison Clarke's perpetual relationship status.

'Wow, Maddison, you're, like, single *single. I don't know how that's even possible nowadays!'*

I feel the last of my Saturday night high evaporate from my body.

There's got to be some way I can get up and leave right this moment without looking like an entire weirdo. A call from a stranded friend, perhaps, or a coronary. Something dire that would necessitate an exit right *now*.

'Hey, Pippa, isn't this your song?' Aiden asks, voice breaking through the silence as he looks over my head to meet Pippa's eyes. 'Why aren't you up there dancing? In fact, why aren't you all up there?'

Pippa's smug face lights up at his comment, but it's honestly nothing special. Everything that has ever been in the top forty is 'Pippa's song'. But I bite my tongue, because it has worked unexpected wonders. Suddenly she's out of her seat, beckoning everyone to the tiny space in the centre of the pub.

'Aiden, come and join me!' She purrs this in a voice at least five semitones higher than her usual register.

She reaches across to grab him, an inch away from hitting my face, but he stares at her hand with an unmoving, remorseful smile.

'I don't really dance,' he says. 'And Maddy here still needs to finish her drink. Can't leave her all by herself.'

It's enough to make Pippa re-register my presence, her smile dropping instantly. She regains composure quickly enough, but I saw the slip and she knows I did. I'd put money on her not even remotely caring.

'Fine, but I'd better see you out there later!'

Then she saunters off to join the rest. I finally exhale, the sound deep and exceptionally loud, much to the amusement of the only other person in the booth. I may not be able to see his face, but I can feel the judgement radiating off it.

'You're staring.' My eyes are still fixed to my glass. 'Why?'

If he expects a 'thank you' for getting Pippa and co to leave the table, then he will be waiting an awfully long time.

'No real reason. It's just, you were awfully quiet when everyone was talking about their relationships.'

'I didn't realise there were points for participation.' I turn my head to him this time, watching his lip curl slightly at my weak attempt at some snark. His eyes darken with curiosity.

'Nothing to contribute?' He scans my face.

'Just didn't feel like sharing with a bunch of acquaintances.'

I counter his stare, taking a swig from my drink as our pupils wrestle for the upper hand. He's judging just how far he can push and I'm wondering just how far I'd really let him. Eventually it's him who breaks, glancing down at his glass for a breather before looking back at me.

'So, there *is* a special someone.'

'Not quite.'

'Not quite?'

Not at all.

He keeps prodding. 'There's a story at least.'

'Everyone has stories. Ask what you really want to ask,' I say, jabbing the paper straw so hard against the glass that it rips.

For a moment, he seems taken aback by my dare; he thought I'd retreat instantly. Admittedly, without two drinks in my system I probably would have. But the gin is burning its way through my body and infusing everything it touches with unbridled confidence.

'Did you ever date anyone at Winterdown?' he asks, vaguely changing the subject.

I shake my head.

'Surprising,' he says.

'Why?'

'Well, you were ...' He drops it. 'Dating someone right now?'

'Nope.'

'How many exes?' he asks.

'One.'

'One?' His eyes grow wide.

I shrug. 'Well, yeah, kind of.'

It's enough to make me shrivel inside myself again.

'It's not uncommon. In fact, it's probably more common than socials let on. Between the limited good options and desirability politics, I don't get how so many people bounce from long-term thing to long-term thing. I've only been with one person I'd consider an ex, and even that is generous.'

My mini rant pours out my mouth before I've even realised that I've started, but he doesn't mock me or let out a single laugh. Instead, he listens quietly and carefully, eyes still affixed to my own.

'Why is it generous?' he asks. 'What happened?'

His eyes trace the crease of my brow as he patiently and delicately awaits whatever answer I feel comfortable enough to give him.

'It was more an arrangement of convenience and it just fizzled out, I guess,' I say. 'He was this guy at uni and I'd never really dated. Honestly, I don't even know if I really liked him. A part of me genuinely liked that he liked me, but a bigger part just wanted to get the virginity thing out the way.'

'Tick off another milestone.' The way he says it is earnest, like he truly understands.

'Exactly.' I smile back. It's weak, but he accepts it. 'What about you? Any girls in the picture?'

'None that I care about,' he answers, shrugging callously.

'Charming,' I remark, as he flashes a teasing smile.

It sparkles more than it should and makes my stomach turn inside out, reminding me of our current proximity. We're still sat knee to knee, squashed in the corner of the empty booth as if everyone else was still squeezed there with us. I can feel our legs brush against each other, see his back pressed to the wall, but I have no desire to spread out and he hasn't asked me to.

'I'm kidding. Honestly, I'm not really into all that right now. When things ended with Luce, I realised it's kinda stupid to get that attached to one person,' he says.

'Luce?' I ask tentatively.

It's the first time I've heard him mention any name outside of a work context and it somehow hits harder hearing that it's a girl. I don't want to prod too hard – I'm worried that if I do, he'll close right back up again. But I want to know who Luce is. I have a strong, presumably gin-fuelled desire to know more about him.

'Lucy Hayward – she went to school with us. We got together in our teens; I thought everybody knew that.'

Her name comes with a weight that pulls my jaw to the floor and crushes my chest in the process. *Lucy Hayward*. Lucy Hayward, who caused me so much pain and, worse, picked her nose throughout primary school.

'She'd stopped eating her own snot by then,' he says, apparently reading my mind.

'Sorry, it's just … You were *dating* her?' I ask.

Years of interactions flash before my eyes, dating all the way back to when we were eight. There was the petition she started to ban my 'stinky lunch foods' and the times she would scrunch my hair and tell everyone it felt like a scrubbing sponge. I thought I was free of her when she didn't stay on at Winterdown to do her

A levels, but she was always there, at every party, making me the butt of every joke until eventually I stopped going anywhere she might be.

I went to university convinced that I would be a stronger, more evolved version of the person that I was before. A resolve that almost broke when I moved into my room and found out that I was to be neighbours with none other than Lucy Hayward. Her eyes narrowed in on me the second she saw me, resemblant of a predator clocking its prey, but that environment was different and so she took a different approach.

'Maddison!' she exclaimed, her forced smile publicly distracting from the snarl in her voice. 'You got in *here*? Wow. So impressive for you.'

Things went from bad to worse after that. I should have switched halls there and then. Maybe even universities.

'How could you not know?' he asks, unperturbed by my shock. 'You guys went to the same uni and we were all over each other's feeds.'

I rack my brain for an instance where I've heard about the two of them being together. I saw them act close and heard that they went to the same parties, but Aiden was a flirty guy and I never thought anything of it. Honestly, the second Lucy stopped going to school with me, I tried to block all mentions of her out of my life. I certainly didn't know that they were in a full-blown *relationship*.

'I never saw it on Facebook.'

'Well, that's 'cos no one our age uses Facebook, Maddy,' he says dryly as he takes another sip of his drink. 'But we were insufferable just about everywhere else. I had to go through and archive over a decade's-worth of posts . . .' He stops as he takes in my face. 'Are you all right?'

I can't even try to hide it this time; I nearly choke on my drink in shock. My cheeks puff out as I attempt to trap the liquid in my mouth.

'A decade?' I splutter, coughing on some stray droplets.

'We dated from Year Nine through college, then off and on again through uni. Long distance is a bitch.' He sighs, nursing his drink carefully. 'I visited her at uni one singular time and it didn't exactly go well.'

I flash back to May Madness, the chaos of it. A week of debauchery and mind-numbing EDM and non-stop parties. If you didn't attend, you may as well not call yourself a student. I was prepared – I pre-wrote my assignments, bought cheap vodka and had new outfits that had FGA approval. By night three I was in my element, or, at least, buzzed enough to pretend that I was a girl who could be in her element like that. That's when I saw him.

'You were visiting *Lucy*. That's why you were there,' I say quietly. 'You never told me that. I guess that's why . . .'

A shiver passes through me. His shoulders tense. This is clearly not the time.

'How did you two end?' I ask at a normal volume.

He relaxes ever so slightly, relieved at the quick diversion.

'With a text,' he replies bitterly. 'She was on a girls' trip, and apparently it couldn't wait.'

'That's gotta suck,' I mumble, studying him carefully.

He did his best to wipe all traces of sadness from his voice, but even he couldn't help the audible clench in his throat right at the end of his sentence. Suddenly he can't look at me, or the bar, or anything for that matter. His eyes fix on an ice cube, following it as it melts, bobbing in his glass.

'That was just the start.' He gives a brief, sadistic chuckle. 'We'd moved in together right after graduation to make up for the years apart, but *she* owned the apartment we shared; her dad gifted it to her. So, after the text, I had three days before she got back to pack up my stuff and move back in with my mum.'

I suck in air through my teeth, my face pained on his behalf. It's loud and harsh enough to make him look up at me.

He shrugs. 'Nothing quite like getting dumped and told you're homeless with a poorly typed message at four in the morning.'

'Four a.m.?'

'She was out clubbing. I reckon she met someone else. Props to her for not just cheating, I guess.'

'I mean … that's not really where the bar should be, is it?'

He chuckles again, but this time the sound is a little lighter. Sweeter.

'You're right – it's not. But that was Lucy. I mean, you know what she's like.'

'You could say that.' I try to cut the resentment from my tone, but it seeps out like venom. His eyes widen awkwardly before dropping back to nervously seeking solace in his glass.

Lucy and I ended up forming a surprising friendship in the year we spent living next door to each other. Or, at least, enough of an acquaintanceship that meant she could relieve herself of all claims of animosity. But it was a plaster on a deep, wide-open wound, which she took great pleasure in ripping off the first chance she got.

I feel his eyes flit over my pursed lips, notice the dipped eyebrows, and come to a rest as they count my shaky breaths. He motions to speak, and my body grows ice cold at the thought of him addressing the elephant in the room.

'I am sorry about what happened at May Madness,' he says gently. 'I was going through a lot and I needed to blow off some steam. And back then, steam meant going out with Luce. But that doesn't matter. What matters is that I was *awful*. I know it now and I knew it back then too. That's why, when I saw you in that boardroom, I thought it'd be better to just pretend I didn't remember you like that.'

My chest has grown tighter, my breath shortening ... I can't relive this yet. Not in this pub, not tonight.

'It's fine,' I say.

He hangs his head low, storming ahead in a rush to get the words out. 'No, it's not. It shouldn't be and I am sorry.'

'Honestly, it's fine, let's just drop it. And I'm sorry about Lucy.' I reach for my glass, quickly taking a sip before nodding heartily at him in solidarity. 'From what I've gathered, relationships aren't all they're cracked up to be anyway.'

He laughs this time. *Bellows*. The sound echoing against the wood and vibrating through both me and the booth.

'Sorry,' he eventually manages to say. 'I don't buy that for a *second*.'

I squeal as he continues to laugh back at me. 'It's true!'

I want to be angry, resent him, even just conjure a frown, but the light in his face forces the corners of my mouth up to my cheeks. I missed the warmth of his eyes and the joyous crook of his brow when we ventured into the May Madness drama. If you ask me, that's even more reason to never bring it up again.

'I had something serious-ish with someone last year and it pretty much solidified that the whole song and dance isn't worth it,' I say.

'Sure, uh-huh. And yet your five-year plan says you should ...'

'Be with a partner that I could consider marrying by thirty. I'm aware.'

He smirks triumphantly, bowing in his seat and accepting accolades from an imaginary crowd. I slap him lightly on the arm just to make it stop. It doesn't work, because his arm's pure muscle and it stops me in my tracks. He laughs some more.

'So, tell me, Maddy. Is this future husband of yours falling from the sky?'

'Hey, it's not that easy!' I try to argue with intention, but my tone falls hilariously short. I can't stop smiling at his stupid face. I blame the booze. 'As you can imagine, there's a whole list of boxes I need to have ticked.'

He nods mock-militantly. 'All dutifully committed to notebook number three?'

'Number four is for the lists, actually.' I take a huge gulp of my drink, noisily slurping the dregs with the straw as he pretends to take a mental note. 'But before I can even get to the list, I need to find a man that's attracted to me. That part is, well, if I'm being honest, currently quite thin on the ground.'

He laughs even louder, still light and hearty in its tone, but now callous given the circumstances.

'Is my lack of appeal *funny* to you?' I ask in disbelief.

I knew it was too good to be true – a couple of shared drunk laughs do not negate who he was and always will be. A prick from primary school who spent years of his life with *Lucy Hayward*, the one person I may dislike more than him.

He freezes the second he notices my scowl, his smile dropping just as quickly. He shifts in his seat to face me as straight on as he can. Our knees brush as he turns.

'OK, no. Never. What is funny to me is that you actually believe that you lack appeal.'

I blink back at him confused.

'Really, you're gonna make me do this?' he asks, eyebrow raised sceptically.

I continue to scowl, mind racing to decipher this new riddle.

'Oh, you seriously don't get it.' He tuts. 'Tonight alone, I have watched *at least* four men in this place almost break their neck trying to watch you walk.'

I feel my cheeks go hot at this new change in direction, but it doesn't deter him. He tilts his head.

'There is no way you don't notice. You must know that you're stunning – you're not stupid.'

His eyelids dip ever so slightly, narrowing in on my face as he patiently awaits my response, but I don't know what to say. Up until this point, I wasn't convinced Aiden even recognised I was a woman, let alone one that he might consider pretty.

'I mean . . . I have my moments? Decent make-up and the right clothes can . . . help, I guess?'

It's deeply embarrassing talking about myself in this way in general, let alone with Aiden. An Aiden who inadvertently just called me attractive.

'Good. Because you'd be stupid to think otherwise.' He slams his glass on the table, caught in his own flow as his words attempt to catch up with his racing mind. 'Like your performance on Saturday? I only saw a video of it and even I thought . . .'

He trails off, his eyes widening. His jaw goes tight, sheer panic smattered across his face as he raises his glass and quickly drains it.

'Even you thought . . . what?'

'Unimportant.' He rushes on. 'The point is there's no way in hell you're devoid of interest. What you lack is the ability to take notice, because you're blinded by your lists and your seven notebooks.'

I let him drop the first one, but I can't let another comment like this go.

'It is important,' I say. 'What did you think?'

'Focus, Maddy!' He tries to mask his fluster with this new, sterner tone. 'What I'm saying is you need to branch out some more. That's the whole point of this bet, isn't it?'

'I thought the point was the job?'

'The end goal is the job, obviously. But you are supposed to stop planning and just let things happen. How's that going for you?'

It's a subject change if I ever saw one. Before I can press him further, I feel someone creep up behind me.

'Aiden!' Pippa whines his name, shimmying over with a couple of new drinks clearly in her system. 'We're dancing! *Now*, Mister.'

She sways ever so slightly, hands on her hips in what I can only assume is her attempt at being authoritative while still cute. He stares from her to me, a pained expression on his face that I can't help but stifle a small giggle at.

'Oh, Maddison, you should come too, if you want,' she adds half-heartedly as she follows his eyes towards my face.

He's begging me not to leave him alone with her, and I do, deeply, want to help. But this is the perfect exit and the idea of him squirming is far more delicious than staying would be.

'I'm actually going to head out!' I say, sweeping my phone into my bag. 'But this has been fun!'

I leave the humid pub behind me and welcome the crisp night air as I step into the street. It's less than five minutes before I feel my phone buzz in my pocket, the message shining bright against the dark street.

Alone with Pippa?! Low, even for you, Maddy . . .

A laugh escapes my lips before I can stop it.

I didn't plan it, just let it happen! Going with the flow, etc. :)

He opens it instantly, the typing bubble appearing the second I've hit send.

Game on. I'll see you next week.

Something shifts in me as I walk towards the bus stop. A warm tingle in my lower abdomen that has nothing to do with the alcohol.

Nudge 18

The Butterflies

Days until the Summer Splash - 120

Days until no more Aiden - 134

Days since our bar chat - 26

Days spent thinking about it - 26

It has been weeks since I sat with Aiden in that cramped little booth, and still the memory of it refuses to die in my brain. I can smell the booze, feel the pull of the sticky dance floor, and the way that his knee brushed against my own. Every minuscule action plays on a loop in my head – the way he smiled, the way he leant, the way his breath felt on my face … It is criminal. One person should not have this strong a hold. Especially not someone like Aiden Edwards.

I've barely been able to think straight outside of work and, if I'm being fully honest, in it as well. I needed something, anything, to clear my mind, so when I received ominous instructions from Kimi via text, I jumped at them, no questions asked.

What are you doing after work? Don't answer. You're hur-
rying home, putting on your cutest athleisure and being
picked up at 6.30.

I have no idea what she's brewing even as she pulls up at my house, with Raina's dogs, Pudding and Pretzel, in the back of her car. She ignores every one of my questions as we make the whole journey across town to Richmond Park, distracting me with small talk and rants about her day.

We wander through the park with the dogs and the further we walk, the less things make sense to me. It's a long way to go on a Tuesday night just for a stroll and a chat. Plus, if she wanted to walk Raina's dogs, then we could have stayed local and we also could have brought Raina with us.

'Do I finally get to know what we're doing?' I ask, as our conversation comes to a peaceful and warranted lull.

She glances over to me, lips pursed into a tightly contained smile as she attempts to trap her excitement behind her teeth.

'We're finding you a man,' she declares proudly.

'A man?'

'Multiple men, potentially,' she continues. 'We've got to see what the options are and then we'll decide on the number.'

'I'm sorry?'

Kimi has come up with many schemes over the years in her self-proclaimed role of Queen Wing Woman. She usually, however, reserves her mischief for bars or clubs, and they never go further than some flirty one-liners or the occasional kiss. Doing it now, in broad daylight in the middle of the week, is truly chaotic, even for her.

'I was thinking about that conversation you said you had with Aiden and he was right about one thing. You are gorgeous and it's time you started embracing it, so you are getting out there, beginning today.'

'Kimi!' I say in protest.

She's known me more than long enough to know she can't just spring things on me, let alone things to do with strange men. I'm not emotionally prepared to flirt and I do not look the part. I'm not even wearing mascara.

'You want romance, the husband, the whole nine yards by thirty. But, babe, your love life is one thing you absolutely can't reduce into a plan. Especially when you're not getting out there. You're not even on any of the apps!'

'Because I *hate* the apps!'

'We all *hate* the apps.' She sighs. 'Which is why we're not at home swiping. We are man hunting. In the wild.'

'At Richmond Park?'

She stops dead mid-stride, before turning to look me in the eye. 'Ruby, my fave paralegal at work, is dating one of the most gorgeous men I have ever seen in my life. She said they met when they physically ran into each other at Richmond Park, and, hey – you know what they say about lightning striking twice.'

'That it never does?' I reply.

'Oh. Well, forget that one. Um, never say never.'

'And the dogs?' I ask, as Pretzel gently tugs on her lead.

'*Everyone's* more approachable if you're walking a dog. Raina understood the cause and Pretzel loves my car so it's a win-win. Now, pay attention. We've got to find our targets.'

Her eyes survey the smattering of people ambling around the park ignorant to her impervious glare. She scans the grounds with the precision of an army-grade rifle, narrowing in on her options before her neck snaps back at me.

'What do you think of the two on that bench over there? Well-shaven, nice sweatpants, no ankle on show.'

I glance over. They're sat laughing at something one of them said, soft smiles and nice faces. I could certainly do worse.

'The one on the left has pretty eyes,' I say.

He's squinting as he throws his head back, his smile stretching across his cheeks.

'How would we even talk to them?' I ask.

But I am talking to the air, because Kimi and Pudding are already six steps ahead of us.

'Excuse me! Hi, hello, I really like your shoes. Where'd you get them?' she asks, hand on hip.

The man on the right beams widely, launching into some story about shoe auctions as Kimi nods intently. She's definitely not listening, but she's doing a fantastic job pretending she is. He is more than sold, although the way that he's eyeing her up says that he still would have been had she not even spoken.

'Oh, that's so cool!' she says with great faux conviction before turning towards his friend on the left. 'This is my friend Maddison, by the way – tell her she's pretty.'

'Kimi!' I scold.

'What? You are. Is she not?'

Kind Eyes chuckles, looking between us and smiling before diverting his attention solely towards me.

'Hey, I need no instruction. Your face speaks for itself,' he says, smiling.

Cute. Cheesy, but cute, nonetheless.

'And you have a beautiful smile,' he continues.

His eye contact is unmatched, his stare waking a few stray butterflies from their hard-to-locate cocoons. I feel their wings flap, first slowly, testing the waters, before taking off on a shaky but warranted flight.

'Thank you,' I reply.

'I'm Benji, by the way. You from around here?' he asks, still staring.

The sun is setting on his features, gracing his skin with a breath-taking wash of golden glow. His eyes are even more mesmerizing up close – deep, dark pools of brown that reflect the pinks and oranges of the sky around us. They catch the light the same way Aiden's do, but this time it's more fun because these eyes look at me like someone that wants to talk to me. My mind drifts to Aiden, our texts and our night at the pub, flashing back to the way our knees knocked and the panic in his eyes as he let slip that he thinks I'm attractive. *Did he mean it? Was it the alcohol?* It shouldn't matter. I cut it off instantly, returning my focus to Benji.

We go back and forth with ease, topics darting from TV to careers to favourite dinners. It's all surface level, but that's where it should be. It's light and it's safe, and a perfect first step. Our eyes never leave each other's faces, blocking out the park, the dogs, Kimi, and his friend next to us. I'm laughing and smiling, and it's not even forced. Light, happy giggles flow out of me with beautiful ease.

'Mads, the park's closing,' Kimi says, giving me a small nudge.

'Parks close?' I ask, still trapped in my daze.

'Let's get going.' She chuckles, tugging lightly on my arm.

Benji smiles softly, refusing to break our stare as Kimi says her goodbyes and encourages me to do the same. We hug goodbye. It's uncomfortable, but in a way that is new, fresh and thrilling. I think.

'I wanna see you again, Maddison,' he says, handing over his phone. 'You got a number?'

My phone vibrates minutes into our walk out of the park, before we've even made our way back to Kimi's car.

Hey, it's Benji. Dinner and drinks tomorrow?

We both squeal as we read it, Kimi grabbing my arm in excitement and cheering.

'We *love* a man that takes action immediately!' she says.

She forces me to recite our conversation word for word as we walk, and again as I sit in her passenger seat. I don't even care that it's late – it's all masked by the buzz of the evening we've just had. I have a date. My first proper date of this year, with a man who actually seems like he may be worth my while.

'Any butterflies?' Kimi asks.

'Sort of. At least three.'

'Three's a start and it's more than there've been in a while, right?'

'Uh-huh.'

She's almost right, I suppose. It was more than there *had* been in years. But recently, the flurry in my stomach has made a couple of brief reappearances in some deeply unexpected places.

I'll give them their dues – the poor babies were probably confused, mistaking a rampant hatred for something radically different. But they flew as a troop, unified and plentiful, and I felt what it was like to have them all beat at once. Benji's butterflies weren't like that – they were small and few. But they were *there* and they were *new*, and that's the only thing that matters.

I press my forehead against the cold glass of the car window, shutting my eyes tight and focusing in on the night.

Nudge 19

The Jeans

> **Raina:** Third one for sure, with the boots.
>
> **Devi:** Agreed. That dress is a 10/10.
>
> **Me:** I'm already wearing the jeans :(

I sent four different outfit options to the group chat this morning, with three interchangeable coat-and-shoe combos, and literally no one replied. When my phone finally buzzed late into the afternoon, I didn't even want to look.

> **Raina:** The jeans are so cute too!
>
> **Devi:** I was actually struggling to choose between 3 and the jeans!

They're both liars – the jeans may be cute, but the dress was better ... I already knew that before I left the house. But I panicked and second-guessed myself ... I don't know what the protocol is any more, and I certainly don't know how to double that up into something I can wear to work first. Even if I'm not in the office today, I at least wanted to keep a professional vibe.

A pair of hip-hugging flared jeans were certainly a risk, but I figured paired with the right top they might be able to pass. And they probably would have if I wasn't working with Aiden, who looked me up and down the second he met me outside.

'Jeans on a workday? That's unlike you,' he said, a confused but intrigued look on his face.

'I'm trying new things, remember?'

It looked like we both were. My jeans looked even more out of place next to the white shirt he'd shown up in. It's the first shirt I've seen him in since the La La Lounge and a huge step up from his usual T-shirt-jeans combo. He nodded back at me, impressed, before we headed inside the wine cellar.

When Evie said she wanted us to hand-select the wines for the party, I imagined something similar to cocktails at the Lounge. That was not the case. This is, in fact, far less glamorous and involves sitting cross-legged on the floor as we inspect the bottles around us and make notes on our terribly balanced laptops.

You see, Evie is a sucker for attention to detail and wants the bottles to mirror the theme perfectly. She's sent us to an extremely niche, international wine cellar hidden just off Camden Market that specialises in unknown bottles from around the world. Before the sommelier guides us through our tasting next week, we must first make our way through their basement of different bottles and research which ones come from our spotlighted countries. It's been a trawl. We have been in this basement since 10 a.m. and not come up for air or light once.

The good news is, it's stopped me from worrying about tonight, or my outfit. Or at least, it did until the texts came through from the girls. I look down at my legs again with my new knowledge of their opinions, the light-wash taunting me as it stretches tightly across my thighs. They're cute, but they're basic. Way too casual. Benji will think I don't try. What if he's used to girls who put an effort into their appearance? Or girls who show up and look effortlessly cute? He'll see my jeans and he'll laugh, and the date will be over before I've even ordered my starter.

Are jeans first-date appropriate?

I nervously type into a private browser, frantically scanning the results for a definitive answer. Before I can get too far, a chocolate bar flies through the air and slides across my keyboard, briefly shocking the breath out of my system.

'Eat,' Aiden says as I look up at him in confusion. 'You skipped lunch again and you're more jittery than normal.'

This task has been so involved that we've barely made conversation, which, while refreshing, is increasingly rare nowadays. For a moment, I even forgot he was here.

'If you don't like chocolate, I've got other options. Strawberry grains, protein bars, a selection of crisps . . .'

'You keep a small pantry in your bag?' I ask, raising an eyebrow.

'I've started to, yeah. You barely eat when you get bogged down with work. Didn't know your snack preference so had to cover all bases. I call it my *Mads-Bag* – like a grab-bag.'

Terrible attempt at a pun aside, the whole thing takes me by surprise. I have sat next to Pippa and Gus for four years and neither have noticed my poor eating habits. I barely notice myself until I'm sitting on the bus feeling dizzy and wondering why. To have Aiden – the man who sees me two days a week and quite frankly probably doesn't care if I live or die – notice is incredibly suspicious. But, regardless, my stomach is growling, so I open the packet and take a bite.

'I chose well.' He is triumphant, watching as I wolf the bar down within a matter of seconds. 'You want some crisps too?'

'What flavour?'

'What would you want?'

'Ready salted?'

'Knew it.' He smirks, shaking his head. 'Although, I did have options just in case.'

He reaches into his backpack, removing a six-flavour multipack from it like the sword of Excalibur and chucking a pack across the table. I waste no time replying, tearing open the packet and shovelling crisps into my mouth. The salt soothes all my worries the second it touches my tongue, and I feel my shoulders unfurl and my breath steady. He slides a second across before I'm even done, waiting for me to snatch it before he indulges in one himself.

'I told you I covered all bases. Isn't that what organised people do? Have plans A to C ready to go?'

'You bought a multipack of crisps – quite literally "small potatoes".'

He flips his middle finger up at me, before taking a couple of crisps out of his own bag.

'So, why so stressed?' he asks, his tone gentler. 'I thought you had the invite wording in the bag?'

Yes, the invite wording that I took a break from wine research to submit before close of play. The wording that I was about to start when the FGA finally replied to me. It's 4.30. I promised Evie this would be with her by five and I currently have three words. They're not even good ones: *Dear Sir/Madam*. What was I thinking? It's too formal. I have to delete.

'You're probably overthinking it. Let me see,' he says, mistaking my silence for a cry for help and reaching across for my laptop before I can stop him.

I try to snatch it back, but I'm not quick enough. He looks over my dubious Google search, eyes scanning it twice for good measure before emitting a deep-throated chortle.

'I knew the jeans weren't for work,' he manages to say.

'It's not funny,' I pout, reaching for it again.

I'm nervous enough as it is – the last thing I need is Aiden mocking me before I've even arrived. It's insulting at best and degrading at worse, and souring up all the goodness of the snacks.

'Who's the guy?' he asks.

'Irrelevant,' I answer.

'Where'd you meet him?'

'None of your business.'

'So, an app.'

'No, hate those.'

His eyes light up at the morsel of information. 'In person? What was it … a bar? A club? Was he at Paint That Mate? What's his name? I probably know him.'

I can practically see the possibilities running through his devious mind.

'You don't know him,' I say, monotonous as can be.

'I *could* know him. What's his name?'

'You're not in the same circles.'

'You don't know my circles.'

This goading is slightly lighter and friendlier than normal, devoid of our usual animosity. He's not trying to attack me and I have no need to go for him. So, I retract my claws and throw him a small bone.

'His name's Benji.'

'Rough name,' he says immediately.

I scrunch my face in confusion at the unprovoked change in tone.

He shrugs casually. 'I've never met a good Benji.'

'How many Benjis do you know?'

'Enough to know they're all losers.'

His lip's curling at the corner, features dancing in delight at the mildly irate look creeping up my face. He's enjoying this far too much and it's only irritating me more, piled on further by the ever-telling look in his eyes.

'I know what you're doing.'

His spine straightens at my assertion, smirk growing wider as he leans forward and takes me in.

'What am I doing, Maddy?' he asks, voice low and seductive.

The tone sends a jolt through me that briefly halts my breath, but I rush past it. It's confusing and distracting – all part of his plan. But I'm smarter than he is. I know a ploy when I see one.

'You're trying to psych me out before my date. Launch me into overthink mode and *you* one step closer to winning our bet,' I say.

'Is that so?'

His voice is so low now it hums, vibrating through my eardrums and travelling down to my stomach. The interruption re-awakens the butterflies in their pit.

'I see right through you.' I ignore them as they flap.

His mouth twists into a teasing smile. 'Do you now? How do I look?'

My cheeks flush instantly, the heat crawling up my face and washing through the rest of my body with swiftness. He can't just *say* things like that. Not on a work outing and especially not right now.

'We're done talking about this,' I say, hands returning to my keyboard.

I direct my gaze back to the screen, quickly closing the tab and opening the invite wording. I type furiously as I will the task to bring my heart rate back down. Out of the corner of my eye I can see him staring at me, his stupid smile still firmly intact.

'It's five – leave,' he says.

I half sing in reply as my fingers tap feverishly on the keys. 'Can't hear you. I'm wording the invite.'

'You'll be late for your date; I'm sure you have a whole schedule planned out.'

Of course I do. I can't quite admit that now, especially since he's so curious. Benji picked a bar in Brixton, which would have been fine if I was in the office in Clapham, but since I'm travelling from north to south, it involves having to brave not one but two hot, sticky Tubes. I'm a Tube hater anyway, but the Tube before a date after I straightened my hair this morning is just cruel. If I leave soon, I *could* get away with adding half an hour and taking two buses instead. But looking at this blank document, I don't think that's happening. I do a silent prayer that my roots withstand the Tube humidity.

'I'll finish the invite,' Aiden says.

I look up from my keyboard, lips pursed as I try to decipher this new trap.

'It wasn't your task.'

'You're right. And you've *never* picked up any of mine.' He rolls his eyes. 'You've got places to be. Boring Benjis to meet. I'll stay and finish – shouldn't take that long anyway.'

'You don't stay late,' I retort.

'I have a bet to win too. A couple of late nights won't kill me and I'll track them in my new work log.'

I can't help but release a small, near-silent chuckle at the way his eyebrows wiggle proudly at the mention of his new log. It's almost undetectable but he picks up on it, meeting my smile tooth for tooth as he nods in acknowledgement.

'You sure?' I ask.

'Positive. Go make Benjamin's night,' he says, returning to his laptop.

It feels weird leaving him behind in this cellar, working. I've never left this close to five, either. Something about it feels almost illegal and I can't explain why. I open my phone camera, checking over my face and applying a fresh coat of gloss to my lips before I get up from the floor.

'Oh, Maddy?' Aiden calls and I freeze, hand wrapped round the cellar door handle. 'The jeans are *definitely* first-date appropriate. He'll be a big fan.'

Nudge 20

The First Date

'We should have got a booth,' Benji sighs as he pulls up a stool, steel legs scraping loudly across the floor.

'Sorry, I just sat where they led me,' I say, attempting to catch his eye as he scans the noisy room for better seats.

Even with the early exit, I still found myself at the bar twenty minutes late. I walked as fast as my heeled boots allowed me, hobbling from the bus stop to the venue in the hopes that he was still there. He didn't reply to any of my three journey update texts and I don't know him well enough to know whether that was a sign of frustration. Turns out it was probably a result of him travelling himself, as I arrived at a yet-to-be-claimed reservation.

He huffs as he settles. 'It's fine. Just not what I'd wanted for us. You deserve the best, you know?'

He gazes into my eyes, waiting expectantly. I force a tight-lipped smile and a faint nod of appreciation, which proves to be more than enough. He smiles back at me, as if desperately attempting to summon a vibe that has yet to appear, before reaching for the singular menu on the table.

'Have you ordered yet?'

'No, I was waiting for you.'

'That's so sweet. You're too sweet,' he says, eyes locked on the card.

'So, how's your day been?' I ask.

'What?' He has to yell as the music grows louder.

I raise my voice too. 'How's your day been?'

'Oh! Yeah, it's been good.'

He waves his arm in the air, beckoning a nearby waitress over as he keeps the menu clutched between his hands.

'Hey – can I get a rum and Coke – it's Happy Hour, right? I'll have two. And the sliders, and the fries on the side.'

'Of course. And for the lady?' she asks.

'Sorry, could I see the menu?' I ask him.

I haven't had a chance to look. When I first got here, I was afraid that, in my state, the mere names of the food would take me from mildly irritated to full-on hangry. He hands it over and stares impatiently as I scan through the items, the weight of his and the waitress's eyes pressing on me, so I narrow in on the first thing I see.

'I'll just take the fries. And ... a gin? Do you do gin? I'll take a gin and lemonade.'

'And two tequila shots,' Benji adds, before turning and winking at me. 'It will loosen us up.'

Forward, but at this point I'll take anything.

The waiter turns on her heel, leaving us at our tiny, tall table, surrounded by the loud chatter of the bar around us. I'll admit, it's not exactly the 'dinner and drinks' vibe I got from his texts, but on the upside my jeans are definitely not out of place. If anything, the boots and top may be a little *too* dressy for the vibe here.

'So, tell me about yourself, Maddison,' he says, reclining on the imaginary back of his stool.

I've always thought 'tell me about yourself' is one of the worst questions you can ask a person. It does nothing on your part to decipher them and puts it all in their hands. It's lazy and callous, and full of ambiguity, along with the presumption that the person you're talking to is basic enough to condense their whole life into a small string of sentences.

'What do you want to know?' I ask, throwing it back at him.

'Everything.' He shuts me down instantly.

His eyes are still pretty, I suppose. The glint appears a little duller drowned in the low light of the bar. But he's *trying*, at least. I can't expect him to live up to the standards I imposed in my head.

'Well, you know that event I was telling you about? I made some headway today—'

'Ah, yes, events – you do events.' He nods with faux profoundness. 'How do you find that?'

'Yeah, I enjoy it. Actually I—'

'I've always thought I'd be pretty good at events. I have some sick ideas,' he says musingly.

'Oh, that's great,' I say, benevolently brushing the double interruption aside. 'You said you are in finance, right?'

'Well, it's actually more complicated than that. I do a bit of this, a bit of that, here, there and everywhere. But, yeah, trading plays a part in it all.'

'Trading?'

He waves my question away. 'It's quite complex. Let's not get into it this early in the night.'

The waitress reappears with our drinks and our shots, saving me from the inevitable forced prying he was expecting. I neck the shot instantly, placing the glass down with a grimace before he has had a chance to finish pouring the salt onto his hand.

'Woah, you don't mess around.' He is clearly impressed.

'Can we get two more, please?' I catch the waitress just before she walks away.

The more I drink, the more his little quirks become bearable and the talk of 'building his empire' becomes easier to stomach. The kind sparkle in his eye returns, murky cloud a thing of the past along with my sobriety. We order a third, fourth and fifth round of shots and two more drinks each, conversation swelling by the time we reach the fourth.

'I like you, Maddison, you're fun.' He's slurring his words and his gaze is deep in a way that feels ever so slightly intrusive, but I let it go because he called me fun. I never get called fun, ever.

'And you're a really good listener,' he continues.

'Thank you,' I reply, my smile real this time.

The fact that I listened so well because he barely let me talk is neither here nor there. Who cares about the rough start? We've ended up here, and under the low bar lights and the influence of many, many drinks, I cannot deny that we do get along.

'I'm sorry – just wanted to let you know that we close in ten,' the waitress says.

The last call bell was a while ago, but the interjection still makes me gasp in surprise. Closed already? How late could it possibly be?

I check my phone and see *23.48* bold and bright on the screen. It taunts me, reminding me of tomorrow's early start and the journey I still have to take to my house.

'Where to next?' Benji asks, beginning to put on his jacket.

Next? It's almost tomorrow! Tomorrow Thursday! Thursday the workday!

'I'm pretty sure everything else around here will be closing too.' It's a half-lie. I don't know if they're open or closed, I just know that I need to get home. I've already missed the last train and I still have to get up for work tomorrow morning. A concern that, apparently, only affects me.

'Cool, wanna just walk around then? I'm not ready for this to be over,' he says, coming over and grabbing my hand.

His hand is warm, albeit slightly moist to the touch. Big enough to engulf my entire palm in the centre of his own. He squeezes it tighter, staring closely, forcing a moment. I stare back, force it too, beg the butterflies to return.

'I should probably get home. It's getting late and I have work tomorrow,' I say, eyes still searching his for a hint of a spark.

'I could come with you?' he says, swinging his hand and mine.

I stifle the giggle desperate to burst out of my mouth. Not only is the offer audaciously presumptuous for a first date, but the thought of bringing him back to my parents' house is laughable.

Hi, Mum and Dad. Here's a man I met yesterday in the park. He's staying the night; we'll see you tomorrow for breakfast!

The thought of their faces is enough to have me in hysterics, but I try to refocus and shake my head.

'Not tonight.'

'Ah, OK.' He huffs, not even trying to mask his disappointment. 'We'll see each other again, though.'

He creeps slightly closer, towering over me and biting his lip. It would be something, I guess, if I wasn't so focused on my perfect view up his nostrils.

'Sure,' I answer, attempting to convince myself too.

I suppose, given how things picked up after the initial awkwardness, I have no reason *not* to see him again. He is cute, and he's tall, and I have no real reason to say no. Isn't the point of this whole thing with Aiden to say yes more often?

'I'd really like that,' I say, doubling down.

'You're really sexy, you know,' he says, forcing his voice an octave deeper.

He shuffles closer to me as his right hand squeezes mine even tighter, left swinging to cup the back of my head (although it ends up being more of a slap). He looks down at me hungrily as he leans in, in a way that makes me want to run. I don't want to *really*. I know that. I'm just being stupid and focusing too much on how fishlike he looks from this angle.

I taste rum and Coke and strawberry vape on his tongue as it forces its way in between my teeth. It's sloppy and drunk, and excitedly flapping out of control, but I do my best to manoeuvre it from my end. We find some sort of rhythm; still choppy, but slightly more to my liking as his hands move straight to my backside. He squeezes both cheeks tightly while pulling me into his crotch, my balance faltering and leaving me no choice but to wrap my arms round his neck. I hold on tightly, my heels lifted off the ground in a way that feels more like falling than flying. His lips are soft, that's a plus, and he seems to like what we're doing, given the way he's moaning into my mouth. But the moans seem forced – he's sounding off because he feels like he *should* – because it's how he saw the moment going in his head. I would fake moan too but, frankly, nothing would give me the ick more, so I focus on his lips and try to drown the sounds out.

'Woah,' he says, finally pulling away. 'You sure I can't jump in that car with you?'

'Not tonight,' I say again. 'I really should get home.'

After one more sloppy kiss he heads to the Tube station, leaving me to wait for my taxi in the dark outside the bar, alone. I finally check my phone properly for the first time since I got to the place, finding a slew of texts, voice notes and missed calls from Kimi.

> Been in meetings all day. Sorry I missed the outfits!
>
> How was it?!
>
> Are you OK?!
>
> If we don't hear from you in five mins we're calling the police.

She's in the group chat as well, all three debating my welfare, complete with screenshots of my location and a physical description of Benji.

> All good, alive, date just ran late! Debrief tomorrow xxx

I make sure to share the details of my ride with them the second I get in the car, before anyone has a chance to report me missing, and then I sink into the leather seat and reflect on the night at hand. The car moves through the night, Brixton a blur to my right, but I do not look. My eyes are glued to my phone, scrolling through my camera roll with a new mission at hand.

I find a blurry but decipherable picture of the shot glasses from the night, empty and strewn across our table. The photo is grainy and discoloured from the bar's terrible light, but it's clear enough to be fit for purpose. The word *online* pops up briefly under Aiden's name almost instantly after I send it, turning the ticks on the message blue before disappearing again.

I lean back in my seat and sigh as I stare out the dark window. *Well, at least tonight can't get any more disappointing.*

Nudge 21

The Residual Flirtation

'Sorry, could you say that again? I lost you there.' The reverb spits my voice back at me in chunky, robot-like fragments.

'I said your signal is shit,' Aiden says, his face so clearly unimpressed in the small, faded image.

'Who says it's *my* signal?'

He huffs. 'I'm restarting the call.'

I woke up this morning with the headache to end all headaches, birthed by those shots and raised by my distinct lack of sleep. At first, I tried to fight it – snooze my alarm and convince myself that I'd be bright and perfect by the fourth time it went off, but it was to no avail. The thought of leaving my house made me want to cry until I was out of tears. So, after a quick call with Pippa about a fake emergency, I managed to switch my scheduled work-from-home Friday for today.

Aiden was thrilled; it meant he got to stay home too and avoid a trip to the Abbingtorn building. The downside? We both have to spend the day working through a Teams call on my hit-and-miss Wi-Fi connection.

'Maddison, when are you folding those clothes? I have washing to do too.' Mum tuts as she barges through the previously closed door.

'I only put them in this morning!' I watch in horror as she makes herself comfortable behind me. 'Could you do that in the kitchen, please? I'm working.'

'Working?' she asks. 'You're in pyjama bottoms.'

'I am working from home,' I say.

'Wrapped in that blanket?' she asks, eyebrow raised.

'It's freezing in here.'

It may be April, but it's the fakest 'spring weather' I've experienced in years.

'Is that your mum?' Aiden asks brightly, connection issues apparently solved.

The male voice triggers her curiosity. She sets her basket down and makes her way back over to me, peering over my shoulder and squinting at the screen.

'Is that Aiden Edwards?' she asks loudly, apparently entirely unaware of how video calls work. 'Oh, he's grown up nice and handsome, hasn't he?'

'Yes, it is, and he can hear you.' I sigh deeply.

'Hi, Mrs Clarke! Long time, no see!'

She coos. 'Aiden! How's your mother? Did she have her surgery?'

'She did, yes, and it was tough, but she's recovering well.'

'Your mum had surgery?' I ask.

'A minor one. A couple of months ago.' He shuffles uncomfortably, glancing down. 'She's fine.'

A couple of months ago, while we were working together. Friction or not, I would have remembered something like that. Disappointment stirs in my stomach. I hate that he didn't feel like he could tell me, and that I never picked up on it. I want to ask more, but it feels wrong of me. Intrusive almost, like crossing a line our newfound acquaintanceship isn't quite ready for.

'I thought you said you were working, not catching up with old friends,' Mum says, turning back to me.

'Mum. Aiden works for Evie, the woman I'm doing that event for.'

And he's not my friend.

'Oh, how fun! I always liked that boy!' she says.

'He can still hear you.'

'I always liked you too, Mrs Clarke.' Aiden beams through the screen.

She smiles widely, proving once again that almost everyone falls victim to the Aiden Edwards 'charm'. I sit with my eyes glued to the ceiling as the two exchange an unnecessarily long string of pleasantries. He's a different person in front of her – sweet, polite and engaging. It's sickening to watch him put it on and even worse to watch her buy it. I let out an audible sigh of relief when she eventually gathers the washing basket and heads for the kitchen, door closing tightly behind me.

'Mums love me,' he says, lip curled. 'And she's great. Shame about her daughter, though.'

I groan. 'Focus, please. How'd the invite copy go down?'

'Evie loved it – signed off the wording, so now it's with Design. How'd the date go?' he asks. 'You had a lot of shots on that table.'

I shout triumphantly. 'So, you *did* see the photo!'

Silence. For a moment I think the connection has dropped again, but then I see him dip his head in shame as he fumbles for a reply.

'It's none of your business anyway,' I say, attempting to hurry the awkwardness along. 'I sent the picture for evidence, not because I wanted to discuss it with you.'

'Oooh, that bad?' he asks, recovering quickly.

'Great, actually. Really fun.' I texted Benji a similar sentiment when I got home and am yet to receive a reply. My stomach dips just thinking about it. I change the subject. 'Where are you at with catering? I think I've found a good Mexican option – small, family-run. They have a restaurant in Shoreditch; we could pay it a visit.'

'So *that's* why you worked from home today.'

'Because I wanted to visit the Mexican restaurant?'

'Because your date went so great. Did you stay round his?'

'Aiden!'

'Hey, there's no judgement from me. I've definitely had sleepovers for a lot less.'

His last sentence triggers a strange wash of jealousy, gone as quickly as it arrived, but deep, strong and burning. I shake it off instantly, putting it down to the lack of sleep. If anything, I *pity* anyone who encounters Aiden.

'Lovely,' I sigh, going for nonchalance. 'Now can you let me know where you're at with the catering?'

'Think I've got the Indonesian in the bag too. Wanna do a double feature? Mexican for lunch and Indonesian in the evening?' he asks.

'Tasting everything from both? Sounds like a lot of food. Do you think I should bring Gus or Pippa in?'

'Hmm.' He is clearly unenthused. 'That could make it a "too many cooks" situation.'

'Aiden Edwards, are you trying to take me out to dinner?'

It comes out of my mouth before I can stop it – stopping me in my tracks as much as it does him. I don't know what's worse, the quickness with which it came or the smooth unwavering confidence that accompanied it. There's no explanation for it other than it being a residual stray, left over from the flirting I was doing last night. My cheeks grow hotter the longer we both stay silent, Aiden's raised eyebrows and pursed lips speaking louder than either of us could.

'Gus and Pippa should come too. Wouldn't want to upset Benji,' he says eventually.

'Great, I'll check their availability and get back to you.' I squeak this as normally as possible.

It's not normal at all. I've ruined the entire moment.

'Cool. Another call later before we log off for the day?' he asks.

We have another hour of this call scheduled.

I hesitate. 'Yeah, sounds good. I'll sort dates for the tasting and you let me know how it goes with the printer?'

The conversation lulls once again, leaving us with that same, offputting silence. I want to burrow into a hole in the ground and I can feel my skin itch at the awkwardness. He waits a moment longer, mouth open to speak before snapping shut and changing course.

'Perfect. See you, Maddy.'

His image disappears, leaving me to stare back at nothing but my pixelated reflection on the screen. I slam the lid of my laptop shut and scream into the abyss.

'What happened?' Mum rushes into the room with a yell, her sleeves rolled up, saucepan poised over her shoulder like a baseball bat.

'I'm fine. Everything's fine,' I sigh, bending my head to rest it on the closed laptop.

'Then don't *scream* like that,' she huffs, reluctantly lowering her weapon. 'And don't forget to fold your clothes.'

Take me out to dinner. Take me out to dinner? Who on Earth do I think I am? Who on Earth do I think *he* is? That was cringey and embarrassing in so many ways and I can only imagine how much worse it looked from his eyes. I can never see or talk to him again. There's absolutely no way I can move past this. What was I thinking? Why would I say that? I close my eyes, take a breath and try to refocus.

I wasn't flirting. I was just confused.

I repeat it over and over in the hopes that I'll start to believe it.

I don't flirt with Aiden. I wouldn't flirt with Aiden. I wasn't flirting. I was just confused.

Nudge 22

The Wet Forehead

BENJI: Hey it's me. Had fun last week. Wanna do it again?

I read it three times before screenshotting and sending straight to the girls. It's been a week and a day since that night at the bar, and it's the first time I've heard anything from him at all. I sent him a text that night, and a follow-up the next day – I even waited until lunch to send it as to not seem too full on. But it's been crickets for a week. A whole week and one day of nothing, only to receive that. No apology, no excuse, no fake family emergency . . . *Had fun last week*. What an absolute bum.

RAINI: He lives!

KIMI: For now. Pls tell me you haven't replied.

DEVI: Ghost him, not worth it.

RAINA: At least hear him out!

They reply exactly as expected and I sit back and debate which of them I should follow. While Raina 'engaged to her high-school sweetheart' is the outlier, her reply is, for sure, the one that I'm most drawn to. Call me stupid or ridiculous, but I just can't help it. There's something inside me that's saying there must be more to the story.

>   **ME:** Don't know what to say

>   **DEVI:** Nothing. He's undeserving of your time.

And from an objective perspective, I know that she's right. If this were any of my girls, I would tell them not to bother – a real man would have followed up a whole lot sooner. But my mood lifted tenfold when I saw his name pop up. I could feel my sunken ego rise from its small pit. This is going to be bad for me – I can feel it. But that doesn't stop me from opening up his chat.

>   I had fun too. Could do sometime next week maybe?

I hit send before I have time to think too hard. It's relaxed, non-chalant, and sent fourteen minutes after his – that's taking a stand if I ever saw one.

I can't stop checking my phone on the bus to work, frantically looking away and back again, hoping that, by some miracle, his reply will catch me by surprise. It doesn't come. Thirty-eight minutes now and I'm still yet to feel a buzz. I start scrolling through my social feeds, searching for literally anything to distract me from my expectations. I want to lock my phone away, miss his response by hours so this time he can be the one anxiously waiting, but I just can't. My phone may as well be glued to my hand.

I'm so focused that I almost miss Aiden on my way in, his loud call of my name making me jump out of my skin.

'What are you doing?' I ask once I finally recover.

It's 8.44 and our group time doesn't start until ten. Of course, since the bet began, he's been coming in earlier, but, even then, it's usually around 9.25. Yet here he is, perched casually outside the building, leaning against the brick wall with his hand in his pocket.

'Waiting for you.' His voice is gravelly. I can only assume I'm the first person he's spoken to this morning. 'We're not going in there today – come on.'

He beckons me closer, before turning on his heel and strolling away. It takes him until he reaches the corner to realise that I'm not following him, but rather I'm frozen in my spot, confused.

'My car's around the corner and it's signed off with your boss,' he says, rolling his eyes at my distrust. 'Come on, I wanna beat traffic.'

It's enough for me. I have too much to think about right now to worry about Aiden as well.

I check my phone frequently during the ride, Benji's absence enough to stop me from pestering Aiden about our destination. We hit the motorway, and nothing. Drive through Surrey, and nothing. We even pull into a car park and still, no text back.

I've been busy for *hours* and he hasn't had time to type one silly little message. Fourteen minutes was too kind – I should have waited at least thirty before sending my last response.

Enough is enough. I put my phone on Do Not Disturb and set a timer for three and a half hours. He may be busy doing whatever, but so am I, and I will focus on that rather than silly old Benji.

'*Dizzy Days Water Park.*' I read the sign out loud as Aiden reverses into a space.

The more I embrace my surroundings, the less I'll think to check my phone.

'That's the place,' he replies. He shuts off the engine before quickly grabbing his bag from the back and ruffling around until he produces a black leather journal. 'I got in touch with a couple of the ride suppliers that your team pulled together, and one of the most cost-effective ones on the list makes the rides here. Figured instead of going back and forth via email, we could see his work in action.'

But I can barely hear him; I've found a new distraction. In his hand are pages laden with diagrams, annotated in detail with highlighted colours and notes. My eyes scan over the scribbles, as detailed as they are concise. It's a masterpiece and it seems to have come from him.

'Is that ... colour coded?' I ask, watching as he flicks through them.

'It's a ranking system. There's a key in the back.' He scratches his head. 'Am I doing it wrong? I watched a sixteen-part TikTok series.'

He stares at me, attempting to decipher the sudden intensity pooling behind my pupils. He's confused, but not as confused as I am, because he's not experiencing the unmistakable heat rising up my body. He made a colour-coded key. He ranked his research. He drew *diagrams*. The mere knowledge of it has twisted my insides into one giant knot. I have no words to reply to him – all I can muster is a weak shake of my head. It's enough reassurance to let him move on and start getting out of the car.

Amusement parks were my idea of a sensory hell as a child, filled with loud noises, rides I was too small for, and far too many people. Even now, as we stroll past the winding queues and screaming vendors, I'm questioning just how long we have to be here. The only thing keeping me going is the fact that, no matter how miserable I am, Aiden looks worse.

'So where do we start, then?' I ask as he stares back at me blankly. 'With the rides. Which one are we going on first?'

'Oh, we're not doing those,' he says, shaking his head. 'We came to look, make notes, watch the reactions of the people that get off them.'

I can't help but stare up at him with a mild expression of disgust. Who drives someone all the way to an amusement park and doesn't go on a single ride? It's idiotic and borderline psychopathic, even for Aiden. But the longer I look at him, the more I suspect that there's more to it. Every ride that soars past makes him grimace. He's more uncomfortable than I've ever seen him.

'I never pegged you as the type to be scared of an amusement ride,' I say, trying my luck.

Honestly, I never considered that he might be scared of anything. Up until recently, I wasn't entirely convinced that he possessed emotions at all. The jury's still out on whether he does.

'I'm not!' he replies. 'I'm just a sensible person who knows to avoid things that could lead to certain death.'

A screeching carriage full of people races past us on the left and he flinches, practically jumping out of his skin. Before he has time to recover, another ride rockets past our heads. He ducks in fear, his eyes darting to the thrill-seekers above before quickly darting to me.

'You see that one? That's a lawsuit waiting to happen,' he says.

In his defence, the ride doesn't look remotely safe. None of them do. But there's something about the one above us, with its large, twirling frame, that has an indescribably dangerous allure. It's so tall and horrifying, and, just a couple of months ago – maybe even one week ago – I would have agreed that I'd never go near it. But I am bolder now, or at least I am trying to be, and there's nothing I feel compelled to do more.

'Let's go.'

'What?' he asks.

'Let's go! You want me to act on impulse? My impulse is telling me to get in that queue and onto that ride.'

'Go right ahead,' he says, lightly shooing me towards it.

'If I'm going, you're going,' I say.

I grab his hand and pull him towards the line, looking back as his face contorts in shock. He stumbles after me, mouth open but lost for words, and ego far too proud to object.

'You're a menace,' he mutters, shaking his head.

'Or am I being a diver instead of a wader?' I ask defiantly.

The silence between us is palpable as we move through the queue, triggering every instinct I have to grab my phone from my bag. But I can't. I won't. I am stronger than that. Instead, I look up at Aiden, his deep-brown eyes glued to the carriages above us. He's terrified, but he doesn't dare admit it. It's not until we're ushered into our own two-person carriage that he once again acknowledges my presence.

'These seats are tiny,' he says. 'It's not looking good.'

He's right – the seats are abnormally cramped. I'm a good few inches shorter than he is and even I'm struggling. But the one benefit to being squashed tightly beside him is that I get to witness him emote in 4K. His jaw is clenched tight, his hands squeezed into fists. He wants nothing more than for this to be over. But me? I want to replay the look on his face for as long as my memory allows me.

'Relax, we're fine,' I say to reassure him, revelling in his discomfort.

The safety bar swings down, trapping us in place, and he jumps at the movement, trying to play it off as a shiver. But I know what I saw and he knows I know too.

'There's no going back now . . .' I can't resist taunting him.

He grumbles, his jaw clenched in terror. 'You're the worst.'

The ride whirrs raucously to life, the vibrations echoing through both of our bodies and the far-too-thin metal. We jolt forward instantly, sealed into our fate, before oh-so-slowly creeping towards our doom. I can feel Aiden's breath catch as we begin our ascent, the vessel climbing the slope so tortuously slow. The speed of the climb makes it all that much worse, and, given how stone-faced he is, Aiden certainly agrees.

'See, it's slow. This is not that bad,' I lie, overcome by an instinct to calm his nerves.

He grunts. 'That's how they get you. They lull you into a false sense of security, and then BAM.'

'Bam?'

'Bam,' he says solemnly. 'See those people in front? They're almost at the drop – listen for their screams.'

Like clockwork, the carriage plunges off the edge and the sound of their shrieks floods the air around us. I can feel Aiden's whole body stiffen as we near their old point.

'Want me to draw a letter on your arm to calm you down?' I say jokingly.

For a moment – literally less than a second – his mouth contorts into a smile. In fact, if I saw correctly, I think a small little huff of laughter escaped from his nose as well.

'Thought you'd be shitting yourself,' he says, diverting the focus.

'Me? Never.' I say, and he scoffs in disbelief. 'OK, I was. But is that not what this challenge is for? Plus, your fear's making it easier to forget about mine.'

He turns to face me, a begrudging smile on his face as he prepares to deny his fear one more time. But before he has a chance, our carriage comes to an abrupt halt. My stomach leaps into my throat in time with the steep drop, the world dissipating into nothing but swirls and blurs. The ride ricochets off more sides than I believe possible, tossing us around like rag dolls in the process. I try as best as I can to clamp my jaw shut – to float through this like I'm entirely unfazed – but I needn't bother. Even my loudest screams are drowned out by the shrieks of the man next to me. I can feel every flex of his annoyingly hard biceps as he bellows and howls, and squeezes hold of me.

We lurch forward as the carriage hits new flat ground, falling back into our seats with a thud. As we slowly coast forward, I'm spared a moment to catch my breath and take in my finally clear surroundings. Once again, all is steady and right with the world. Better in fact, because I now know that Aiden Edwards screams like a baby.

I shriek with laughter, the sound vibrating through my body and rippling into his chest. He still hasn't let go and a part of me hopes that he'll keep me trapped in his arms just a bit longer. It's nothing to do with him, of course, but there's an odd comfort in his embrace. A small pleasure to be found in the feel of his warm body pressed against mine.

I snuggle closer without thinking and await his inevitable recoil, but it doesn't come. Instead, he pulls my body closer so he can lightly rest his head on top of mine. The effect is more dizzying than the death-defying drop we just survived on the rollercoaster.

'I can feel it coming,' he says.

'What?' I ask in a daze.

He's fretting. 'The next drop. I can feel it. We've been flat for too long.'

'You think there's another one?' I ask.

'You don't?' he replies, his chin rustling my hair each time he speaks.

'I don't know. I figured one might be enough.'

'One is never enough for the maniacs who build these things.'

Screams sound faintly in the near distance, echoing their way back to our terrified ears. Except this time, they come with a grand finale, culminating in a definitive and spine-chilling splash.

'There's *water*?'

My features contort into unbridled fear. Speed, I can do. Drops, I can manage. But water? Water is where I draw the line. I did not account for water. I did not wear the right clothes, or right shoes, or right hair to get wet today.

'It's a water park, Maddy,' Aiden says dryly, regaining some of his trademark bravado.

'Not every ride at a water park soaks its victims. If I knew I would have brought a coat or plastic bag or something.'

'It's just a bit of water,' he says. 'We'll be fine.'

'You, with less than one inch of hair and no make-up on, may be fine,' I tut, shifting from his shoulder to try to get a look ahead.

'If it's that important to you, why didn't you check if this was a super soaker beforehand?'

'Because I didn't plan this, remember? I just dived in,' I huff, turning to face him.

His features soften for a moment, a part of him almost proud, before his brow furrows and he starts to jump into action.

'How long do you reckon we've got? Ten? Fifteen seconds?'

'Not helping,' I say, the nerves rising in my stomach.

I've never been good at being caught by surprise – a lesson my parents learnt very early on. The poor pair found themselves having to make scheduled itineraries for every single planned family day out. One time they tried to be cool parents and take us out of school for a surprise day trip, and I was so outraged that they had no choice but to turn the car around and reschedule for a day when I had fewer commitments, and prior notice.

The older I got, the more life hammered it out of me because you can't throw a tantrum like that as an adult. But that doesn't mean I don't still get the feeling inside – the thudding heartbeat and sweaty-palmed panic that comes with the unexpected. And right now, I can't think of anything worse than being unexpectedly hit by what sounds like a tsunami's worth of water.

'Looks like we have enough time for this,' Aiden says, starting to strip down to just his T-shirt.

'We're about to be soaking wet ... You want to be cold too?' I ask, trying my best not to glance down at his briefly exposed lower abdomen.

'I mean, I'd rather not. But you seem like you need this more.' He shoves his hoodie towards me with urgency. 'Wrap it around your body; use it to cover your head ... Whatever makes the big bad water go away.'

'Are you sure?' I ask, dubiously trying to make sense of his sudden random act of kindness.

'One hundred per cent, if it stops you from moaning all day,' he teases. 'We're getting closer – hurry up. And stop checking me out.'

'I wasn't! I wouldn't—'

'Maddy, chill.' He smirks.

I snatch the hoodie from his hands and wrap it around my head, clinging onto it as tightly as humanly possible. His eyes look over me with a confusing intensity, softened only by the bemused pout of his lips. He tilts his head, gaze frozen on my face with something I'd almost mistake for affection, before breaking his hold with a fond shake of his head.

'What?' I ask, perplexed.

'Nothing,' he says, attempting to swallow his grin. 'Now hold tight. This one looks like a heart attack waiting to happen.'

He scoops me back under his arm, gripping tightly for good measure. A string of profanities leap from both of our mouths as we plunge into a drop even steeper than the one before. Our screams meet each other's in perfect harmony, the volume climbing with every metre that we fall. I would try to close my mouth, but gravity won't let me, so the sound lives on, punctuated by an almighty crash of a wave.

I feel the slap of the water before I have time to see it, overcome with an ice-cold bite as it floods the floor. The wave soaks through every inch of my clothing and invades every orifice, bringing with it a cold and uncomfortable chill. I expect to feel sick, or enraged, but as we coast towards the end, I feel quite the opposite. Instead, I'm overcome with an electric surge of adrenaline. The fabric of the hoodie has absorbed most of the water, leaving my hair and most of my face mercifully dry. Endorphins flood my system more than the water ever could, and my skin feels on fire with the thrill of the ride.

We turn one final corner before the ride comes to a halt, the safety bar raising and the sound of crowds returning. Aiden wastes no time at all leaping from his seat and clambering out to plant his shoes on solid ground. He turns back to me, reaching out his hand in what I can only assume is an act of solidarity. I take it and he silently pulls me across the gap from the carriage back to the land. Our eyes meet the second my soggy sneakers hit the ground and I can tell, even through his grumpy façade, he enjoyed it as much as I did. The adrenaline in the air is thick enough to taste; we're both coming down from the same deliciously dangerous high.

I can see his shoulders relax as we head for the exit.

'Let's do that again!' I say, heart still threatening to jump.

'Fuck, no.' He shakes his head. 'Unless you really, *really* must?'

I shake my head, satisfied by the knowledge he would face such a huge fear again if I asked him nicely enough.

The grin stays plastered to my face all throughout our descent, from the purchase of overpriced gift-shop towels to the reveal of our disgusting souvenir picture. I look like a drowned rat, but Aiden physically flinches at the expression of pure terror on his face that the camera caught in deliciously high definition. That's more than enough for me. I buy it on a strip, a keyring and a fridge magnet, much to his dismay. He huffs as I pay and grimaces as they bag it, but I catch him smiling at the Polaroid strip when I come out from the toilet after fixing my hair.

As we walk through the park, patting ourselves dry, I can see him eyeing up some of the other rides with curiosity.

'Which one next?' I ask.

'I think one was enough.'

'I really don't think Evie would agree,' I say. 'Where's your sense of adventure? Your spontaneity? This is not the same boy that jumped in that brook.'

'You need to calm down. And maybe lay off the fizzy drinks.'

He watches fondly as I pull a face at his teasing advice, before fixing his eyes on a spot on my forehead.

'You're still dripping, here.' He reaches for his own towel and shuffles closer, lightly touching it to the edge of my forehead and diligently patting it dry. He works with intense skill and precision, carefully studying my face as he softly completes his mission. The water is gone, but his hand still lingers, as does his gaze. His eyes are locked in now – fixed gently onto my own, only breaking to steal fevered glances at my softly pursed lips. My breath catches in my chest, held in place by the force behind his gaze and the sudden stillness of everything around us. Something's shifted. Something that's made my mouth go dry and the rest of the world cease to exist.

He feels it too, the force between us pulling him in, his face coming closer and mine willing it with every step.

His hand moves to cup my head and he gulps.

'Maddison, I—'

A piercing screech sounds from my pocket, breaking us apart. We spring from each other, and I fumble around and reach to turn it off as the noise gets steadily louder and more intrusive.

'What was that?' he asks, still recovering from the sudden interruption.

'A timer. Must have accidentally had it set or something.'

It's a feeble excuse, but less pathetic than the truth and a perfect distraction from whatever *that* just was. I unlock my phone and take a quick peek . . . Three and a half hours is up and still no message from Benji. I look at the chat, in case there was a message that didn't pop up on the home screen. Nothing. Not a thing this whole entire time.

'So, what next?' Aiden asks.

'Lunch?' I say.

I don't know what just happened between us, but I'm attributing it to adrenaline and the lack of food, so an overpriced hot dog has never been more alluring.

'Works for me – I'm buying,' he says jokingly, wiggling Evie's company card as we make our way towards the closest kiosk.

He carries on as normal and I try to follow his lead.

This is Aiden. Aiden Edwards. The Primary School Prick.

I check my phone as he orders us both jumbo hot dogs with extra fries.

Still nothing from Benji.

Nudge 23

The Messages

'Did you get my email?'

'Which one?'

'The diary request for next week.' Pippa sounds annoyingly chipper even with the shoddy call signal.

I flick through to my inbox. There in blue sits an unopened email from three minutes ago.

Diary Request

Title: Mads x Pippa :)

Date and Time: Thursday 15th April, 15.00 – 16.00

Location: Boardroom, Abbingtorn House

Comments: Empty

'Yeah, I just got it,' I say in a tone that I hope reads *please wait more than three minutes before following up.*

'Perf – that works for you, right? I never know any more with how busy you've been with Evie,' she says.

I ignore the passive aggression. 'Would you mind clarifying what it's regarding?'

'Mads x Pippa smiley face' doesn't paint the most descriptive picture.

'I just figured, with how busy you've been with this event, I'd book some time for us to catch up and discuss your progress,' she says innocently.

'Oh, you've rescheduled my appraisal?' I ask.

Since my last attempt in January, Pippa promised that she'd reschedule asap. Then Evie entered the picture and Pippa's saltiness rose to levels that could fill an entire ocean, with all my hopes of me ever getting recognition at Abbingtorn sent there to drown.

She coos. 'Let's not call it that. There's no need for us to put labels on it – makes it far too formal.'

Of course there isn't. If she calls it what it is, or formalises it, then I'd have reason to argue for the pay rise and promotion I deserve.

'It's more of a catch-up,' she continues.

'Where we talk about my progress?'

'And other things. All good things, of course!'

'Thursdays are an Aiden day – I'll have to move him to one of my Abbingtorn days – are you OK with that?' I ask. 'I can see when he's free and confirm with you over email.'

One perk of remote working is supposed to be the minimal contact with Pippa. The quicker I get her off the phone, the quicker I can get on with my work.

'God, you two never miss a beat, do you?' She giggles awkwardly.

If I'm not mistaken, there's a tinge of jealousy in her tone. I just don't know whether it's triggered more by the running of the Summer Splash, or the alone time with Aiden.

'We've got a pretty strict timeline, very little room for missed sessions.' I am only half engaged as I start typing out a message.

> Can we do Tuesday & Wednesday next week? Pippa
> drama . . .

He views it instantly, typing before Pippa's even finished her faux-cheery response.

> Already blocked out Wed & Thur in my planner in ink. But for
> you? Anything.

I chuckle involuntarily.

'Maddison?' Pippa asks.

Looks like I managed to tune her out to a point where even she noticed something other than the sound of her own voice.

'Sorry,' I say, hoping she didn't hear my little giggle at Aiden's message. 'Yes, Thursday's all good. Anything else?'

'Well, actually, while I have you here . . . My dry-cleaning? It's urgent. Sent you an email this morning . . .'

'Already arranged for me to pick up tomorrow lunch,' I say instantly.

'You're a star,' she says, before hanging up.

A star that is overworked, underpaid and growing duller by the day, sure.

> Thank you!! Pay u back with another trip to Dizzy Days? We
> never got to ride the Flumes of Death . . .

I vow it will be the last message I send before I get back to my serious work-from-home work. But then he replies, again, almost instantly.

> Let's just call it even.

I write back at once.

> Thought so. See u Tuesday.

'Who are you smiling at?' Mum asks, making her way through the living room faster than I have time to pray for schools to go back already.

'No one. I'm working.' I hope it's enough of a clue that she should, once again, leave my makeshift office.

'That wasn't a work smile.' She purses her lips in a smug, telling way that only a mother can pull off, then makes herself comfortable, nestling into the sofa and switching on the TV before I can stop her. Usually I'd protest, or take the remote for myself, but between Pippa's recent attitude, Evie's promise and all my Summer Splash work, I'm pretty tapped out when it comes to regular Abbingtorn days anyway. So, I leave her to it, stealing glances at her show as I half-heartedly click away at my laptop.

'Was it that boy you're seeing?' she asks, feigning a casual air that I know is nothing but a thinly veiled front. 'The one who took you out for drinks?'

She's been dying to know more about Benji since I first brought him up – a thing I only did because she coaxed it out of me. I needed some sort of explanation for that first late weeknight, and the one that followed last Friday after his 11 p.m. U about? text.

I leapt out of bed, donned the most cleavage-heavy top I owned, and showed up at his friend's gig with Kimi. We played it cool, letting them know that we were 'just swinging by' after our own 'fun and significantly better' night out. The whole thing went over well, just as I expected. He couldn't take his eyes off me, and, later that night, his lips. But I still jumped in a cab with Kimi because he didn't deserve to go home with me after it had taken him over twenty-four hours to respond. When I wandered through my front door at 3.30 a.m., my mum, ever the night owl, was shocked at my return, and incredibly eager to know everything. Thanks to the copious amount of alcohol in my system, I was more than happy to sit down and share with her.

She keeps pushing. 'It seemed like a boy smile.'

'I'm working,' I say as I focus myself on my screen once more.

'How is he anyway?' she asks.

'He's OK – we just needed to swap days next week.'

This is why I don't tell like to tell my parents about men. If she gets too happy, then I will too and I'll convince myself that it has potential before I know if it does.

'What days? Were you planning to meet up with him again?'

Benji. Not Aiden. She's talking about Benji.

'I meant work, that is a work thing. You're distracting me!'

'Understood.' She mimes zipping her mouth and tossing the key behind her shoulder. 'But I like him if he's making you smile like that. That's the last thing I'll say on the matter.'

She's right, Benji should be making me smile. And he does . . . I think. At least he does when we actually talk. Which, frankly, isn't enough, and is mainly in person thanks to his stupid week-long text intervals. But I'm done waiting around. If I want this to stand any sort of chance, maybe I need to make more effort to drive us into something more serious.

I reach for my phone once again, work laptop a prop at this point, and pull up our thread of spaced-out, barely-there messages. I type, pressing send before my brain can stop me. This is diving. This is acting without thinking first.

U free tonight?

To my surprise, he responds thirty-three minutes later. A personal best at this point.

Yh, kinda tired tho. U can come round mine if you want?

Not exactly what I expected, but a sign of interest nonetheless.

I push back my chair, ready to run to my room and grab my list journal for a quick pros and cons session, but I stop myself in my tracks, pulling it back in and taking a deep and much-needed breath.

Don't think, just do.

I like this guy and we were leading up to this anyway, so why not just get it out of the way now? It has been more than a while for me and I have needs just as much as anybody else does. Plus, as much as I hate to admit it, I have been feeling a fair bit of pent-up frustration since that weird moment with Aiden at the water park. That forehead wipe awakened something in me that had been dormant for far too long. Something one night with Benji could sort if I were to actually give him a chance.

Everyone has casual sex nowadays, so what's stopping me having it with someone I mostly like? Someone I have been on multiple dates with! That is, if you count our Friday swing-by as a date.

Don't think, just do.

I've already thought too much and if I carry on, I *know* I'll talk myself out of it.

Send me your address, be over around 7 x

Seven would give me enough time to shower and shave my entire body.

His next response comes even quicker, leaving a mere five minutes between my message and his.

A thumbs-up.

Followed by his address.

Let's hope he's saving his enthusiasm for when I get there in person.

Nudge 24

The Head Pat

I had no feelings while I was getting ready; no anxious thoughts or pangs in my gut. Nothing to steer me away from what I was about to do. I was just as calm the whole ride here. But now, standing outside his door, I feel my fight or flight activate. I pull up our few messages and cross-reference his address with the door in front of me. It's correct.

Are you coming down?

I write, following up from the Outside text I sent eight minutes ago. If he doesn't appear soon, I don't know what will happen first: me getting metaphorical cold feet or me getting actual hypothermia.

Three more minutes pass. I wish I'd brought a proper coat.

The intercom crackles and fizzes as it comes to life, before beeping as the front door springs open.

'Second floor up – first door on the left. Be quiet – my flatmate's in.'

My stomach starts to quiver, but I put it down to lack of food and keep going up the metal staircase, to find him leaning against the open doorframe in anticipation.

'Quick.' He briskly ushers me through the door, past the living room and straight into his bedroom.

Everything is black or dark grey, from his walls to his bedsheets to his shelves and the various things scattered on them. His carpet is prickly, even through the thin layer of protection afforded by my socks. A lampshade-less lightbulb hangs from the ceiling, switched off to allow for his table lamp. I would like to think he chose it to set the mood, but I fear that it may be to hide the fact he's barely cleaned up.

'One sec, just gotta finish this.'

He lies on his bed, shirtless, and far more focused on his console than my presence here. After a few minutes, he changes the screen from whatever video game he was playing to Netflix.

'D'you like superheroes?' he asks, flicking through title cards.

'Erm, I've seen a couple with my brother but . . .'

'Cool, there's a new one on here,' he says, before clicking a button and getting comfy for the opening credits.

It's not until after the full five-minute sequence that he notices me still hovering awkwardly in the corner by his door. I would have moved sooner or followed him, but he left me no space and he didn't bother with any sort of invitation.

'You look nice,' he says, finally taking a moment to look me over.

'Thank you.' I try to hide my creeping smile.

I have no idea what you wear when the sole purpose of an outing is to get laid, and it took a *while* to properly decide. After a lot of panicked scrambling through my wardrobe, I settled for a subtle-but-effective push-up bra, a low-cut T-shirt, an unzipped hoodie and a pair of bum-scrunch leggings. The aim was to look unbothered and yet still effortlessly hot in a barely trying, every-day way.

He shuffles over to his left, patting the small-but-something-I-guess free space that he's created next to him. I take it as the only sign I'm going to get and scurry over, squeezing in the best that I can. He throws his arm round my shoulder, proud smile on his face as he pulls me in tighter and leans in. I feel his tongue down my throat before I have time to breathe. It moves clunkily, flapping around like a fish out of water.

'You're so fucking sexy,' he grunts into my mouth as he paws clumsily at my chest. 'Take this off.'

He tugs impatiently at the lapel of my hoodie, making no effort to remove it but all the effort to whine about it. So, I quickly adjust from my position and shrug it off, before diving in for kiss number two.

Kissing him is a task – it starts rough and unrefined, but with time he gets bored and lets me take the reins. Usually by attempt two or three, we get somewhere passable and I actually end up having a good time. As I start leading with my tongue, I make a silent prayer that the same practice doesn't extend to everything else. I don't have time for that tonight. I still haven't eaten and I was planning to be home before 10 p.m.

'And this ...' He makes a half-hearted attempt to lift up my shirt, but my hand comes swinging down to stop him.

I chose the most oversized T-shirt I own so that it wouldn't have to come off. I don't need him seeing the crease of my stomach, or the way my boobs seem to shrivel to nothing in the cold. And I don't want him to look at my naked body with those horny, hungry eyes. But as we pause, I realise that stopping his hand was one step away from killing the mood entirely. I recover the moment, slipping his palm into mine and squeezing it tight before guiding it under my shirt.

'Wow, you're ready to go,' he says smugly, watching me shimmy my leggings off with haste.

I'm more than ready. He takes the hint, legs scrambling as he rushes to pull off his sweatpants. It takes him far too long to unhook my bra under my top, ignoring all my offers to do it myself, but, eventually, we get there, clawing at each other's skin as we kiss, the movie an irrelevant whir in the background. I close my eyes, trying to focus on the touch of his hands and turn this into something at least a little bit sensual, but it's no use. His actions are just far too robust to be anything other than what they are: the clumsy pawing of a selfishly horny man.

'What are you doing?' I ask, opening my eyes and straightening to see what's happening.

He freezes, propped on top of me, penis in hand ready to slide it inside me.

'What does it look like I'm doing?' he replies, confused.

'Have you got protection?' I ask, startled that I even need to.

'Are you not on the pill?'

'Have you been tested recently?'

'I don't have anything, I'd know if I did,' he laughs, rolling his eyes.

'Well, I'm not on the pill. Or anything else, for that matter,' I lie, watching as his face remains unchanged.

Transferring disease is clearly not a worry to him, but I was hoping that something like pregnancy would be.

'I'll pull out,' he says.

I can't help but laugh. What kind of seventeen-year-old-boy-level response is that?

'Yeah, we're absolutely not doing that.' I gently shoo him off me.

He doesn't know me at all if he thought something like that would pass.

'OK, calm down!' he says, blatantly ignoring my deathly calm and frankly apathetic exterior. 'There's still other things we can do.'

He softly strokes my hair, licking his lips before he leans in for another kiss.

The upside is we've been at this long enough tonight that we've reached the point where his kissing has significantly improved. It's a little less wet now and he seems to have got the message that your tongue shouldn't just whirl around lawlessly like a sock in a washing machine.

I moan softly into his mouth. This is what I came here for – this feeling. This feeling will make me forget. I lose myself in the kiss, in the movement of his lips and the intense grip of his hand in my hair ...

Then I feel it.

The head pat.

The push of his hand against the top of my head, trying to shove me under the covers.

I fight back, pretending I don't understand and trying to bring us back to that brief moment where everything felt good. I grip his head with both hands, doing my best to distract him with a tantalising lip bite and a heavy dose of tongue, but he has one goal in mind and he will not give up. His hand pushes harder and harder until he realises it's no use and resorts to words.

'Give me head.'

It's blunt and tactless, making it only more evident that he's undeserving. But I decide to adequately test the waters before I decline. I am nothing if not reasonable.

'You first,' I say.

His eyebrows lift at the request, mouth opening in utter shock and horror.

'Yeah, I don't do that. Especially not the first time.'

'Then neither do I,' I say, pulling away as he leans in to kiss me again and shoots his hand straight to the top of my head to audaciously try his luck a third time.

'What do you mean?' he asks, genuinely wide-eyed and confused.

I roll my eyes and attempt to make it as clear as day. 'If you won't go down on me, then I won't go down on you.'

He snorts in disgust, the space between our bodies growing cold as he pulls away. 'You being serious?'

'Why wouldn't I be?'

'Because that's not—'

'That's not what?' I ask, ready to fight.

He catches the glare on my face, his dissipating within seconds. He knows he's lost this and I'd go as far as to say he's a little embarrassed.

He slides in close again, warmth returning as my chest touches his and his arms cradle me tight. His head dips down slightly, a trail of saliva forming on my neck, each new patch cold and uncomfortably wet.

'I'm sorry,' he says between soggy neck kisses. 'Let's not argue about this – it's not worth losing what we have.'

He orders us pizza and we watch the rest of the movie, him frequently pausing it to fill me in on the context I've missed. It's cute and domestic – an inviting change of pace and a chance to see him in a different light. His arm stays wrapped around my shoulders, squeezing me closer every time it gets 'scary' in the hopes that I'll jump and let him protect me, but I hold my own. After what Aiden and I went through last week on that water ride, nothing can make me jump for the foreseeable future.

We kiss goodbye at the door at 10.18 p.m.

'Next time I'll be more prepared,' he says, swinging my hand in his.

'You'd better be,' I reply and turn to leave, hoping I can at least be in bed by eleven.

My taxi pulls up right on time, just as I let myself out of the apartment block's door. I get into the back and sigh, more than ready for my own cleaner and better-smelling bedroom.

The shower I take is enough to wash off the general smell of his room, and the fresh pair of pyjamas are soft enough to comfort me ever so slightly after our frustrating end. I reach for my phone to message Aiden the second I slide into bed, typing out the (massively condensed) story three times. My finger hovers over the send button, nervous and timid. I can't do it. I hit delete and put my phone down to charge.

Spontaneous or not, this is one thing that doesn't feel quite right to share.

Nudge 25

The Meeting

I got home OK. Thanks for a fun night x

I cringed as I sent it, but I felt like it had to be done. Then I woke up in the morning and there was no reply, and I deeply considered breaking into his house just to delete the message.

Three days later, still left with no reply, I caved and reacted to his story on Instagram. It was nothing too extreme – no fire emoji or heart eyes, just a little *100* to remind him that I still existed.

Still nothing. No response, no meaningless emojis back, just radio silence for two more days.

On the sixth day, I heard the buzz and flocked to my phone to find a singular sign of life ... He'd reacted to my first message with a thumbs-up emoji.

A thumbs-up emoji. After six whole days.

Day seven and I have moved on and decided that we're simply no more. Blowjob-Beg Benji is now a figment of my past and I have made a promise to live in the here and now.

'Aiden!' Pippa screams his name, barrelling towards him as Gus and I follow slowly behind.

She throws her arms around him, swaying back and forth while she traps him in a tight hug. At first, he looks startled, but then he accepts his fate, swaying along with her.

'Long time, no see,' he says jokingly.

It might be the funniest thing she's ever heard in her life, the way she throws her head back and screeches. I can't help but roll my eyes at the whole ordeal, but I make sure that it goes unnoticed. At least, it almost does. I can see Aiden catch it out of the corner of his eye and smirk. I have to smirk right back.

'Nice dress,' he says to me.

'Gee, thanks,' I reply, matching his sarcasm.

'I was being serious.'

'Oh. Well, thank you, then,' I manage to say, surprised by his sincerity.

I look down at the short satin skirt of my dress, sat a risky few inches above my knee. When I first tried it on, I was ready to storm out from behind the partition and tell Anika it was too short for a workday. But she twirled me in front of the mirror and I marvelled at the way it pinched at my waist and flowed at my hips, landing perfectly mid-thigh. I hoped the stunning embroidered detailing, dotted about the fabric, would be enough to distract from the scandalous length.

Up until this moment, it has, but the longer Aiden's eyes linger, so does another beadier, more calculated set.

'It's weird seeing Maddison dressed up, isn't it? She's always so *businessy* at work,' Pippa says. 'Or at least, she tries to be!'

She links his arm as she says it, tapping him playfully as if they're sharing some private joke at my expense. He doesn't go along with it. Instead, he looks at her, confused, dulling her bravado with one awkwardly long silence.

'Aiden, my man!' Gus uses the opportunity to sandwich himself into the conversation.

Aiden goes in for a handshake. Gus goes in for some form of 'fist-bump, high-five, turn, pose' combo. It's incredibly cringey and deeply hard to watch, and I desperately need us all to go inside.

'Where's Evie? Has she already gone in?' I ask him, praying it's enough to end this outdoor charade.

'Yeah, she's already in there. So are Oliver and Maxwell,' Aiden replies. 'I came out to get you.'

I sigh with relief, using the moment to lead us inside and leave the desperate attention-seeking behind in the street. The others follow, Pippa upping her stride to ensure she enters first, smile plastered on her face ready to greet our bosses.

Clients are often reluctant to do the Abbingtorn midway check-in, insisting it 'should just be an email', but Evie welcomed the opportunity with open arms. Her one stipulation? We 'avoid the stuffy boardroom'.

I figured that probably meant a meeting round hers, but then she booked us in at one of the most prestigious sushi spots in the city. A-list prestigious. Bodyguards-at-the-door prestigious. Strict-formal-dress-code-even-at-one-in-the-afternoon prestigious.

The waiter leads us across the unbearably dark dining-room floor and through a deep-red curtain to a private room. Within it stands a large, emerald circular table, seating Oliver, Maxwell and an impeccably dressed Evie.

'Oh, my God, you did it, you wore the dress!' Evie cheers, bypassing Pippa and rushing towards me. 'Anika *raved* about it after your fitting and I was oh-so hoping that I'd get to see it in person.'

She grabs my hand, twirling me so she can get a 360.

'Hi, Evie,' I say as she continues to examine me.

I also do my best to throw Oliver and Maxwell a silent 'hi' and a welcoming wave to where they stay sitting at the table. They wave back, observing mine and Evie's closeness with pleasant surprise. If I still had hope, I would pray that this would make them put me face to face with clients more often.

'Oh, my God, Evie, I *love* your jumpsuit.' Pippa creeps closer to give it an unwelcome stroke. 'Is that Prada's Spring collection?'

'It's custom, actually,' Evie answers, doing her best to subtly shuffle away from her. 'Shall we get seated?'

Evie and Gus sit first, moving towards the back of the booth and leaving one more space near them and two closest to the front of the room. Pippa hovers by the front.

'After you!' She waits for me to sit and leave her next to Aiden.

'Doesn't it make the most sense for me and Maddison to sit up front? We've got the presentation,' Aiden says.

It's so satisfying to watch Pippa's face fall in real time that I almost forget where I am and break into a smile. But I don't. Instead, I swallow my glee and do my best to nod nonchalantly. She hesitates for a moment, but eventually whacks on a smile, reluctantly sliding in next to Gus.

Evie insists that we do not begin presenting until everyone has sampled at least one bite of each dish. She ordered the special tasting-menu before we got here and says that we have not *lived* until we've had a bite of their truffle gold-crusted salmon sashimi. Naturally we obey, spending almost an hour picking at everything and exchanging light-hearted pleasantries.

'Question . . .' Aiden whispers, lips pressed to my ear. 'How does Pippa eat sushi with her mouth so busy kissing everyone's arse?'

I choke on my tuna roll, rice attempting to fly from my nose as I stifle the laugh that's rolled up my throat. The entire booth goes quiet, concern washing over everyone's faces as they turn to watch me suffer in high definition. I can feel my cheeks burning, which only makes the sushi in my mouth fight harder as I attempt to swallow it down without incident. It's not working. I start to choke some more. I take one long, forced swallow and give a reassuring thumbs-up, hoping it's enough to keep everyone's eyes off me again, but I can see Aiden smirking deviously out of the corner of my eye. I make a mental note to not dare look at him again until my food is safely down my throat.

'You need to stop,' I hiss once we've both calmed down and the conversation around the table has moved on. 'You are going to get me in trouble.'

'You could use a little trouble.' He pops another roll into his mouth.

Eventually the chopsticks clatter and the plates get swept away, and Evie excitedly gives us the floor. We run through everything, from on-the-day details to our PR plan, to how we've managed to still remain in budget, complete with printouts of spreadsheets, further mood boards, my meticulous timelines and Aiden's brilliantly annotated diagrams. The room fills with chatter as Oliver, Maxwell and Evie praise the detail with which we've approached everything.

'This is top-notch work – well done, you two!' Oliver says.

Maxwell nods. 'That's what we expect from an Abbingtorn girl!'

I can practically see Pippa's skin turn green as they speak, but she tries to brush it off with a quick, telling flick of her hair.

'Yes, it's super impressive,' she says, her tone sickly sweet. 'I'm so proud of you, Maddison. I've been training you for a moment like this!'

Of course she'd try to take the credit for this when she has done absolutely nothing, training or otherwise. Maxwell and Oliver are eating it up, but I can see Evie's unimpressed face.

'That's so interesting, Pippa,' she says, much to Pippa's shock and excitement. 'Tell me, what have you done to get Maddison to this level? I'd love some tips, manager to manager.'

Pippa's face freezes in terror. It's so cartoonish that even Gus is purse-lipped, struggling to keep it together. We make eye contact for a moment, subtly sharing a nod of solidarity.

'Erm, well, I – it's kind of a mix of everything,' she stammers. 'I just feel like where she's been under my wing, she's managed to pick up quite a lot over these four years.'

'So, you've led on an event this big before?' Evie asks plainly, already knowing the answer.

Pippa's cheeks are growing redder by the minute. She keeps taking sips of her cocktail but all that's left are the dregs, and each fake sip makes that fact even more obvious.

'Well, Abbingtorn's never really had an event to this scale . . .' Pippa answers eventually, unable to meet Evie's narrowed eyes.

'And, Maddison, you are doing an amazing job handling the company's first one,' Evie says, giving me a warm smile.

It is a takedown of beauty – classy from start to finish with the kind of cut that goes deep without too hard a strike. Oliver and Maxwell are stunned and Pippa, bless her, is still too stressed out to realise just how hard Evie's shut her down. Evie is everything I want to be and more, wrapped up in beautiful, pristine packaging. I wanted the job before, but now I *need* it, more than I need to breathe.

'So next steps,' Evie continues, clapping her hands together and snapping everyone back into business mode. 'How rigid are these timelines?'

'We can certainly make amends if you think they're needed,' Aiden answers.

She nods in acknowledgement, carefully flicking through the printout and hovering over a selection of dates.

'I'm going away just before the Summer Splash. Aiden – cancel the house-sitters for that first weekend. I want you two to schedule an overnight.'

'An overnight?' I say.

'By the time of the event, I need you two to know my house and the grounds better than you know yourselves. I'll get two of the spare rooms made up, you can go up Friday night and Aiden can spend Saturday and Sunday getting you better acquainted. I'll stock the fridges and pantries – I want you to feel like you've *lived* there. It will make the event run better and have my guests feel more at ease.'

It's wildly unorthodox, but so is Evie, and, somehow, it makes perfect sense coming out of her mouth.

'Aiden's house-sat for me before – he can assure you there are no ghosts or anything of that sort,' she adds in jest. 'Does that work for you?'

'Yeah, I can fit that in,' I say, mentally flicking through our timeline.

I feel a flutter first, and then a stampede of butterflies kick at my poor, sushi-filled stomach. My breath hitches, but I vow to remain in control, grappling for the folder on the table and zeroing in on our notes.

Aiden's hand slides over the one I still have under the table as he gives me a small, reassuring pat on my clenched fist.

'Chill,' he whispers. 'The diary can wait. We'll rearrange things together after this meeting.'

It doesn't help anything. The butterflies grow more ferocious from the moment his skin touches mine.

'I'll handle the overnight expenses, of course,' Evie says, head flicking between Oliver, Maxwell and Pippa. 'So, are we done?'

We all nod because everyone knows by now that if Evie Eesuola says we're done, then we are definitely done.

Nudge 26

The Coward's Way Out

Days until the Summer Splash - 42

Days until no more Aiden - 56

Days since latest 'disagreement' with Benji - 11

Days since I last got a response from him - 6

I deserve better. I know that. I am not in denial. But then Benji texts me and I smile, and my memory grows selective.

I went through the removal process – deleted his name from my phone, archived the chats, even had a mock wake with the girls. I was done – I swore I was, and I like to think that I meant it. But then he texted. Sorry, life's been hard. And I folded instantly.

We discussed his terrible texting in great detail over the phone a couple of weeks ago, when he asked me why I was 'being so pissy with him'.

'I feel like you don't want to talk to me,' I said, trying not to sound too whiny.

'Of course I do, otherwise we wouldn't talk,' he said.

'Then why the gaps between replies?'

'I'm just busy.' He brushed my frustration aside. 'But you're my girl whether we talk or not.'

Not his girlfriend, of course. That would be far too much commitment and he's made it clear that 'that's just not where he's at right now'. Instead, I'm his 'girl' – a vague moniker that feels far more like an anchor than a term of endearment. When I went through it with Kimi and Devi over drinks, I could tell by their faces that they were not fans. I get it, I totally wouldn't be either, but I just can't shake him, no matter how hard I try. And I've *tried*. It's been 'over' more times than I care to admit. But I'm not getting any younger, or less single, and he is better than nothing. Plus, he does make me laugh and smile every so often.

What about Saturday? X

It's been three weeks since we last saw each other in person, him claiming it's because I'm never free when he is. He 'trades' from home for a living. He could literally be free whenever, but I'm trying to play it cooler, so I've chosen to let that go.

'Are you texting Benji again?' Aiden asks, returning to his seat.

I used his quick toilet trip as an excuse to be on my phone, since he's already called me out countless times over the last month for texting Benji too much. It's not my fault – the boy loves to pick arguments in the middle of my workdays. That is, when he's actually replying. It's embarrassing, so I've learnt to hide my phone usage better in the office, texting behind my handbag or pulling up Messenger on my laptop. But we're not in the office today and being sat across from each other at a table doesn't leave much room for hiding.

'Sorry.' I place my phone, screen down, on the tablecloth. 'Was just trying to sort some things, but they can wait. You and these fishcakes have my full attention.'

And they do. We went to a fair few food tastings all over the month of May after we got over take-me-out-for-dinner-gate, but now June has rolled around we've had to start getting serious and locking down our final choices. Castries Kitchen was one of the first St Lucian options we tried and I have not been able to stop thinking about their oxtail since. We've been back and forth about final menu choices with them for the last three weeks, and I have been counting down the days until we could be back here sampling the final options.

We both lift a miniature fishcake from the sharing platter in the middle, raising them in an air-toast before taking a bite. The crunch of the batter is immaculate, immediately echoing around the small, empty restaurant floor. I close my eyes as I chew, taking in the flaky fish, the chilli, the seasoning, all at once.

'We've got to serve these,' I sigh in pleasure.

'Agreed. They might be better than my mum's,' Aiden nods.

I gasp. 'Blasphemy!'

He shrugs. 'Hey, the bar's high, but these might just be higher.'

I reach for another, then another, and pray the next course comes soon. If it doesn't, I might have to ask them to take this tray away . . . or at least put the food in some Tupperware for later. It didn't occur to me until that first bite that, despite it being nearly 3 p.m., I haven't eaten or even drunk anything today. I am hungrier than I thought. And incredibly thirsty. I've forgotten what hydration feels like.

My phone buzzes against the table and I can't help but instinctually whip it around and check for Benji. It's not him. Of course it's not. It's Kimi, actually, once again stressing why chasing him is not a good idea.

'Wow, you two don't stop, do you?' Aiden says.

'That's us!' I lie, shrugging as I put my phone back down.

I may have exaggerated how well things were going with Benji to Aiden. I couldn't help it, I needed some world in which Benji and I were a perfect couple. It started with innocent bouts of omission but the more I said, the more I started to believe my own lies. The lie to Aiden was my comfort. A safe space among the barrage of blue ticks and gaslit phone calls. Omission became embellishment, and that embellishment straight fiction. A fiction where Benji actually acts like he likes me and I actually enjoy his company.

Kendrick, the owner, comes over, a gleeful smile on his face as we once again praise the fishcakes in all their entirety. Then he whisks them away, replacing them with a cone of what look like small corndogs.

'I got creative with this one,' he says with pride. 'They're battered and deep-fried plantain.'

I gasp.

'Calm down, Maddy – you look like you're about to start drooling,' Aiden says as Kendrick chuckles.

I can barely hear them. I'm too focused on the cone of deep-fried golden goodness placed in front of me.

'I'll leave you to it,' Kendrick says before walking away.

'Do you need a moment?' Aiden asks.

'I need several,' I whisper.

He laughs deeply, throwing his head back before reaching across the table and grabbing a stick. We bite into them in tandem, eyes widening at the sheer, rich, deep-fried nectar that befalls our mouths.

'A definite yes,' he says.

'No question.'

Kendrick clears our plates away and pours us more water as we wait for the mains. I guzzle it down quickly. So quickly, in fact, that Aiden slides his own glass over before my empty one has even touched the table. I nod back in thanks and he shrugs it off instantly, watching as I knock back his too.

'So, what's Benji saying?'

I stare back blankly so he nods towards my phone, reminding me that I am supposedly in good, regular contact with Benji.

'Oh, right, yes. Nothing important.' I'm babbling. 'We were just trying to make some plans for this weekend.'

It's not entirely a lie . . . I *have* been pestering Benji for at least his availability so I can try to plan something nice this weekend.

'Plans with Benji?' Aiden's eyes grow weary. 'This weekend?'

'Yes,' I say, confused. 'It doesn't go against the bet. You said I could make plans a week in adva—'

'You can't. You're busy.'

I blink. 'What?'

'*We* have plans this weekend.'

I roll my eyes before shaking off his weak attempt at a joke.

'I'm serious,' he says.

'Yeah, sure,' I say sarcastically. 'What are we doing, then?'

'Maddy. The overnight.'

I stop dead in my tracks, my blood running cold at the thought as I frantically reach in my handbag for our *PLANS* binder. I plonk it on the table and flick through it maniacally, desperately searching the timeline and scanning for this weekend's dates. Lo and behold, *OVERNIGHT* stretches from Friday to Sunday in perfectly printed ink.

'It's that time already?' I say.

'You didn't put it in your calendar?'

'Nice try. I haven't used a personal calendar in almost five months.'

He feigns a scowl, doing his best to act mad at the revelation, but I can see how impressed he is. 'Well, I have.'

He whips out his counterattack.: a deep-orange suede book, the year embossed on the front. He pauses dramatically, waiting for me to take it all in – let the book and me really have our moment. Once I'm done, he flicks through to the month of June, where *Overnight* is written in purple from the eighth to the tenth.

'I use purple for everything work-related,' he says boastfully.

'You need to stop talking about your colour coding; I'm getting emotional.' I'm half-joking.

'Weirdo,' he says teasingly, as I quickly message Benji again.

Acc, can't do Saturday ... Next weekend? Xx

'So I'm guessing you haven't packed, then,' Aiden continues.

I huff in response. 'You'd be right.'

And, come to think of it, I haven't done any laundry in a couple of weeks ... Kimi deleted my reminders when she deleted my calendar. It's been a struggle.

'Bring jumpers – Evie's house gets really cold at night,' he says before calling Kendrick over and asking for two more glasses of water. 'How are you getting there?'

'I don't know ... Bus? Train? Something.'

It got thrown our way months ago and I only looked up the route once. That's unheard of for me – even *I* can barely believe it. Neither can Aiden, apparently. He stares at me, mouth ever so slightly agape.

'I'm gonna drive so if I work from your office Friday, you can leave with me?' he says.

I nod in agreement; it beats buses and trains for certain. Plus, over the last couple of months, I feel like Aiden and I have been so busy with work that we haven't had time to drive each other too mad.

Benji still hasn't replied by the time I get home. Nor has he by Wednesday night, two whole days later.

> We've talked about this.

I cannot keep having this same conversation. I understand that he's busy – I am too – but I make time for his messages and he should be able to do the same. I can't think about packing.

I type a quick message to Aiden.

> I'll get the train to Evie's. I think I'll need to come home to pack on Friday night.

I can't think about anything but the unopened text bubbles that lurk beneath my lock screen. One time would be fine. Twice, I could get over. But I cannot keep *doing* this over requests for basic conversation. And with him, it is *basic*. Basic as can be. There's no way it could be anything else – for that, he would have to reply. The phone vibrates and I dive for it, but it's just Aiden.

> Getting the train makes no sense. Throw some clothes in a bag and bring it to the office with you.

My overnight bag sits empty on my bed, mocking me less than forty-eight hours before departure time, but I'm in no state to pack a bag. I need answers, and quickly. The type that only Instagram can provide. I roll onto my stomach, unlocking my phone and scanning the row of profile pictures across the top for Benji's, to no avail. It's suspicious for someone who posts to his story all day and every day (and still doesn't have time to text me back). I go for Plan B. I open the search bar and . . .

Nothing.

No account when I search for his name.

No fragmented chat where our message history once was.

My heart drops to my stomach.

> Can one of you search Benji's @ and let me know if his profile comes up?

It's a mildly unhinged request, but one the FGA take on with no question, each one sending through the same screenshot of his clearly active profile.

He's blocked me. A week after we got on the phone and he *begged* me to 'take it easy and just give him a chance'.

He blocked me. Like a coward. And I hate to say it, but there's a part of me that's not even that surprised.

> So, guess we're over?

I text, blood hot as I type, attaching a screenshot of the *username not found* message.

He's online instantly. It's the quickest he's ever opened a message and the longest he's ever spent typing a response. I can't look away. I wait for what feels like hours as the bubble keeps moving – taunting me each time it wiggles. Eventually it comes through . . . One sad little sentence. One long, nervous wait for a dull, thoughtless end.

It all got too much. Gd luck with everything.

And just like that, the bubble bursts. It's over – for real this time.

Nudge 27

The Lesson

Are you allowed to call a break-up a break-up if you were never technically in a relationship? It was barely a situationship – I can't claim he used me for sex, because he was too lazy to even meet up for that. And yet, the way he ended it has made me feel absolutely worthless.

A week ago, I was questioning why I was even seeing someone who's asked me one question about myself since the first time we kissed (The question? What you wearing?, sent at 11 p.m. He was asleep by the time I replied five minutes later). Now I'm replaying all our interactions back in my head as a reel of best bits, and blinking back tears. I'm acting like a war-widow. It's pathetic.

'What's going on with you?'

I turn to see Aiden, eyebrow raised sceptically. His eyes linger for a moment. Or, at least, as long as they can before they have to flit back to the road ahead.

'Nothing.'

'You haven't said a word this whole journey. You just keep staring out the window like you're in a music video.'

I sigh and turn my head in the opposite direction, watching as the cars slow on their way back to the city.

'See, usually that would have got me a laugh.' He pauses, his tone softening as he risks a second glance. 'Seriously, what's up with you?'

I snap at him. 'Shouldn't you keep your eyes on the road? I'm not in this car with you by choice; we don't have to make small talk.'

It is entirely uncalled for, but, in my defence, so is his incessant checking-up on me. If I wanted to talk about it, I would, and I would do so with literally anyone else in the world.

'Wow. Well, next time we go to Evie's, you can drive yourself,' he says jovially, my snark rolling right off his back. 'You're one of those super cautious, annoyingly rule-abiding drivers, aren't you?'

He's trying anything now, angling for any kind of bite.

'I bet you passed with a perfect score,' he continues. 'Come on, what was it? You can tell me … Or maybe it wasn't so perfect! Is this where I learn that you're actually a rule-breaking speed demon?'

'I don't drive,' I sigh, desperate to shut him up.

'Why? Environment? Road tax?' He gasps. 'Suspended licence?'

'I haven't passed,' I say. 'Never even took my test.'

It slips out, a result of my desperation to quell his relentless attempts to fill the silence, but I immediately wish I could swallow it back up again.

Aiden pulls the handbrake up at a red light, taking the moment to properly turn towards me.

'What?'

'I don't have a licence,' I say through gritted teeth.

'You don't have a licence,' he says slowly.

'Well, what do I need a car for? Buses, trains and taxis exist.'

'This journey, no?'

He's too smiley, too light. He's having too much fun sparring and it's only souring my mood more.

'I said I'd get the train,' I retort.

'And I said I wouldn't let you, because that was a pointless idea,' he says.

'Well, then, you don't get to lord it over me. And you don't get to act all superior just because you can push some pedals.'

Silence drowns us yet again, the air stale and awkward. I painstakingly count each raindrop that slides down the glass. I know he meant nothing by it, and usually I would have taken it on the chin, but today is not the day for anyone to test me.

But Aiden, annoying as he is, isn't Benji, and for once isn't the person actively making my life a misery. I can't take everything out on him; it just isn't fair and it would prove for a very awkward forty-eight hours. I glance over. His eyes are now fixed on the road, his grip tight on the steering wheel, arms and jaw tensed.

'It was just one of those things that I just never got round to doing.' I attempt to defuse the tension. 'I tried at the start. Began learning the second I turned seventeen. Booked in ten lessons starting the day after my birthday. I had the test booked for the summer because that gave me enough time to get my forty-five hours of practice in.'

He nods curtly, stealing a fleeting glance at me. He doesn't speak, but his grip on the wheel loosens ever so slightly.

'Then what happened?' he asks.

'I just wasn't very good behind the wheel,' I sigh. 'I was convinced I'd whizz through it and have my licence by June, but then ...'

'When you weren't meeting the timeline, you pushed it away,' he says with an understanding nod. 'If you change your mind, you could always try again.'

I shuffle uncomfortably, avoiding a response.

I still see giving up on driving as one of my biggest failures. I avoid talking about it at all costs, shy away from showing anyone I still have my provisional. There's a dark cloud over my head every time I have to run for the bus – a voice that tells me I'm too old for this to be my commute. But Aiden makes it feel easy, like a small blip in the road. 'You could always try again' like it's a choice, not a failure.

He taps his fingers on the steering wheel. 'Did you learn manual or automatic?'

'Manual,' I reply.

'So, you like struggle.' He grins. 'Me too.'

He checks his mirrors and tugs down on the gearstick sharply, before twisting the steering wheel with a flick of his wrist. The car and I screech as we make a sharp left. Car horns sound off all around us, but Aiden pays them no mind, continuing his joyride off the packed main road. Within moments, the angry orchestra fades into nothing and he pulls us over on a small country path.

'What are you doing?' I ask.

I scan his face for any sign that he plans to murder me in this car, but he is, of course, as unreadable as ever as he finishes parallel parking on the side of the road. Once the engine has stilled, he turns his head towards me, a small but intriguing smile on his lips.

'Wanna practise?' he asks.

I stare back, my clear confusion prompting a swift eye roll from him.

'Driving. Do you want to try driving?' He gestures boldly to the steering wheel in front of him.

'You'd really let me drive your car?' I ask, eyebrow raised.

He's being so calm, it's borderline sociopathic.

'Come on, how often d'you get a free driving lesson?'

It must be some sort of joke or empty gesture to test my new 'don't say no, go with the flow' attitude. There is a difference, however, between not saying no to an after-work drink and not saying to no to something that could quite easily kill us both.

'I could kill us,' I say.

'So be it. I've lived a good life.' He shrugs nonchalantly. 'But you won't – I'm a really good teacher. Taught my sister, actually.'

'You taught your sister to drive?' I repeat.

'Sure did, so I'm still insured for a learner to use my car … I think. Now, come on, we do have to get to Evie's at some point.'

He opens his door and walks around to the passenger side before I have another chance to argue. He waits impatiently, tapping his foot as I unbuckle my seatbelt and scurry around to the driver's seat. A fizz of excitement bubbles from my feet to my chest.

'Adjust the chair,' he says as I stare blankly at the dashboard.

I turn to face him, wondering how on earth he expects me to do that, but he stays silent. Time to get creative. I turn back to the buttons and dials, pushing one with a small picture of a seat and some squiggly lines. It lights up and I push back on the chair, expecting it to move, but get a slight warming sensation spreading across my lower back instead.

'Oh, we're really starting from square one – got it,' Aiden laughs, switching off the chair heating before pointing to the other side of me. 'There's a lever to your right, just under … exactly. You've got to press it a few times to move the seat. Go forward and up until you can reach the pedals properly and see out the front window.'

I reach down and start pumping, getting fully comfortable in the seat. It's still warm, the leather soft and beautifully broken in. He lets out a chuckle.

'What?' I ask.

'Nothing. You're just so short.'

'I'm only like . . . a couple of inches shorter than you,' I say.

'Five, at *least*. Six if I'm in the right shoes,' he retorts. 'Right, let's start easy. Put your foot on the clutch.'

I stare back blankly.

'The one furthest left,' he says, smiling at my evident lack of knowledge. 'So, first find the bite on that clutch; press it all the way to the floor and keep lifting until you feel the shift.'

'What shift? What will shift?' I ask.

'Don't worry, you'll feel it.'

'Feel what?'

'Stop thinking, just try.'

His words are strong but careful, actions gentle and so attentive. It's exactly how he was in the boardroom and on the stoop of the La La Lounge. I move my left foot, trying different pressures until the front of the car lifts slightly.

'I think I've found it!' I say.

'Amazing. Do you think you can hold it there for a bit?'

I nod, my eyes fixed ahead of me as I refocus all my energy on keeping the ball of my foot exactly where it is. My calf is shaking just thinking about it, but I power through.

'Cool, let's see how good you are at keeping the clutch in place – go into first gear and lift the handbrake.'

He says it so steadily, like we're playing with a little toy and not a giant metal cage that could take someone out.

I jerk the gearstick upwards and the car makes a horrible

metallic crunching sound. I shriek and instinctively pull back on it sharply, which causes an even louder crunch.

'You've got to put your foot down on the clutch when you change gears,' he says with a small chuckle.

'Why didn't you tell me?'

'I just did!' He leans back, smiling.

'Yeah, great timing.'

'Shut up and try again,' he says.

I slam my foot down and push the gearstick. This time it slides across easily, guiding me into a false sense of security. I lift my foot. The car shudders and lurches forward before the engine cuts out entirely. Adrenaline shoots through me and I feel my cheeks flush with a strong, shameful, burning heat. This isn't a fun little test. I could do real damage if I'm not holding the clutch correctly. This is why I should not be driving and this is exactly why Aiden's not a qualified instructor.

'Maddison. It's OK,' he says, picking up on my panic. 'Give me your hand.'

I shouldn't trust him, but his steadiness compels me to, so I reach out my left hand, breathing as deeply as I can. He holds it for a second and I focus on his palm, warm, strong and safe.

'I can't do this. I'll just fail again.'

'Yes, you can,' he says immediately. 'Maddison Clarke, you are many things, but you are not a failure.'

I turn to face him, bracing myself for the mocking look and the curl in his lip that will give away his ridicule, but instead there's nothing but warmth.

'Come on,' he says gently. 'One more try, then we'll switch back and never speak of this again.'

'Promise?' my voice squeaks. It was supposed to be a joke,

but it comes out as a desperate whimper. He smiles and nods emphatically, so I start the engine, and gently depress the clutch again. He guides my hand towards the gearstick with his and our fingers close around the leather, acting carefully as one as we slowly slide the stick all the way into first. He lets go, prompting a sharp intake from me at the now sole power of my hand over this machine. Before I can form a full thought, he reaches to release the handbrake.

All the air in the car shoots into my lungs and my arms lock straight as I brace myself for the inevitable disaster, but nothing comes. We stay still on our small country road, nothing moving but the rain outside our windows.

'Impressive!' Aiden says. 'I didn't master my clutch control until four, maybe five, lessons in.'

'It's probably a fluke. Or the fear,' I say.

'Give yourself some credit. You've done this and you'll do more if I have anything to say about it. Now, shall we move it?'

I want to decline, but the unwavering support in his eyes convinces me that I can and should do otherwise. So instead, I nod and lift my sole *slowly* off the clutch until the car begins to roll forward.

'OK, a bit more on the accelerator.'

'I'm good with this speed,' I say.

He chuckles, shaking his head at my very valid nerves.

'Have you checked said speed?' he asks.

I glance over. Six miles per hour.

'We're crawling,' he says.

'Everyone's got to start somewhere.'

'Move your foot,' he says firmly. 'I promise you that we don't have to go past fifteen.'

We drive up the same country road, round the same bend and back around to the start again as many times as it takes me to feel comfortable and stop making shrill noises every time I have to turn a corner. Eventually his handholding becomes more of a light hover, leaving me to lead us round our empty country route. I'm a pro by the end, swivelling round our circuit with style at an impressive seventeen miles per hour and going up to second gear. That is, however, until we meet our first obstacle, an ignorant and incredibly brave pigeon walking in the road. I gasp as I spot it, panicking as my hands start to swivel and I immediately forget what a brake is. We head straight for a brick wall, but Aiden comes to the rescue, practically leaping from his seat and flinging his arms around me to steer us right back on track.

'Brake!'

I slam my foot on the brake, the two of us lurching forward as the car starts to vibrate uncontrollably.

'Clutch. Maddison, clutch foot down now,' he says, clearly very panicked but still not raising his voice.

He moves the gearstick into neutral and pulls up the handbrake. I turn the key in the ignition, cutting off the engine, and we simultaneously collapse back into our seats as the car comes to a very relieving still. There's a moment of silence, quickly followed by us both launching into fits of hysterical laughter.

'OK, that's enough for one day,' I say in between my fits of giggles.

'Agreed,' he says, his arms still wrapped around me.

And then I glance to my side and see his face, almost touching my own, and it's enough to instantly cut my laughter short. He grows silent as well, processing my own face, and his arms and the lack of distance between us.

'So, what's the verdict?' he asks, voice shaking, but body staying put. 'Would you do this again?'

'With you teaching me? Anytime.'

If I'm not mistaken, I could've sworn that his eyes left mine for a moment to steal a fleeting glance at my lips. My stomach flutters, dips, goes through a loop at the thought of what could possibly be running through his mind. But that just wouldn't make sense. Not for Aiden and certainly not with me.

'You need to stop looking at me like that,' he sighs, making no attempt to look away. 'It's lethal. And really unfair to your man.'

'What man?' I ask instantly, my confusion breaking the spell.

'Benji . . .' he replies. 'Or are you guys not at the label stage yet?'

'Oh . . . yeah.'

In all of the madness behind the wheel, I completely forgot about Benji and the hole he left me with. Forty-eight hours of tears and rock-bottom self-worth eradicated with one twenty-minute driving lesson.

'There's no more Benji,' I say.

It's the first time I've said or typed the words without feeling a pit form in the depths of my gut. It's liberating for me, and apparently for Aiden too. His eyes light up, flicking from happy to mischievous in a heartbeat. My own heart quickens.

'Is that so?' he asks, not even bothering to mask his excitement with some sarcastic comment.

'He ended it on Wednesday.' I watch his reactions carefully. 'I only found out after he blocked me.'

He tuts. 'Coward.' He's happy – it's clear. I hold my breath. 'Why on earth would he do that?'

'The real question is, what are you going to do now there's nothing to stop you?'

I don't know where the words come from, but I feel them in my core. Almost as if they were always there. Aiden wastes no time analysing, closing the final gap and locking his lips perfectly on mine.

Kissing Benji was a process. It took effort and brain power, and made me have to think and try, but kissing Aiden's not like that. Not even close. Kissing Aiden feels like diving. Kissing Aiden feels like home.

We engage in a perfect conversation without words. He moves as I move, his mouth working with grace and passion as it comes together with mine. It requires no thinking, no instruction or verbal communication.

I grip the back of his head, desperate to feel more of him – we're as close as we can physically be, but it's still not enough. I need every part of him pressed up against me, and I know he needs it too with the way his hands are sliding over me. I moan softly into his mouth, giving him all the consent he needs to cup me, first gently and then with far more intention. The butterflies soar in my stomach, their wings flapping triumphantly.

Aiden tries to pull me closer – I try to get there too, but the car's stupid gearstick is in the way. I emit a huff of frustration as I knock it with my knee, which prompts him to chuckle lightly into my mouth. He pulls away, much to my dismay, but my anger dissipates instantly at the sight of his face.

'We are going to be late to Evie's,' he says, punctuating each word with a light kiss.

He's smiling softly at me, looking past my eyes and straight into the depths of my soul. He thinks he's lucky. That *he's* the lucky one because *he* got to kiss *me*.

I sigh, reluctantly crossing my arms. He's staring straight ahead now, preparing to leave the car and switch places, but he can't stop grinning. Neither can I. It's infectious. It's all I want to do.

'Since when have you cared about punctuality?' I tease him, still breathless from the kiss.

He shakes his head fondly. 'What can I say? You're rubbing off on me in more ways than one.'

He lifts my chin with his hand and leans in once again, our lips continuing where they left off. I feel fire course through my body, settling at my core and begging for more.

'Seriously, we do have to go,' he says, thumb tracing my lips as I pout back at him in disappointment. 'Don't make me move you out of my seat.'

'Do it.' I reach out to run a fingertip over his biceps. 'I'm sure you could lift me, easy.'

I can't lie, I've thought about it. I've thought about it more times than I care to admit. I blame Devi and her constant commentary on the size of his arm muscles.

He struggles for a second, the brazenness of my actions almost tempting him past the point of no return. But instead, he resists, which makes me just as proud as it does frustrated. I guess one of us has to be the sensible adult, even if it leaves us both high and dry.

We switch places again and get back on the road towards Evie's, just as we were less than an hour ago. Except this time, his left hand is planted on my knee, creeping further up with every road sign that we pass.

Nudge 28

The Overnight

'After you.'

Aiden grins with pride as he holds open my door, beckoning me out of the car. My heart is still racing, more so when I look him in the eyes, but I try to stay cool. It's too early to show my cards.

'Cute,' I say plainly. 'Probably would have been cuter if you hadn't made me wait here while you ran around to let me out.'

He tuts. 'Whatever happened to "thank you"?'

'Whatever happened to efficiency? We could have both been inside by now.'

I square up to him, standing as tall as I can to at least meet him eye to eye. The fire behind his pupils burns bright, flashing and sizzling before coming down to a deeper, more intense simmer.

'Are you trying to rush me inside?' he asks, pulling me close until we're pressed chest to chest.

I breathe in his scent. Rich and powerful. One more sniff and I'll melt.

'We don't have to . . .' I say, bluffing, my breath heightening.

'Oh, but we do.' He traces the curve of my lips with his eyes. 'It's a crime that we're not already upstairs.'

His head dips down to meet mine, hand cupping my chin as he teasingly hovers millimetres from my face. I close my eyes, waiting for the inevitable brush of our lips. But it doesn't come. Instead, he breaks us apart, snatching our bags from the back seat and leading as I chase him to the house. There's an undeniable spring in his step as he resists all urges to break out into a run. He stops at the front door, looking me up and down with an unbridled lust and a glimmer of concern.

'Are you sure you want to do this?'

I nod, silently gathering the words to tell him just how much I want to do this, but just as I grasp them the door swings open and knocks them clean out of my brain.

'There you are!' Evie says, as we both stare in shock. 'It's getting late – I was worried you'd got lost.'

'Evie!' Aiden says.

It's more of a yelp than a word, but he swallows it down and tries once again. 'I thought your flight was this morning?'

'It got delayed,' she sighs, before beckoning us in. 'They're putting us up in hotel rooms tonight – a pre-trip slumber party. But I thought I'd treat you both to dinner before I headed off.'

She leads us through her grand foyer, down the hall and into her dining room, where her large ornate table is set for three.

'Malia, my nutritionist, hadn't left for the weekend yet, so she agreed to prepare a nice spread for us all,' she says.

I haven't recovered from the whiplash I got when Evie opened that door when her nutritionist emerges from the side door, the decadent platter in her hands making my jaw drop. The smell of the freshly sliced steak hits me before I see it, and when my eyes home in on it, I almost sob with appreciation. It's a charcuterie board. A steak charcuterie board. Sliced steak, fans of cheese, lightly toasted bread slices and grilled vegetables lie among small ceramic bowls of creamy sauces and mashed potatoes.

'You two must be starving – you're so quiet.' Evie pulls up a seat at the head of the table. 'Sit! Eat!'

I catch eyes with Aiden as we both lower into our seats, positioned opposite each other, either side of the table. He smirks knowingly. It sets off the cascade of butterflies and I lower my eyes to the table.

'Are you two OK?' Evie asks, her tone growing concerned.

'Yeah, was just a long drive,' Aiden manages to say, swooping in to our rescue.

'Ah, I see.'

She doesn't buy it, but decides to leave it there, leaning across the table and grabbing some sliced fig. As she leans, she catches my face, pausing to take a closer look at it.

'Maddison, babe, you look really flushed. Is it hot out there?'

I catch sight of myself in one of the twisted metal candlesticks on the table. My reflection is horribly distorted, but clear enough to show wisps of hair escaping the bun I threw my hair into post-kiss, and the light sheen of sweat on my forehead.

Aiden barely stifles his chuckle.

'Very,' I say, trying to drown out his interruption. 'Don't let the rain fool you – it's something else out there.'

'Really? I found it quite chilly.' Aiden leans back in his seat, smirking at the new scowl I send his way. 'You sure you're OK, Maddy?'

I thought we were a team in this, but the gleam in his eye says otherwise.

'Pretty sure,' I say, giving him a pointed look the second Evie redirects her attention to her plate.

He huffs a laugh to himself, smugly spearing a head of asparagus with his fork and maintaining eye contact. Looks like this dinner just became the latest in our series of games.

'Why don't you tell Evie about the drive?' I ask curtly. 'Those country roads were intense.'

I purse my lips and stare at him. He shakes his head back. The night is young and we're just getting started.

We are at each other's throats the rest of the way through dinner, but differently this time. It is teasing, and flirty, and takes place in the intensity between our eyes and the occasional nudge under the table. But as we finish up and wave goodbye to Evie, the reality of the situation starts to set in. Before I know it, I am up the stairs and locked in my room before he's had a chance to say a word.

'You did WHAT?' Kimi screams, managing to shake the room even through the tiny speaker on my phone.

'Quiet!' I whisper. 'But I know. Trust me, I'm just as shocked as you.'

'I'm not shocked,' Devi says, detective face in check. 'With the tension you two have and his arms, it was bound to happen at some point.'

'So, what happens now?' Raina asks, as all three of them wait in silence.

'I don't know! Why do you think I called you?' I say.

'How was the kiss?' Devi asks.

'Unbelievable,' I sigh.

The moment plays on a loop in the back of my head, the mere thought of it sending a shiver through me. It felt like liquid electricity, coursing through my veins, both exhilarating and terrifying.

'What am I doing kissing *Aiden Edwards*? Who do I think I am?' I say.

Kimi frowns. 'Don't do that, babe. *He* is the one who should be so lucky.'

'No, I mean . . . it's Aiden. *Aiden*. It just doesn't make any sense.'

I try to think back to a few months ago – to school – to the nightmares, but they're all tarred over with a burning, irrevocable lust. None of it matters – all I can see is the Aiden here and now. The Aiden whose hands traced my skin delicately like it was made of silk.

My thoughts are jolted by the sound of three taps at my door, each one clear, precise, and intentional.

'Is that a knock?' Kimi asks.

'It's a knock,' I say.

'It's a knock!' Raina squeals. 'It's gotta be him, right?'

'Oh, my God,' Devi gasps.

'Guys, be cool!' I hiss.

'Maddison? You awake?' his voice sounds as he tentatively knocks again.

Kimi screeches in dismay. 'What are you doing sitting there? Use your feet and go get him!'

My body is on autopilot as I rise from the bed, practically floating towards the door and reaching for the handle. He's standing there in grey fleece shorts and a T-shirt, freshly showered and shaven. He smells like cocoa butter, the scent elevated by a slight hint of aftershave he was trying to be subtle about.

'Can I come in?' he asks quietly.

'Yeah, of course.'

I'm trying my best to be cool and it's almost believable, bar the small quiver that comes towards the end of the sentence. I glance over to my phone, girls silently freaking out in my palm, hidden from him behind the white wooden door. I jab once, twice, three times at the red button to end the call, and my phone starts vibrating as messages pour in. I know they're cursing me in the group chat, but I can worry about that later. There are more important things at hand right now.

He strides in slowly as I carefully shut the door behind him. When he reaches the bed, he hesitates – I can see his mind whirring as he debates the best etiquette. Eventually he positions himself lightly on the edge of the bed. A suggestion, with the clear intention of leaping up if he's read it wrong. My heart's back at it again, thumping hard against my chest. I worry it may burst through my ribcage.

'Is that what you sleep in?' he says jokingly, looking me up and down.

I needed advice so badly when I got to my room that I didn't even think about getting ready for bed before calling the girls. I'm still in the jeans and oversized fleece I've been wearing since this morning, while he sits comfortably on my bed and mocks me.

'Haven't had time to change,' I say, still frozen.

'Fair, but how are you still in the fleece?'

Take it off me, I desperately want to say, but the nerves keep me quiet.

'I thought you'd be in bed by now, getting an early night for tomorrow,' he continues, filling the silence.

'And yet you still knocked on my door.'

'Yeah, of course I did. I thought you'd be in bed,' he says slowly.

The full impact of his words hit, sending a shot of heat straight through me. His face has never looked better, even in the dim lamplight of my room. His eyes roam my body with an unbridled desire before he unflinchingly meets my gaze. He wants me, dare I say it, as much as I want him. He's just waiting for me to make the next move.

My legs feel like jelly. I worry that if I move from this spot, I may crumble to the floor under the weight of his gaze, but there's a reassurance and comfort in it that tells me that I can do no wrong. I hate how much I like it. I hate how much I want it. I want him right now more than I've ever wanted anyone.

'You're thinking too hard,' he says, calm as ever. 'Again.'

I raise an eyebrow, which makes him laugh. He looks me up and down with both compassion and a deep, insatiable hunger, each one fighting its hardest to take the top spot.

'What's on your mind?' he asks, his head tilted as he takes me in.

You, and your tongue, and what's under your shorts, and how quickly I can be there too.

'That you need to stop looking at me like that. It's lethal,' I say mockingly.

His smirk curves into a smile, shaking his head at the accuracy of my impression of him in the car. He rises from the bed, moving to stand in front of me before my brain has time to catch up.

'Is that what you want? Me to stop looking at you?'

I shake my head. He wraps his fingers around my wrist.

'Good, because there's so much I have yet to see.'

I feel my back hit the door before I have time to process, my arms above my head, wrists cuffed by his hands. The weight of his body presses against mine as our tongues intertwine, eager and desperate for more. I fight back a groan as one arm keeps me in place and the other one snakes around my waist. He flicks the lock behind me and it clicks reassuringly. It's just us. Alone. In this giant bedroom.

I roll against him, moaning softly as he matches my rhythm and releases my hands. My senses have taken over and I can tell his have too. We are drunk on lust and excitement, and the ridiculous amount of tension that has finally come to a boil. I drag my hands across his body, down his arms, up his incredibly sculpted back, anywhere and everywhere I can touch. His fingers trace patterns up my sides before they slide my zip open, and he swiftly parts our lips to pull the fleece over my head.

'God, you are gorgeous,' he whispers, looking me up and down.

I can't help but squeal with delight as he lifts me off my feet and carries me over to the bed.

'You have no idea how long I've wanted to do this,' he says, positioning himself on top of me.

But I do have an idea, because I've been right there too, desperately trying to convince myself I didn't want this.

'All those late nights, that cramped meeting room, your endless notetaking and those *jeans*.' He lists each item frustratedly, punctuating it with kisses. 'And that video of you dancing . . . God, you have made this so hard.'

His mouth moves to my neck, the sensation of each kiss shooting volts of electricity from my head to my toes. Our eyes meet, both of us smiling as his hand reaches for the zipper of my jeans before quickly rolling them down to my ankles and chucking them across the floor. He adorns my legs with kisses on the way back up, before hovering at the top of my inner thigh. One lick and I feel my whole body set alight.

'Come here,' I whisper, keeping my eyes trained on him as he comes back up to join me, kissing his way up my body as he does.

I grab his head with both hands as our mouths meet again, this time far more forcefully. It knocks all the air from my lungs and makes my pupils glaze over. He watches it happen and grins widely. I'm under his spell.

He pulls back momentarily, taking a foil wrapper from his pocket and giving me a small, questioning look before tearing it open.

I raise an eyebrow. 'You came prepared.'

He looks bashful for a moment, eyes briefly dropping. 'I thought I'd put these on my just-in-case list.'

'Your "just-in-case list"?'

'I categorised my packing list.'

'That is the hottest thing you could have possibly said.'

It's all the approval he needs to power forward. His shorts fly across the room as he gets himself ready, kneeling over me with glee. Even from this angle, every inch of him is irresistible. It would be annoying if it weren't such a turn-on. He uses one hand for balance, the other to spread my thighs apart in one swift yet assertive play of dominance.

I'm a lost cause from the very first thrust, the feel of him making me whimper underneath my breath, but the little noises ignite something in him, spurring him on further as he works his magic. And it sure is magic. I can feel his hand caress me as it slides down my side, tracing over my hips before leading into my thigh. I scratch my nails down his back and suddenly I'm not the only one moaning – the vibration tingling my lips as we continue to kiss. He looks like a Greek statue, jaw clenched as he focuses on me, abs rippling in the golden lamp light.

His eyebrows shoot up as I roll us over, move his hands to my outer thighs and settle on him comfortably. His eyes devour my new angle from top to bottom as I sit straight and let him take all of me in. There's no part of me worried about stomach rolls or small boobs or the potential double chin. In this moment, I want nothing more than for him to see all of me for who I am.

We both gasp in tandem as I roll my hips for the first time. Our eyes lock as I continue, an invisible string between us making us move as one, thrust as one and soon, finish as one. I don't even have to tell him when I'm close, he reads it in my eyes and thrusts harder, gripping me tightly. With one final kiss, I keel over onto him, my whole body growing weak as tremors ripple through me from head to toe. He hugs me close, his moans and gasps sounding in my ear as I feel him erupt inside me.

'That was . . .'

'I know,' he says, still trying to catch his breath.

He wraps his arms around me, scooping me off him and onto the bed, before enveloping me from behind. I'm safe in his hold. Trapped in a blanket of his warmth as he slowly traces patterns on my arms.

It's silent for a moment. My mind whirrs as I start to process what we've just done, what he's just said, what we've both been *waiting* for.

'I meant what I said, you know,' he murmurs into my ear. 'I've wanted to do that for a very, very long time.'

'I know. Me too.' I bring his arms closer in.

'So, what's stopped us? Stupidity?' he asks before yawning.

He nuzzles my neck as he does. It's subconscious. On instinct.

I scoff. 'Stupidity? Maybe you, but could never be me . . .' I smile with pride as he laughs heartily in response.

'I'm serious, Maddy. This is *something*. Something we should have done so many years ago.'

His voice is deep and stern. The mood shifting as the patterns stop swirling and he grips on to me tighter.

'Didn't you ever think about us?' he asks.

The butterflies are different now. Elation surpassed by trepidation. This is brand-new territory, with far shakier ground. So much further to fall, even with the smallest misstep.

'I think about you.' His voice slurs slightly, drowsiness taking over as his arms grow heavier around me. 'I've always thought about you and how much I regret not telling you that night . . .'

His words fade into a deep, unconscious sigh. I sigh too, with relief, as my stomach starts to steady. The words play in my mind as I drift off to sleep, my stomach skipping on the same loop.

Nudge 29

The Safe Space

I wake up the next morning and reach over to feel an empty space where Aiden lay the night before. My heart stills, breath catching as I rub it again just to check, as if his body will suddenly materialise out of thin air.

It wasn't a dream, it couldn't be.

Although a dream would be better than a reality where he woke up and left in regret. I turn over and hear a crackle. A small page from his journal lies on the pillow beside me.

This is what they do in the movies right? To let you know it wasn't a dream?

Breakfast downstairs when you're ready xx

I rush to shower, brush my teeth and begin to rummage through my bag. If I knew how this weekend would go, I would have packed way cuter clothes. And maybe that bra I have that actually makes me look like I have cleavage. But, unfortunately, I'm stuck with the result of a last-minute, tear-filled, broken-hearted rampage through my room. It's nothing but sweats, baggy jumpers, and old ratty leggings, the complete antithesis of effortlessly sexy.

As I stroll down the stairs, clad in tiny sweat shorts and an oversized off-the-shoulder sweatshirt from my uni days, I can see him clanging about in the kitchen, spatula doubling as a microphone as he sings along to his playlist.

There's a deep warmth to his smile as he catches me watching him from the door. He beckons me over, eyes following my every step towards him.

'What you making?' I ask, immediately inspecting his work.

A chocolate-chip pancake sizzles quietly in the pan, the bowl of mixture next to it on the counter.

'There's more in the oven. Here.' He reaches under the stove, emerging with a stack ready to go. 'I didn't know what time you'd be up, so I had to keep them warm.'

'You cook?' I ask.

'I'm a man of many talents,' he says. 'There were a few years where my sister refused to eat anything that wasn't accompanied by a stack of pancakes. I've perfected the recipe.'

He spins around again, this time grabbing a tray and sliding a myriad of toppings my way. I immediately reach for the whipped cream and chocolate sauce, pile them high and shovel bite after bite into my mouth without chewing. They are perfect.

We polish off the pancakes within minutes, stealing quick, smiling glances at each other as we eagerly make our way through our plates. Then, as soon as we finish, he marches over to me, scooping his hand around my waist and pulling me in for a long morning kiss.

I wrap my arms round his neck, leaning into him so far that

my heels leave the floor and he takes on my weight. His hands run down my hips and round my back, grabbing hold of my bum and giving each cheek a firm squeeze before lifting me in the air. It was hot the first time and it's hotter the second. I never knew I had a need to be lifted like this, but now I can never go back.

I follow his lead, instantly wrapping my legs around his waist as he effortlessly places me on the kitchen counter, making sure that our lips don't part, not even for a moment. His right hand moves from my back, fingers creeping slowly up my inner thigh before sliding their way under my flimsy excuse for shorts. They toy at the band of my underwear, pausing cruelly as they await my small but desperate plea for more. I glare at him impatiently. He chuckles lightly, the sound bouncing off the tiles and filling the kitchen with his mischievous joy. I can see his mind whirring – he's debating leaving it even longer – but one glance at my pouting face and he knows I'll combust if he does.

His fingers dip beneath my waistband, lightly teasing before travelling further down as he kisses my neck. He starts with one finger, stroking gently and listening out for my reactions before upping it to two and increasing his speed. He has rendered me speechless. It's so good I can barely think straight as his mouth travels further and further down my body.

'Wait,' I pant, sense quickly snapping me back to life.

He freezes, eyes full of concern.

'Doesn't Evie have cameras?'

He breathes a shaky, relieved sigh. 'Not in here. I know the blind spots. I've added them all to the tour.'

He raises an eyebrow, silently asking if he can continue. I nod and he jumps back to work, leaving a trail of kisses across my stomach and down my outer thigh before working his way up my inner.

I close my eyes and give in to the feeling of his mouth on my skin, climbing its way up to where I need it most . . . But then it stops.

My eyes open instantly as I stare down at him, the spots on my thigh starting to grow cold. He pays me no mind, pulling my shorts and pants off in one fluid motion.

'Hey, Maddison.' He is looking up at me with a smile that sends that fire rushing through me. 'Tell me which letter I'm drawing.'

Then I finally feel his tongue press against me, and we make our way through less than half of the alphabet before he has me quivering helplessly on the countertop. As he re-emerges and comes up to eye-level again, I can't help but roll my eyes at the all-too-pleased grin on his face.

'I will get you back. I was promised a tour of all blind spots, remember?' I threaten.

'Of course, I remember. And you're welcome,' he says smugly.

Once I recover, he shows me around Evie's illustrious grounds, takes notes, and presents me with the most beautifully annotated map I've ever seen in my life.

'I drew it up back when Evie first told us this was happening,' he says, shrugging as he hands over my copy. 'There's a key and some codes, and everything is to scale. I've also mocked up where I think the rides and stalls should go, but I printed those onto reusable stickers so we can rearrange them how we want before finalising.'

It is the sexiest thing I've ever heard a person say, and I jump on him before he even has a chance to put the map down.

Eventually I suggest lunch, offering to sort it since he made us such a delicious breakfast, but he shakes his head and whisks me down to the bottom of the garden, unlocking the door to Evie's greenhouse.

I recognise it from a lot of her spring and summer content, but that can't even begin to compare to the site in real life. Vines weave their way up the walls and slope across each side of the slanted glass roof. They perfectly frame the room, meeting in the centre above the wide, marble table adorned with woven wicker décor. Behind the table, on the back wall, sits a man-made waterfall, with large rocks built to cascade into a small pool. Aiden shuts the door behind us, blocking out the outside and leaving us with the trickling noise of the flowing water. It's a refreshing change to the modern, sculpted grounds; a tranquil oasis among the hustle and bustle.

He leads me over to the table and I realise the decoration is a picnic basket, two glasses and a bottle of wine.

I squeal, dropping his hand in astonishment. 'When did you have time to do this? I've been with you all day!'

'I packed the basket this morning and brought it down while the pancake mix was resting.'

He brushes it off like it's nothing. He doesn't even notice I've frozen in shock and he cracks open the bottle, pouring the wine into two wide yet delicate glasses.

'You look like you're buffering,' he says, finally looking up and laughing at the stunned expression on my face.

He pulls me to him, kissing the shock away as I melt into his hold.

'That's better,' he whispers, guiding me towards the table and proudly pulling out my chair.

He unpacks the basket to reveal two hefty-looking sandwiches, chocolate bars and three packs of ready salted crisps.

'I had to make do with what Evie had in,' he says, divvying it up. 'You get two packs of crisps because you always eat one straight after the other.'

'I do not!' I say.

'Yes, you do.' He slides my portion over to me. 'It's cute.'

How he made a *sandwich* – arguably one of the most boring of foods – so unbelievably delicious, I do not know. It's rich with mustard, salamis, olives, onions and more – layered, decadent and all for me.

'I'd like to raise a toast,' he says, leaning across the table to top up my glass.

I lift it halfway in the air in anticipation, eyebrow cocked as I await his next words.

'To us,' he continues with a small smile. 'To the Summer Splash, to this weekend, and to last night. *Especially* to last night – I mean – that deserves its own toast. But if I start . . . well, I'll be here all day. So, to us, I guess – to everything to do with us. God . . . You make me so bad with words.'

His eyes leave mine only to dart around frantically, dropping and lifting in time with his fragmented sentences. His nerves overcome him, spilling out and turning his words into small little murmurs. It's so cute and tender, and deeply unlike him, and I can't help but stare as I take every morsel of this new Aiden in.

'You've never been bad at *anything* – trust me, I have waited for you to be bad at something.' I laugh softly. 'You've been great at everything since the day that we met, and every day after.'

His lips twist back into a smile, eyes returning to mine. The warmth in them sets my heart on fire.

'You think I'm great at *everything*?' he asks smugly.

'I'm not saying it again.'

He chuckles. I smile. My heart flutters.

'You were wrong about me before, you know. I don't just float through life expecting things to work out. I just don't need to track it across seven notebooks.'

He softens the last part with a good-spirited eyebrow raise and a refill of my glass.

'Oh, really, so what are your goals, aims, objectives, then?' I ask, eyebrow raised in jest.

I expect him to shut it down, keep it a secret, but he doesn't. Instead, he springs to life, babbling on eagerly.

'I want to start my own business. Build something from the ground up, like Evie. I mean, obviously not like Evie's. I have an idea, but ...' He tails off. 'I just want to do something that leaves my family with a legacy and keeps my mum and sister sorted for the rest of their lives. I have the plan – pages of it, ready to go. I just need to make the jump.'

'What is it?'

He launches into a well-constructed, clearly deeply thought-out plan for a non-profit carpool/shuttle-bus service for parents whose children need lifts to and from activities. He glows as he talks about it, radiating a passion so deep it burns a hole through the floor. I feel it shine on me too, as hot as rays from the sun.

'It sounds like you've got it all worked out. Have you started working on it?' I ask.

'It's not the right time,' he says, stalling.

'Why not?' I ask. 'For someone who insists I dive right in, you're being awfully wade-y.'

His laugh starts light, but sinks quickly into a bitter chuckle, twisting his smile into something far more introspective.

He sighs. 'Every time I get close to taking the leap, I think about all that money, and how I might need it if something happens to my mum again.' His eyes drop straight to the table, only taking a break to steal quick glances at my still, timid face.

I think back to my house, our Teams call, and my mum's question.

'How's your mum? How was her surgery?'

I didn't ask back then because it wasn't my place. We weren't friends, were barely colleagues, and I had no right to know. But now, as we sit here, after the night we just had, something has shifted. It's new ground – shaky ground – and I don't know how even it is. But I've got to try. He's given me an in – I've got to take it.

'Again?' I ask, hoping he understands that I can't manage more.

He does. 'My mum had a heart attack, which, erm, led to some pretty bad complications.' He takes a gulp of his wine, hand shaking ever so slightly. It's hard to tell whether the shake is from rage, sadness or both. 'I got a call mid-seminar, booked a last-minute train ticket and was by her hospital bedside by lunch. It was rough. Really rough. "Say your goodbyes" rough.'

There's a pinch in his throat through the last few words, so tight that he's forced to break for air. I want to squeeze him, ease the pain away and promise that he'll be OK, but it feels far too intrusive. Instead, I settle for a palm, stretched across the table. He grabs it instantly, exhaling deeply as he squeezes it tight, and I trace soothing shapes across his skin with the pad of my thumb.

'I felt like my world was going to end that day. Nothing mattered. Not school, not friends, not even Luce.'

I shift uncomfortably, but he doesn't seem to notice.

'All I could think of was my mum, and our house and my little sister, and what would happen if . . .' He trails off. 'I wasn't ready to be her guardian and I'd never really thought about my future, but suddenly it was there. I panicked. Hard. Ended up slumped on the waiting-room floor, trying to figure out why I suddenly couldn't breathe.'

'I've been there,' I whisper, recalling that day in the boardroom.

'Yeah, I know,' he says softly, 'A nurse taught me that soothing technique, actually. I'm glad I was able to pay it forward.'

'Yeah, me too,' I say, mirroring his shaky but gentle smile. 'So, what happened next?'

He swallows his smile instantly, face contorting back into that of a scared little boy. It's so quick that it can only be muscle memory. He's back in the room. Back reliving the worst day of his life.

'She spent the next three, four months in and out of hospital. My dad's not around, she can't drive, and my sister was thirteen at the time, so I applied for extenuating circumstances and did the rest of the year from home.'

'That's a lot.'

It's not nearly enough of a response, but I can't help it – he's stunned me. All these years and I had no idea.

'Yeah, it was.' He sighs, voice laced with resentment. 'I can't lie – it fucked me up for a while. I couldn't focus, couldn't think of anything but my mum, and her heart, and how we were gonna survive. I don't think I slept for more than three hours at a time that next year. And I sure as hell didn't talk to anyone for three months straight.'

'So, your friends . . . ?'

'Didn't know. A lot of them still don't, to be fair. They've never been the best when it comes to the serious stuff. But Lucy knew. She didn't get it, and she *hated* how miserable the whole thing made me. If I wasn't with my family, I was busy arguing on the phone with her. In fact, the only time I left my mum's side during it all was a couple months in, when she forced me to visit her . . .'

'During May Madness,' I say.

'Yeah ...' For a second, he looks back at me confused, before completing the puzzle for himself and snapping to life.

'Oh, shit. I'm really sorry, I didn't ...'

'Not right now,' I say, trying to brush it back under the carpet.

I thought I was ready to talk about it with him, but right now I can't think of anything worse. Not after last night. Not after this greenhouse.

He shakes his head, searching deep into my eyes and forgetting about his troubles as he narrows in on mine. I can read his face without him speaking.

'Maddison,' he says.

'I am over it, no point dwelling on it.' I shrug, reaching for my glass and draining the contents. 'How's everything with your mum now?'

He pauses before continuing, less than happy but willing to concede. 'Really good. We're all good. Mum had open-heart surgery at the start of this year. It was scary as hell, but she's been thriving ever since. And Sara's smashing it, obviously – she takes after her brother. Studying medicine at uni, wants to be a heart surgeon one day.'

I can see a small smile return as he immediately untenses.

'That's really lovely,' I say, my smile growing too.

'Yeah. She's my everything. They're my everything,' he says. 'And I will do everything in my power to make sure they're always secure. It's why, I don't know, sometimes I think maybe the business thing should just stay a pipe dream. I've got a secure thing here with Evie, and she's finally starting to see my potential and consider me for promotions. I reckon I'd make a pretty good manager someday.'

'You are a manager though – a talent manager is still technically a manager,' I say.

He pauses.

'Honestly, that's just Evie-speak for personal assistant. It's a fancy title with no actual responsibility,' he says. 'In all my years with her, I've been waiting for a chance to show I'm worth more – that I can do more than just take her notes and run errands. So, when I got the Summer Splash . . .'

'You knew it was your chance to prove yourself.'

'Exactly,' he says.

It's like hearing my own diary parroted back to me. All the arguments and eye rolls and refusals to back out weren't because he didn't care, but rather because he *did*. He cared just as much as I did the entire time. He just had a different way of showing it.

'And you almost gave it up.' I search his eyes for an answer.

He shrugs into himself, clearly desperate to look away and drop it. But he doesn't. He stays firm and continues to match my stare, his eyes glazed over with a wordless apology.

'I was making you miserable and I knew how badly you wanted it too. I didn't want to be the thing standing in front of your dream,' he says. 'But then she was so proud of our presentation, and my mood-board idea, and it was my first taste of seeing just how much I could do this. I didn't think it would cause the reaction it did though – sorry. I genuinely am so sorry about that.'

'I've told you already – the panic attack wasn't about you.'

'I know that now.' He squeezes my hand tighter. 'But at the time, I felt like I was ruining your life and I spent all weekend stressing about it. Maddison, please look at me when I say this. I never want to be the thing that makes you upset again.'

My eyes drop to the table, briefly overwhelmed by the beauty of this place, our conversation, and the warmth of his hand as it cradles mine, but even as I look down, I feel his eyes before I see them, burrowing into me with a stern but kind gaze. The sheer force of it makes me dizzy – alcohol be damned. I don't think I will ever get used to the way he looks at me.

'I brought you here, to this greenhouse, because I wanted you to see my favourite part of this place.' He rises to his feet and beckons me to follow as he begins to conduct a mini tour. 'It's way out of bounds for any of her guests, so I can usually escape when the people or her parties get too much. I tell her I need to go get more napkins . . .'

He stops at an old chest nestled in the corner and opens it to reveal endless stacks of napkins.

'Genius,' I say, nodding at the display. 'But I can't imagine you of all people needing to escape a party.'

Back at Winterdown, the words 'Aiden Edwards' and 'party' were synonymous. He was the life of each one and they could not happen without him. I'd come in on a Monday to endless retellings of Aiden's exploits at yet another party I didn't go to.

'I like my alone time too, I'm just not snooty about it,' he says teasingly, arm coming in for a playful pat.

I catch it on its way in, gripping his fist in my palm and staring back at his shocked little face.

'Impressive,' he says.

'Thank you.' I smile smugly. 'And thank you for bringing me here. For sharing your secret escape with me.'

I drop his hand and make my own way around the space, ducking under low vines and twisting my way around the plants. It's like something out of a movie – a magical land of mystery, a world apart from whatever lies in wait outside. He watches me as

I wander through the foliage, sniffing flowers and stroking leaves on my way. I turn around quickly, attempting to catch him in the act, but he owns his stare proudly, sauntering over and grabbing my hand in his. We face each other, me looking up as he looks down, some magnetic force pulling us close. I feel my lips part, teeth flashing to mirror his as best as I can. It's not the same, though. *His* smile makes my heart shoot through my chest.

'I was kind of thinking that, maybe this time around, we could consider this *our* escape?' He shrugs. 'You know, a safe space that we could both run to if the Summer Splash gets too much.'

His hand shakes in my palm as he says it, eyes suddenly glued to the floor. He's nervous – shy to share his place with someone else. I drop his hand, reaching for his chin and bringing it closer.

'Will there be a picnic every time?' I joke to ease the tension.

His jaw unclenches immediately, whole body relaxing as he shifts back into his naturally cool state.

'If that's what it takes, then so be it.' He laughs with me before pulling me in for a triumphant kiss.

Nudge 30

The Promise

'Is that mine?'

'What?'

With the day nearly over, it's time to pack up our stuff so we can head out first thing in the morning. I hoped he wouldn't notice the new addition to my wardrobe, but now that he's packed and ready to join me for bed, he's already spotted it. It's my own fault, I suppose. I lost any advantage of being sneaky the second I insisted that we spend the night in my room.

'Don't play dumb, Maddy.'

'Me? Dumb? We both know that's impossi—' An ear-piercing screech leaves my mouth as he lifts me into the air, twirls me around and lands me very effectively out of the way of my duffle.

'Yep, just as I suspected.' He removes the oversized sweatshirt from my bag.

'I've worn it all evening! Reason dictates it's mine now.' I march back over to him and reach for it, ready to snatch, but he is far too quick, stretching his arm above his head. I jump over and over again as he jerks backwards with a smile on his face.

'You done yet?' he asks, far too proud of himself.

'Aiden, that's discriminatory. You can't use my height against me,' I say, pouting.

'I thought you were "only a few inches shorter than me"?'

'I am. But you have freakishly long arms,' I retort, jumping again.

His fake-fight face crumbles instantly, revealing a melting pot of joy underneath. He attempts to keep his mouth straight – fight back against the creeping smile – but he can't help it, try as he might. I bring it out of him and I take pride in the fact that there's nothing he can do about it.

'That was mean, Maddy.'

'I said what I said,' I say, standing tall as I attempt to square up to him.

It's no use. Both of us are too elated to even try to fake mad after the weekend we've had.

'Well, these freakishly long arms do come in handy ...' He hooks the other one around my waist and pulls me in until we're chest to chest.

The closer I get to him, the more his scent overwhelms my senses and makes me absolutely feral. I throw my arms around his neck, bringing him down towards me until our noses brush against each other.

'That's better,' I sigh, lips brushing his teasingly as I speak.

He dips even closer. 'Was this your plan all along? Get me close enough to kiss again?'

'Oh, I wanted you close,' I say, thumb stroking the back of his neck. 'Close enough for this.'

I break us apart, ripping the sweatshirt from his newly relaxed arm as I go, and make an overly dramatic beeline for the bed. He lunges but I'm too scrappy, swerving under his arms to roll across the duvet and make my final play, triumphantly placing the shirt back in its rightful place in my bag. I sigh contentedly as I finish, lightly tucking it in and smoothing over the creases before zipping the bag up for good.

'That was low.' Aiden wanders over to the bed. 'You are only supposed to use your sexual prowess for good.'

'That *was* good. I had fun and I got my top back.'

'You are unbelievable,' he says, a wide grin on his face.

His hands reach for my shoulders, pushing against them until I lie flat on my back against the silky duvet. His eyes have darkened, the pools of hunger growing clearer and clearer as he climbs on top of me and pins my hands above my head. I tilt my chin up, lips pursed as I move towards his, but then he swerves. Pulls back as I let out a small whimper.

'You tease me, I will tease you right back,' he says, an all-too-smug smirk on his face.

'Aiden.' I don't have it in me to say anything else. But it doesn't deter him. He keeps his grip on my wrists tight, peppering teasing kisses down my neck and across my collarbone.

'What's wrong, Maddy?' he asks.

He adjusts his hands to secure my wrists together with one and uses the other to tug lightly at the hem of my shorts. They drop to the floor, his fingers returning to trace unbearably teasing patterns over the thin fabric that's left. He delights in my stilted breaths, glancing up at me to fully take them in, his fingers still steadily taunting me over the lace of my underwear.

I huff. 'This is cruel and unusual punishment.'

'Really? You don't sound like you're being punished,' he says teasingly.

He punctuates his sentence with a far more heavy-handed stroke, his finger quickly dipping beneath the fabric. I try to bite back a moan, but it seeps through, making his ears prick with glee.

'Consider this payback for the sweatshirt I'm letting you keep.'

'You're letting me keep it because I rightfully won,' I say breathlessly.

He presses harder, my body jolting at the sensation as he brings his mouth to my ear. 'How does that win feel right now?' he asks, the whisper sending shocks through me.

He gives my lobe a light bite for good measure, dragging his teeth across it before kissing his way down my body unbearably slowly. I wrestle against his hold, but there's absolutely no use. The strength of his singular single hand is too much for me while I'm in this kind of state.

'Aiden, I swear, if you don't . . .' I gasp as the vibrations from his chuckles send shockwaves through my body.

'You are in no position to be making demands right now, Maddy.' He runs his hand back up my body, coming in for a kiss.

It's a peck. Barely there, rubbing more salt in the wound and bringing him far too much joy as he pulls away. He looks down fondly at my disgruntled face, brushing a stray hair from my forehead.

'Have I ever told you how cute you look when you're mad? It's adorable.' His finger traces the same endless circle around my nipple, unbearably light to the touch. 'See, that face – that face you're pulling right now – all scrunched-up and stressed? Very hot.'

He moves his fingers the second I open my mouth, turning what would have been a perfectly biting response into an uncontrollable moan. There's no point in fighting; he's got me right in the palm of his hand and he knows it just as much as I do.

He scoops me up into his arms the second we're done and we lie there in silence, sweaty and tangled in each other. I want to say I could get used to this, but I don't think that could possibly be true. This isn't something you acclimatise to, this is not something that will ever stop being earth-shatteringly delicious.

I hug his arm closer to my chest as he follows suit and squeezes me tight. It's different to before. Not as soft or carefree. He's holding me like he's scared I'll escape if he doesn't.

'What are you thinking about?' I ask, tracing patterns on his skin.

'Huh?' he asks, breaking out of his daze.

His tone's sleepy, slower and feigning an air of confusion, but I don't buy it. I roll over, parting from his hold to come face to face with his features, shining even through the darkness.

'Tell me.'

The command is soft enough to not push him too far but firm enough for him to know I won't give up. And he knows. It's clear by the worried gulp that follows as he casts his eyes away from my face.

'It's all good.' He lies terribly.

'Aiden.'

'Maddy,' he says, eyes glinting in the dark as they return to meet mine.

The worry in them is enough to make my heart still, setting off alarm bells in my head. I look away. I try not to, but I can't help myself. Something doesn't feel right. He doesn't feel right.

'Look, if you've changed your mind ... If you regret this at all, I'm cool with that. It was probably stupid anyway. I mean, I know who we are and I know that we're different and ...'

The words slow as they battle with the lump forming in my

throat. I can't look him in the eye, or the face, or anything for that matter. I stare down at the mattress in between us, the gap bigger from the space I seem to have created.

'Maddison. That's not it at all. I was thinking about you, and ... *this*, yes, but not like that. I just ...' He pauses. 'I know that you don't want to, but I think we should talk about May Madness.'

My heart sinks further, this time for a different reason. A stronger reason. The kind of reason that I can't bear to relive.

'No,' I whisper.

'Maddison, we need to at least—'

'It happened; you apologised back at the pub; I think we've done all we need to do ...'

He grabs my arms with his hands, steadying what I thought were my well-hidden shakes. I can tell by the look on his face they weren't hidden well, or at all. Before I can stop it, the moment plays, cut for cut, in my head. As vivid as the treacherous day that it happened.

I was understandably shocked when he walked into the cramped kitchen of whatever house that day's party was in, having not seen him since school. I watched him stroll across the room, his preoccupied, pinched expression dissolving into something else entirely the second he saw me. In my evolved, newfound confidence I struck up conversation and found we actually had a lot to talk about. We got into heated debate over the best *New Girl* character and exchanged notes on how uni compared to sixth form. We ended up standing in the corner talking each other's ears off for most of the night. In fact, there were several moments where anyone watching might have mistaken us for old friends. That was, until Lucy showed up.

I smiled at her, thinking she would come and join us, but her mouth snapped closed the second I did, eyes looking over me from head to toe. I can still feel the breath I held as her eyeballs took in every pore and every bump. She let no curl go unturned, making sure to hover scathingly at the fat on my noticeably bare lower thighs. In the seven months we'd been neighbours, I'd never seen her like this. She hadn't looked at me like that since we were at school.

'I can't believe she is still following you around!' Her lip curled with each word, delight ripe across her features. 'God, Maddison, you were always such a piece of work. Drove Aiden here up the walls – he could never stop going on about how irritating you were.'

I looked to him for back up – confirmation that she was wrong. He bowed his head, silent for the first time all night.

'What do you think, Aiden? Does she seem any different?' she asked, her voice loud enough to capture the attention of everyone within earshot. 'I mean … She dresses different. I wouldn't say better, but *different.*'

The comment set off a chain of sniggers behind her as people listening whispered callously to each other. Suddenly the playsuit the FGA had hyped up earlier over FaceTime felt stupid and ugly and so obviously not me. I folded my arms across my chest, shrinking into the lack of material and praying that I could be literally anywhere else. I tried not to show fear. Even then, I knew that was the worst thing I could do. Plus, my flatmates were watching, and I was barely cool enough for them as it was. The last thing I needed was to crumble in front of a campus It Girl. But before I could stop it, the alcohol soured in my stomach and bile rose up in my throat. I couldn't help it – I spun around and instantly threw up into the sink behind me.

'Luce, we should go,' Aiden whispered, tugging at her arm as I retched.

She sneered. 'You're right, we are wasting our time. Bye, Maddison. I'm sure I won't be seeing you around campus.'

I watched as Aiden turned on his heel and left my already shaky reputation in tatters on the floor. He didn't even care. Why would he? He clearly hated me. Lucy had pretty much made sure that everyone at that party did too.

I spent the last semester in turmoil, barely leaving my room unless it was to attend a seminar. Any assignments not pre-written suffered badly and I submitted one a week after the deadline, which sank my overall grade so low I considered retaking the year.

I'm broken from the memory as Aiden scoops his hand under my chin to pull me eye to eye with him once again. I catch my breath the second he makes contact, tremors of worry stilling in their place. They can't move – I can't move.

'What Lucy said that day ... the way she said it wasn't true.'

Her words echo in my head as if she were right here saying them.

'God, Maddison, you were always such a piece of work. Drove Aiden here up the walls – he could never stop going on about how irritating you were.'

His arm swings around me, pulling me close until my head rests on his bare chest.

'I called her out on it after we left. We argued for *hours*. Broke up for like three or four days after that.'

'That couldn't have been easy ... arguing over some random girl from school,' I murmur.

He was so warm, so open when he stared at me that night. I would have never pictured their evening ending that way.

'Oh, you weren't random.' He chuckles, pillow rustling as he shakes his head. 'That's the one thing she said that *was* true – I could never stop going on about you. I think she could tell, even back then, that I was a little *too* preoccupied. That's my bad. It wasn't fair to her and it certainly wasn't fair in the way it got taken out on you.'

I scoff. 'You weren't preoccupied with me.'

'Maddison. Even back then, you consumed most of my waking thoughts.'

He's so resolute. Nothing hidden, nothing left behind. It's as scary as it is exciting, and I can feel my heart triple in speed.

'I just need you to know how sorry I am,' he continues, his arms tightening their hold. 'I would never let anyone make you feel like that again. You'll always know exactly where you stand with me. I can promise you that.'

'I believe you,' I whisper.

And I do, wholeheartedly. The man across from me would never let anything hurt me. I can tell by his gaze, by his hold, by the way he speaks. I'm safe with him. He's safe with me. No matter what's in our past.

I turn back around and he cradles me, softly resting his chin on the top of my head. I'm encased in his arms, back pressed firmly against his chest. He's got me, now and for ever. At least, that's what I can't help but hope.

Nudge 31

The Group Chat

'**G**ood morning.'

His lips brush against my skin as he whispers into my ear, voice gravelly from our lie-in. Then he turns to face me, his tongue eagerly exploring my mouth.

'Good morning to you too,' I whisper in between kisses.

He laughs softly into my mouth, teeth grazing my lower lip. The small nip drives me wild. I grab on to him tighter, clawing at his arms as our kisses grow deeper and deeper.

'We need to stop.' His lip curls as he eyes my frustrated face. 'If we keep this up, we are never leaving this place. We've still got to tidy up and get you home.'

He punctuates his warning with a teasing tap on my nose, which is scrunched in a very forced anger as I scowl back at him. I want to mean it, but I'm too damn happy to give off anything that looks mildly believable.

'One more hour,' I say in protest, stroking down his arm.

'And mess up your Sunday routine? Never.'

'I don't have a Sunday routine!'

He scoffs. 'Liar.'

'I haven't since you dared me not to.'

'Well, I do.' He jumps out of bed. 'And *you* dared me to stick to it. So, we need to go!'

I don't know what's worse – how determined he is to stay organised or just how sexy I seem to find it. I have no energy left to be mad at the cold space between us, I'm too busy resisting the urge to jump on him again. I need to cool down – it's ridiculous. I'm like a cat in heat. One look at him and I lose every ounce of sense I have.

'You OK?' he asks, smirking far too much for my liking.

'Mmhmm.' It's not remotely believable.

'Sure … Well, I'm gonna shower. You coming?' he asks, hand reaching down to the bed.

'I fear for our time management if I do,' I sulk, slapping his hand away.

He laughs wholeheartedly and leans in for one last kiss before heading to my ensuite.

I lie flat on my back, my hair bonnet rustling against the silk pillow as I replay the events of the weekend in my head. They burn in vivid colour, as rich and vibrant as they were when they happened, drowning out the water that runs faintly in the distance. Me and Aiden. Aiden and me. It's something I never dared dream of and somehow everything I've ever needed.

It feels too much like a dream – something that could only exist between Evie's tall walls. My heart murmurs slightly, in time with the thought of what happens when we leave – when the bubble bursts and we're back to who we were before we got here.

Will he still like me?

My stomach drops. The thought grows with each passing second.

You're being stupid. It's been five minutes.

I try to shake it off, but it's no use. The pit in my stomach is too deep and there's only one cure for it, or rather three cures waiting for me in our group chat.

I reach across the bed for my phone, stretching as far as I can without moving. It feels foreign in my hand, the way I've ignored it for the past few days. But it's time to get back to business and soft launch reality, if you will. I need a second, third and fourth opinion before my head explodes on this expensive bedding.

I squint as it turns on, the lock screen aggressively shining back at me as I wait for my eyes to adjust. The wallpaper flashes to reveal a smiling girl, dressed in a full leotard and holding a trophy. It's not my phone. A message lights up the screen, causing the previously stacked ones to unfurl. I drop it immediately, but not before I catch my name, multiple times.

I shouldn't. I know that. It's not good for me. Not good for us and whatever this is.

I trust him.

I don't know him.

I need to know what it says.

The shower's still running, the water echoing across the bathroom's marble walls and mingling with whatever joyful tune he's humming. He's not leaving any time soon and I don't plan to have a full look, just a peek to set my mind at ease.

It's probably nothing.

I shouldn't do it.

But what if it's not?

I can't start whatever this is on a foundation of distrust!

Fuck it. It is definitely better to know. It'll be nothing, and I'll feel stupid and will never need to look again.

I trust the gnaw in my gut and the shake in my hands. They wouldn't do this over nothing. With one final glance at the bathroom door, I take a breath, reach out my hand and bring the screen closer.

> Maddison Clarke? This has to be a joke …
>
> Not Moany Maddy?!
>
> Thought u were just tryna steal her job lol
>
> Not a single girl in years and now HER? Bro …
>
> Nah u can't go from Lucy to that, come on …
>
> You dog!

They go on and on, back and forth with each other longer than I can stand. It's too much, too real. The same boys from school saying the same things they said every day for years of my life.

I can feel my heart slow, blood running colder as I let the phone fall back onto the mattress where I should have left it.

'It's all yours!' Aiden practically sings as he strides through the room. His stupidly wide grin shrinks the second it takes in my now sunken frame. 'Wait, what's wrong?'

He rushes over to grab my face, his eyes laced with worry. He checks my temperature, and then my body for any signs of injury. I can't speak. I lean into the comfort of his hold a mere second before it makes me recoil. I can't let him do this. Can't let him keep making me feel protected. I'm not safe with him. He and his friends have proven that I never will be.

He looks closer, fear running up his face as he twists my head and studies for any sort of sign. I don't know what he's searching for, but I can tell that he won't stop until he finds something.

'Y-you have a message.' My words trip over themselves. 'Loads, actually. From your boys.'

I gulp back the tears that threaten to follow. It's not the time to cry. It's time to be strong, prove I am OK.

He freezes, fear and worry dissipating as they are quickly replaced with a newfound confusion. His eyes squint back at me for more context, but I can't speak without breaking my glare. I manage a quick nod towards his phone on the bed, which he follows instantly. My chin falls forward as he drops his hand from my face and ventures over to retrieve his phone. His eyes widen as he scrolls through the hours of chat, breath catching more with each message that he reads. His teeth clench firmly, face falling back to unreadable stone as he clutches the device tightly and looks over at me.

'I didn't go through it on purpose,' I say, a shake evident in my voice. 'I thought it was mine and then I saw my name, and I just . . . well, I couldn't stop.'

'How much did you read?' he asks gruffly.

He's trying not to shout, but his nostrils have started to flare.

'I don't know . . . Not all of it, but enough,' I say. 'I kind of got the gist . . .'

The bed sinks as he sits on the side, back facing firmly away from me. He throws his head in his hands, heavy breaths leaving his mouth. 'I don't even know where to start.'

I get it, I do. I shouldn't have looked and there's a big part of me that wishes I never did. But then there's my breath that's growing steadier and my heart that's beating faster, letting me know that I did what I needed to do. The lust-filled bubble that we have lived in this weekend was just that: a see-through, deeply fragile bubble. It had no choice but to burst, and it was better for it to happen now than later, before we took it too far.

'You should get back to your room,' I say.

'What?' Aiden asks weakly.

It's the first time he moves, turning to look me in the eye. His brow is furrowed, face flustered. He knows he's been caught out and not even he can think of a way to spin it.

'We have to go, right? And I need to shower before we do. You should go back to your room. Maybe start on the tidying.'

'We need to talk about this.'

He's so solid, yet also ready to collapse. I have to look away.

'There's nothing to talk about.' I wrap the sheets around me as I sit up. 'You guys said what you said and I'm sure you'll say more.'

'Us guys?' he says. 'Maddison, I wasn't involved – you saw the messages.'

'Some of them, yeah, but they had to start somewhere, right? My name wouldn't have come up like that without you setting them off.'

I can feel my wrists start to shake, my body waver as I think of their thousands of jokes at my expense. I can still remember their laughs and their impressions. They echo non-stop in my ear, making me wish I could disappear.

'You think I would do that? Encourage that?' He spits the words out in anger, eyes still trying to catch mine.

I stare down at the crumpled duvet, fixing it tighter around my naked body and trying to shut out the noises in my head. This isn't like then. This is somehow ten times worse, because this time I actually thought I was safe. I was an idiot, who threw decades of opinions away after one stupid kiss in his stupid car. An idiot who should have stuck to her guns and never taken him on in that stupid tent.

'Why not? You've done it before, time and time again.' My words grow louder and stronger. I'm not the girl at the house party any more. I won't be the one that feels bad.

'Seriously? Maddison. I told you last night that I would never do that to you again.'

'And then look what happened this morning,' I say.

'I wasn't involved!'

'They're your friends, Aiden. That doesn't just come out of nowhere.'

'I barely talk to them!'

'Then how did they know?' My voice cracks.

'I just … I don't know.' He gestures, grasping for words. 'I just needed to tell someone about you. Someone who knew—'

'What a joke I was to you?'

'What you meant to me. Still mean to me. I thought they would get it. I don't know, I thought they'd understand.'

I feel his hands slam into the mattress long before I hear the thud as the bed rocks ever so slightly with the strength. It's not enough to derail me. I shut my eyes tight and focus all my energy on my senses. What I can touch, what I can hear, what I can smell, taste, can't see. I rub the sheets between my fingers, grip on to them tight and record the sound. He can't hurt me now. Not here. Not *ever* again.

'Look, Aiden, this weekend was fun, but we both know that it was only for the weekend, right?'

I wait for him to exhale or smile with utter relief that poor Moany Maddy hasn't accidentally fallen in love with the guy who just wanted a quick fuck. But he doesn't.

'Maddison,' he says, a pleading in his tone.

'We've spent a lot of time together, and we're only human and we needed to get it out of our systems. And we did. All weekend. So now we can forget about it and go back to being us.'

'Out of our systems?' His voice is low.

'Well, this obviously isn't a *thing*, right? I mean, I'm me and you're *you*. We both know how that works, and even if we didn't the whole outside world sure does.'

I swivel towards him to stress my point with a gesture to his phone, but I make the mistake of looking at him in the process. He's frozen, dejected and confused.

'You don't mean this,' he finally manages to say.

His eyes are clouded with a disappointment I almost believe. But I saw those messages. I know the real him and I'm sure he is disappointed in a different way. Disappointed that I caught on before he could make me the butt of his big joke. He got me all through school and even uni, so it's not working this time.

'Of course I mean it.' I raise my chest proudly and try to relax into a cool, nonchalant state. 'I mean, you and your friends were right. I'm sure if I told my *girls* what I'd been up to, they'd say even worse.'

'They would?'

They wouldn't. But the pained croak in his voice, while biting, almost makes the lie feel worth it.

'We are who we are – two people who have never got along. The event's just over a month away. There's no point in pretending any different now.'

'Uh, yeah. Sure,' he says, slowly blinking back to life. 'You're right, I guess.'

He rises and gathers his things. I feel the last of my heart rip in two, but it's needed.

'Exactly,' I say, nodding back. 'We get ready, we go home and then we smash out this party. One of us gets their dream job, the other walks away, just like we planned.'

After everything, it's that sentence that finally stops him dead in his tracks, head swivelling to take me in in sheer disbelief.

'You still want the job?' he asks.

'Of course. Do you not?'

It's why we're here. I have to remember that's why we're here.

He hesitates before he answers, studying my frame closely.

'Yeah, I do. Guess we just … got distracted.' He sighs.

'Exactly. But that's over and now we can focus.'

He nods firmly and my stomach sinks at his confirmation. But we both know it's for the best; we are at our best apart from each other, and this little blip back together is just that, a blip. His friends and my friends would all agree.

I rise from the bed, holding the duvet around me as I make my way towards the bathroom to drum in the point. His eyes follow me as I go. I can feel it, but I know that it's not the same. This isn't a look of desire – it's a look of goodbye.

My chest tightens.

'So, I'll meet you downstairs when I'm dressed?'

One more word and my voice would have broken.

'I'll start on the tidying.' He nods.

And then he turns the doorknob and wanders out into the hallway, leaving my room and my heart emptier than it has been the entire weekend.

Nudge 32

The Passport Holder

'You're an idiot,' Devi snaps at me, less than thirty minutes after I've rolled through my door.

I made the mistake of sharing my eye-wateringly expensive taxi's ETA with them when I left Evie's house. The girls showed up at my door before I'd even unpacked my bag, and they wasted no time with their interrogation. We went through it all, with gasps and cheers at the highs and an uncharacteristic silence at the inevitable lows. That was, of course, until Devi worked up the courage to say what the other nodding pair were apparently thinking . . . That my reaction was possibly just a teensy, little, tiny bit unfair to Aiden.

'You didn't see the messages in all their gross boy-chat glory,' I say. 'They were just a reminder that he will never get over who I was in school. And I am and will always be that girl.'

'Are you?' Raina asks sceptically.

'He still calls me Maddy, for God's sake.' I collapse on my bed beside Raina.

My stomach flips on itself when I think of the breathy way he said my name in bed. Followed quickly by another wash of sadness as I remember the worry he injected into just three syllables when he saw me after his shower.

'Honestly, Mads, you've been a whole lot different lately.' Kimi gets comfortable at the foot of my bed. 'A few months ago, would you have even considered jumping into bed with a guy on a *work trip*?'

I lie. 'Maybe.'

But it's no use. I'm hit with a wave of synchronised screeching laughter.

'That's not the point,' I say. 'The point is that to him and his friends, I will always be Moany Maddy.'

'And he'll always be our Primary School Prick,' Kimi says. 'Doesn't mean we won't like him if he makes you that happy.'

Raina and Devi make sounds of agreement, and I close my eyes trying to block it all out.

'The happiness was a lie,' I say.

'Babes, I can't lie, I still don't get how you've reached this conclusion …' Kimi's face is scrunched tightly into a firm, puckered ball. It's her trying face. Her 'I will not judge you, but I really, really want to' face.

'I read their group chat.' I enunciate each word slowly.

'And you saw how many messages from him?' Raina asks.

'I was reading previews on his lock screen. I wouldn't have seen messages from him anyway.'

Devi chimes in. 'So, zero. I heard zero.'

'And when you tried to avoid the subject, he insisted you talk about it?' Raina asks.

'Well, yes, but—'

'Just like he did when he *finally* made you talk about May Madness and apologised for his *small* role,' she continues. 'Which, by the way . . . I love you, Mads, but you had massively overplayed how involved he was in that.'

'He stood there while she mocked me! Using his words!' I say.

'A total dick move, of course.' Devi nods. 'But you've always made it sound like he was the one throwing the punches.'

'Because it felt like he was!'

'Because you've always liked him!'

'Devi!' Kimi and Raina scream in unison.

I sit up, horrified. They grow silent, passing scared but knowing looks between them. None of them dare look my way as Devi scrambles for more words.

'I'm s-sorry, it just slipped out,' she stammers.

'What? What's going on?' I ask.

They stay mute, deeply guilty frowns on their faces.

'Guys?'

The silence continues. Eventually, Raina takes one for the team, letting out a long, pained sigh as she lifts her eyes back up to my face.

'We always said we weren't going to say anything,' she says, as the others nod softly. 'We were waiting for you to figure it out for yourself, if you even wanted to. But then you kissed him and he knocked on your bedroom door, and we were hoping we'd be over pretending that you haven't always been pining for him.'

I instantly choke on my spit, coughing and spluttering as Raina rubs my back and Kimi screams at me to breathe.

'I'm fine,' I pant, trying to regain my composure. 'I just – what? Pining for *Aiden*?'

'Mads, *no one* stays that obsessed with someone for that many years,' Raina says, softly shaking her head. 'Even if they felt like they made a fool of them at uni.'

'If it helps, he is as equally into you,' Devi adds.

Kimi muses, 'Maybe even more so.'

I instantly shake my head. 'You guys are so wrong. I read—'

'The group chat.' They finish for me in high-pitched, mocking voices.

'His friends are trash – we know this. But I think you're too quick to assume he's the same. From what you've said, it sounded like he was mad at them too,' Raina says.

'You don't know that.'

'And neither do you, because you didn't give him a chance to talk about it!' Kimi says. 'You got scared and ran, and I get it, I do. But you made us promise we'd stop you from wading and get your butt diving, so that is what we're going to do.'

'He's in your office tomorrow, right?' Devi asks, as the three of them reanimate.

'Yep, and then every day until the Summer Splash. We had to amend our initial schedule.'

'Perfect!' she says, before glancing over to Raina's ready-to-burst face. 'Raina, go on.'

'Go to him!' Raina says. 'Apologise for overthinking and tell him that you want to see where this goes!'

'Whoa, slow down,' I say as I watch the usually-so-cynical Devi and Kimi nod in agreement. 'I get it, I jumped to conclusions. But we don't even know if *he* wants to see where this goes.'

'Yes, we do, you moron! He basically screamed it with his sadness!' Devi huffs. 'And you will find that out when you sit down and have an *honest conversation* with him.'

'Exactly!' Kimi says. 'You will go in tomorrow and you will tell him how you feel, in the lowest-cut top and shortest skirt you can get away with in the office.'

But it doesn't feel that easy, even after the pep talk from the girls. No action feels big enough. When we argued in that bedroom, I watched his face drop in front of me and every shred of trust we'd worked up shatter into a million pieces.

I lie back on my bed the second they leave and scroll through the months of text messages between me and Aiden. There are hundreds of them, thousands maybe, dating back to the first day I sent him that video from Paint That Mate. What started as the occasional bit of proof quickly grew into day-to-day conversation, little anecdotes and inside jokes. I flick through bored selfies from Meeting Room H, scribbled drawings of event concepts, the stupid pictures of us posing in the aisles of the supply warehouse, and even the Polaroid strip from the water park that he insisted on keeping. At some point, without realising, Aiden Edwards and I became friends. Quite soon after that, we were openly flirting with each other. And I threw it all away on some stale history and an angry assumption.

I barely sleep Sunday night, too anxious for the morning and the sheer amount of making up that I must do. On Monday, I keep my outfit simple but intentional, pairing a smart top with the bell-bottom jeans he noticed months ago. I take no risks ruining my light make-up, or the forty minutes spent on my hair, and leave early enough to make it to the office stress-free. My stomach quivers every minute until 9.45, as I await his arrival and my imminent plea for forgiveness. But I embrace the queasiness. It's a sign that I'm able to feel something for him. That he is worth the stress.

The shrill, piercing ring of my desk phone makes me practically jump from my seat, but my heart recovers just as quickly. It's time. I hold it firmly to my ear.

'Package for you.' The receptionist quickly hangs up.

My stomach drops, but it's fine. He's simply not here *yet*. He still has fifteen minutes. He'll get here, he always does. In the meantime, I have more than enough work to distract myself with, including whatever is at Reception.

Pippa asks what it is the second I come back upstairs, whining like a child until I agree to open it at my desk. I gasp immediately as I unravel the last of the tissue paper. There, in my hands, sits the first Abbingtorn x Evie exclusive passport cover.

'It's gorgeous,' I whisper as I stare down at it.

The leather is soft in my hand, boasting the beautiful artwork.

Pippa cheers as she peeks over my shoulder. 'Design really came through!'

'This one was all me and Aiden,' I say.

A few months ago, in the midst of all our event madness, Aiden and I got sick of the back-and-forth with the design team. They wouldn't respect me enough to go forward with my ideas, insisting they weren't possible or that they just knew better. I have a sneaky suspicion that it had something to do with Pippa's work husband heading up the team.

Sensing my frustration, Aiden suggested we design a concept for ourselves, putting it forward with the others for Evie's selection. We worked late nights and early mornings, doing it in our own time and ensuring that it didn't hinder our actual Summer Splash tasks. He would draw as I threw fragmented ideas at the wall, weaving them into exactly what I had in my head. Our final design was a masterpiece that we were both proud to call ours, and it won Evie's heart by a landslide. Now here it is, a product of the two of us and our hard work, resting between my palms.

'I can't wait to show him,' I say, clutching it to my chest.

'Oooh, can I join the call too?' Pippa asks. 'I'd love to see his face when he sees it.'

'Why would I call him? He'll be here any minute now.'

Her smile grows exponentially. 'Wait, you don't know?'

I stare back at her blankly, the corners of her mouth shooting further up her cheeks the longer I stare. It's too smug, too gleeful to be good news. My stomach starts to churn.

'Max and Olly got an email from Evie last night. It said that you two are at a point where he can stay in Evie's office for the final stages of this,' she says. 'I was very surprised, I thought you were joined at the hip. And I'm really shocked he didn't tell you himself.'

She tries to fake apathy, but she can't stop the smile glued to her face. It stings just as sharply as her last sentence.

I'm really shocked he didn't tell you himself.

I lie. 'Yeah, sorry, he did. It totally slipped my mind.'

Then I put on a pair of earphones and turn my music up loud, reverting my eyes back to my open spreadsheet before she can question me further.

I can't focus on the spreadsheet, or the music, or anything else; all I can think about is how he's not here and won't be here again. He can't stand to see me and he couldn't even tell me himself. This can't be it. I still have so much to say.

I open up a blank email, close it and reach for my phone, keying in a few numbers before dropping that too. It's not good enough – nothing is. He doesn't care any more, because I panicked and pulled away from something that really could have been worth caring about. And for what? An old rivalry and some stupid remarks from people whose names I barely remember? I should have let him talk, but I was too proud. Too afraid of what he might have said.

It's all too much. My head's spinning like it was in that boardroom and my heart's beating so loud I can hear it in my ears. My breaths are coming too quickly, lungs shaking as they try to keep up with the demand. My vision closes in and my fingers tingle as I feel fear overcome me.

But I can't today.

I will not.

Not in front of Gus and certainly not in front of Pippa.

Let's breathe together. Copy me – in and out. Aiden's voice sounds in my head, smooth, sure and steady.

I shut my eyes and obey it, remembering how it felt when his hands traced patterns on the back of my arm. Breath by breath I get slower, chest rising and falling to the command of the man occupying my thoughts. I lay one arm firmly on my desk, using the other to softly trace letters across the surface of my skin. *A-I-D-E-N* I spell out, slowly and surely, as I feel my lungs settle into their usual rhythm.

'Maddison?' Pippa asks. I pause the music and look up. 'My report? It's due later.'

I nod back at her, shaking off what almost was and diverting my attention back to my screen. The report will get done, but first I have bigger matters at hand.

I open up a new window, keying in the website and clicking *purchase* before I can change my mind. He'll complain, but, unfortunately, he has no choice. I need an escape and he is my only solution.

Bought a train ticket. See u this weekend x

I type, ending with a kiss for extra emphasis.

I mentally pack my bag for the rest of the day. It's time for a break. Time to go back to university.

Nudge 33

The Escape

He's standing at the station in a puffer coat despite the twenty-five-degree heat, scrolling through his phone with no awareness of his surroundings at all. But, regardless, my heart grows three sizes and I barrel towards him, enveloping him in a hug.

'What the hell!' Anton jumps out of his skin.

I don't care. I keep squeezing despite his protest.

'I've missed you,' I sigh, feeling him finally give in.

He grunts, reluctantly hugging me back. 'Missed you too.'

Anton called me the second he read my first text, convinced that it was some sort of practical joke.

'It's too spontaneous. You don't do spontaneous,' he said.

'I need to get out of London and I miss you!' I explained. 'Do you have a spare bed? The same-day return was too expensive.'

Though he didn't quite buy the relaxed attitude, he went along with it for my sake. However, I see him steal worried glances at me the whole bus ride to his flat.

His house is cleaner than I expected, which isn't saying much considering my expectations stemmed from the state of his room at home. There's a typical student-housing light layer of grime, but it's not the dirt-riddled cesspit I assumed he would occupy.

'Our sofa folds out into a bed!' one of his flatmates says to me, excitedly leading me to it.

Her name is Jul, and I've seen her in his tagged photos and clicked through out of curiosity of her weird username. She seems nice enough, and, so far, is the only one who's said more than a nervous 'hi' to Anton's older sister.

'We've been waiting for a chance to test it out!' she continues, kneeling on a cushion as she reaches for the sofa's lever.

After a brief struggle and some help from Anton, the two of them unfold the sofa to reveal a makeshift bed. It's laden with crisp crumbs and old lint that has slipped through the cracks over time, but looks sturdy enough.

'I can take this, and you can take my room,' Anton says, catching my grimace as I eye the sofa.

'Thanks, but this is fine!' I look away before I see too much. Given the option of this sofa bed or the mysterious man-cave of my twenty-year-old student brother, I will take my chances on the dodgy sofa bed any day.

'We're going out tonight, if you wanna come!' Jul says. 'Some of my med friends are coming round for pre-drinks.'

'I didn't pack for a night out, but thank you,' I say as politely as I can.

Jul is the kind of girl I wish I could have been at uni – optimistic and friendly, and down for a night out. I feel like I spent my three years focusing on deadlines and societies and upping my CV. I made friends for necessity and I went out to fulfil social contracts, but I was never that girl who just had a good time. The one time I

tried, it ended so disastrously that I never dared to try again. Jul's
bright eyes cause a pool of regret to rise in the pit of my stomach.
She's having the time of her life, as she very much should, before
the world inevitably swallows her up.

'You can borrow something of mine!' she offers happily.

'I'll see how I feel,' I say in the end.

It's more than enough for her. She skips away gleefully.

Alone again, Anton leads me to their kitchen, boiling the kettle
before I even have to ask. He ruffles through the cluttered cup-
boards, eventually striking gold with a polka-dot pastel mug and
crumpled box of Earl Grey tea.

'I don't have teabags … Or a mug. But the girls do and they
won't mind if I borrow one for you,' he says. 'I don't have milk
either, but Jul drinks this pea milk stuff. She says it's good, so …'

He haphazardly splashes in a glug from the carton. Then he
ushers me back to their living room, proudly presenting me with
the worst-looking cup of tea I've seen in my life.

'Thank you,' I say, faking a welcome sip.

'No worries, let's sit. What's wrong with you?'

He asks it before I've even sat down, his face firm and assured
that he will get an answer.

'Sorry?' I ask, scrunching my face right back at him.

'You heard me, what's wrong with you? Is Dad sick?'

'What? No! Why would Dad be sick?'

'Why would you just up and leave London to come here? Is
it Mum?'

'Everyone's fine.'

'Then what's wrong with you?' he asks for the third time.

He's annoyingly stubborn, even more so than me. I blame my
mother for giving us both her most irritating trait. But the last

week has shown me I need to overcome it, and now is as good a place as any to start. His mouth stretches into a satisfied smile as I sigh and place my mug on the table.

'Everything's a mess,' I say, watching the swirls appearing on the surface of the tea.

'What's everything? What's a mess?' he asks carefully.

I shut my eyes to the world for a moment, exhaling deeply and with it, blowing away the dark cloud masking my issues. I can't bear to look him in the eye; it's too hard.

'Too much to count.'

I'm supposed to be the adult when it comes to us – the one that's supposed to help *him*. Now here I am, washed up on the shore of his student accommodation, running from my problems and having to admit that I've fucked up my life.

'I'm stuck in this rut. I can't get a pay rise to save my life, but the world keeps getting more expensive. And Raina's getting married! And Kimi's on track for partner despite being way below the average age, and Devi just bought a house, and I am so happy for them all, but I can't help but feel like I'm the only one struggling.' I gasp for breath, choking on a stray tear. 'I can't talk about it with them, or anyone, because I just sound bitter. I want them all to do great, of course, but is it wrong to wish that I was up there with them?'

He gently nudges a roll of kitchen towel my way. I tear a piece off and dab at my face furiously.

'And I finally get the opportunity to maybe prove that doing the right thing for years wasn't just for nothing, and I hinged it all on a stupid bet that I don't even know if I can win, or even want to win. And now Aiden ...'

I can't finish. The words won't come. Aiden's makeshift toast in the greenhouse comes rushing back to me.

God . . . You make me so bad with words.

My mouth is dry from the salt from my tears. I take a large gulp of tea, forcing myself to focus on something other than the painful throb in my chest.

'Aiden from school,' Anton says. 'What is this bet?'

I rip another piece of kitchen roll off, dragging the coarse paper under my eyes.

'It doesn't matter,' I say. 'Honestly, I don't even care any more.'

'Then why are you crying over it?' he asks, peering at me gently.

I whimper. 'I'm not. I'm crying because I've spent so long wanting to get somewhere to practically no effect. I'm nearing thirty and I don't even know if I want anything I have written on my list any more. I've wasted years – decades – of my life climbing from step to arbitrary step, for what? It all feels so hopeless and – I don't know – I just wish I could go back and start over again.'

'Then start again,' he says plainly.

'I can't,' I say, whinging. 'Didn't you hear the part where I said I am nearly thirty? That's no age to start over again.'

I can't stop crying. It's embarrassing, but he doesn't dare judge. Instead, he leans from his seat and embraces me in a bear hug. We stay like that for several moments, until I reach up and yank his earlobe. He pushes me away roughly and I let out a watery laugh. The first real laugh I've had since leaving Evie's house.

'We're going out tonight,' he says firmly.

'I appreciate the offer, but the last thing I wanna do is party with a bunch of twenty-year-old med students that are already cooler than me,' I sigh.

'Yeah, I'm not gonna go to that party. *We're* going out,' he says.

'Where?' I ask, subtly pushing the cup of tea away.

'Get dressed.'

'Anton . . .' He's grown up with me, he should know that I need more information than that.

'If you can hop on a train last minute, then you can get dressed without knowing where you're going,' he says. 'Go wash your face and get ready. I'll text Jul – I'm pretty sure she has a spare clean towel.'

Jul did, in fact, have a spare towel and it was by far the cleanest thing in the whole bathroom. How the two girls in this flat get by I do not know, but I commend them for being two of the world's strongest soldiers.

After freshening up and changing out of my grubby travel T-shirt, I join Anton at the foot of his stairs and wave goodbye to his flatmates, now at least three drinks down. We wander haplessly through the back streets and I have to bite my tongue to stop myself from going full mum and questioning his safety. But eventually we arrive at his students' union, heading through the foyer and straight up the stairs.

My ears fill with noise the second we turn a corner, music and laughter filling what looks like the union's common room. The place is packed full of students, lounging across sofas, gathered round pool tables, and reaching for cups filled with ominous liquids.

'The ACS have these casual hangs every Friday night,' Anton says. 'I swing by every once in a while, when I need a pick-me-up.'

He guides me through the room, swerving breezily through the different groups with fist bumps and head nods, and quick stops for private jokes. I've always known Anton was social – he's never at home – but seeing him in his element is something different entirely. He's so calm and comfortable, and it fills me with peace knowing that he's found a community when he's away. He stops at one specific group, greeting a guy with locs and two of his friends, before being handed a drink and turning around to introduce me.

'This is my sister, Maddison. Mads, this is Monts, Sam and Tyrell. Monts is my ACS older brother,' he says. 'We're on the committee together.'

'You're on the committee?' I try to hide my shock, but I can't help it – it's so unlike him.

'You're not the only one who knows how to join a society, Ms Twelve Extra-Curriculars,' he says jokingly.

The guys laugh behind him before introducing themselves again, Monts pouring me a drink as he does so.

'Ants, you never said your sister was this fine,' Tyrell says, throwing me a flirty nod.

'Never say that again,' Anton warns them off before I have a chance to respond.

They nod before shuffling up on their sofa so we can squeeze in and join the fun. Anton glows while he's around them, approaching their conversation with wit and charisma I never get to see. I nervously tap the plastic cup with my nails as I listen to them talk between themselves, throwing in a stray laugh from time to time so as not to seem like some awkward bystander. They race through topics quicker than light, breaking only to shout their favourite lines of the songs that sound off in the background.

'So, what's your deal, Maddison?' Monts asks me softly as the other three depart to find us another bottle.

'Well, I work in events at a baggage company—'

'That's not what I meant,' he replies, cutting me off. 'Why are you here with us tonight? Anton said something was up.'

Of course he did. Apparently, I can't trust my brother enough to understand that my breakdowns should remain secret.

'Hey, relax,' he says, noting my tense demeanour. 'He didn't say *what* was up, just said you might need a chat. I'm pretty good at getting people out of their funks.'

'Are you?' I ask, chuckling softly at his mock-therapist voice.

'Ask your brother. I've helped him through a couple of things before,' he says. 'So, go on, what's the issue? Uncle Monts' ears are open.'

I shrug it off and wait for him to get bored, drop it and move on, but he continues patiently waiting. He may not be Anton's biological brother, but he sure has the same annoying willingness to wait for my confessions.

'I'm just getting closer to thirty and stressed about where my life's headed. You wouldn't understand,' I say.

No one would in this place because they don't know how lucky they are. Uni was the last place where I still felt like my future had hope. So, to share all of this with some ACS member who's still in such a malleable stage of his life is pointless.

'Actually, I would understand more than you think.' He leans back on the sofa and looks me in the eye. 'I'm twenty-nine.'

'What?'

I hate the tone of it the second the word comes out of my mouth. Luckily, he laughs off my shock.

'Yeah, I get that a lot,' he chuckles.

'So, you're what? Doing your masters? PhD?' I ask.

'Undergrad. Second year, like your brother.'

I clench my jaw tight to avoid any more reactions I'll regret. He takes my silence for the question that it is and takes a relaxed sip of his drink before continuing.

'I didn't want to study anything when I left school. Went straight into a job as a plumber. Seven years into that, after some pretty big life events, I decided I wanted to be a psychologist. Turns out, that requires a degree and a whole lot of training. So, here I am, three years later.'

'So, you started at twenty-seven,' I say, doing the sums in my head.

'Yep, and will hopefully start my doctorate by the time I'm thirty-two. But who knows about that yet.' He shrugs.

'That doesn't scare you? Starting over so . . .'

'Old?' he asks, laughing at my embarrassed face. 'Twenty-nine is nothing. Thirty is nothing. If I wanted to start again at fifty, I would. Time is just that – time. It dictates too much of our lives already for us to start letting it dictate what we can and can't accomplish.'

'But how do you stop it from dictating everything?' I ask, staring at him intensely.

I can't help it – the booze has seeped into my system and I'm suddenly desperate to hear his advice. He pauses to look up at the ceiling, arranging the words in his own head before imparting them to me.

'You gotta get to the root of your issues. Figure out *why* it's so important for you to reach your dream life by a certain age. It's your dream life, not your dream thirtieth year; you literally have your whole life to go through the motions and figure things out.'

I don't know if it's the drink or the music or the long sentences, but his advice leaves me more confused than where I left off. He can instantly tell as he looks down at my face, my lips parted and eyes wide as I stare back dumbfounded.

'OK, let's try something else,' he says, shifting his stance so he can stare at me head on. 'Speed round – no thinking, just answer straight up. What are your biggest goals for thirty?'

'House, promotion and fiancé,' I say, the alcohol drawing them out of me with ease.

'And what happens if you don't achieve them by then?'

'I fail,' I say, obviously.

'Fail what?' he asks.

'Life.'

'Why?'

'Because ...'

But I don't know, I don't have an answer. I haven't thought past that point, or even about what that point looks like if I don't succeed. When I think about it now, I guess I'd still just be me. Still lost and behind, trying to reach the goals I set out for myself.

'Look at me.' He waits until my eyes meet his before he continues to speak. 'Answer honestly. Would you call me a failure?'

'Of course not,' I say. I've never seen someone calmer or more confident in where they need to be.

'Well, by thirty I won't have a house or promotion – I won't even be qualified for my dream job yet. And as great as my girl is, I can't see us getting married till I've graduated, so I probably won't have a fiancée either. Is that OK?' he asks.

'Yeah, of course,' I say.

'So why isn't it OK for you?'

And just like that, it makes sense. All the pieces arrange themselves in front of me, delving inside and freeing the knot in my chest. I flick through pages of goals and charts in my mind, each one revealing itself to be more superfluous than the last. I hear a voice, see his face without closing my eyes, repeating the same thing he's been telling me since he re-entered my life.

'Nobody asked me to do all this but me,' I say.

Monts cheers. 'Exactly! Couldn't have put it better myself.'

And I couldn't either, because none of those were my words. They were the echo of a man who will barely talk to me now. A man who saw all this months ago and tried his best to coax me through seeing it for myself.

'You all right?' Monts asks, leaning to catch my eye again.

'Yeah, sorry. Thank you,' I say. 'Honestly, this was exactly what I needed to hear.'

The boys return with more booze, top up my glass and get back to their banter without missing a step. But I can't focus, can't think of anything but Aiden and just how badly I've screwed this up. He saw through all my worrying and tried to help me before I even knew I needed his help. And now he's gone, thanks to me and the conclusions I jumped to because I was too scared to let him in properly.

I make it through the night, the next morning, the hug goodbye with Anton, with thoughts of Aiden pushed as far back as I can manage. But as I sit on the train home, back to life, back to London, there's one thing that dominates my mind, clear as day.

It's time for a change. To take a leap that's been years in the making.

Time to believe in myself.

The Edge

Days until the Summer Splash - ZERO

Days since I've seen Aiden - 37

Days since I made my choice for today - 31

Days I've considered backing out and keeping things as they are - 31

'The train would have been so much faster. I don't think I can be in this car for another minute!' Pippa whines as she rolls down the window of our stuffy taxi, dramatically fanning herself with her hand.

'We're almost there.' I don't even bother to hide my disinterest.

'How would you know? Your eyes haven't left those papers since we got in the car.'

'There's a lot to be done,' I say, circling vital words with my pen. 'We've got two, maybe three hours before the first guests start arriving.'

I booked a taxi weeks ago for an 8 a.m. pickup, but Pippa insisted that was wildly unnecessary. One 'casual convo' with Maxwell and some BS about 'surge pricing' later, and I was forced to push the time back to ten o'clock. I wanted to fight back, or find a workaround for myself, but Aiden sent a curt little text insisting that I needn't do either.

> I'm driving up early, no need for both of us to. Just get there when u can.

Then he amended all pre-11 a.m. actions to just include him.

'I'm surprised you didn't stay up the night before! Thought Evie would have handed over her deed to you by now.'

I can't help but look up at her, dragging my eyes from the colour-coded Gantt chart Aiden prepared to keep track of today's tasks.

'What's that supposed to mean?' I ask.

'I mean, you can't deny that Evie treats you *preferentially* because you're both ... you know ...'

'You think Evie treats me well because I'm Black?' I ask bluntly, saying the quiet part out loud since she won't.

Her eyes widen, breath hitching as soon as the words land, and a rosy, panicked hue starts to rise up her face.

'No, no, but the dresses, the overnights, the days out of work, the fancy meals ...'

She looks over to Gus, for help, I assume, but he won't look up. He, if I'm not mistaken, looks quite disgusted.

'I'm running her event. I've seen you do all that and more with clients,' I say.

'Well, yeah, but ...' She casts about for something to say, before snapping at me, 'I'm head of the department, Maddison.'

This is usually the part where I drop her snide remarks and move on. But not today. Today I have nothing to lose.

'And?' I ask.

'The fact you're running this event in the first place is just ...' She trails off once again, aware that, in a world with HR, she should probably stop while she still can. But she's already said more than enough for me. I unzip the rucksack at my feet, digging around inside before finding one sharp corner. I clasp the envelope firmly between my fingers, the paper cold and calming to the touch, before dropping it in Pippa's lap. I was going to wait until tonight, but I guess if there's one thing I can thank her for, it's making this part so much easier to follow through on.

'What is this?' she asks, ripping it open.

'My letter of resignation.'

After four years of bogus tasks and stagnant progression, an email seemed so lacklustre. I needed to see her open it, read it, and look her in the eye so I knew there was no going back.

'Maddison,' she says. 'You don't have to—'

'Yes, I do,' I say firmly. I can see Gus try to hide his smile.

'Is this about money?' she whispers, leaning forward. 'If your new job is offering you more, we can match it.'

'There is no other job.'

'OK, so you want more money. Fine. We'll book a meeting in for Monday, get that sorted asap.'

She types into her phone fervently, the meeting invite buzzing through to mine within seconds. I resist the urge to roll my eyes.

'Pippa, it's not needed. I've already started on a comprehensive handover,' I say. 'I can even help you look for my replacement.'

'You can't leave!' she says, her voice growing higher by the minute. 'We won't find a replacement quick enough.'

She's right – they won't find anyone who will put up with as much nonsense for as little pay. In fact, the more I dwell on it, the sourer I feel about fact I've spent four years of my life with them.

She grabs my hand. Her grip is cold, just like the look behind her eyes. 'I'm serious, Maddison. You and I, we've been through so much. You can tell me if something else has come up.'

The desperation on her face almost makes me feel sorry for her. But then I remember what she's put me through over the years and the little I've got in return, and that feeling dries up long before it has time to settle.

'Pippa, HR already have my resignation email. I am leaving.' My tone is final.

I try to wriggle my hand out of her tight squeeze, but her grip grows vice-like as she looks me over.

'So, you'd rather be unemployed?' she asks grimly.

A scary word. A fear tactic, meant to push me back down. A few months ago, it most definitely would have worked. But I have a new voice in my ear and it's saying *jump, no matter what lies below*.

'I'll figure it out.'

And for once, I genuinely believe I will. The thought sits with me, swells, filling me with peace. I will figure it out. No matter what happens, I will be all right.

'Maddison, the job market is no joke right now. You'll be *lucky* if you can even get an interview,' she says, her voice growing colder and spine growing longer as she launches into her new tirade. 'You have no idea. You haven't *done* this as long as me. We took you in straight after uni ...'

'I think she'll do great,' Gus interjects, much to Pippa's dismay and my own surprise. 'Good luck, Maddison. Any company would be lucky to have you.'

He smiles at me. It's soft yet firm, and packed full of support. As little as we may talk, I know what it means without him having to say any more.

Step one done; all that's left now is the jump.

The Jump

We did it. After six months of long nights, extensive research and precarious planning, we turned Evie's infamous grounds into an almost unrecognisable water resort. The kind that brings 'resort style' into the glamour age.

'I'm *obsessed*!' a guest is yelling to her phone as she walks past me, livestreaming. 'This whole place is incredible. Like and follow for a three-sixty tour!'

I cross-reference her with my guestlist, scribbling a wonky asterisk next to her handle so I remember to request the analytics from her livestream. I'm so engrossed in my clipboard I barely notice the two men who appear in front of me.

'Great job, Maddison!' The sheer volume from Maxwell makes me jump out of my skin and look up from my board. 'And you scrub up well!'

I run my fingers over the beads of my dress. 'Thanks, Maxwell. Really appreciate it.'

Evie insisted Anika dress me for the Summer Splash, stressing that it was mandatory as a 'face of the event' to put my best foot forward in the most fabulous pair of shoes. Three mid-week consultations in Anika's loft and many video calls with Evie later, and we finally settled on the winning outfit: a jewel-toned minidress with cutouts and the kind of intricate boning and beading that has me worried I'll break something if I so much as breathe wrong.

'Well done, Maddison – you really did Abbingtorn proud!' Oliver adds.

I nod back at him, my stomach soaring at the validation before sinking with guilt at the knowledge I've just resigned. I wonder if Pippa's already told them. Surely they wouldn't be so kind if she had. Or maybe they would – maybe they'd try to guilt-trip me into staying.

A carriage loop-de-loops above us, carrying a barrage of screaming passengers and saving me from my guilt-ridden spiral. My breath catches as we all look up at it. I know this one well. I tested it myself. Tested it with Aiden.

They continue their compliments and run through their event highlights, but I barely hear a word. All I can think about now is him. I harken back to that day, to his hold, to the way he made my stomach fizz.

My phone buzzes in my clutch, giving me an excuse to walk away and be saved from the onslaught of small talk.

Need u upstairs, hurry pls.

I politely excuse myself and make my way upstairs to Evie Eesuola herself.

'Oh, you look stunning!' she shrieks as I enter the room, immediately running over and upsetting her full glam team. 'Turn around – let me see! Anika was so right about the hair.'

Anika demanded that the outfit be worn with a voluminous

high ponytail. I told her I didn't have any hair that would work in such a ponytail, but I could make a sleek middle-part work. Next thing I knew, I was shipped a full range of extensions and clip-on ponies from Evie's latest collaboration.

'Are you excited?' she asks, as her glam team come and join us to further fuss around her.

I nod along, despite being past the point of excitement. The party started an hour ago and I've been on my feet for the last four. Evie's only so excited because she's yet to make her fashionably late entrance.

'What you've done here is amazing. You should be so proud of yourself.' She places her hands on my shoulders. 'I have told the board *everything* and I've already been inundated with emails since they've arrived. I cannot wait to announce you and Aiden as the heads of my new events team.'

'The job is ours?' I ask in disbelief.

There is no way that it's taken less than an hour for the board of Evie's whole company to see what Abbingtorn couldn't see in my four years with them. But her smile stretches wide across her face, eyes squinting with unbridled glee as she nods and claps her hands with excitement.

'It sure is – congrats, Mrs Head of Events!' She brings me in for a hug, to the further annoyance of her glam team. 'I am thrilled to have you on my team and I'm sure *Mr* Head of Events will be even more thrilled than I am.' She finishes the sentence coyly, pursing her lips and raising her eyebrows knowingly as she waits for me to slot the final piece into the puzzle. She's not going to say it if I won't, but she won't stop staring until I do.

'He told you?' I ask, testing the waters.

Either that, or Aiden wasn't as sure of those blind spots as he thought. If it were the latter though, I'm sure she wouldn't be smiling. She'd probably be demanding some sort of cleaning fee.

'He didn't need to,' she laughs, putting my chest at ease. 'I saw the change in him from the second that you showed up. Five years with me and I've never seen him walk with so much spring in his step. You challenge him.'

'He challenges me too,' I say.

Or at least, he did, back when he would talk to me.

'I know he challenges you,' she continues, eyebrow raised yet again. 'I told you already – when I see potential, I do everything I can to make it grow.'

'The Summer Splash,' I mutter.

'And the overnight, and the co-head position,' she says. 'The second he told me he was interested, I realised you'd make the perfect pair. And I was right, obviously – you're great partners. You should really look into why that is.'

She does pretty much everything she can do with her face but wink – I fear if she did wink, the woman doing her eyeliner would swing for her. But everything else is enough. Evie has many great qualities, but subtlety is not one of them.

'You want us to date?' I say.

'I want you to get *married*!' She throws her hands up exasperatedly. 'But, I suppose, yes, you could start with a date. With the chemistry between you, I'm surprised you haven't already explored *something*.' She laughs but stops quickly, catching my darting eyes before I have time to cast my guilt into oblivion, then shrieks in excitement. 'Oh, you have! Recently?'

I nod, still stunned.

'Well, good. It's about time you two did this properly.' She beams from ear to ear.

I sigh. 'It's not quite that easy.'

Thanks to me it may never be again.

'His request to work separately,' she says musingly, connecting the dots. 'He said you didn't need him in the office any more. I thought it genuinely came from a mutual place.'

I have spent the last few days desperately trying to avoid the creeping sadness I've felt loom every time I think of Aiden. But as she shares her side of the story, I visualise his lone working request in 4K. It's too much – the image stabs me square in the chest and I feel a tear roll down my cheek. Evie gasps and sends a glam team member to lightly dab it away with a cotton pad.

'Come here!' she says, shooing her glam team away and bringing me in for a big bear hug. 'Go on, tell me what he did.' She brings my face close, not afraid of make-up stains on her silk robe.

'It wasn't him.' I sigh again, trying to keep my voice steady and keep the rest of the tears at bay. 'It was me. I overthought things and ruined them before they started. And now it's been weeks and he's barely spoken to me.'

I hug her tighter as I speak, afraid to let go and return to facing the big, bad Aiden-less world of my creation. That's when I feel the vibration ripple up through her chest to her mouth. A small giggle sounds as I pull away to verify it.

'Oh, honey, if you think that this is *your fault* then you two are going to be absolutely fine.'

She pauses for a moment as she spots my expression and realises that she may have missed the mark just a bit. So, she readjusts, calms herself and ushers me over to her vanity to join her in the chairs before she continues.

'Maddison. He hasn't stopped talking about you this whole time. You may have set things back, but the ship is definitely still docked.'

My body goes still, time slowing around me as Evie's words sink in. I'd lost all hope but a tiny flicker of a light, nestled deep in the furthest crevasse of my heart. As Evie speaks, I feel it flicker in time with her words. Evie Eesuola, influencer extraordinaire and apparent fairy godmother, is convinced that the clock hasn't struck midnight just yet.

'You think I can save this?' I ask softly.

'Oh, absolutely,' she whispers. 'Go get him.'

I feel a glow within my chest, the small flame of hope burning brighter.

'I will,' I nod, giving her a fleeting smile. 'But first, I'm so sorry – I need to talk to you about this job.'

She settles back into her chair and fixes me with one of her trademark, penetrating stares. So, I take a deep breath, nervously meet her eyes and dive into my pre-prepared speech.

I leave Evie's room with a fire under me like no other, barrelling down the stairs, through the kitchen and back to the grounds. I run across the green, barely dodging a tray of gourmet tacos and scouring the sea of people before spotting a familiar face. It's not the one I want, but one that could possibly help me.

'Gus – have you seen Aiden around?' I ask briskly.

He jumps as I grab his elbow, almost dropping his bespoke cocktail.

'Maddison! I'm so proud of you!' he says, loud and joyful, coming in for a hug that I assume is egged on by the drink. 'You're out of here and you should be! I never understood why you've stayed so long! You've got something special, you know? You're so good at this and Pippa knows it. It's why she keeps you down.'

'Really?' I ask.

'Yeah, I see it. And, honestly, it sucks. I've mentioned it to her in one-to-ones – tried to bring you into my projects, but she shuts it down every time. I can't stand it. It's no way to grow.' He pauses, taking another sip. 'I've been debating leaving too. I just think, if she's blocking you from progress, she's probably blocking me too, you know?'

The pieces start to connect – the rescheduled meetings, the menial tasks, the fact that I'm still a PA four years on despite making it clear that I want more ... It isn't Abbingtorn, it's *Pippa*. She's the thorn in my side, blocking my blessings left and right. I should be angry or shocked that the thing I've assumed has finally come to light as truth. But all I can do is giggle at the flushed face of the man in front of me. I haven't seen this side of Gus before. Other than the 'predictable' comment, I wasn't aware he had opinions of me at all.

I guess work colleagues can be strange – sometimes they become your best friends and sometimes they stay strangers you work with every day, but know nothing about. Maybe if Gus and I had talked to each other more, we could have been the type that were friends. Maybe this last month of my notice could be the first step we need to at least band together against a common enemy.

'I'm gonna miss you, Gus,' I say, and, honestly, I mean it.

He smiles softly. 'I'm gonna miss you too, Maddison.'

We can't hug again – the first hug was weird enough; it's not us and we're not there yet – but we exchange two small, knowing nods as we match each other's gaze. It feels light and new; the start of something that could be nice. A connection with someone who truly gets it.

'Don't be a stranger,' he says.

'I'm here if you ever need to rant.' I return his smile. 'Now, have you seen Aiden? It's important.'

He springs back to life, startled by my new jump to action.

'Yeah, erm …' He frantically searches his tipsy mind for clues. 'He said something about getting more napkins. But that was a while ago and there are loads beside …'

I am gone before Gus has time to finish his sentence, speeding down the hill to the bottom, heels be damned. I should've known he'd be there – he told me he would be. I burst through the doors of the greenhouse, past the vine arch and find Aiden perched on top of the napkin chest.

'What are you doing here?' he asks.

With the way he changed the schedule, I haven't seen him in his party outfit yet. He's in smart trousers and a crisp, aqua shirt, the exact colour to compliment my dress. It's deep, soft and beautifully inviting – the complete opposite to the burning anger painted across his face.

I don't dare look away, taking in all the rage while I let Evie's words play through my mind. This isn't over. He cares about me. I can fix this. I just need to try.

'You scare me,' I say.

The words come out as more of a strained pant, as I'm still catching my breath from the run. But they come out, which is the part that truly matters. I've made a start. I've laid the first brick of our bridge. He gives me a confused look, before anger clouds his features again.

'OK, cool, I scare you. We done now?' he asks.

'No, we're not,' I say, moving closer as my breath starts to steady. 'We have been at war for years and yet I am addicted to your smile. That scares me. You make me bolder and brighter, and push myself so much harder, and, honestly, that scares me too. But I have learnt in the last six months, that sometimes the things that scare you are the things that help you grow as a person.'

The words flow out of me this time, that flame of hope forcing them out, lighting the path. He looks up at me, face still stony but so much less angry as he moves to stand in front of me.

Up this close, I can practically taste each note of his aftershave. I've missed this. I've missed *him*. I can't lose us again. He takes my arm, sending a volt of electricity through my skin and directly up my spine. I have to chew on my bottom lip to keep myself grounded and keep the butterflies at bay.

'Do you remember what you said to me in the back of the taxi? The night we were getting back from the La La Lounge?' he asks.

I shake my head. I blacked out that portion of the night. Knowing what alcohol does to my internal filter, that's probably for the best.

'All this time, I couldn't tell if you didn't remember or if you were just trying to pretend,' he says.

'Was it that bad?' I ask, grimacing at the thought.

I was peak hatred – I could have said *anything* back then.

He keeps his expression neutral, but there's a light hint of a sparkle in his eyes, indulging in the way that I squirm as I await a response to my evident worry. He doesn't give too much away, but he does edge closer, leaning over so we're both nose to nose.

'Well, we'd both had loads to drink, so I figured I'd take the chance while I could and ask you why you hated me so much, after all these years.' He pauses to check if it triggers anything for me, but it doesn't, as much as I wish that it did. I can't think of anything right now but him and this moment. 'There was, of course, the chunk where you kept calling me the worst and insisting that hating is just what we do . . .'

'I'm sorry,' I whisper.

I can't even try to defend myself. It's the exact kind of thing that I would have said.

'Don't apologise yet. There's more.' His lip is curling, tone lightening as he chuckles a little and cups my chin. 'You told me that I had ruined your life in the worst possible way because I had made you realise that there was more to life than just achieving things. That impressing me meant just as much to you as achieving your goals. And that you knew that I'd never know what that felt like because I didn't even notice you.'

A wave of cringe runs through my body from head to toe, chilling me to my core.

'I was drunk,' I say.

'And it made you honest. I like honesty.'

He stops again, his thumb diverting from the patterns it was drawing on my cheek to gently circle the shape of my lips. I inhale deeply, lips parting almost on cue and willing him to move closer. He considers it briefly, before swallowing deeply and snapping back into focus.

'So, here's some honesty from me,' he says, hand firmly in place. 'You were wrong. I don't remember when it was that you became more important to me than air, but I pushed it down further and further, and hoped it would disappear because I never thought I was or could ever be good enough for you.'

'You don't mean that,' I whisper, searching for a trace of insincerity in his eyes.

He continues. 'I *begged* Evie to let you run this project alone at first. I knew that if I spent this much time with you again, those feelings would come flooding back. Every day that you've been back in my life, my feelings for you just kept growing stronger. I love you, Maddison.'

There it is.

The four words I swore I'd never hear him say. *I love you,*

Maddison. Just like that. Clear and honest, and all for me. It's everything that I didn't dare to let myself dream of as I struggled through my teen years next to him.

'You're awfully quiet,' he says nervously.

I can't help it; it's all too much. He loves me. Aiden Edwards loves me.

But, after everything I've been through today, my brain has too much to process.

'I quit this morning. Gave Pippa my letter of resignation in the car,' I say, the words rushed.

'You what? Maddison!'

He doesn't get mad at the change of subject, or the fact I haven't said I love him back. He's too caught up in my happiness, grabbing my arms and squeezing them tight in triumph.

'It was long overdue.' I'm still in shock.

'And perfect timing!' He whirls me around, rejoicing. 'I don't know if you've chatted to Evie yet, but—'

'I turned down the co-head position too,' I say.

He halts instantly, my shaky words wiping the elated smile clean off his face. He drops his arms from their hold and goes to rub the back of his head in distress.

'Maddison, what? I know the last month or so has been weird and we had the whole agreement and everything, but you have to know that I wouldn't actually want you to turn down your dream job.'

I smile at his sincerity. 'It's not because of you, or the bet, or the last few weeks. It's because of me. *For* me. I need time to figure out who I am without deadlines, or structure. What I want outside of achieving rigid, unnecessary goals.'

'And you told Evie that?'

'I did. Earlier today. I had a whole rehearsed speech to ensure that I actually went through with it, and then I saw her face and forgot it all instantly,' I say. 'It didn't help that I'd been crying over you like ten seconds before.'

'Really?' he asks, sinking back down onto the napkin chest.

'Yeah, but, somehow, I managed to say something. And once I was done pouring my heart out to her, she laughed in my face.'

It's his turn to do the same, apparently. His guffaw bounces off the glass, echoing around the walls and filling the space between us. I think back to that room, and how she flicked her hair behind her, looking down at me kindly with a puzzling yet deeply comforting smile.

'Maddison, honey, I get where you're coming from and I truly do love this journey for you,' she said. 'But you don't have to blow up your *entire* life to figure out who you are and what you want to be. In fact, by the looks of it, you've done a lot of that work in the last few months without having to give up *anything*. It's OK to want things. It's OK to have goals. You just need to put less pressure on yourself to achieve them. From what you've said, the problem with your five-year-plan wasn't the content at all, but rather the timeline.'

I snap my focus back to Aiden.

'Sounds like Evie,' he says. 'She wants you on the team so badly, she was not taking no for an answer.'

'You're right – she did not. She told me to take three months. Spend some time with myself and figure things out before I join the team. Apparently, there's this guy I'll be heading the department with who's pretty capable of managing until I start. I'm not so sure though ... Don't tell Evie, but he sounds kind of cocky. I don't think I'll like him much.'

He chuckles, this one deep and hearty, filled with the joy and comfort I've come to crave since we stopped talking. He rises from his seat, walking towards me until we're toe to toe, his breath tickling the skin on my face.

'Any plans for your time off?' he asks, his lips brushing lightly against mine as he speaks.

'No idea, but I'm sure I'll figure it out. I'm pretty well-known for going with the flow nowadays,' I say teasingly.

His mouth parts widely, throwing his head back to laugh before bringing it down until we're nose to nose.

'You know, I hate to say it, but I think that you actually may have won this bet,' he says.

I raise an eyebrow. 'I don't know ... Your organisation impressed me. Didn't you say you went as far as your *own* five-year-plan?'

'That I did,' he says. 'But it wasn't nearly as detailed as yours. In fact, there was only one thing I wanted to achieve.'

He breaks us apart yet again, reaching for his pocket and pulling a torn-out sheet from a space in his wallet. He unfolds it carefully before taking my hand and sliding it gently into my palm.

In five years' time, whatever I'm doing, I'd better be doing it with Maddison Clarke by my side.

I sigh. 'Aiden.'

'Don't,' he says, snaking his arm round my waist and pulling me in until we're chest to chest. 'We've done enough talking. Just promise to help me achieve it.'

His lips brush against mine again as he speaks, each movement so deliciously teasing. But I'm done with the teasing – I cannot take it any more. I grab the back of his head, our lips crashing together with more urgency than ever before.

Our first kiss, and every kiss that followed, was incredible, life-changing in so many ways, but this one is something else. This one is propelled above by its extraordinary level of honesty. I am kissing Aiden Edwards, the man whom I love. The man whom a part of me has always known that I love. And now I know that he loves me too. Loves me with every stroke of his tongue and every teasing bite of my lip. I pull away from him slightly.

'What?' he asks as he pauses to study my face.

Beneath the swollen lips and flushed complexion, I assume I must look quite bemused. I can't help it.

'This dress is very structured, so we have to be careful with sudden movements,' I say with a small smile. 'But, seriously. I just can't believe this is *us*. This is where you and I have ended up.'

He smiles sweetly, the two of us exchanging giddy looks of disbelief before he looks me up and down again, hunger returning. I sink to my knees in front of him, eliciting a pre-emptive sigh, before I reach behind him and snatch a handful of napkins from the cabinet. I rise and flash a triumphant smirk at his stony expression.

'Come on, we have an event to run,' I say, holding out my hand.

He huffs a laugh and reaches out, his fingers slotting perfectly between mine. I give his hand a small squeeze, a silent promise that whatever happens next, I won't be letting go.

Epilogue

Three years later

'Are you wearing a tie?' I ask, leaning against the doorframe of our room and ogling shamelessly as Aiden fixes his collar in the mirror.

'What, is it too much?'

He glances down, awkwardly adjusting it with a mild panic. His breath quickens, eyes focused as his fingers twirl the fabric between them. I stride towards him and our hands brush as I take it from him, flipping the fabric over itself and smoothing the material down before using it to pull him closer.

'Not at all. In fact, you should wear ties more often.'

He relaxes instantly, the lines in his forehead softening as he brings his face down to mine for a sweet, tender kiss.

'I asked Anika what colour your dress was and had her source me something that would coordinate without looking too matchy,' he says.

I can't even try to control the soft noise of pleasure that leaves my mouth. It's barely there – a scratch above a whisper, and probably would have gone unnoticed in regular circumstances. But here, pressed up against Aiden Edwards, a man who worships every step and breath I take? It stood no chance. His lip curls at the sound and he shakes his head in mock judgement.

'This little nerd fetish of yours is getting out of control,' he says teasingly.

'It's not nerdy to appreciate preparedness!' I shuffle closer between his legs. 'And you love it.'

'Only because I love *you*.'

The words vibrate against me, tickling my lips before they're parted by his tongue. It slides in slowly at first, lightly caressing my own before delving deeper as his hands slip around my waist. I lose myself in the feeling, body writhing in his firm hold as heat rises in my blood. His hands roam the surface of my dress and another moan escapes me, but he catches it in his mouth, making the corners of his lips curl even more.

'I love you, too.'

His hands travel south, caressing my hips before scooping me up into the air in one swift move. I gasp, wrapping my legs around him as he twirls me around and places me atop our chest of drawers.

'We shouldn't.' The words are breathy and soft and lost in my gasp as his lips touch my neck. 'I need to be downstairs.'

'Tell me to stop and I will,' he whispers, teeth grazing my ear as his hand lightly cups me, sending a new wave of tingles down my spine. 'Just say the word and I promise to go away ...'

I grapple at his shirt, all sense a thing of the past. The silken tie slips through my fingers to the floor, and I reach for his buttons, working as quickly as my hands will allow.

Then we hear it. A knock, and a loud voice that follows.

'We're coming in, make sure you're decent!' It's Kimi.

The door swings open and less than a second later she walks in with Devi by her side, the two of them shielding their eyes. Raina walks in behind them holding an intricately iced cake. It's beautiful – the kind of cake you'd see on a vision board, *my* vision board to be precise, the one I made at twenty-five.

I squeal, jumping down from the furniture. 'Girls! You really didn't have to! We bought food, we have a cake.'

I take in the swirls of blue and white icing that frame small cursive piping.

For Maddison
Here's to being thirty, flirty and thriving!

A single candle sits in the middle, flickering gently and lighting the three eager faces behind, urging me to blow it out. I close my eyes before blowing with all my might, no wish needed. I have everything I could want right now. They all clap and cheer, Aiden coming up behind me to give me a tender kiss on the temple.

'So, when you said you'd come over to help prep ...' I say.

'It was all a ruse!' Devi finishes for me, unveiling a large gift bag from behind her back.

'We couldn't let you turn thirty without an FGA pre-party – come on, now, Mads,' Kimi tuts, producing a knife to slice the cake.

'Sent you up here to "rush Aiden" so we could light the candles,' Devi adds, before turning to him and scowling. 'When we told you to distract her, this is not what we meant.'

He rolls his eyes at her faux-disapproving glare.

'I'll be downstairs *actually* prepping for tonight, then. You ladies enjoy your pre-party,' he says. 'First round of guests were told to be here in about an hour, so I'd say you've got a solid two.'

The door shuts behind him and all eyes focus on me, the glow from their smiles placing me under the spotlight. They break into the worst rendition of Stevie Wonder's 'Happy Birthday' that I've ever heard, complete with an awful yet confident three-part harmony and synchronised twerk circle. By the time they're done, there's no air left in my lungs to thank them. All of it escaped my system as I belly-laughed my way through their performance.

'I love you guys,' I finally manage, as they grin in response and embrace me in a four-person group hug.

'Thirtieth and a housewarming all in one day. You must have been pulling your hair out,' Kimi says.

I smile. 'Honestly, this was all Aiden. I've been so busy with work that he's done all the heavy lifting.'

'Really?' Raina asks. 'But there's all these little touches – the staggered arrival times for family and friends. The matching out-fits? It's so ... you.'

'I guess I really have rubbed off on him in more ways than one,' I say jokingly.

At first, I worried that dating and working so closely together would be a recipe for disaster, but I quickly learnt that when it comes to us there can never be too much of a good thing. We did our best to keep the work talk to the office, and only ever *occasionally* blurred the lines with a few late-night office dalliances. It turns out that Evie was right from the start – when we work together, we are magic. Together we've conjured the highest conversion-to-sales from events numbers that Evie and the Evielution board have ever seen.

I expected to feel sad or scared or something more daunting

when Aiden told me he was planning to leave Evielution, but those feelings never came. I was overcome with pride as I watched him finally take a chance on his real dream. One year down the line and Aiden's non-profit has started to gain a name for itself, and I am now the solo *director* of events at Evielution. Together, we make a comfortable(ish)-enough amount to rent our first place in London.

The girls hand me the gift bag and wait impatiently as I unwrap the seemingly never-ending assortment of gifts. There are things for the house: vintage plant pots with accompanying plants, gold-rimmed wine glasses, framed pictures of us, the cushion covers I drooled over while window-shopping with Devi, a label maker, a set of gorgeous glass Tupperware with an array of separators to break them into compartments. I try to insist it's too much, but they all shut me down and say that nothing's too much for such a big milestone. Then they point me towards the final present in the bag, wrapped up neatly in soft tissue paper.

I unfurl it carefully, ripping back the layers to reveal a beautiful mint-green leatherbound notebook with my name embossed in gold on the front.

'It's one of those fancy ones you're always raving about, but are too proud to buy,' Devi says.

'Do I talk about it that much?' I ask. 'I just think that—'

'No planner should cost upwards of forty-five pounds!' they all say.

I flick through the pages excitedly, scanning over the prompts and the spaces for lists and the weekly breakdowns.

'It's beautiful,' I say as the girls shake their heads.

'We figured you needed a special one to kick off your thirty-first' Raina says.

'Yeah! You can track your meetings, vision board, write your new five-year plan ...' Kimi shuffles over to look through the pages with me. 'What is on the list for the next five years? I need inspo for my own in a couple of months.'

'Nothing,' I smile.

The girls stare at me in shock, and I laugh. I look back at them, closing the journal and setting it down on the side before hitting them with the same words that struck me over three years ago.

'I have things I want to do, but there's no point setting a timeline. Let's just see what happens.' I shrug. 'I've decided to let life surprise me.'

It's Kimi who breaks first, her eyes shining with pride as she pulls me into a tight hug. Soon the four of us are enmeshed in one big cuddle on my bedroom floor, taking care not to lean on the gorgeous cake in the middle.

Life can surprise you, and I am finally giving myself permission to let it do just that. I don't know what the future holds for me and Aiden, I don't know how long we will live in this flat on the edge of south London, or how long I will work in events for, or if I'll ever get married. What I do know is that, right now and for the foreseeable future, I'm happy. I'm surrounded by love, and laughter, and that is all that matters.

Acknowledgments

Right, strap in, grab a drink, I fear this is going to be a tad too long and incredibly gushy. But in my defence, this is my first ever published novel, so I have an insurmountable bucket of feelings that I need to expel.

Firstly, can we please take a moment to acknowledge the fact that I am even writing this? I have published a novel – this has been everything that six-year-old me wanted to do. I am quite literally living my childhood dream, and I get to put these words in the back of a book. I still haven't processed that and, as I write this, I am unsure that I ever will. I sincerely hope that everybody reading this accomplishes their biggest dream too, because this feeling is so incredibly indescribable. I want everyone to experience it just once.

Of course, I haven't made my dreams come true by myself by any means. Publishing a book is a long and comprehensive task and it well and truly takes a village. Thank you to Literary Agent extraordinaire Silé Edwards, who took a chance and sent me an email that changed my life forever. My heart stopped when I read your words 'Have you ever thought of writing a book?' and I stared back at my many saved-down manuscripts and theorised how to reply without sounding geeky and desperate. You are my Fairy

Godmother, and I will never be able to thank you enough for being so patient with me and holding my hand through the process of writing this brand-new book from start to finish, and everything that has followed since.

When it comes to Dialogue, I would like to thank Alexa, firstly, for reading said manuscript and deciding it was worthy of publication. Writing a book is scary enough, but worrying no one will buy it is something entirely different. Thank you for showing your passion and excitement for this project from our first meeting. And thank you to the whole team for all the effort and commitment involved in bringing *Quarter-Love Crisis* to life.

I would like to thank my family for always being there for me and making me believe I was special even on my most average days. Particularly my parents, Dionne and Hugh, and my favourite (and only, but who's counting) sister Mia. You have done such an amazing job raising me to believe that I can do anything as long as I put my all into it, and I hope this book and any that follow do you proud, as they are all a product of the belief that you poured into me. I would also like to give a special shoutout to my Auntie Claudia, who has been supporting and pushing my goal of being an author since I was in primary school. Your support has meant the world to me, and I couldn't have done it without you either. Also, one day, we will go for that dinner.

To my Baby Got Books girls, Eni and Crystal, thank you for being my sounding board whenever I need you. Thank you for the many shouty wine nights, for the never-ending stream of advice, and for being my willing test readers (sorry Mum ... especially if you are only just finding this out). You are more than friends to me at this point, you are solidly family, and you have been the most amazing support during this whole wacky process.

To the rest of Salt Squad: Alice, Amaris, Titi, Rachel, Phoebe, Charmaine, Sarah, and Mia. To Enya, to Leia and to Graham, I am truly honoured to know each and every one of you. Your friendships have helped teach me what good friendship looks and feels like, and it is the reason it was so important for me to include strong themes of friendship within this book. So basically, you're all responsible for the best characters here, the FGA.

And to the man who snuck up on me and made me fall in love . . . I did not know you when I drafted this, but you have been my biggest supporter during everything that has followed. Thank you for your help and constant encouragement, and for surpassing even the best of book boyfriends. (I'm sorry, this part is so cheesy and I've made myself a bit sick, but it's a romance book so gotta go all in, right?)

Bringing a book from manuscript to what you are reading is a team effort.

Renegade Books would like to thank everyone who helped to publish *Quarter-Love Crisis* in the UK.

Editorial
Alexa Allen-Batifoulier
Saida Azizova

Contracts
Stephanie Evans
Sasha Duszynska Lewis
Isabel Camara

Sales
Megan Schaffer
Kyla Dean
Dominic Smith
Sinead White
Georgina Cutler-Ross
Kerri Hood
Jess Harvey
Natasha Weninger Kong

Design
Carla Orozco
Chevonne Elbourne
Charlotte Stroomer
Sara Mahon
Sasha Egonu

Production
Amanda Jones
Kelly Llewellyn

Publicity
Alice Herbert
Corinna Zifko

Marketing
Mia Oakley

Operations
Rosie Stevens

Finance
Chris Vale
Jonathan Gant

Copy-Editor
Suzanne Clarke

Proofreader
Gabbie Chant

Jasmine Burke is a writer, marketer, and lifestyle content creator from London, who grew up with an obsession with both reading and writing. She credits her love of books to her parents, who fed her passion from the age of three, in the hopes that Baby Encyclopaedias would stop her from asking so many questions about how the world works. She spent her primary school summer holidays hauled inside (when allowed), writing stories to read to her little sister. It's fair to say that those stories have grown since then, and she is excited to share her latest one(s) with the world.